Don't surrender your freedom.

Domers

12-1-2010

Thanks!

David Couzins

This is a fictional work. Characters and incidents are products of the author's imagination and should not be construed as real. Any resemblance to actual events or to any persons living or dead is purely coincidental.

Published by Airstream Publishing Company (USA)
1163 Ridgewood Circle
Lake in the Hills, Illinois 60156

Library of Congress Control Number: 2010915373

ISBN-13: 978-0-9830863-0-7

To my wife Gilda and our boys
Kevin, Nathan, and Jonathan
Thank you for your love and support.

"I do not want to settle down in the houses you would build for us. I love to roam over the wild prairie. There I am free and happy. When we sit down, we grow pale and die."

– Setanta (White Bear), Kiowa Chief (1815(?)-1878)

1.

Countless rough-hewn boulders littered the barren ground. A persistent wind raged from the north and built mounds of fine sand high against each of the jagged, rust-colored rocks. The partially buried rocks looked as if they were burrowing to escape their harsh desert home. Low in the eastern sky, a bleary hot spot marked the position of the sun as it struggled to pierce a veil of white haze. A vast ocean of rippling dunes flowed to the distant horizon where it blended seamlessly with the haze and blurred the distinction between ground and sky.

Among the endless chaotic sea of desolation, a tiny portion of order, mechanical and precise, toiled without complaint at the behest of its creator…

Programmed instructions arrived from Earth seven minutes after their transmission. The incoming electronic signal routed through a receiving antenna and into the central computer onboard NASA's Mars Rover No. 64. The computer interpreted the new instructions and relayed the appropriate commands to actuator motors controlling the rover's robotic arm. Moments later, the rover transmitted a return signal which raced through space for another seven minutes carrying back to Earth image data from several onboard cameras.

Jonathan Corant, Mars rover controller, hunched forward in meticulous study of all four video display screens in his command center. Jonathan broke into a wide grin after confirming that the instructions he just beamed across millions of miles of outer space had successfully positioned the rover's collector drill above the Martian surface. Great care would be needed to program the next set of instructions that would initiate the drilling process into the planet's crust. Jonathan picked up the input stylus in his right hand and began tapping the touch screen that displayed a schematic of the Mars rover. Although he was alone in the room, the remote rover driver spoke his plans aloud to steady his pace and sharpen his focus.

"Okay, move the drill arm down twelve-point-six centimeters to bring the drill head into contact with the surface; next, set laser depth gauge to..." His concentration was shattered by a shrill voice from the next room.

"Jonny, dinner is ready! Come to the table, please!"

One mother's shout and Mr. Jonathan Corant, 'expert Mars rover driver,' was transformed back into Jonny Corant, nine-year-old elementary school student working to complete his 4th grade science class assignment, and his command center was reduced to nothing more than the average kid's bedroom.

"But, mom," Jonny whined in protest. "I'm doing my science assignment and I only have fifty minutes left before I lose my turn with the Mars rover!" Jonny shouted his plea through his open bedroom door but no response was forthcoming from his insistent mother. With a heavy sigh, Jonny tapped the logout button relinquishing control of the rover to a classmate. Now he would go to the end of the line and likely not get another turn to remotely control the rover until Wednesday.

Jonathan dropped the wireless keyboard and control stick beside him onto the plain blue bedspread and jumped to his feet. He took a quick look around the room, then, despite the setback with his school work, Jonny bounded out of his bedroom without a care.

The scene beyond his cozy bedroom was a stark contrast to his comfortable place of school work and sleep. Jonny stepped through his doorway and into the 100-foot diameter circle of central living space that dominated his home. The huge gray space was empty except for an eight-seat dining table and four large couches set end-to-end in a partial circle. The curved line of couches faced a giant display screen that hung suspended from a domed ceiling that arched upward to a central apex twenty-two feet overhead. The smooth surface of the high vaulted ceiling was bathed in soft indirect lighting whose random patterns of muted pastels changed every morning.

Six additional bedrooms, some configured like Jonny's, and two full bathrooms lined one half of the perimeter of the cavernous space. The other half of the domed central chamber was encircled first by a large playroom that these days also doubled as a music room, for it had been years since it was a nursery for infant Jonny. Next to the playroom was an open gym space full of exercise equipment, then came some locked maintenance closets housing the mechanical heating and cooling systems, then the dome door to the airlock that led to the Outside. That door held bad memories for Jonny; he tried to never look at that. Continuing around the perimeter on the other side of the dome door was another maintenance closet containing air filtration systems, water heater, and 600-gallon water tank; next came the laundry, then the kitchen, and completing the circle was a store room that among other things contained three months of food rations in the event of an emergency.

Jonny scrambled into his customary chair on Grandpa Frank's end of the table. At the opposite end of the table Cynthia Corant shook her head and glared disapproval at her youngest son. "Good of you to join us, Jonathan."

The hand of big brother and best friend, Tom, playfully rubbed the top of Jonny's head.

"Bow heads for grace, please," mother Corant continued. "Dear Lord, we thank you for the food we are about to receive. We ask your blessings upon everyone in this dome and upon the domes of our loved ones. May you bless those on the Outside and keep them strong against the harsh life they endure. In Jesus' name we pray. Amen."

A chorus of 'Amens' sounded from those around the table. Counter-clockwise from Jonny was brother Tom Corant who, at twenty-four, was much older than Jonny's nine years. Tom was tall, handsome, and his frame well-muscled thanks to hours spent in the family gym trying to keep up with oldest brother Steven who was the next Corant at the table. Steven Corant was only one year Tom's senior but Steven held the informal title of Man of the House ever since their father's fatal heart attack six years ago.

The seat at the head of the table was vacant. That was Paul's chair.

Cynthia Corant sat opposite Steven. This dome was hers and had been since she and Paul moved in twenty-six years ago on the 16th day of June, 2054. Per government regulations on dome habitation, she and Paul were married that very day via video conference by the minister of their church, with their respective families and scores of friends watching the ceremony via the video conference from within each of their own dome homes.

The twins were next—Lucy and Linda, identical and inseparable. They shared a bedroom despite there being one empty and available child's bedroom. The girls were in their last year of high school and were anxiously awaiting the results of their skills assessment test. The test results were crucial because the government assigned a person's career based on his or her performance on the test.

Cynthia's father, Frank Bellows, sat at the far end of the table. Frank was a first generation domer. Between the years 2019 and 2028, the entire population of the United States moved into millions of family-sized, hermetically sealed domes free of dust and germs. The planning and construction of the windowless, reinforced domes began in 2013 after a cargo vessel entered Boston Harbor in the middle of a workday and blasted the city off the map with an atomic bomb hidden in a lead-lined container. The dome skeptics were silenced one year later when a sister device from the same stolen MIRV warhead went critical at 18th and Pennsylvania Avenue, two blocks from the White House. Planning for the Washington attack had been so thorough, the Secretary of Agriculture was the first person in the line of succession left alive who could be sworn in as Acting President. After the Washington blast, eight more thermonuclear bombs from the missing MIRV remained unaccounted for. Loose nukes, the Islamic jihadist bio-terror attacks that killed hundreds of thousands in Los Angeles, Minneapolis-Saint Paul, Frankfurt, Paris and Naples, wide spread violence caused by world economic turmoil, the deadly flu outbreak of 2015, and the genetically engineered oil-consuming bacteria that mutated into a flesh-consuming organism that devastated South America and came dangerously close to North America before being stopped—all those attacks and terrors as well as others made the safety of the domes very appealing and eventually mandatory for the citizens of the United States. Of course, the conspiracy that provided the true impetus for forcing the country into domes was only just taking shape at the time the cherry blossoms were vaporized.

Frank Bellows—Grandpa Frank—went under the dome in 2022 at age eleven. Frank was the only person at the Corant dinner table who had ever seen the sun.

Tom reached out to rest a hand lightly on Jonny's shoulder. "So, you must have been having a lot of fun controlling the Mars rover, eh, buddy?"

"Yeah, Tommy, it was great! But I got the drill all ready, and now Billy Wilcox is gonna' get the fun of drilling into the crust."

Seventeen-year-old Lucy Corant twirled a small bit of spaghetti with her fork and looked across the table at her silly little brother. "Drilling into sand on Mars? That doesn't sound so fun to me." The giggling grew louder as twin sister Linda joined the teasing.

Tom gestured to Lucy to pass the pasta sauce and chided his sisters, "Lucy, Linda, I'm going to tie your blond ponytails together like I used to."

Before Cynthia could chastise Tom for the ungentlemanly comment, she saw Steven playfully jab his younger brother's arm with an elbow. Steven didn't sport the sandy hair and strong jaw of his siblings. He inherited Paul's curly black hair and pointed chin—the same sad eyes, too...Cynthia caught herself before the reminiscing went too far. She wanted off the anti-depressants that were packed in the family's weekly ration bundle. Maybe this was the year?

Grandpa Frank cleared his throat, leaned to his left and, head lowered, looked Jonny squarely in both eyes, "Young man, you should dig wherever you want to dig." Frank straightened himself up in his chair and continued, "Of course, when I was your age, I didn't use robots to dig for me. I used my own hands to dig in the ground, real good dirt too, and at night I could watch Mars move through the stars."

"Dad!" Now Cynthia had to intercede. "Dad, you know you aren't supposed to..."

"I know," interrupted Frank. "I know. The government doesn't want people who have been Outside to talk about it. Heaven forbid we might start a revolt or lead a mass exodus."

"Dad," but Cynthia didn't go any further. Frank was staring down the length of the table, passed Paul's vacant chair, and even passed the dome walls. It was the look Frank gave when he shut down. And Cynthia knew hers wasn't the only anti-depressant prescription in the ration packages.

"Hey, everybody," Steven broke the awkward silence. "Come on, we should be living it up, right? We only have Tommy living with us for one more week!" Steven slapped Tom hard in the back of the neck and in almost the same motion, leaned forward and put his other hand gently on Cynthia's shoulder. "Now, don't get all emotional, mom. Most kids get married and leave the nest after all."

Tom threw up both his arms high in the air in mock celebration. "That's right! You all have only one more week to kick around Thomas A. Corant!"

Tom reacted quickly when he saw the smile vanish from Jonny's face. Tom had been more like a father than a brother to Jonny the last six years. "Hey, Jonny, you're not going to have time to miss me." Tom extended his fingers and thumbs and brought his hands up on either side of his face imitating a picture frame. "See this face, Jon?"

Jonny nodded meekly.

"Well, you're going to see it every day, but a million times bigger up there." Tom stretched one arm to point to the huge ten-foot by forty-foot display screen suspended from the ceiling toward the rear of the dome.

"Yeah, I know," Jonny conceded reluctantly.

"That's right," snapped Cynthia. "We will see Tom every day. I wouldn't let him leave if he wouldn't agree to that."

Tom matched his mother's smile. "Okay, then. Let's eat. Mom, I will definitely miss your cooking. I know everybody receives the same government rations, but from what I hear from some of my friends on the Net, it sounds like you are way above average in how you finesse the food."

"Thank you, dear. Tell Jenny that if she needs any pointers, she can buzz me anytime."

Steven swallowed a mouthful of noodles and chimed in. "Tell Jenny? Mom, I say you teach Tom your cooking secrets. Jenny starts her job as a remote assembly line controller at the dome fabrication plant in a few weeks. With average family sizes on the increase, the dome business is booming. And I understand a few other countries are considering joining the US in going under the dome."

"Good point, Steven. Oh, and Steven," Cynthia lowered her voice to a whisper and leaned closer to her son. "You don't need to report Dad's little outburst do you?"

Steven Corant worked for the arm of the Federal Communications Commission that policed the Net for subversive activity. The "Net" wasn't the same Internet accessed by the rest of the world. The seventy-five million domes that constituted the United States were connected to a separate information and communications web that was completely isolated from the Internet. Content control by the FCC was much simpler that way. The country had to be protected from hackers and cyberterrorists after all. The official name for the domer web was SNet, an abbreviation of the marketing nickname, 'SuperNet." Over time, the 'super' adjective gradually fell out of use, either because it was easier to just say 'Net' or because the widely known content control practiced by the government made the term 'super' seem…ridiculous.

Steven read the concern on his mother's face and whispered, "Don't worry, mom. I know Grandpa doesn't mean any harm."

"I know you are talking about me down there." Frank had returned his attention to the family dinner. The room was silent and the air full of apprehension. Frank tried to pull closer to the table but the foot plate of his wheelchair would not let him move forward any further. A widower for the last three years, he had held out alone in his dome against his children's wishes until last year when a stroke forced him to move back in with family sooner than anticipated.

"Look at all of you. Like every other day of your life, you are all sitting here wearing the same baggy, dull gray shirt and dull gray pants made out of God knows what synthetic. You eat the same irradiated, foil-packed, infinite shelf-life food—nothing fresh, because you aren't allowed a refrigerator. Once a week I hear the clank behind the inner dome door that says the ration package is here with free dried meat, free dried fruit, free flour, free powdered milk, free rice and beans, all courtesy of our generous United States government!

"And that's a farce if there ever was one—*government.*" Frank snarled and spat the word. "The President and her cabinet all hiding under domes of their own, nine other domes each with a Supreme Court Justice, 500 more domes containing House and Senate members representing states that don't even exist anymore. It's absurd." Frank sighed and lowered his slowly shaking head.

The look from their mother told Lucy and Linda to begin the drill. The girls rose from the table and took Jonny with them to the music room and shut the door.

"Dad, we keep telling you we are doing okay. We are *safe* in here. We don't have to worry about nuclear weapons or nerve gas attacks. No more subway bombs, flu epidemics, or violent crime." Cynthia paused and tried to think of new points, these had all been covered before.

"Yes, Grandpa, things are better now," Tom added as he usually did. "We are safe from nuclear, biological, and chemical weapons. None of the dangerous natural or man-made micro organisms on the Outside can harm us."

"Young man, you are just giddy about finally moving in with your online girlfriend so that you can stop playing with yourself."

Steven laughed. "Ouch! Nice one, Grandpa!"

Frank wagged a finger in Steven's direction. "Don't think that I don't know what you do all day, mister. You should be ashamed of yourself, trolling the Net looking for things to censor. Your kind has wiped out every video and photo of the Outside that shows the natural beauty of this planet—all in the name of protecting the sanity of everyone under a dome."

Tom didn't return the ribbing he received from Steven as he knew Grandpa Frank was hitting a sore spot with his older brother.

"Boys…" The cue from Cynthia was clear and Tom and Steven left the table for Steven's room. Cynthia swished the linen napkin off her lap and onto the table as she stood, then walked toward her father. Tears were flowing as she knelt beside his wheelchair and laid her head on his arm. Cynthia felt Frank's other hand, trembling slightly, still unsteady from his stroke, rest lightly on top of her head.

"I'm sorry, Cindy." Then, after another moment, "You know, it's a good thing the government doesn't allow cosmetics in ration packets, or you would really look a mess right now."

Cynthia laughed between sobs. But she really didn't understand. She was safe and she had her family. Why would anyone want to live on the Outside?

* * * *

Tom followed Steven into his bedroom and closed the door. Steven dove onto the bed and turned on his side, head propped up by an arm and elbow while Tom dropped into the recliner a few feet away.

Tom turned to his older brother. "Boy, Grandpa was in rare form tonight."

"I'll say. He was certainly a bit more surly than usual."

"Do you think he is developing Dome Syndrome?" Tom saw Steven visibly wince at his suggestion—probably because 'Dome Syndrome' was one of the potentially subversive phrases Steven said he tracked for the FCC. People who didn't adjust well to dome life were generally classified as having Dome Syndrome. Effects of the syndrome varied from minor to severe claustrophobia or depression, and in some cases, severe psychosis and/or suicide. The concept of Dome Syndrome was widely known because it affected so many first generation domers—people like Grandpa Frank who had years of exposure to life on the Outside prior to going under the dome. Steven had mentioned scrubbing renegade postings on the Net that hinted the worst effects were much more common than most people realized and might be spreading beyond first generation domers to second generation domers who had never seen the Outside. Tom dismissed the thought. Anyone could write anything on the Net after all, true or not.

"I don't think so, Tommy. He has been under the dome for almost sixty years. I think it has more to do with losing Grandma three years ago. Back before domes, surgeons might have been able to save Grandma when the cancer didn't respond to other treatment. As far as Grandpa is concerned, our dome society killed Grandma."

Tom nodded. Steven's theory made sense. Complex surgery wasn't available to domers. Indeed there were surgical and dental field kits that could be specially delivered to domes that allowed doctors to remotely conduct less complex surgeries. One of the men in Tom's army unit came down with appendicitis last year and the Army sent two devices to his friend's dome. One device was remotely controlled by an anesthesiologist to keep the patient sedated and the other device was a small, odd-looking metal frame with half a dozen miniature robotic arms that was placed over the patient's abdomen. A team of surgeons and nurses remotely controlled the small robotic arms that held scalpels, retractors, sutures, and lasers. Today, Tom's teammate was as good as new.

"So, come across anything really interesting on the Net that needed scrubbed lately?"

Steven smiled. "You know I am not supposed to talk about that!"

Tom threw his head back against the chair cushion and laughed. "You break that rule every week just like I tell you about my military exploits. We're both smart enough not to blab that info to others over the Net."

Steven put his forefinger up to his lips. "Shhhhh! Quiet."

"What? Steve, you don't think the government has hidden microphones and cameras planted in all the domes?"

"No, I don't," Steven answered without hesitation. "There is no evidence of that."

Both men knew their doming history. When people first went under domes there was a tremendous amount of work done to assure citizens that there were no such hidden listening devices. Private contractors from non-American firms scoured every square inch and investigated every electronic component.

"On the other hand, audio, video, and text transmitted over the Net..." Steven pointed to the dark computer display panel on his wall, "...that is another story—that communication can be tracked."

Tom studied the blank video screen on Steven's wall. His brother had explained several years ago that the government didn't have the resources to monitor all communications sent over the Net but it did have computer software that automatically searched audio and text streams for words and phrases that might indicate subversive activity. Tom considered other Net rumors as well. "Right, the government can tap into any communication over the Net that it wants to but what about Black Shine's claim that the government can use the cameras and microphones in the video screen units even when the power is switched off?"

Steven lifted his free arm into the air in half a shrug. "I suppose that *might* possible, but I don't buy it. Be careful, now. Remember what I said about using the name of that rebel…"

"Yeah, I know, sorry." Steven had indeed warned him previously to never put those two words together in text or speech over the Net. Nothing would attract the attention of the FCC faster than search hits that located Net traffic containing the name of the mysterious underground anti-government movement known as Black Shine.

"Okay, just be careful," Steven warned. "Now back to your original question, nope, no new juicy Net rumors. How about your world of robot soldiers? Is England still paying you to kill pirates in East Africa?"

"Correction, Great Britain is paying the United States Treasury for the use of certain US Army assets, yes, that is correct. We're planning an operation right now."

Steven rolled onto his back then after a few quiet moments asked, "Tom, do you ever think much about Grandpa Frank's ramblings against dome life? I don't. I mean life—well, except for losing Dad—life seems pretty good to me."

Tom leaned forward, rested his elbows on his knees and thought about Steven's question. He had a great job, a loving family—including Grandpa Frank even if he got ornery every once in a while—he had hundreds of friends all over the Net, and he was about to move into his own dome, get married and start a family. Why trade all that to live in fear on the Outside?

"No, I don't put much stock in his complaints either. Life seems pretty good to me, too. In fact..." Tom jumped to his feet and clapped his hands together. "In fact, things are great and I am going back to my room to talk with the young lady that I am going to marry next week!"

Tom slapped his brother's leg on his way to the door. He swung the door open but before stepping across the threshold Tom turned and tugged on his shirt. "One thing though. . . on the Net, I have seen a lot of pre-dome photos of people from all over the world, and these gray pajamas we wear all day—not very stylish—I might have to give Grandpa Frank that one."

Steven dismissed his brother with a wave. "Who needs fashion when you never leave your home? Say 'hello' to Jenny for me. And for Grandpa Frank's sake, you two better not get carried away and get too loud."

After a sarcastic 'yes, sir,' Tom was gone.

2.

Tom finished his shower, wrapped a towel around his waist and walked out of the bathroom toward his room two doors further down the dimly lit dome perimeter. To his right, the spacious central living area was a black void. The automated lighting was in nighttime mode, keeping the entire space too dark to clearly see the far side, one hundred feet away. It was late and everyone was presumably in his or her bedroom. Tom shut his door, threw his towel over the chair and slipped into bed. He sat upright with a pillow between his back and the headboard. He said one word: "Jenny," and the large panel display on the opposite wall popped on in an instant. Two seconds later, his fiancé's image filled the screen and Tom welcomed her into his bedroom.

"Hello there, Gorgeous!"

Jennifer Salem beamed a broad smile over the Net. Like Tom, she sat in her bed with her back against the headboard. Her full, dark brown hair flowed down both sides of her face, over her smooth white complexion and high cheekbones and then onto the bed sheet that covered her chest. Jenny's wide, dark brown eyes stared lovingly through the display screen.

"Hi, sweetheart. I missed you!"

Tom matched her beaming smile. "Was this morning really such a long time ago that you've had time to miss me?"

Jenny gave one exaggerated nod of her head, "Yes, indeed, Mr. Corant."

Tom clasped his hands together behind his head and leaned back. "Did your day go okay?"

"Yes, it did, thank you. I received my first work schedule. I start next month on the 14th as expected. So once we move into our own dome next week, I will be remotely building domes in one room, and in the next room you will be fighting the scourge of the Earth—at least until quitting time."

"After which, we'll find something better to do," said Tom with a playful wink. "Is that what you are thinking, young lady?"

"Maybe," came the coy response. "So how was your day, Tommy?"

"It was okay until Grandpa had another episode." Tom recounted for Jenny Frank's comments during the family dinner and also relayed Steven's theory explaining the behavior.

"Yes, honey, I think your brother is probably right about that. Doesn't sound like Dome Syndrome to me. He misses his wife. I think that is sweet and I feel sorry for the poor man."

"Yeah, losing Grandma hit him hard. But I'm worried about how he is influencing Jonny. Jonny is asking a lot of questions about the Outside that I never bothered about. What if, like they say, excessive curiosity about the Outside can eventually lead to Dome Syndrome?"

Jenny brought her arm across her chest to hold the bed sheet in place as she leaned over to grab the glass of water on the nightstand. After a quick sip, she answered Tom. "Well, honey, you have known me for nine months now and you know that I am a little closer to Jonny's side than yours in that regard. Do you still maintain that you have no interest at all in what it's like outside these domes?"

Tom didn't hesitate. "No interest at all, baby. You saw the gruesome pictures of Boston and Washington atomic bomb victims that they show every seven-year-old in second grade. *That's* the Outside. I say 'no thanks' to that world."

"Sure, I saw the pictures. If they weren't censored from the Net, I bet the pictures of our retaliatory strikes on Iran and Yemen are just as gruesome. But the world has to be so much bigger than just those places, Tommy.

Wouldn't it be something to get to the Outside and just run, run as far you wanted!?"

The excitement shining from Jenny's face made Tom grin, not because he shared the sentiment, but because it highlighted her best features. He loved that smile, but he shook his head at her question. "No, I'm not sold, Jen. What about all the dangers out there?"

"Tom, there already *are* people living on the Outside in the United States."

Tom knew Jenny was right on that count. There were small groups of "Outsiders" not living inside domes. A few thousand lived in scattered strongholds built by rich individuals who realized their wealth was useless inside a dome. But the government permitted the establishment of only a few strategically located strongholds which were expected to supplement automated physical security of important infrastructure like factories, power plants, waterworks, and food stores. The remaining super wealthy individuals who didn't like the idea of life in a dome bought citizenship in another country and left America for good. There were a few others who refused to go under the dome and hid in the wilderness long enough to avoid compulsory doming. They were referred to as "Stragglers" and had been resourceful enough to evade capture by the government's "Rat Patrols" that hunted them. Anyone who evaded capture until the final dome was sealed in 2028 was on their own, but at least they were no longer hunted. There was a small group of military on the Outside and thousands of farm laborers descended from Hispanic illegal aliens, all performing tasks that current robot technology could not yet replicate efficiently.

The last group living on the Outside was much larger—over two million Native Americans. The American Indian community, despite being comprised of many different tribal cultures, was surprisingly unified and exceptionally defiant toward the concept of living inside domes. The government eventually conceded that going under the dome would be voluntary for members of Indian tribes and as a result, nearly half of the Native American population chose to remain Outside. But in exchange for their forbearance regarding the forced doming policy, the government made agreements with several Indian nations to act as an Outside defense force, protecting the borders of the United States, and assisting the strongholds with protecting the four regional dome farms and all agriculture and manufacturing infrastructure in the country. An agreement with what became known as the Treaty Tribes was quickly reached before the first group of US citizens went under dome in 2019. Included in the agreement, at the insistence of the tribes that traditionally lived on the Great Plains, was the obligation of the government to reconstitute the great bison herds that once roamed the country's central plain. Consequently, throughout the years of planning and building the dome society, certain resources were diverted and tasked with planting prairie grasses and hastily ripping up thousands of miles of highways, railroads, and fences in order to eliminate barriers that could interfere with reestablishing the migration patterns of the buffalo.

"Yes, there are people living on the Outside, but it must be a very insecure existence," noted Tom.

"Tom, you drive combat robots. You must have seen a lot of the Outside through the robot video feeds. What does it look like out there? Fear of Dome Syndrome has the Net is so scrubbed of outdoor pictures and video, no one can get a good idea."

"Actually, I see satellite imagery and I do get video feeds from robots and aerial drones, but nothing in the visible light EM band. What I see of the Outside is extremely distorted and certainly not very appealing because the thermal infrared cameras assign colors to temperature variations in the environment. I never see things the way the human eye would see them."

Jenny's frown contrasted sharply with her beaming smile of moments ago. "So you don't want to....to...say, touch a tree?"

"Why? I've read descriptions of them."

"See a cloud?"

"Why? Net articles say they are just groups of ice crystals."

"Swim in a lake?"

"Can't swim."

"Breathe fresh air?"

"The air's just fine in here," insisted Tom. But he sensed Jenny's growing frustration and realized if he had any hopes of transitioning into a more intimate session with his bride-to-be, he better pursue a different track. "You're not wearing anything under that sheet, are you?"

"I thought I was the one asking the questions here, Thomas," scolded Jenny in mock anger.

"Ah, I thought so. Well, that makes two of us!" Tom grabbed the top of his sheet and threw it off his body.

Jenny giggled as she watched Tom's bare, reclining image on her display screen. "You are incorrigible and immodest, Mr. Corant."

"Right on both counts, Ms. Salem. Would you like to see me go for salacious?"

"Sure," Jenny responded demurely. "Let's see what you've got."

"Alright, but let's not wake Grandpa Frank."

3.

"That's checkmate, Tom."

"Ari, you crush me every time! Can't you let me win just once?" Tom had known Ari Goldman since third grade. Their weekly chess game ended the way it usually did, but their games were recreational. Serious chess players would scoff at the way Tom and Ari chattered back and forth during the game.

Tom liked to keep up with advancements in robotics and enjoyed discussing the subject with Ari who remoted into the big robot works near Columbus, Ohio to perform his government-assigned job as a robotics engineer. Technological breakthroughs were happening more often now that the country's resources weren't dedicated solely to building huge numbers of domes or automating entire industries so they could be run remotely in a world where people were never permitted to leave their home.

Programmable robots and remote teleoperation of factory equipment by domed workers had allowed the United States to become a manufacturing giant once again. Factories churned out superior products at low cost since there were no salary, healthcare, or pension costs built into the price of goods. No currency—tangible or electronic—flowed through the private side of the US economy because food, shelter, healthcare, and all needs were provided by the government. The pool of available workers was so large, the average person worked only nine hours a week; consequently there were no labor shortages and no labor unrest. High-quality steel was stacking up in western Pennsylvania for domestic use and for export. Farm equipment, computers, military vehicles, electronics, robotics, aircraft, ship building, nuclear power, pharmaceuticals, weapons, and industrial chemicals were just some of the industries that produced product for export via teleoperation of factories and transport vehicles.

With all industry owned by the government, the revenue poured directly into the US Treasury.

Tom Corant's career was not in the manufacturing sector but his work did occasionally contribute to the Treasury. Tom was a US Army sergeant who specialized in remotely operating heavy infantry fighting robots, nicknamed "combots" by the troops that drove them. When not fighting for US interests, the government rented Tom and his combot-driving colleagues to other nations as paid mercenaries. Other military men and women sat in their domes and remotely flew aerial drones, or controlled automated military transport vehicles on land and sea, or they controlled any number of support robots that loaded ships, maintained vehicles, managed supply depots, and so on.

"You are getting better, Tom...really." Ari's smiling round face floated in a window to the left of the chess board on Tom's bedroom display screen.

"I don't believe that, but thanks, Ari."

"Sure, Tom. Next week, say a prayer before we play. Maybe that will help."

Tom found himself pondering Ari's suggestion for a moment. He thought about sitting on the living room couch every Sunday with his family as they and thousands of others joined Reverend Bixby's Methodist Church service videoconference. He listened to the sermons and mouthed the lyrics of the hymns when they scrolled along the screen. But was there really anything to all that?

"Ari, do you really think a prayer will help me?"

Ari hesitated for a moment, puzzled by Tom's unusually introspective demeanor. "Well, sure Tom, don't you?"

"I am beginning to wonder about that."

"That's not an unusual sentiment, Tom. One of my father's favorite topics of dinner discussions is the effect of dome life on religion and faith. He sees a marked decline in faith among several religions. Domes have taken away Fear and government provides for all needs. Mind and body are so content under domes, some people are forgetting about their soul. As for my people, we have been running and hiding and fighting for so long, this little stint under domes won't put a dent in our faith. You, however, are cut off from nature and might be a little more vulnerable. You're on a dangerous path my friend. God is real. If you are having doubts, think about talking to my father or my rabbi."

"Thanks for the offer, Ari. I might take you up on that someday soon. Hey, I have to go. I have to kill pirates in East Africa for the Brits in a few minutes."

"The British are paying for US mercs? Why don't they just send in their SAS?"

Tom shrugged. "I think we end up being cheaper than the Special Air Service. Plus, this is a very remote location with no friendlies in the area. If something goes wrong, we don't have to worry about extraction. If we get into serious trouble, we just blow the self-destruct charges on the combots and we're done."

"All right, I will catch you later, Tommy." Ari's face disappeared from the screen.

Tom took a sip from his water cup on the night stand and lifted himself up into a more comfortable position with his back flat against his headboard. He logged into the mission grid with his password while biometric sensors on his display screen and keyboard confirmed he was indeed Sergeant Thomas Corant and was authorized to participate in the mercenary operation. The mission status display indicated the combot transport vehicle (a standard, teleoperated 18-wheel tractor/trailer) would reach the demarcation point in eighteen minutes. The transport had already rolled through Ethiopia and driven across the border into Somalia. The rig drove through

Galkayo without incident and would reach the destination of Hobyo momentarily.

Tom logged into his combot unit and began a systems check. He would be driving a standard M18 unit armed with dual, fully automatic M4 carbines and carrying an 8,000-round ammunition load. Heavy infantry combots were about the height of the average man but in no other way did they resemble their human controllers. The top portion of a combot contained a weapons package that consisted of dual machine guns, or dual grenade launchers, or one of each weapon enclosed within a hardened dome that could rotate 360 degrees. The weapons dome sat above a circular skirt of armor that contained the power plant and batteries. The power package was in turn connected to the top of the locomotion package. The most common locomotion package was a quadruped unit with tracked rollers in each of the four feet for moving on smooth surfaces. Each appendage also had ankle, knee, and hip joints to allow the robot legs to mimic the motion of human legs when crossing more difficult terrain. The weapons inside the domed turret had their shoulder stocks removed so they were significantly shorter than human-operated versions. The shorter length meant the turrets had a diameter small enough to allow combot units to easily walk or roll through doorways. In the end, most combots were merely squat cylinders with rounded domes on top and four legs projecting beneath.

All systems checked out okay: weapons, power, gyroscope, infrared camera, satellite link. Tom and his combot were ready for the fight.

Tom watched the text of the mission update ticker scroll along the bottom of his screen. He wiped his moist palms on his domer pajama pants and waited anxiously for the trailer doors to open so that he could survey the desert battlefield. The update ticker reported that hostages were in the area; then noted the transport rig was now stopped on the roadway. The driver of the car behind the combot transport was being told through an external loud speaker mounted on the trailer to drive around the transport rig and proceed down the road ahead of the truck. The driver refused and turned around.

That was a bad sign, thought Tom. The man's refusal to drive down the road probably meant landmines or some form of ambush up ahead. Tom wasn't surprised to see the message flash on his screen indicating the cargo door was opening.

"Okay, here we go," Tom muttered to himself while he cracked his knuckles and wiggled all his fingers to limber up before taking the controls. The top portion of Tom's display screen now showed the thermal infrared image from his combot's camera. Currently, the IR camera looked straight ahead at the background red glow of the truck trailer's hot metal side while in the foreground were several rounded cylinders of combot bodies represented by a cooler blue color. The bottom portion of his screen showed a three-dimensional map of the lawless coastal town of Hobyo, Somalia. The map indicated confirmed enemy positions and also tracked the position of each of the twenty-two combots as they rolled out of the transport truck and swarmed like an army of mechanical ants toward the town. For the time being, squad leader Ryan Belamy moved Tom's combot and the other nine combots of the second squad. Tom would take charge of maneuvering his individual combot when the heavy house-to-house fighting began. Shortly after his combot emerged from the trailer into the hot, bright Somali desert, an urgent message flashed on his screen that warned of incoming small arms fire. The message turned black and faded off the screen when the hostile fire was neutralized by return fire from the leading combots. The pirates had tried to set up a road block with 55-gallon drums filled with sand but concentrated machine gun fire from the combot on point killed the three armed pirates keeling behind the drums.

Although Tom did not yet have maneuvering control, he was able to rotate his combot's thermal IR camera to watch the other mercenary robots of his squad march through the small town of single story houses made of cement and clay brick, each with a sloping roof of corrugated tin—at least that is what the briefing session indicated they were made of. Many of the houses were surrounded by walled courtyards. The thermal IR camera was sensitive enough to show hints of the geometric paint patterns with which some of the houses were decorated. But the images Tom and the others saw through the thermal IR cameras were far different than what the normal, visible light images would have looked like through a human eye. In thermal infrared, the relatively cool sky displayed as a backdrop of dark purple. Houses were various patches of yellow and green walls with tops glowing red due to the hotter surface temperature of the metal roofs. People were either fuzzy dark silhouettes or bright glowing monsters depending on the time of day and the temperature of the surrounding environment. Tom used to hate looking at the Outside through the crazy patches of false colors that thermal infrared sensor systems assigned to objects according to the amount of heat they radiated, but he was accustomed to IR sensor displays now. His trainers told him it was easier to spot bad guys, day or night, with thermal IR. Grandpa Frank said there was another purpose for the weird sensor displays—the lack of detail and the patchwork of false colors prevented domers who remotely operated equipment on the Outside from seeing how beautiful the world really was.

Tom and his maneuver partner Meg Thatcher's combots neared their assigned compound and squad leader Belamy finally gave the squad full control of their robots.

"Okay, Meg, you ready?"

"Let's kick some ass, Tommy!" Meg wasn't as demure as most girls Tom knew.

"Southeast corner, then sweep counterclockwise."

"Roger that, Tommy. I've got your six and your right flank."

"Follow me into the first structure, Meg. I am going to use my bot to kick down the door."

Tom maneuvered his combot up to the wooden door and initiated the unit's pre-programmed mechanical door breaching procedure. The combot automatically shifted its balance onto three legs then used its fourth, free leg to deliver a powerful horse kick to the door. Audio pickups relayed a dull thud followed instantly by the sound of cracking and splintering wood. Thermal IR showed no signs of occupancy or movement. Tom swiveled his camera and watched Meg's combot come up behind his.

"Okay, I am going out the back." Tom repeated the door breach procedure and used subtle joystick movements to walk his combot outside the structure. Through the combot's loudspeaker, he played the language file that shouted stern commands in the local dialect to order everyone out of their homes. A hail of small caliber bullets clanged against his combot's frame in defiant response to the computer-voiced evacuation order.

"I'm taking fire, Meg!"

"Me too, Tommy. Let's rip them up!"

Both combot controllers drove their robots into the adjacent one-story rectangular building in the southwest portion of the compound where the hostile fire originated. Tom's thermal infrared camera showed half a dozen yellow, people-shaped blobs pointing weapons and firing. Muzzle flashes exploded as pulses of white lightening in the thermal infrared picture. Tom and Meg each used a standard four-second burst of automatic rifle fire to rake through the enemy pirates. Only one of the six men showed any signs of life after the barrage. The wounded pirate writhed in pain on the floor. Tom turned down his audio pickup so he didn't have to listen to the screams and fired a quick burst into the wounded pirate.

"Okay, Meg, we're clear. Follow me to the northwest building."

The remaining two buildings in the compound were empty but through the window of the last building, Tom's camera spotted a yellow blob carrying a rifle and scrambling over the rear wall. Much of the pirate's rifle still radiated a bright hot glow indicating it had been recently fired.

"Runaway out back!" Tom yelled into the microphones built into his bedroom's display screen.

Tom and Meg put their combots in gallop mode and ran the robots out the front gate and around the corner to find the unknown combatant running away from the compound. Tom blasted through the combot loudspeakers the indigenous language audio file that ordered "Halt!" but the pirate continued his flight into the desert.

"I will take the first shot at 300 meters," said Meg into her head set.

"Why do you get first shot?"

"I called it, Tom."

From bedrooms inside their separate dome homes, Tom Corant and Meg Thatcher watched the pirate flee into the Somali desert. They both switched their respective robot's weapons to semi-automatic manual firing mode and took aim. When the laser rangefinder reported the fleeing criminal was three hundred meters into the desert, Tom heard Meg's combot discharge one round. The man stumbled off stride, obviously hit, but didn't fall.

"Damn it," Meg pounded her mattress in disappointment.

Tom aimed carefully, compensated for the slight signal delay, and transmitted the shoot command. The bark of the carbine was mercifully muffled by the software controlling the combot's audio sensors—no need to transmit the full force of that uncomfortably loud sound back to the combot operator. One second later the running man flopped motionless onto the desert sand.

"Hah! Winner and still champion—Thomas Corant!" Tom pumped his fist in the air in celebration.

"Stop your gloating, Tom. I will get you next time."

Moments later the lieutenant in charge of the mission called a cease fire. Combots controlled by the beach team had rescued the hostages and prevented the pirates near the shore from launching missiles and grenades to destroy the captured vessel.

"Nice work everybody," said the lieutenant over all frequencies.

Tom maneuvered his combot toward the main road at the southwest end of town. Standard procedure called for him to establish a defensive position while awaiting clearance to load his combot back onto the transport which would drive back to Djibouti to begin a discrete exit off the African continent. Tom thought he heard a brief rush of muffled noise then he lost all battlefield audio and his combot's video feed went black. Every effort to reestablish contact with his combot failed. Tom muttered curses under his breath and called Meg through a standard Net message window to see if she knew what happened.

"Hey, Meg, what's going on? I lost contact with my combot."

"Wow, Tommy, your bot is in *pieces*! You must have stepped on a land mine or someone touched off an IED."

"I'm dead?"

"You are so dead! The Lieutenant is going to tear you a new one."

"Well okay, if I'm dead then I'm going for coffee. Bye, Meg." Tom had been chewed out for losing robots before, this wasn't the first time and wouldn't be the last.

4.

Shabbakasha was a warrior of the Penateka division of the proud Numunuh people, or in the language of the frightened turtles hiding in their shells, he was Roving Wolf of the Comanche Nation. He sat high and supremely confident in the saddle, familiar with every sound and movement of his mount. His riding pants were US Army desert battle fatigues. The matching shirt was folded inside a saddle bag since the dark complexion of his bare torso was more than a match for the weak winter sun. He wore his jet black hair the traditional way, parted in the middle and twisted into two thick braids down to his waist. The sunglasses weren't traditional, but they would preserve his sight for later years. Slung across his tanned back was a buffalo skin quiver full of arrows, each handmade from the wood of a dogwood tree. Strapped to the left side of the saddle was a bow carefully crafted from buffalo horn that he could string and fire his first arrow within five seconds, all while riding at a full gallop. Tucked along the right side of his saddle, for good measure, was a fully automatic Colt M4A1 carbine, heavy barrel variant. Night scope and M320 grenade launcher attachments were packed in a readily accessible saddlebag.

He had followed the men since they forded the Rio Grande near the small town of Presidio and turned north along US Route 67—six Mexican army soldiers on horseback, traveling quickly and not taking good care of the twelve horses in their company. The six spare horses were already saddled and carried light packs. Roving Wolf guessed the extra mounts were getaway horses—horses used in emergency pursuit or retreat situations usually after riding the first mount to the point of exhaustion.

The Mexican patrol traveled during the day and stopped each night to bed down inside an abandoned building. With most US citizens under domes, there were millions of abandoned buildings across the country available to travelers but fifty years of neglect and weathering resulted in some structures being more serviceable than others. They stabled their horses under roofs as well. Late March nights in this arid country could easily dip below freezing. Roving Wolf suspected the horses were stabled more from concern about being seen by the infrared camera of a military surveillance satellite or an aerial drone rather than concern about the health of the animals. Being discovered was a dangerous proposition given that the United States enforced border security with a long standing shoot-to-kill order.

Half past ten in the morning of the third day, the Mexicans left Fort Davis, still traveling north but now on Texas State Route 17 heading toward Pecos. They had yet to spot a single soul during the trek. Every small town building and private ranch along the way was deserted, dilapidated, and clearly showing the effects of fifty years of complete neglect—the normal conditions found in any county across the United States these days. Only a handful of Outsider strongholds or town areas frequented by Native American bands were properly maintained.

On the trail ahead, the small Barilla mountain range grew steadily closer. The brittle shrubs and dead prairie grass patches of the desert lowlands gave way to juniper, oak, and pinyon pines as elevation increased and as they skirted the eastern boundary of the Davis Mountains.

Since the mid-morning sun wasn't in a position to reflect off the lenses, Roving Wolf took a quick look at his quarry through his binoculars. He was forced to keep a significant distance between himself and the Mexican patrol in order to minimize the chances that the soldiers would see dust plumes kicked up by his horse. But the men he followed were moving into the mountains now and he would be able to close the distance soon.

Roving Wolf trailed the invaders under the cloudless, deep blue Texas sky and speculated about their possible mission objectives. Their destination seemed certain, for the soldiers were on a direct course toward the southernmost boundary of the Texas dome farm. Located largely in the area known as the Staked Plain, the Texas dome farm contained 30 million domes within an area the size of West Virginia. The dome farm began just north of Amarillo and continued down through Lubbock, Midland, ending near Fort Stockton and was wide enough to include a portion of eastern New Mexico. The balance of the seventy-five million domes that housed the country's population was spread among three other dome farms, one in southwest Arizona, one on the border between Arkansas and Mississippi, and one straddling the border between North and South Carolina.

The incursion by the Mexican patrol was the first of its kind as far as he knew. One would think that an armed foreign force only forty miles away from the southernmost domes was a high priority matter. Roving Wolf had used his portable SATCOM uplink kit to beam a situation report to the domed military officer directing his scout mission along the Rio Grande, but there didn't seem to be much concern. His orders remained the same: discretely observe and report but do not engage the enemy unless they threatened the spring cap or water station at San Solomon Springs outside the town of Balmorhea. The twenty million gallons of water per day that bubbled up through the ground at San Solomon Springs was a major component of the water supply for the dome farm and must not be compromised.

Just before the highway pressed through the pass between the Davis Mountains to the west and the Barilla Mountains ahead, the Mexican soldiers abruptly turned their horses due east. The change in course meant the waterworks at Balmorhea was safe, for the moment.

Roving Wolf believed that the scouting party was now using the south side of the Barilla range as cover for maneuvering closer to the dome farm that began across Interstate 10 just east of Saragosa.

Late in the afternoon, Roving Wolf broke off the direct chase to graze his horse before turning north to enter the hills and locate water. The Mexicans would be doing the same in two hours when they reached the end of the small range of hills. Roving Wolf planned to use the cover of darkness to approach the men and hopefully listen in on any campfire conversation. His Spanish wasn't perfect, but he would also setup a listening device that would capture sound and transmit any conversation to his Army handler for translation.

Before setting off on his mountain hike, Roving Wolf confirmed a tall clump of mesquite brush was free of any lurking animal dangers then sat down in its shade to text another report to his handler. The scout unfolded the antenna and opened the sturdy case of the SATCOM unit. His fingers punched the keyboard aggressively as he included in his message yet another plea to eliminate the threat. The presence of Mexican soldiers in *his* territory and so close to the domes and to his own family in Pecos stoked a growing anger—maybe this time he would get clearance for lethal action.

5.

The hot shower felt good after a strenuous workout in the family gym. Tom dried off and slipped into his domer wear. He draped his towel around his neck, opened the bathroom door, and stepped into the clean gray expanse of the dome central living chamber. His mother now sat on one of the four couches in the middle of the room; she must have emerged from her room while he showered. Her head tilted upward and her gaze was fixed on the giant main view screen, the far corner of which was directly above Tom's head so he couldn't see what was displayed. Although his mother's eyes never wandered from the screen, she was aware of his presence and gestured for him to come over.

"What's up, mom?"

Tom turned to look up over his shoulder as he walked toward the couches. Jenny's face filled the left quarter panel of the screen. Her smile widened when Tom walked into view of the cameras.

"Hi, honey. Your mom and I were just talking about the big day tomorrow."

Tom dodged the coffee table and sat on the couch next to Cynthia. "Is that so?" Tom gave a quick wink in his mother's direction and then turned back to the huge screen. "So, is everything all set?"

Cynthia nodded. "Yes. Dome Services confirmed that the transport vehicle will pick up Jenny at 7:00 a.m. The transport will then dock with our dome door at approximately 8:41 a.m."

"Be sure to be in the airlock on time, Tommy," instructed Jenny. "Dome Services stressed that for our safety, the transport will dock for only a few moments."

"Baby, there's no way I am missing that ride. Don't worry." Tom didn't admit to feeling more nervous as the transport time neared. He didn't believe he had cold feet.

Acute apprehension before such a significant life event had to be normal after all.

"I won't let him leave you at the altar, Jenny," Cynthia promised. "You should both arrive at your new dome around 10:10 a.m. Reverend Bixby and your dome counselor will be on the main screen waiting to speak with you. At 11:30 the video conference will begin. It looks like we will have about 630 logins from domes of friends and family. Reverend Bixby expects to start the ceremony at 12:00 p.m. sharp."

Like every engaged couple for the past sixty years under domes, Tom and Jenny would be transported to their empty new dome to begin their married lives. The marriage ceremony would be conducted via video conference soon after arrival. There would be no rings to exchange, no wedding dress, no cake or flowers, no reception, and no exotic honeymoon travel—total cost of the wedding: $0.00.

Cynthia briefly reminisced about her and Paul's first day in their dome. The same simple wedding ceremony performed remotely with the big view screen carved into a couple hundred small squares, each showing the face of a guest, some display windows showing a whole family group, especially in the case of invited relatives. But after the ceremony, the big screen turned off, the barrage of well wishing chatter disappeared and she was all alone with her new husband. The dome was so big and so quiet. It was no wonder their minister and dome counselor recommended starting a family right away. Cynthia smiled when she recalled that she and Paul had done just that—they didn't even make it to the bedroom that first time.

Tom listened to the banter between his mother and Jenny while he rubbed the towel against his damp hair. He was all set for tomorrow. There wasn't anything to pack. Domers didn't have any possessions.

Cynthia tapped Tom's knee. "Now, Tom, be sure to buzz back here daily to speak with Jonny. This won't be easy on him at first. I know how he looks up to you and that you spent a lot of time together, especially after Paul died. Don't give him a chance to miss you."

Tom nodded. "Sure, mom, I won't be a stranger to Jonny." Tom saw Cynthia's eyes take on a pre-tear glisten. He knew it wasn't only Jonny who wanted that daily call.

Jenny's voice blared down from the giant screen again, "Cynthia, I will make sure Tom doesn't forget to call. I had to practically give my family and friends a detailed schedule of when I would check in with them."

Tom stood, fighting a slight stiffness that set in after the heavy workout. "Okay, I am going to leave you two to finish your plans." Tom blew a kiss to the screen. "Talk to you later, baby!"

"Bye, Tommy. I love you."

Tom walked over to the kitchen and prepared two cups of coffee before checking in with Steven for one last bull session with his big brother—last *in-person* session anyway.

6.

First Lieutenant Kevin Benson sat in his dome bedroom studying the map of West Texas displayed on the wall-mounted screen above the foot of his bed. The young army officer used the control stick built into his wireless keyboard to zoom in to the portion of the map containing navigation detail on the small Barilla range of hills that rose from the Texas desert 200 miles southeast of El Paso.

A blinking icon in the lower right corner of the screen indicated someone was requesting a conference. The name on the icon was Kevin's superior, Major Charles Lassiter. The junior officer tapped the keyboard to accept the call and Major Lassiter's face appeared in a window that hovered over the map.

"Anything new on the Mexicans, Kevin?"

"No, sir. They have spent a second day camped in the hills observing the dome farm with some high-powered optics. They are about four miles from the nearest dome. Blue-21, says they have no heavy weapons or significant amount of explosives," reported the Lieutenant who used the codename for the Comanche scout he directed on the surveillance mission.

"What have the Mexicans seen over the last two days, Lieutenant?"

"About what you'd expect, sir, some Dome Services vehicles delivering rations and picking up waste. There have been two small systems maintenance vehicles that made service stops at four different domes in the area—servicing HVAC and air filtration systems. There was one morgue unit that removed a body from an area dome but that operation might have been beyond their notice. The extraction was over a mile and a half north of the perimeter domes. There was also some eastbound traffic down I-10, an eight-truck convoy. I don't know what the trucks were hauling but the remote operators had them moving at high speed. Two of the Mexicans did actually ride north to the Interstate the day after the convoy but they turned around moments after reaching the highway."

Major Lassiter nodded silently as he took in and contemplated the information. I-10 was part of the road system that connected the four dome farms across the country. The highway was far enough south that it wasn't destroyed to accommodate buffalo herds like the more northerly roadways in Oklahoma, Kansas, Nebraska, and South Dakota.

"Our scout has gotten close enough to record a bit of their conversation but they aren't talking much business. They do seem concerned about being caught on US soil," added the Lieutenant.

"Of course they are concerned. We are within our rights, and within our rules of engagement, if we shot those bastards dead right now."

From within his dome home, Major Lassiter studied the same map Kevin Benson studied. "Maybe they are just conducting a basic 'observe and report' scouting mission?" suggested the major.

"Maybe, sir. But why send six guys, then?"

"Survivability…in case of trouble, enough men to fight their way out? You reported earlier that they don't seem to have a long range transmitter. That means they have to live to tell their tale."

"Yes sir, unless they are on a one-way mission."

The major considered that possibility for a moment. "Still doesn't make sense. And you said earlier they have foil blankets to help hide their infrared heat signature? It's a good thing they don't know how little we have in the way of satellite assets. Anyway, this 'invasion' has been reported all the way up the chain. According to the general, the National Security Advisor and the Secretaries of Defense and Homeland Security are pondering this situation right now and if they know about it, the President knows."

"I still can't give the order to Blue-21 to take them out?"

"Negative, Lieutenant. Everyone wants to see what they are up to first. Do you think your scout could take all six of them down if such an order is ever given?"

Kevin laughed. "Sir, they wouldn't stand a chance."

7.

Tom held the coffee cup handles with one hand and rapped on Steven's bedroom door with the other. The door opened quickly and Steven ushered Tom inside, taking the cup of steaming black coffee that Tom offered.

"Hey, thanks Tom." Steven plopped down on his rumpled bed covers and set his cup on the night stand. Tom sat in the recliner and placed his cup in a cup holder built in the chair arm.

"You still working, Steve?" Tom asked and gestured in the direction of his brother's wall-mounted video display.

"Yeah, I ran into some Net traffic claiming that the US government is secretly working with the United Nations to put the entire world under domes—just a wild conspiracy theory at this point that isn't generating much discussion yet." Steven picked up his keyboard. "Let me just clear my screen. By the way, I have a new Dungeons & Dragons campaign starting in an hour. I suppose you still aren't interested—silliness I think you call it?"

Tom shook his head. "Everyone has different views on what's fun."

Steven reached for his cup. "As I recall your fun comes from playing poker?"

"Yes."

"And extensive use of your highly developed social networking skills?"

"Yes."

"And cybersex with Jenny?"

"Yes, again. Of course I will be getting the real thing tomorrow." Tom grinned proudly. Was that the cause of his increasing anxiety about tomorrow? He didn't think so.

Steven carefully sipped his hot brew. "You are still sure that Jenny is the one for you?"

"Of course she is," Tom insisted. "Why? You don't think I'm doing the right thing?" Tom's lingering anxiety deepened further. Was Steven sensing a problem or doubt about the wedding, too?

"Oh, I don't know, Tommy. Jenny is a great girl, certainly. But, can you spend the next sixty years in a dome together? That's what I wonder about regardless of the couple—not just you and Jenny. The government gives everyone one shot, no second chance. If you get a divorce you move back in with mom and can't ever marry again."

"Believe me, I am fully aware of that." Tom squirmed in his seat and sank further into the cushions of Steven's recliner. "Between the mandatory sessions with the government health counselor and the talks mom has arranged with Reverend Bixby, I do understand what I am getting into." Jenny and he had completed an exhausting battery of government forms and hours of interviews. He remembered Jenny's tears and heartbroken look the day they received the government recommendation that they not marry. What did they know, anyway? Tom still didn't understand the recommendation and wasn't about to follow it. Jenny and he got along so well together.

Both brothers saw the message icon pop onto Steven's screen. "Well, there is your bride-to-be right now." Steven smirked and used a voice command to open a video conference window.

An instant later, Jenny's smiling face appeared in the window. "Hi, Steve. Is Tom in with you?"

Steven adjusted the camera to allow Tom into the picture. "Hi, Jenny. See for yourself."

Jenny perked up considerably when the camera found Tom. "Hi, Tom! Thanks, Steve."

"Hello, Jennifer darling. Couldn't wait until our usual time?" Tom turned to his brother. "See how much she loves me?"

"I am not calling because I love you, I am calling to confirm you sent video conference notices to everyone," teased Jenny.

"Yes, mom helped out with that. We're all set on this end."

"Thanks, Tommy. What are you two up to? One last in-person brotherly chat?"

Steven held his extended index finger in the air then leveled it at the screen, "Yes, exactly."

"So Steven, tomorrow you will see Tommy's face up on your screen next to mine. Are you ready for that?"

"More than ready, Jenny. It will be good to have Tom out of here. The man can never remember to wipe down the gym equipment when he is done, or rinse a coffee cup, or pickup his soiled domer wear. He leaves his slippers in the unlikeliest of places. You will learn all these things and more for yourself soon enough."

Jenny giggled and whisked a clump of her long hair back behind her shoulder. "Hey, Tommy, do you think we will see any of the Outside tomorrow during the ride to our dome?"

Steven turned to Tom. "You are right, an unusual obsession with the Outside."

"I knew you guys were talking about me. I am not obsessed, just curious."

"Just curious about what the Outside *looks* like right? You surely don't think life on the Outside is better than life in a dome?" Steven had never talked with anyone who suspected the Outside was better—except Grandpa Frank.

"Of course she doesn't think the Outside is better. Look, all of us wrote our freshman English papers comparing life before domes and life after domes." Tom recounted some of the positive aspects of dome life that made it into most of those high school research papers. Crime of every kind was virtually non-existent unless someone in your own family snapped; no spread of infectious diseases; no homeless; no abuse of illicit drugs or alcohol because they were not allowed in ration packages; no worry of riots or strikes, no car accidents, no guns. There were no money problems because money was no longer needed or used, except by the US Treasury—the government provided everything. In addition to protecting against nuclear, biological and chemical man-made horrors, the domes were strong enough to protect against natural disasters like tornados, hurricanes, floods, or blizzards—and domes were not built in regions known for strong earthquake activity.

"My own paper focused on how family life is better under domes. The nuclear family is strong again with parents and children never leaving the home for work, school, or play. Divorce is very rare because there are no financial pressures, no possibility of infidelity, and because of government regulations that forbid remarriage after divorce."

"I never fully understood that," inserted Jenny. "I think everyone aspires to marry only once but humans are complex emotional creatures and things happen. Should the government really be in the business of preventing remarriage? I don't think so"

Steven scratched the top of his head and leaned back against his headboard. "I always understood the government's position on that was due to limited resources. The number of domes is limited and the resources needed to move people to and from domes are limited. That's why couples living in different domes farms aren't allowed to marry. The government doesn't have the resources for continually shuttling people among the four dome farms in Arizona, Texas, Arkansas, and the Carolinas." Steven went on to explain that the same resource limitations were responsible for other government policies such as not allowing single adults, or gay couples, or heterosexual couples who didn't want children to move into domes—someday those restrictions would be lifted, but the rebounding economy could not be burdened yet with a major dome building spree unless it was a foreign contract that generated revenue. Unlikely to change, however, was the ban on allowing multiple persons without family ties to live together in one dome because of a host of potential problems that would require too much intervention. Non-familial dome populations were limited to a small number of prison domes and domes housing those with the most severe physical or mental disabilities.

"I guess that makes sense," Jenny conceded.

"Gee, Jen, are you thinking we won't grow old together?" Tom joked.

Jenny slapped her crossed legs. "No, of course not!"

"I am just teasing, sweetie. Look, I don't see much on the negative side to dome life. The biggest negative I can think of is fewer life prolonging options for treating disease and old age because doctors can only work with patients remotely."

"I can think of a couple other problems…Art for one. People are writing and making music but no one is painting or sculpting because of the strict limitations on what materials can come into domes."

Steven nodded in agreement with Jenny. "And, just so you know, I have seen Net traffic complaining that all forms of Art are anemic these days and that condition is attributed to our separation from Nature and our lack of *physical* social contact as opposed to the current norm of social contact by video screen only. Of course, there continue to be complaints about landscape artworks being banned from the Net."

Tom agreed and added, "Grandpa misses sports like baseball, football, and basketball. We need to remember that Grandpa is a first generation domer so moving into a dome was much more of a hardship for him because there were things he had to give up. The three of us are third generation. We haven't lost anything, right? The way I see it, there are a whole lot of things in the positive column about domes and very few things in the negative column."

"That's my read, too," added Steven.

Jenny's head shook slowly back and forth. "I disagree. I can't help thinking we are missing out on *a lot* on the other side of these walls, gentlemen."

Tom snapped the recliner upright and leaned forward. "Baby, once we are together tomorrow, you won't have any lingering feelings about being unfulfilled."

Jenny laughed. "Well, someone has a rather high opinion of himself!"

"You see what I have been putting up with all these years!" exclaimed Steven. "I wish you much good luck, Jenny."

Tom jumped out of his chair. "Come on, honey. I know when I am not wanted. Let's finish this conversation in my room."

"Good night, Jenny," said Steven as he threw a pillow into the back of Tom's head.

Tom picked up the pillow and drew his arm back to throw. Steven held up an arm in a defensive position. "No, no, don't spill my coffee!" Tom heaved the pillow anyway which Steven nimbly dodged.

"Good night, Steve. You two are such brothers." Jenny meant that in the most loving and rambunctious sense.

8.

Tom shook Frank's hand. "Goodbye, Grandpa. I will miss you. But you're going to see me on the screen all the time. I'll be checking in often. It will be like I never left."

"Good luck, young man. I hope you get all the way out someday."

The Corant family gathered in front of the inner dome door. Even Jonny stood near the door despite his trepidation. Tom hugged both of his sisters. Lucy and Linda were smiling but they both soaked his shirt with their tears.

"We'll see you on the big screen in a couple hours for the wedding ceremony, Tom," said Linda. Lucy nodded in agreement but she was too emotional to add anything further.

"Sure. Of course. Don't miss me now," insisted Tom.

Steven reached out his hand which Tom shook vigorously; then the brothers embraced with Steven slapping Tom on the back before they broke.

"Good luck, Tom. Fill that dome full of kids."

Tom smiled. "I will work on that."

Jonny stepped up to Tom who knelt down on one knee and put his hands on his little brother's shoulders.

"Hey, Jonny. I see you managed to get close to the dome door. It's not so spooky, is it?"

"No, I guess not," but Jonny didn't sound too convinced.

Tom knew full well the source of Jonny's dread. His younger brother was only three years old when Steven and Tom carried the body of their dead father into the airlock. Jonny was supposed to be in his room with the door shut. Only later did the family learn Jonny had peered through his cracked door to see Steven and he take their father through the dome door but re-emerge without him.

Tom gave his little brother a long tight hug and now he too had to make an effort to choke back tears. "Jonny, you are going to see me all the time, I promise. I will be as big as a dome up there on the main view screen. Other times, I will be on your bedroom screen and it will be just you and me again. Okay?"

"Yes, Tommy." Then Jonny lost his battle to hold back his tears.

Tom stood after one more quick squeeze with Jonny.

Cynthia Corant was shedding tears so profusely Tom was afraid she would dehydrate and shrivel up right before his eyes.

"Come on, mom. Don't make this so hard."

Cynthia hugged her son for a long time. Tom was the first child to leave her dome. She knew this emotional trial would come someday and that it would be a gut-wrenching experience, but now that the moment had actually arrived, the impending separation was even more difficult to face than she imagined. Yes, she would see him bigger than life all the time on a giant view screen. But how could that be the same? Yet Cynthia did recall that when she left her childhood dome, she found herself calling back to her parents and siblings freely at any time and after a while, seeing their smiling faces daily, things really did settle down into a comfortable place. She hoped it would be the same with Tom.

Tom finally stepped back from Cynthia. "Gee, let's cheer up everybody! I hope you are in a better mood when I see all of you up on my big screen at the wedding!"

"It's time, Tom," said Steven. "You better get into the airlock." Steven punched the code to open the inner dome door.

Jonny stood in front of his mother who rested a hand on both of Jonny's shoulders. As the dome door swung open, Cynthia felt Jonny push backward against her.

Tom took a deep breath then stepped into the airlock. That was the official name for the eight-by-eight foot chamber but it really wasn't an airlock in the sense that it served to transition people between points of differing air pressures. The chamber was originally designed as a decontamination point for persons coming in from a hostile outside environment. Fortunately, sensors had never reported any radiological, biological, or chemical hazards outside their dome. Also, dome society policy changed after the government's initial dome plan—under the final plan, people would not be permitted to have the codes required to operate the outer door and exit their dome.

The door slammed shut with a hollow metallic clank. Through the small window Tom saw his mother standing with Jonny in front of her. Linda and Lucy were on either side of Cynthia, each with an arm around their mother. Grandpa Frank sat beside Lucy in his wheel chair. He stared at the door latch, not up through the window at Tom. Frank's face was twisted into a contemptuous scowl. Steven stepped over to put an arm around Linda and waved. Everyone but Grandpa Frank picked up Steven's lead and started a goodbye wave which Tom quickly returned before the protective window cover closed and his family was gone.

Tom turned around and leaned his back against the cold metal door that had just locked shut. He took another deep, deliberate breath hoping to purge some of the heavily charged emotion coursing through him. His eyes swept around the bare, empty chamber. Eight feet in front of him was the outer dome door. Beyond that door was the Outside; the Outside that his parents feared; the Outside about which Grandpa wistfully reminisced; the Outside that generated such curiosity within Jenny and Jonny; the Outside that Tom wanted nothing to do with.

Tom's wandering thoughts refocused when he heard the faint scraping of metal. He walked forward toward the outer door. Before he reached the door, the upper portion slid away into the left wall with a slow, grinding screech. Beyond the opening was the dim, enclosed interior space of the transport truck bed. On the far side of the otherwise empty cargo space, Jenny sat on a bench frantically waving both arms.

"Hi, honey, jump in!"

Then another voice echoed from speakers attached to the forward wall, "Climb aboard quickly, Mr. Corant, we need to get moving."

Tom obeyed the voice of the driver who remotely controlled the transport. He planted his hands on the lip of the opening then jumped off the floor pulling both legs up and rolling awkwardly onto the floor of the transport. He was on his back laughing and looking up at Jenny when the automated door of the cargo hold cranked closed.

"Is this really how everyone starts out their married life?" he joked while still on his back.

Tom rolled over and pushed himself off the floor then shuffled over to Jenny who was strapped onto the seat by a restraining belt. Jenny reached out with her arms as Tom knelt on one knee and they kissed for the first time.

"Hello, *Mrs.* Corant!!"

Jenny giggled, "Whoa, not yet, mister. You still have a wedding to go to!" Jenny said as she leaned forward for another kiss.

"Hey you two, you'll have plenty of time for that later," admonished the voice of the unseen remote transport operator. "Mr. Corant, sit down and fasten your seat belt, please."

Tom reluctantly complied, breaking Jenny's embrace to sit next to her.

Jenny grasped one end of the seatbelt and reached across Tom's lap for the other piece.

"Works like this," she said while demonstrating. "Flat end into the buckle, click, and pull this strap so the belt is low and tight across your waist."

After the 'click' Tom grabbed Jenny for another kiss. "Got it, baby—thank you!"

The transport accelerated away quickly causing the couple to lurch sideways.

Tom held his hand against the side of Jenny's head, feeling her soft hair that he had longed to touch for so long. Finally her sparkling brown eyes were looking at *him,* not an image of him on a video screen. It was a completely new experience that shot joy like an electric shock through every nerve in his body. "Wow, Jenny, it is so good to finally touch you!"

"I know, I wonder…," Jenny cut off her words with a startled shriek when the transport bucked violently upward.

"Whoa!!!," Tom yelled as they felt the transport leaning far to the left.

The transport tipped too far to recover and with a loud crash slammed onto its side. Tom's and Jenny's heads jarred hard against the transport's left—now bottom—side. The deafening reverberations of metal scraping along concrete pounded violently into their ears as the vehicle ground to a halt on the roadway.

"What the hell is going on out there!" exclaimed the transport controller from his dome bedroom 1,700 miles away in the Carolina dome farm. Jack Bekin had a spotless, trouble-free record for the last twenty-nine years of remote controlling Dome Services transport vehicles, but now his gasoline powered panel truck with modified dome door docking attachment was lying on its side, immobilized. Jack's stomach twisted into a knot of confusion and anger. "Are you guys okay in there?"

Tom rolled his head to his left and was relieved to see Jenny smile back at him. "Are you okay?"

Jenny nodded carefully. "Yes, what was that?"

"We are okay except for a ringing that is still pounding in my ears," Tom answered the remote driver.

"Okay, hang on you two. I am contacting the Dome Services emergency channel."

Jack clicked on the call button for emergency services and the duty officer popped onto his display.

"What's the problem, Driver?"

Jack looked at the face of the young woman who answered his call. She looked too young for what must be a rather important position. "Hello, officer. Are you running the shop? How old are you, officer?"

"That's not the way to get on my good side, Driver. State your emergency, please."

Well, all business, anyway. "My personnel transport overturned with two occupants. Nobody hurt. I sent the coordinates already. Here is a link to my video feeds…"

"Got it, Driver. Reassure your passengers. We'll have an emergency transport there in twenty minutes."

"Thank you, Services."

The loud bang on the rear doors of the transport startled Tom and Jenny. Then came another bang . . . and still another.

"What's that?" asked Jack. He picked up the loud noises from audio sensors on the transport.

"I was hoping you could tell us," said Tom.

After another bang, Jack saw the picture from the outside rear camera disappear.

Jack closed his audio feed to the transport so Tom and Jenny wouldn't hear his next call to emergency services. "Officer, are you seeing and hearing all this? You better get some military help out there. I think somebody did this on purpose and now they're trying to break into the vehicle!"

"I'm ahead of you, Driver. I already alerted dome farm security."

One more loud bang and the heavy "lower" rear door of the panel truck swung open and crashed onto the hard road surface. Tom and Jenny had to shield their eyes from the bright sunlight that flooded into the back of the truck.

After a moment came the stomping of several pairs of boots and excited voices talking in Spanish. Tom and Jenny were still strapped to their seats, disoriented, and suffering from mild shock when several pairs of strong hands grabbed their arms and forced hoods over their heads.

"¡No mueva!" The shout echoed through the overturned truck. The Mexican soldier wielding the hammer smashed the interior camera and Jack and emergency services lost the picture of what was happening to the passengers.

Tom and Jenny were unbuckled and snatched roughly to their feet, their hands quickly bound with rope.

"Tom, what's going on? I can't see anything," came the desperate cry from Jenny. The rope dug painfully into her wrists and the pungent body odor of the men was nauseating.

"¡Cállese!"

Tom heard the command for silence directed Jenny's way, then a muffled thud and then a shriek of pain from Jenny. He lunged in the direction of the man shouting commands and bowled one of the men to the ground, landing on top of the outlaw. Other hands grabbed him and rolled him onto the floor. Heavy boots pounded his chest, thigh, arm, and grazed his head.

"¡Vayamos!" Several more hands jerked Tom to his feet.

The squeak of metal and loud bang on the top of the transport told Tom the other rear door must have been thrown open by another one of the bandits.

Tom and Jenny were pushed roughly out of the truck. Tom was reassured to feel Jenny's hands find and grasp his left arm. The breeze was chilly but at least it dispersed the smell of sweat and body odor that fouled the inside of the transport. The road surface that the kidnapped couple shuffled along was much harder than the padded dome floor they had walked upon all their lives; their thin house slippers did little to cushion their feet against the uncomfortably hard concrete.

Tom heard more voices now, all talking too fast or with too much slang for him to follow with his limited exposure to Spanish. The hood over his head was terribly disorienting and was beginning to adversely affect his balance. The air that seeped under his hood carried a strong, musky animal smell that Tom didn't have the experience to identify. He heard the clopping sound of many footsteps on the concrete as well as occasional heavy snorting sounds all of which led Tom to correctly assume they were in the company of horses. He had seen enough indoor animal zoological videos to recognize the sound. Tom heard their captors say something about "*caballos*" which solidified his assumption. That was one of the few vocabulary words he remembered from class all those years ago.

Half a mile away, Roving Wolf watched the scene unfold through binoculars. There just wasn't enough brush to provide the necessary cover for closer observation. His horse was hidden a further half mile away, grazing in an arroyo. The Comanche scout used his SATCOM gear to text an urgent message to Lt. Benson reporting the attack on the personnel transport and the kidnapping of the couple. He again asked for permission to intercede but was again denied.

Roving Wolf watched the Mexican soldiers make several attempts to push both of the kidnap victims onto the backs of getaway horses before they were ultimately successful. The hands and feet of both victims were tied to the saddle and stirrups so the novice riders would not fall.

The party galloped west down I-10 away from the crime scene and toward an unknown destination. Roving Wolf sprinted to his own horse to take up the chase. After three miles the kidnappers led their captives south of the highway toward the cover of the increasing vegetation growing on the initial slopes of the Barilla range. The Mexicans stopped to water their horses near Lake Balmorhea and then turned due south to climb deeper into the mountains. Roving Wolf followed but with extra caution since the enemy soldiers would be watching their rear for signs of pursuit.

* * * *

Tom wondered desperately if the terrifying day was ever going to end. They had stopped briefly only twice. During the first break, one of the kidnappers rolled his hood up over his mouth so he could take a few gulps of water—that was the extent of the hospitality. Since they still couldn't see and were not allowed to speak, Tom and Jenny improvised a signaling system whereby they both coughed every once in a while just to confirm for the other that they were still alive and nearby. During the last stop, both he and Jenny stood next to each other and suffered the humiliation of urinating in front of their captors. Their wrists remained bound in front and the hoods on their heads blinded them to all, but Tom heard the whistles and cat calls and the laughter when he felt Jenny squat to relieve herself.

Earlier in the day, they had traveled swiftly over flat ground. Now Tom noticed that the pace had slowed and the trail was more difficult. He was forced to lean in all manner of directions for balance as his horse negotiated the steep, winding trail. His wrists were still bound together and tied to the horn of the saddle; his feet were bound to the stirrups. Tom's stomach growled with hunger and he had a thirst like never before in his life, but worse than anything else, worse than the thirst, and worse than the hunger and the fatigue, was the burning in his legs. Every part of him that touched the saddle protested painfully. He wondered if it was possible for skin to rub right off the bone. Tom thought about Jenny and hoped they would both have the strength to survive this horror.

9.

The air grew noticeably cooler and conversation among the Mexicans increased. Tom caught enough to know some of the men wanted to stop and start a fire but others argued against that course, probably out of concern about being seen, or so Tom guessed.

After a few more moments and a number of wild gyrations in his saddle, the ground leveled out and Tom heard some excited conversation among the lead men. Two minutes later the group halted.

Tom and Jenny exchanged cough signals. Soon rough hands were untying Tom from the saddle and pulling him off the horse. His captor made an initial effort to catch him in mid fall but Tom's foot caught in the stirrup and the kidnapper let him tumble the rest of the way to the hard ground. More hands pulled him to his feet. The soreness in his legs and buttocks and the chafing of his inner calves and upper inner thighs were remarkably painful. He walked the best he could with legs bowed outward as if he were still in the saddle. The laughs Tom heard were surely at his expense and due to his awkward gait.

After a few painful paces, Tom was pushed down to the ground. He was prone on his back with wrists still bound in front of him when he felt Jenny fall against his body. After a moment Tom risked a whisper, muffled by the ever-present blinding hood.

"Jenny, are you okay?"

"Tom, my legs…I can barely walk. It hurts so much."

Tom heard Jenny's struggle to keep from breaking into a plaintive cry. The pain and hunger were acute, but being able to talk to each other again lifted both their spirits.

"Can you see anything, Tom? I can't, but I think it might be nighttime."

"No, nothing. I haven't seen a thing since the transport. "

"Who are these thugs and what do you think they want with us?"

Tom shook his head inside his hood. "Probably Mexicans. I keep trying to catch what few Spanish words I know. They certainly reference Mexico a lot. They also reference "the general" and a couple times I heard the name "Mejias." I am sure they are referencing General Juan Mejias—the guy who led the overthrow of the civilian government, what—ten years ago? As far as what they want from us, who knows…ransom money from the government maybe?"

Jenny let a whimper of pain slip as she tried to roll into a more comfortable position on the hard ground. "Tom, I have never heard of such a thing, people being kidnapped from domes and ransomed?"

"Me either. Well, you wanted to see the Outside. I still say, what's so bad about the domes?"

"We have been outside all day but I haven't been able to *see* anything," corrected Jenny.

Tom and Jenny continued to discuss the day's events, discuss their families who would be wondering what happened, and they talked about when the government would rescue them.

The kidnappers had been lucky enough to come upon a canyon where water had drastically eroded a softer layer of the lower sedimentary rock which resulted in a significant overhang of harder rock twenty feet above them. That circumstance allowed the soldiers to build a fire that could not be seen from ground or air.

"Whatever they cooked smells pretty good. Do you think there is anything left for us?" asked Jenny.

"Don't hold your breath, honey."

"Part of me wants to roll closer to the fire so I can warm up, but then I would be closer to those animals."

"I can help a little with that, Jen." Tom lifted his tethered arms over his head and rolled onto his side, pressing close to Jenny so they could share body warmth. He also lifted his right leg and set it on top of Jenny's legs.

"That was painful."

"But appreciated. Thanks, Tom."

"You know, this isn't exactly how I imagined our first day together would go."

Tom heard Jenny's muffled laugh. Then Spanish-speaking voices were getting louder and coming closer. Someone grabbed his arm and pulled him into a sitting position. Jenny yelped when she received the same treatment.

Finally the cursed hood was pulled off his head. Tom looked left and saw Jenny, also hoodless now. Their backs were to the canyon wall which angled out over their heads and then faded into the dark night. Tom estimated the camp fire was roughly thirty feet away. He watched as three of the Mexicans cleared the remnants of the evening meal and prepared their bedrolls for sleep. The bandit who grabbed Tom was now busy tying Tom's feet together. The fifth Mexican set Jenny upright and examined a fistful of her thick brown hair. Tom thought he had heard at least six men on the trail but no one else was in sight. Beyond the fire was a pitch black void. Anything could be out there.

* * * *

Tom watched one of the Mexicans pound two metal stakes in the ground halfway between himself and the fire. When the man finished hammering he announced, "Está listo," then stood and tossed the hammer in the direction of the three bedrolls spread out by the fire.

"Bueno," responded the foreign soldier who clutched Jenny's hair tightly in his fist. The man turned and stared at Tom. Campfire glow flickered onto the criminal's face and lit his malevolent grin. He stood and pulled Jenny up by her hair as he rose. Ignoring her squeals of pain, he spun Jenny toward him and pressed her close while planting a hard unwelcomed kiss on her lips.

Jenny recoiled at the stench of the kidnapper but she could not break the embrace. Tom was bound too tightly to help and the man kneeling beside him put Tom in a choke hold to further immobilize him.

The Mexican soldier holding Jenny pulled her by the hair toward the stakes that were hammered into the earth. He pushed her to ground and was joined by another comrade who helped untie Jenny's wrist bindings only to re-tie her arms wide apart to each of the stakes.

Tom's eyes widened and his heart pounded faster in is heaving chest. He struggled mightily against his bonds and against his captor, but he was helpless. He shouted a loud, desperate "Noooo!" that was ignored by the kidnappers and lost to the black night.

The harder Jenny kicked and screamed, the louder the laughs and taunts became. One of the men unsheathed his knife and used its sharp point to lift Jenny's house shirt which was already ripped and torn from the day's ride.

The scream from the Mexican near the bedrolls was unexpected. Tom jerked his head to the right and saw the man on both knees with an arrow protruding from just under his sternum. It was then that Tom noticed the man closest to the fire was twisting on the ground and clutching at his throat. There were no screams coming from that man, only a sickening gurgle sound from blood passing over a pierced windpipe.

In the next moment, a gentle whoosh of air grazed Tom's ear followed by a dull thud when an arrow pierced the chest of the man restraining him. The soldier who helped tie Jenny to the stakes went down to the ground next, screaming with an arrow impaling his right kidney.

The Mexican manhandling Jenny took the next arrow into his groin.

As soon as he loosed his last arrow, Roving Wolf stepped over the cold body of the Mexican lookout and repelled thirty feet down to the canyon floor.

Tom watched the shirtless man with long hair braids and wearing US Army desert camouflage pants emerge from the gloom behind the fire and calmly walk to each Mexican, stopping just long enough to slice each man's throat.

After cutting the man nearest to Tom, Roving Wolf cut Tom's bonds. He then moved to Jenny and the last two Mexicans. He cut Jenny free before approaching the last soldier with the pierced groin. Roving Wolf put a knee on the Mexican's chest and commanded, "¡Cállese!"

The Mexican reduced his screams to a whimper when Roving Wolf pressed his knife to the bandit's throat and asked, "¿Por qué está usted aquí? ¿Qué desea usted?"

The wounded man shook his head violently and managed a weak response, "Mi capitán dijo hacer problemas."

Roving Wolf dispatched the invader as he had the others then turned to Tom who had scrambled to Jenny and was helping her sit upright. "Are either of you injured?" he asked.

Tom shook his head. "No, I mean, apart from being sore and hungry, thirsty and tired from the ride today. Who are you?"

Roving Wolf hesitated. Sharing names was a much more intimate exercise for many Native American cultures than it was for cultures with a European background. But he decided to humor the battered domer.

"I am Shabbakasha of the Numunuh people. You may say, 'Roving Wolf.'"

"Numunuh? I am not familiar with that tribe."

"You say, Comanche."

"Oh, okay. My name is Thomas Corant—you can call me Tom. This is my fiancé, Jennifer Salem."

"Jenny," added Jennifer, trembling in Tom's arms and still shaking off shock.

"You need rest. Food must wait." Roving Wolf helped Tom and Jenny with setting bedrolls near the fire and brought them some water and blankets. Roving Wolf left the company of the couple to remove the bodies from the camp, check on the horses used by the Mexican army patrol, and transmit a situation report to his handler.

Jenny lay close against Tom. Her trembling had eased and she had time to consider the situation and the violence that nearly befell her. "Can we trust him? And what does he mean food can wait? I'm starving."

Under the blanket, Tom put his arm around Jenny. "Trust him? What choice do we have? And yes, I think we can."

"But the way he killed those men without a thought…"

"Are you having sympathy for those animals after what they have done and were about to do?"

"No, I guess not. It's just that this has all been so…I don't know. I can't even describe it."

Tom knew what Jenny meant. The ordeal that had unfolded over the last twelve hours was a violent trauma unlike anything else in their previously sedate lives.

Tom watched the fire for a few moments; then he stared out into the blackness of the night. Before he realized it, fatigue pulled him into a deep sleep just as it had done with Jenny moments before.

10.

Roving Wolf woke Tom and Jenny well before first light and gave them a large plate of rice, dried tomatoes, and peppers sprinkled with a little hot sauce—all items from the packs of the Mexicans. The early morning was dark and cold. Tom and Jenny huddled under the same blanket near the small fire and scooped rice into their mouths like they hadn't eaten in weeks.

Jenny watched Roving Wolf return from preparing the horses for travel and she took the opportunity to inquire about the situation. "Will you be able to take us to our dome, or is someone coming out to get us?"

"No. I made a report about this fight. I have no instructions about you."

Tom finished his last pinch of rice and asked, "Are you a scout for the Army?"

"Yes."

"Great. I know I told you my name is Thomas Corant, but I am actually *Sergeant* Thomas Corant, US Army. I drive infantry combots. Are you saying that no one is coming to take us to our dome?"

"Correct. I won't leave you here. I will bring you to my village in Pecos—forty miles north."

Jenny was incredulous. "What? We can't go into our dome? What are we going to do?" Do our families know what happened?"

"I have no instructions about you," Roving Wolf repeated. "I will ask your questions when I make my next report. We must go."

Tom and Jenny looked at each other. There wasn't enough light to read each other's faces or the face of the man who had just told them they weren't going home. Tom didn't see the tears on Jenny's check but he felt them when she leaned over and touched her face to his.

"What are we going to do, Tom?"

"We'll figure it out. Don't worry, baby."

"Here, put this on." Roving Wolf handed Tom a small metal tin. "Inside is aloe vera gel, only enough for your most painful spots."

Tom thanked Roving Wolf. The prospect of more horseback riding was only slightly more appealing than staying in the desert to die. The aloe was soothing; he and Jenny wished there was more of it.

Roving Wolf helped the couple make the painful climb onto their mounts. He gave them each one of the Mexican infrared-masking foil blankets for warmth until the daytime temperatures rose. After a ten-minute crash course in horseback riding, Roving Wolf grasped the lead line and led the string of eleven horses out of the canyon. The twelfth horse was left behind. Roving Wolf had evaluated the horses during the night and that one he deemed too skittish and disruptive—probably going lame as well. Leading that many horses at once on a long ride was tricky and he didn't need problems. Fortunately, half of the horses were getaway horses that were already accustomed to being on a lead line.

It was still dark fifteen minutes later when the group emerged from the canyon overhang into a more typical mountain valley. Tom looked up at the twinkling lights in the night sky visible for the first time.

"Jenny, are you seeing this? Wow!" The shimmering stars took Tom's breath away.

"I am. It's wonderful."

As the group travelled down the slopes and out of the small range of hills, pre-dawn glow began washing away the fainter stars. Tom and Jenny watched in fascination as the eastern horizon cycled from purple, to red, then to orange. Roving Wolf noticed the couple's curiosity and halted.

"Why did you stop?" Jenny asked.

"So you don't miss your first sunrise. Be careful for looking at the sun, you can damage your eyes."

Tom and Jenny watched intently as the solar disc peeked above the earth and cast the day's first splash of sunlight into the sky. Fingers of wispy cirrus clouds pointed westward like a giant hand. Multiple shades of red and orange light washed through the clouds highlighting millions of ripples carved by the high altitude winds.

The sun was high enough to shine in full golden glory before either Tom or Jenny spoke.

"That is so amazing!" offered Jenny.

"Spectacular and beautiful, I had no idea." In that moment, Tom realized how profound was his ignorance regarding the natural world beyond the dome walls. He felt as if he were being born again.

"See, Tommy, this is the kind of thing I had in mind when I would muse about the Outside. Not nuclear blasts, or plagues, or poison gas attacks, or even Mexican brigands..."

Roving Wolf started the train of horses moving again. Meanwhile, daylight brought a million wonders to Tom and Jenny. Tom marveled at the vast open expanse of land in front of him. Massive, jutting rock of the Davis and Barilla ranges loomed behind them. Ahead was a sea of sage brush sometimes broken by ridgelines large and small. In other places, great tables of ancient rock in the form of buttes and mesas rose above the desert floor. Tom had seen sketches of those landforms, but never a photograph, and certainly never in person.

Jenny marveled at the scene as well. The land and sky were enormous. Equally fascinating were the glimpses of life flitting about the arid landscape. Rabbits darted among the scrub. Birds chirped excitedly when disturbed from their bushes by the convoy of horses plodding northeast.

"Tom, this is incredible!"

"Yes, sorry. I have been a bit speechless—just trying to take it all in."

Tom and Jenny chatted incessantly with each new discovery they shared. They found that mentally cataloguing the diverse wonders of earth and sky actually made the pain of saddle soreness and chafing seem intermittent rather than constant. They stopped just before the junction of Texas Route 17 and I-10 in order to water and graze the neglected Mexican horses.

Roving Wolf suggested they get a couple hours rest because most of the journey still lay ahead, but Tom and Jenny were too excited about investigating the Outside. Roving Wolf returned with two dozen canteens from the Mexican gear. He didn't trust the Mexicans' source of water and handed the canteens to Tom.

"Here, dump the water out, rinse, and refill from this stream. "

Tom took the canteens strung on a line. "Sure. Glad to help." He realized this was their first real good look at Roving Wolf. The prior evening had been too dark to define detail and in the past two daylight hours of riding, they saw his well-muscled and tanned back as he led the party, but saw little else. And, of course, they chased hundreds of distractions as they observed the vibrant new world that sparkled all around them.

Roving Wolf looked much younger in the light of day. His dark eyes looked as if they were interrogating everything and everyone they fell upon. His thin lips rarely betrayed a smile or a frown. (Tom did catch the Comanche scout grinning while watching Jenny scratch at the sun-baked ground with a bit too much fascination.) The desert uniform shirt that he wore against the chill of the night was again packed away in a saddle bag. Roving Wolf also wore a military web belt with a sheathed eight-inch combat knife on the left and a holstered M9A1 pistol on the right.

Tom set the canteens down near Jenny and knelt down to help rinse and fill, but he looked back up to Roving Wolf. "Look, I want to thank you again for saving us from those barbarians."

"You are in a world you do not know."

"What is it like living out here? Aren't you afraid of disease or one of the biotoxins that terrorist agents are starting to use?" ask Jenny as she pressed a canteen into the stream.

"Life is good here, free as the wind."

Tom pressed Jenny's question. "But in a dome you are safe from nukes and plague and terrorists and criminals, you always have food, the government gives you everything you need, you can visit friends and family all over the country via video conference in an instant."

"So the shell you live in takes your fear away?"

"I guess it does, yes."

"If the price of conquering fear is loss of freedom, I say that is too high a price. Because you don't know freedom, you don't value it. Our medicine chief says: 'conquer fear with faith, not with walls.'"

11.

President Barbara Phillips would celebrate her 60th birthday next week. She was born in 2020, the same year her parents went under the dome. The playroom in her dome home had long ago been converted into the office space she used for conducting the government's business. Her five children all lived in domes of their own. Now, it was just Barbara, her mother, and her husband Ben. Her father passed on twelve years ago and Ben's parents lived in his brother's dome.

Barbara set her cup down on the coffee table and pulled her legs up onto the couch. The left hand portion of the six-by-eight wall panel display began to fill with the faces of the meeting participants. Her own face filled the right hand quarter of the screen but with the meeting not yet called to order, her image was not yet transmitting out to the other meeting attendees. For a moment she regarded the image captured by her screen camera. Her thinning shoulder length brown hair seemed to have more gray streaks with each meeting. By the looks of her full cheeks, she needed to consider cutting back a bit on her share of the rations. Finally the last invitee logged in and saved Barbara the trauma of conducting a deeper self-evaluation. She pressed the appropriate button on her wireless keyboard to call to order the 9th meeting of the National Security Council during her presidential term. The meeting would automatically be recorded for the confidential archives.

"Hello, good to see everyone. I know this meeting was unscheduled but I see things with Mexico are heating up. General Pruitt, will you get everyone up to speed on the incursion and last night's military action?"

Air Force General Joshua Pruitt was only two months into his appointment as the Chairman of the Joint Chiefs of Staff, his predecessor having retired early due to declining health. For thirty-seven years he had attended to military matters from a spare bedroom in his family's dome home. He wore the same gray house pajamas the President and every other citizen wore, not the battle dress or the class A uniform decorated with medals and service ribbons worn by his pre-dome predecessors. Pruitt and the Chief of Staff of the Army had received a full briefing from the theatre commander several hours ago.

"Yes, Madam President. Five days ago, six junior Mexican army personnel on horseback entered the United States at Presidio, Texas." A map appeared on the right side of each participant's video display.

"The group was discovered and shadowed by a Comanche scout working for Army Intelligence. They moved due north 120 miles to the Barilla Mountains and spent two days observing the extreme southern limit of the Texas dome farm. They did not have heavy weapons or a radio transmitter so the threat was minimal.

"Yesterday morning, the Mexicans moved out of the Barilla range, crossed Interstate 10 here, and attacked a Dome Services personnel transport that carried an engaged couple moving to their new dome. The Mexicans kidnapped the couple and retreated back into the mountains.

"Last night, the kidnappers staked the female hostage to the ground and were preparing to rape her. That's when our Comanche scout moved in and terminated the threat. All six Mexicans were killed. Brief questioning indicated their captain ordered them to the dome area to 'make trouble.'"

"We were probed, General?" asked Belinda Ashmore, Secretary of Defense.

"I believe so, Madam Secretary. They sent in a small, expendable force to poke us and observe our military and political reaction."

National Security Advisor, Alan Sayles cleared his throat and joined the conversation. "Look, we know Mexico has been building up troop concentrations in central Sonora west of the Sierra Madre and east of the mountains in Chihuahua. Those are clear threats to our Arizona and Texas dome farms. "

"So General Mejias is growing even more ambitious?" asked Donald Sullivan, Vice President of the United States.

Secretary of State, Carter Mason put a hand up to his face and waved dismissively. "Mejias is a lapdog. Does anybody disagree that this impending invasion by Mexico is being orchestrated, or at least facilitated, by China?" With no murmurings of disagreement forthcoming, the Secretary continued.

"China has been seriously pissed at us since we brokered the deal early in the century that turned North Korea away from China, reunified the Korea's, and reconciled Korea and Japan. Then we rubbed salt in that wound by bringing Korea and Japan in as partners in helping India develop over the last fifty years."

"I agree, Madam President," interjected Judith Zaranski, Secretary of the Treasury. "The cooperation among the US, Korea, and Japan politically, and the developing of India into a huge market, have significantly reduced China's economic influence. And, of course, the doming of America has supercharged our own economy. We have zero need for foreign oil, we are a manufacturing country once again and the goods we produce and sell around the world are made with zero labor cost. We are moving closer to our goal of requiring no import of manufactured goods so we have trade surpluses with almost every trading partner. Finally, Carter indicated the Chinese are angry with us for turning Korea, et cetera. Well, that's nothing compared to how steamed they are about their US debt handling fiasco."

Everyone in the meeting knew the Treasury Secretary referred to the fact that just before the United States went under domes, China sold its US debt holdings cheap—mostly to Eastern Europe—betting their investment would soon be worthless. But once under domes, the United States was no longer burdened with the crushing $150 trillion in unfunded liabilities due to massive entitlement programs like Social Security and Medicare. That debt was wiped clean and the value of the dollar skyrocketed. Eastern European countries friendly to the United States became wealthy and China looked foolish.

President Phillips nodded almost imperceptibly. As President she had access to the confidential archives of previous administrations. She knew the truth about the motives to move the country into domes—and it didn't have anything to do with fear of loose nukes, terrorists with weapons of mass destruction, or natural and manmade biological hazards.

"I too concur with the Secretaries of State and the Treasury," indicated Anthony Covelli, Director of National Intelligence. "We have photographic and other evidence of high-level Chinese officials present in Mexico who aren't connected with the ministries of foreign affairs or trade. Chinese weapons—that Mexico cannot possibly afford—have been trickling into Mexico for years, ever since Mejias staged his military coup."

"General Pruitt," Secretary Mary Loveland of Homeland Security caught the attention of the JCS Chairman. "Do you still believe that Mexico plans to invade the United States?"

"I do, Madam Secretary."

Director Covelli interjected, "The invasion is coming and will happen soon. Unfortunately, we have allowed our Western Hemisphere surveillance satellite resources to dwindle to near zero. We have very little satellite intel. We have done limited penetration of Mexican airspace with a few Predator recon sorties, and there are occasional clandestine incursions by Apache and Comanche scouts. Other than that, we are blind."

"So the alert to the Treaty Tribes last month to mobilize for war is proving a wise move," the President said rhetorically.

Six weeks ago, Secretary of State Mason and Secretary of Defense Ashmore rang the satellite phones of the leaders of the Comanche, Apache, Navajo, Cherokee, Kiowa, Cheyenne, Arapaho, and Lakota Sioux nations—the "Treaty Tribes" that had agreed to act as an Outside protection force in return for certain considerations such as emergency food rations, hygiene rations, ammunition, and continued assistance with re-establishing the bison herds.

Secretary Mason nodded. "One problem there, Madam President. The Lakota, who have gathered an impressive 18,000 warriors on horse have stopped their march and pitched camp in southeastern Colorado. They won't continue south unless their demand is met."

"You mean the demand about giving them the Black Hills? Damn it, they have free run of the place now that we are under domes!" offered the perturbed Vice President.

"Nevertheless," Mason continued, "they want us to officially cede all land ownership rights to them for the establishment of their own sovereign Lakota country. It is not a trivial matter. There has been an offer of monetary compensation for the land on the table for two hundred years and to this day, the Lakota have refused to take it."

"Dan?"

Attorney General Daniel McInnis answered the President, "Madam President, as you know, the Constitution hasn't quiet caught up with the realities of our society under domes. We still elect Representatives and Senators based on a person's geographic district at the time of his family's first doming. But we no longer have any state legislatures, state executives, or state courts. An act as extraordinary as relinquishing a large portion of territory should be codified in the Constitution. Article V governing amendments the Constitution requires that three-fourths of state legislatures or state conventions ratify proposed amendments. Since it's impossible to comply with Article V, I suggest that, at a minimum, we require three-fourths of the House and three fourths of the Senate to approve any such action.

"Also, we can't "establish" a country for the Lakota people. We can give up the land, but it would be up to the Lakota people to take it from there. And that could be somewhat problematic in that the Cheyenne and Crow might have something to say about that given they lived in some of that territory before the Lakota pushed them out."

"Also, Madam President," interjected Secretary of State Mason, "The other Treaty Tribes are indeed gathering and moving their forces but, until they convene a combined war council and discuss the situation, there is no guarantee that any of the tribes will fight with us."

"Or, we could hit the Mexicans with nuclear weapons tomorrow and dispense with the need for coordinating a defense with the Indians," proposed Cecil Harbaugh, Deputy National Security Advisor. Deputy Harbaugh was the junior Council member present and one of his duties was to propose radical ideas for discussion that more senior Council members might not be comfortable proposing themselves.

Defense Secretary Ashmore shook her head. "No, too many radioactives would blow into Arizona, California, and Texas. And you could forget about any future cooperation from the Treaty Tribes. All of those Native American nations have expressly indicated that if we ever use nuclear weapons on or near American territory, they will consider the treaty broken and refuse future requests."

"Presently the Treaty Tribes have very good relations with each other and with us," said Secretary Mason. "The Treaty Tribes and scores of other tribes continue to meet every summer at the All Nations Pow-wow near Muskogee for a Sun Dance and three weeks of festivities. Forty years ago, President Gardner established the Muskogee gathering as a time for the warriors of each nation to conduct war games and for joint training with our military forces. That foresight has led to a highly trained, formidable land army. I say we shouldn't jeopardize relations with the tribes."

President Phillips decided quickly. "Let's have Joshua and his generals develop battle plans both with and without nukes. Betty. . .?"

"Yes, Madam President?" responded Betty Saville, Chief of Staff to the President.

"After this meeting, let's you and I discuss getting the Congressional leadership onboard with the issue of the Black Hills.

"General Pruitt—initial battle plans for neutralizing the Mexican threat—can they be developed in three days? Is that doable?"

"Yes, Madam President."

"Do we feed the story about the Mexican incursion to the press?" the Vice President asked.

National Security Advisor Sayles believed that alerting the press was a profoundly bad idea. "I strongly recommend against going public. Citizens being kidnapped from their dome is unprecedented. Knowledge of the incident will cause panic. That also means the couple rescued by the Army scout can't ever be allowed back under dome—one, because their story would get out and two, they've seen the Outside. We spend too much effort washing the Net of pictures and descriptions of the Outside as it is."

The President nodded in agreement. "General, have the scout escort the couple to the nearest stronghold. What were the families told about the incident when it happened?"

Mr. Sayles added, "That they died in a freak accident with the transport. The transport driver and Dome Services emergency duty officer are the only possible leaks there and they have been told to keep quiet as this is a matter of national security. Their communications are now being monitored full time for compliance."

General Pruitt added one more important item. "Madam President, some sort of address to the nation about Mexico will be required immediately. We need to take a number of preparatory logistical steps to defend ourselves and those steps require the remote help of many citizens. If we don't explain what is going on, rumors of all sorts will flood the Net."

"I believe you are right about that, General Pruitt, thank you. Anything else from the military side on Mexico? What about the Mexican agricultural workers living in US territory? Do they pose a security threat in relation to the apparent plans of General Mejias?"

President Phillips referred to several hundred thousand farm workers, many of whom were descended from illegal aliens, and who now worked crop harvests in California to Washington State and in Florida and Georgia. At the time of doming in the 2020's millions of illegal immigrants were deported, however several hundred thousand were allowed to stay permanently in order to harvest crops, especially delicate fruit products where human dexterity and senses of sight and touch still outperformed machines by a wide and economical margin.

"No, Madam President. The farm workers are far removed from Mexico at this point. They don't receive any money to send home. They have free housing, food and hygiene rations if they need them, and they have access to the same remote healthcare domed citizens receive. They are in a much better situation than the citizens of Mexico. They won't want to risk what they have.

"Anyway, we can review the war plans at your convenience anytime after Thursday, Madam President. Maybe a couple other items worth mentioning; Mr. Jeffers is mobilizing his stronghold in Phoenix; and we are gathering as many aerial drones and M18 combat robots as we can find to send to the Southwest. Strength estimates on everything will be in the plans."

"Good. Now before we adjourn, I'd like to hear updates on our contracts with Great Britain, France, Georgia, and India regarding the mercenary services we are providing..."

12.

Roving Wolf kept his new charges moving at an easy pace, both to help Tom and Jenny avoid the worst of the saddle soreness and to keep the horses attached to the lead line from interfering with each other's movement. The horses did not make trouble and were responding well to their new, more conscientious master.

They traveled north on Texas State Route 17 and despite the slower pace, the flat terrain allowed the party to make good headway toward the Comanche village at Pecos. The clear sunny day warmed into the 60's so the foil blankets Tom and Jenny had wrapped around themselves in the morning were now packed back into saddlebags. Roving Wolf had fashioned two hats from twigs and pieces of another foil blanket and presented them to the domer couple to wear. The scout was afraid that even the weak winter sun would burn the pale skin of Tom's and Jenny's face and neck.

For Tom, the six-hour ride up Highway 17 was much easier than the frenzied ride through the wilderness of yesterday. The road course was smooth and instead of bouncing up and down all day, Tom was able to roll with the motion of the horse and keep contact with saddle. Jenny rode ahead of him and Tom noticed that she was as busy studying the fascinating surroundings as he. The land and sky stretched out forever. They did not tire of the wonder. Tom once again found his thoughts drifting to time spent growing up listening to Reverend Bixby on Sunday's. He couldn't quite articulate and parse his feelings yet but something about the onrush of natural wonders was changing more than just the physical description of his world. The universe—and his understanding of it—was changing too.

The land was flat as a tabletop in all directions now. As they approached the small desert town, the frequency of dilapidated rancher style houses lining the roadway increased. Sage brush, creosote, mesquite, and prickly pear cactus grew in scattered clumps throughout the parched land.

They crossed under the I-20 overpass and the complexion of the town changed. Scores of traditional Native American tipis rose from cleared patches of ground to the left of the roadway. Finally some signs of life as a small group of Comanche children scampered across the road ahead then stood and waited for a good look at the travelers. The village youths, all wearing a mix of cotton shirts and deerskin leggings, held up their right hands to Roving Wolf in a respectful salute. Jenny waved at the children and called 'hello.' Tom gave a similar friendly sweep of his arm and the children giggled, two returned his wave. Tom wondered why the giggles then realized he certainly must look as odd as Jenny did with Roving Wolf's homemade foil umbrella perched on his head.

Roving Wolf pressed on into town. Some of his fellow villagers were busy about the tipi clusters while others buzzed around houses abandoned long ago by families that disappeared into domes. The scout halted his convoy of horses in front of a small rancher with freshly applied white paint. A young woman emerged wearing a simple print dress that fit loosely everywhere except where it stretched around her swollen abdomen. Her long black hair whipped behind in her wake as she rushed off the porch to embrace Roving Wolf once he dismounted his white mustang. After a brief round of dialogue in the Comanche tongue, Roving Wolf led the woman toward Tom and Jenny. Roving Wolf assisted Tom with his dismount and the young woman helped Jenny with the same maneuver.

With one hand still gripping the lead line, Roving Wolf gestured with his other arm toward the woman.

"This is my wife. You call her Red Sky. She works hard, but she is lazy with white words."

Tom shook his head.

Jenny noticed Tom's confusion. "He means she doesn't do well with English—'white words'—get it?"

Tom and Jenny both greeted Red Sky who did manage a polite, "Hello." Roving Wolf explained that children of all Native American nations learned their native language first, but were taught English as a second language in order to communicate with other nations. Fluency in English, or the lack thereof, varied widely among individuals however warriors like Roving Wolf who worked for the Army were expected to be especially knowledgeable.

"I told my wife you will stay with us. Go inside. I need to take the horses."

Tom took Jenny's hand and they both walked slowly, painfully to the door. Red Sky easily beat them to the door and opened it, all the while muttering to herself out of concern for the condition of her guests.

Red Sky ushered the couple into the small living room. She pointed to Tom and then to the heavily worn couch. "Tom, sit." In her next breath she announced, "Jenny, clean." Red Sky grasped Jenny's forearm and led her down a narrow hallway into the bathroom. The Comanche homemaker twisted the creaking faucets then, to Jenny's surprise and embarrassment, Red Sky helped her strip and step into the tub. She lowered herself with her host's gentle assistance into the hot water. Jenny relaxed her head against the back of the tub, closed her eyes, and let out an audible sigh. The caress of the hot water soothed her screaming muscles. Red Sky flashed a satisfied smile and left the room.

While Jenny soaked in the tub, Red Sky went to work in the kitchen preparing dinner. She didn't give Tom a second thought as he lay on his side on the couch to relieve the pressure on his tender buttocks. Tom briefly glanced around the sparsely furnished room but in moments he was asleep.

After twenty minutes of soaking, Jenny opened her eyes to see Red Sky back in the room motioning for her to stand. Jenny stepped out of the tub and Red Sky did the drying. Once dry, Red Sky produced a tin of white ointment and proceeded to apply the soothing cream to Jenny's chafed skin. Jenny's muscles stiffened noticeably as Red Sky unabashedly spread the ointment even in the most intimate of chafed areas. Red Sky helped Jenny slip on a white pullover blouse and a simple ankle length print skirt, then led her back to the living room.

Red Sky reached for Tom's hand. Tom shook himself awake and forced his protesting legs against their will to lift him off the comfortable sofa.

"Tom, clean," the command issued from Red Sky and she led him away to the bathroom. Jenny's eyes widened when she realized Tom might get the same level of attention as she. Jenny briefly thought about interceding or assisting, but sitting on the soft couch felt too good and she instinctively knew that Red Sky meant no malice while dutifully attending to her guests.

Tom finished his turn with the tub and pulled Jenny from the couch. The couple moved to the kitchen table and made an unsuccessful effort to engage Red Sky in conversation. Moments later, Roving Wolf returned from caring for the horses and securing his weapons. The Army scout vanished into the shower to wash away the last two days of accumulated grime. Roving Wolf returned wearing fresh jeans, flannel shirt, and cowboy boots. Tom looked with envy at his host's comfortable clothes; too tall to fit into any other clothes in the house, Tom was forced to wear an old tattered woman's robe.

Roving Wolf sat with his guests as Red Sky brought a small roasted chicken, cornbread, and beans to the table which she previously set with plates, utensils and plastic cups full of water. Jenny watched Roving Wolf tear a leg off the chicken while his wife carved portions for Tom and her. Jenny thoroughly enjoyed both the roasted flavor and succulent texture of the poultry—her first ever experience with meat that wasn't salted and dried into jerky or processed into foil packages.

Near the end of the meal, they heard the front door creak open and slam closed followed by the voice of a young woman chattering happily away in the Comanche language. The source of the bubbly chatter turned the corner and burst into the room. Jenny saw her first. She was maybe nineteen and stunningly beautiful. She wore a tight white tee shirt and even tighter blue jeans. Her chest-length black hair was arrow straight and shimmered in the incandescent light. The young woman saw Tom and her large green eyes widened and her full red lips parted in surprise. The loud, confident Comanche chatter turned into bashful white words with a soft, "Oh, excuse me."

Jenny's cheeks flushed red with fury when she witnessed the unmistakable flash of mutual interest that the woman and Tom shared.

Roving Wolf made the introduction. "This is my sister. She is called Sun Rain. She knows white words very well. Sister, this is Tom and Jenny. They are from the place of the frightened turtles," said Roving Wolf, referring to one of the Native American nicknames for domers.

Sun Rain smiled and apologized for interrupting. "I am so sorry. I heard my brother had returned from his scout and I wanted to welcome him home." She bent down from behind Roving Wolf and wrapped both arms across his neck and chest and squeezed.

Tom smiled. "No need to apologize." He didn't notice the cold look from Jenny.

Roving Wolf patted one of Sun Rain's arms. "Go prepare a room. Tom will sleep here tonight. Jenny will stay next door with you and Grandmother."

Sun Rain snapped upright. "Yes! I will tell Grandmother. Welcome Tom and Jenny!" Sun Rain bounded out of the room with a brief look over her shoulder before disappearing out the door.

"Forgive my sister. In our language, her nickname translates to what you call 'dust devil.'"

Coincidentally, Jenny hadn't known what a dust devil was until today when Roving Wolf pointed one out during the ride up Route 17. Yes, the whirling mini cyclone of wind and dust, full of wild energy did seem an apt description for the energetic Sun Rain. But this dust devil was far more dangerous, thought Jenny.

* * * *

After dinner Roving Wolf walked Tom and Jenny outside and led them across the yard to the small, one story house next door. They climbed two steps onto the open porch with an overhang of sturdy construction but clearly added as an afterthought.

Roving Wolf grasped the handle of the screen door and turned to his guests. "Wait here. I will speak with Grandmother. This is her house." Roving Wolf disappeared inside.

Tom looked at Jenny and shrugged. "I guess we have to be announced?"

"No." Jenny folded her arms. "I think more like he needs her permission to bring us in—just a matter of respect and protocol."

Roving Wolf appeared after a few moments and opened the door, gesturing for Tom and Jenny to enter. Tom followed Jenny inside. They found themselves immediately surrounded by the main room of the small house. The living area had just enough room for two couches on either side of a narrow wooden coffee table. At the far end of the table Grandmother sat in a rocking chair. Her long dark hair was heavily streaked with gray and pulled back behind her head. Her wide face was weatherworn and wrinkled, thin lips didn't hide several gaps made by missing teeth, but her eyes were clear and sharp and carefully regarded Jenny, then Tom. The bright orange Mumu she wore betrayed her as the procurer of the many framed paintings of fruit bowls, flower vases, and landscapes that covered every inch of the living room walls making the room a dizzying cauldron of vivid, clashing colors. Although the décor was not consistent with Jenny's more conservative sensibilities, the house was cleaner than Jenny thought possible given the desert surroundings—there was no dust in here.

"Tom, Jenny, this is my grandmother. Her name means Angry Dove."

They took turns bending down to clasp Angry Dove's hand. The old Comanche woman used both her hands to grasp the hand her guests offered and she held each for a period of time that seemed longer than a routine greeting allowed. While in the grasp of Grandmother Angry Dove, Tom and Jenny both felt some discomfort with the intense, penetrating stare of the old woman.

"Hello, Tom and Jenny. Sorry, I white words no good." Angry Dove apologized for her limited knowledge of English.

"No need to say sorry," offered Tom. "Thank you for letting Jenny stay in your house."

"Sun Rain says you from the frightened turtle place."

Sun Rain finished putting away dishes in the kitchen and rushed over to join the gathering in the living room. "Yes, Grandmother. Tom and Jenny were on their way to be married."

Angry Dove gasped and used a wrinkled hand to cover her gaping mouth. She addressed her grandchildren in a flurry of rapid-fire Comanche dialogue. Roving Wolf and Sun Rain were clearly trying to calm their excited grandmother.

Angry Dove struggled to her feet and shuffled forward to grasp Tom's forearm in one hand and Jenny's forearm in the other. After a few more Comanche phrases delivered with what seemed to be sincere passion, Angry Dove turned and limped into the rear of the house.

Tom loosed a nervous chuckle and glanced at both Sun Rain and Roving Wolf. "I hope we didn't say something wrong?"

"Not at all," Sun Rain assured Tom.

"What did she say?" Jenny asked with more than a hint of concern in her voice.

"Not to be worried, Jenny," Roving Wolf offered. "Come, Tom."

Sun Rain stepped up and took Jenny's hand. "Jenny, let's get a place ready for your sleep." Sun Rain led Jenny to the back of the house while Tom followed Roving Wolf outside and returned to the house of his host.

As they walked Tom asked Roving Wolf if he would translate his grandmother's thoughts and make some sense of the bizarre scene that just unfolded.

"Grandmother feels you and Jenny do not belong together as husband and wife."

Tom puzzled over Roving Wolf's words for a moment. "Is your grandmother able to divine the future?"

"Many people seek her wisdom."

* * * *

Jenny found Tom in the back yard leaning on a fence post, head looking toward the sunset. Tom straightened upon her approach but kept one hand resting on the fence post and moved his other arm to sweep Jenny to his side. The sun was a bright orange ball as it touched the horizon.

Jenny matched Tom's stare across the western plain. "Grandmother says you and I shouldn't get married."

"Yeah, Roving Wolf told me what she said. She just met us, Jen. I don't believe she is right."

Tom watched Jenny's brown hair toss in the breeze as she looked ahead. He couldn't see her face and so was deprived of a valuable clue to her current mood. He also wondered why she had seemed so aloof through the evening meal.

Several silent moments passed then she offered, "You like her, don't you?"

Jenny's terse accusation surprised Tom. "What?"

"Sun Rain. I saw the way you looked at her."

Tom pushed off the fence post and reached for Jenny's shoulder turning her toward him. "What are you talking about, Jenny? How did I *look* at her?"

Jenny pushed her hair from her face and looked at Tom. "Like you wanted her."

Tom shook his head. "Jenny, we are being hit with new sights everywhere we turn. We've been under a dome all our lives and suddenly we are out experiencing a whole new world, meeting people, *in-person*. I probably had that same look—whatever it was—a hundred times today, starting with the sunrise."

Jenny blinked away the beginning of tears. He was right of course. There were new experiences rushing at them from every direction. And it was true, he *did* have that same look watching his first sunrise. That didn't explain the way Sun Rain looked at Tom; but Tom was right. She owed him the benefit of the doubt.

Jenny leaned her head into Tom's chest as a tear fell from her cheek. Not just new experiences flooding in—new emotions too.

"I'm sorry, Tom. I don't think I am quite myself."

Tom lifted Jenny's chin until she was looking up at him. "So, it turns out there is a great big, beautiful world beyond the dome walls—but you are the one who puts the real sparkle in the Outside for me."

Jenny rubbed tears from her eyes and her smile widened. "God, that is so corny." Tom nodded, returned her smile, and pulled Jenny close for their first truly passionate kiss as the last orange beams disappeared below the West Texas desert.

13.

When Tom awoke the next morning he was upset to discover that he had missed watching another the sunrise. He was also still somewhat perturbed that his hosts were keeping Jenny and him apart. But Tom's lingering annoyance was strangely tempered by the unexpected and conflicting feeling of relief on his part that Jenny and he were not yet sharing a bed. Until the kidnapping, Tom had been lustfully looking forward to consummating his relationship with Jenny at long last. But between the pain, the violence, the fatigue, and the overwhelming sensory overload caused by the onrush of new sights, sounds, and smells of the Outside, Tom was having a difficult time nurturing feelings and thoughts of romance and he believed Jenny was in the same place. Then there was grandmother Angry Dove's pronouncement the previous night that he and Jenny didn't belong together. He was still working through that one.

Tom stood stiffly and then much of his initial sour mood drifted away after seeing that laid out for him on the dresser were a tee shirt, jeans, and a pair of hiking boots. He was glad he wouldn't have to don the old, tattered woman's house robe of the night before. He felt quite self-conscious with everyone else in normal Outsider clothing while he walked about in a robe that didn't cover much of his hairy legs and care had to be taken to keep from accidentally exposing too much of himself. He dressed quickly and smiled when he discovered the clothes fit him comfortably. Comfortable was a relative term. He had worn the gray domer pajamas all his life. He wasn't quite accustomed to the touch of the new clothing and footwear—he felt like a completely different person. Unfortunately, he had no idea what to do with the strings that were threaded through his boots.

After dressing Tom stepped out of the tiny bedroom and followed voices to the kitchen. Jenny, Sun Rain, and Roving Wolf were conversing around the table. There was no sign of Red Sky.

"Good morning, everyone. Were you going to let me sleep all day?"

"Are you sorry we didn't wake you?" Jenny asked.

Tom sat down at the table with an audible groan. "No, I guess not. It was good to get the rest."

"What happened to your robe? I liked that," joked Jenny.

Tom was heartened to see a smile from Jenny. "The robe is retired. My thanks to whoever provided the clothes. I figured out how to work the belt and the buttons and the zipper in the pants—not bad for a man who has worn pajamas with Velcro fasteners all his life, but I wasn't sure the best way to connect the strings in the boots." Tom moved one of his legs from under the table to display a loose boot.

Sun Rain stood up and laughed at the condition of Tom's footwear. "Here, let me show you how to tie boot laces, Tom." She knelt at Tom's feet and gave him a slow, step by step lesson in tying shoes. Tom applied her instructions to his other foot and managed to clumsily tie his first boot.

"Good, Tom." Sun Rain nodded her approval and retook her seat.

"Thank you, very much. I have a lot to learn."

"Are you still feeling the pain of the saddle?" asked the inquisitive Sun Rain.

"I am. Muscles are still sore but the burning caused by chafing is much better thank you; and many thanks to Red Sky. Where is she?"

"My wife is on the other side of town. She helps welcome more peoples."

"Yes," confirmed Sun Rain. "It's very exciting that so many are coming this way."

"What is happening?" Jenny asked.

Roving Wolf set down his cup. "The President called the Treaty Tribes to gather for war."

"What?!" came the simultaneous reply from Tom and Jenny.

Tom continued, "War here, with Mexico?"

"Yes, with Mexico."

"You mean, because of the attack on Tom and me?" That idea seemed absurd to Jenny.

"No," answered Roving Wolf. "General Mejias is gathering men for many days. The President's mobilization of the Treaty Tribes began last month."

Jenny and Tom looked at each other. The bright new world they found outside did still contain horrors after all.

"Tom, would you like some coffee?" Sun Rain asked and stood. "Or something else? We already ate but there is more."

"Sure, thank you. Wait, Roving Wolf, is that why we saw the hundreds of tipis set up when we came into town?"

"Some of those dwellings are from the travelers, others, no. Not everyone in my band lives in a house. Some always live in tipi." Roving Wolf explained that all Native American nations were actively practicing and teaching the old ways of living because they did not want to be dependent upon the government for survival. Electricity, motor vehicles, rifles, etc... were not being shunned, but no one was assuming those items would be available forever. Young braves of many nations hunted buffalo once again but were permitted to use only horse, lance, and bow to conquer the large, powerful animals.

Sun Rain brought Tom the remnants of breakfast and coffee. "Here, Tom. Jenny, do you need anything?"

"No, thank you, Sun Rain." Jenny caught Roving Wolf's eye. "Did you ask your superiors about when we can go to our dome?"

"Yes. They said that is not possible. I am ordered to take you to El Paso."

"But..." Jenny's jaw dropped and she shook her head. "Tom, I don't understand. Why can't we go back? What is in El Paso?"

"El Paso is the closest stronghold," explained Roving Wolf.

Jenny understood. She and Tom had discussed strongholds before. She never dreamed she might have to live in one. Could she adapt to a society that mirrored the feudal system of Middle Age Europe? Each stronghold had a ruling class, a trade class made up of people knowledgeable in key infrastructure areas like engineering, construction, engine mechanics, and a farmer class that worked the land to grow food. All stronghold classes provided troops for security forces because danger still lurked on the Outside in the form of bandit bands comprised of stragglers who escaped doming, mixed with some malcontent ex-stronghold members, Indian criminals excommunicated from tribes, and several groups of escapees from maximum security prisons who weren't recaptured before the final dome was sealed. There were only three dozen strongholds in the country and only a handful that had 1,000 or more people.

"You rest today. We will move west in the morning." Roving Wolf stood. "I must go prepare for the journey."

"So soon?" Jenny sighed.

"Yes," Tom added. "The thought of getting on a horse again makes me cringe."

"I will be on the horse. You will ride in a truck," said Roving Wolf.

"Okay, I like the sound of that. But you know that we have no experience driving a truck?" warned Tom.

"Sun Rain will drive. And she knows how to handle the .50 caliber machine gun."

14.

Cynthia sat listlessly on the couch. The tears she shed for Tom over the last day and a half were temporarily stanched. Crying for that long wasn't just emotionally draining but physically draining too and she needed a break before the flow of tears resumed. A rare Presidential address to the nation was scheduled to begin momentarily and that occasion provided her with an opportunity for such a break.

Steven trudged across the large dome living chamber and dropped onto the couch near his mother. "Jonny and the girls and I missed you at dinner yesterday, and at breakfast this morning. How are you doing, mom?"

Cynthia appreciated the concern evident in her son's words and voice. She suspected that her absence from the dining table, her red, puffy eyes and the tear-soaked handkerchief that she fumbled with in her lap told her son much of what he wanted to know. She felt somewhat buoyed by the fact that she had summoned the will to emerge from her room so maybe things would improve from here, even if slowly.

"Hello, Steven. I am doing the best I can. How about you?" Cynthia asked with audible concern.

"Mom, I'm doing okay. I have to tell you, I don't think Tommy is gone. I don't know why, but I think we have been lied to about what happened to Tom and Jenny."

For a moment Cynthia worried about her son's state of mind. His words were delivered with absolute conviction, or was it delusion? "So, you are dealing with this by pretending Tom is still alive?"

"I know it sounds crazy, mom. Sure, I could be wrong, but don't accuse me of wishful thinking just yet."

"I looked in on Jonny last night and he told me that you said the same thing to him. I don't want him strung along with false hope, Steven."

The door to Lucy and Linda's room swung open and the girls walked over to watch the speech on the giant main screen. Lucy sat on Cynthia's right and Linda squeezed in between Cynthia and Steven. Both twin teens brought handkerchiefs to muffle the sniffles that remained after a fresh round of sobbing.

The sharp crack of foul curses from across the living space could only mean that Frank Bellows was trying to negotiate his wheel chair through his doorway. No one stood to help Frank, they had all learned their lesson on that long ago. Frank rolled over the floor and pulled up next to the sofa arm.

"Hi, Dad, I am glad you can join us." Cynthia put her arm around Lucy's back and rested her hand on her father's arm. Frank didn't come out of his room much anymore except for meals, and sometimes not even then.

"Well, I want to hear what the woman has to say. I am going to reserve the right to not believe a word, but I will listen nevertheless," grumbled the old man.

The presidential seal blinked onto the main dome screen. After a moment, the seal was replaced by the stoic face of Barbara Phillips. The President stared directly into the eye-level camera and began her remarks.

"Good evening, My Fellow Americans. I must speak with you tonight about a troubling matter unfolding in the ever-dangerous Outside. The leadership of Mexico is conducting training drills for a number of its soldiers in the Mexican states of Sonora and Chihuahua. While Mexico's intentions are not known, I must be ever watchful of our nation's security. Operations by the Mexican army must be monitored given the proximity of some of our dome farms to the international border. The Mexican government has not been cooperative regarding questions about their intentions posed by the United States. I feel the only prudent course is to begin a series of proactive measures designed to insure the safety of our homes. For security reasons I will not detail those measures here. Understand that I will do everything in my power and use every resource in my control to affirm the safety of all citizens.

"As you know, the wise planners and builders of our dome infrastructure constructed and populated all four of our dome farms concurrently over a fifteen year period. As a result of the careful planning, none of us knows in which dome farm we live or in which quadrant of our unknown farm our individual dome exists. Many of you know how close some of our domes are to the border with Mexico. You or I or members of our families could be in one of those border domes right now. Again, there are no conclusive indications of hostile intent by Mexico. My message to you this evening is merely to keep you well informed about matters that affect our nation.

"Some of you may be asked to alter your normal job routine in order to assist with the security measures that we feel are important to keep our country strong and safe. I trust you will provide your full cooperation if called upon.

"I have every confidence that we will move beyond this issue and that we will remain the strongest and safest nation on earth. Thank you and good night."

The President's image faded to be replaced by a few seconds of the seal, then the big screen went black.

"Well that was short and sweet," commented Frank.

Cynthia reached across Linda and grabbed Steven's arm. "Steven, do you have any insight into this situation? Is there a chance we might go to war with Mexico and if so, would we win?"

Steven shrugged. "Mexico hasn't had much money to spend on vehicles, aircraft, or weapons systems but you can see from the Net News archives that General Mejias has indeed been building a large infantry force ever since he overthrew the civilian government. I don't know what the numbers look like, but Mexico has to have a lot more soldiers than we do. But we have nukes if things get desperate, so I wouldn't worry, mom."

15.

Army General Bruce Beckett logged into the three-way video conference and the computer-generated voice of the secure, encrypted communications system announced his presence: "Joining conference, Commander, United States Northern Command..."

After the announcement, the faces of the other two conference participants appeared on General Beckett's display. The frown and furrowed brow on the face of Joint Chiefs Chairman, General Joshua Pruitt were evidence of an unusually heightened state of concern. The third four-star general on the call, Air Force General Roy "Hop" Hopkins who, like General Beckett, led one of the few Unified Combatant Commands that reported directly to the Secretary of Defense. General Hopkins' charge was the United States Strategic Command.

"Hello Josh, hello Hop. Sorry I am a few seconds late."

"No problem, Bruce," offered JCS Chairman Pruitt. "And thanks again Hop for joining the call. I just wanted a quick sanity check on the plan among the three of us before the civilian leadership joins the fray."

General Hopkins laughed. "The plan is still germinating, right Bruce?"

General Beckett smiled in agreement. "Details are still being worked, that's correct. But things are moving fast gentlemen."

"Who is in charge of the battlefield, Beck?"

"My two best, Pru. The Mexicans are threatening on two fronts so I put Mark Tanner in charge of our Western army and Kathleen Singer is leading the Eastern army."

"The best, yes, but I thought there was bad blood between those two, no?"

"Blown way out of proportion, Josh. Just friendly competition, that's a better description."

"So what is the situation and what have your battle staffs come up with?" asked Hopkins.

"Well, we have known for some time now that General Mejias has been moving and concentrating men and equipment into two areas." General Beckett activated a map display that each of the men could view on their individual screens. "The largest concentration is west of the Sierra Madre Mountains in Hermosillo, Sonora, which is about 170 miles south of the Arizona border. The other force is east of the Sierra Madre, here near the city of Chihuahua about 150 miles from the Texas border."

"Direct and obvious threats to our Arizona and Texas dome farms," noted General Pruitt.

"Right. The strategy isn't difficult to guess. Mejias likely plans to use his larger western force to capture the Arizona domes which stretch from Yuma along the Gila River valley toward Phoenix. That move also cuts us off from a good portion of our food supply in California. From there he marches due east where he combines with his eastern force to take the Texas domes. From there he keeps pushing east to capture the dome farm on the Arkansas/Mississippi border and finally on to the Atlantic coast and the domes straddling the North and South Carolina border. With that, presto, he owns the United States, minus Alaska and Hawaii."

"And China owns *him,*" Hopkins added.

"What do the troop numbers look like?" asked the JCS Chairman.

"The Western Force/Mexico estimate is 275,000 men facing Western Force/USA with 62,000 men. The Eastern Force/Mexico estimate is 50,000 men facing Eastern Force/USA with 13,500 men."

"So we are outnumbered 4 to 1 on both fronts?" posed Hopkins rhetorically. "A few well-targeted ICBM's and this threat can end this afternoon, gentlemen."

General Pruitt chortled. "Hop, you're just saying that because you're pissed STRATCOM isn't in the fight."

"Hey, we airburst the warheads to maximize blast damage and minimize fallout, that's all I am saying."

General Beckett shook his head. "And if you are unlucky with the winds, you get radioactive fallout drifting across much of the country. True, the domes would protect from direct effects, but we'd have to worry about contaminated crops and water. And we'd piss off our Native American protectors on the Outside, maybe even turn them against us."

"Make your worst case plans using nukes Hop, but don't expect them to be implemented. Beck, how good are those strength estimates?"

"Well, I'd rather have confirmation via satellite but that's not possible."

All three men understood that the country's surveillance satellite network had still not rebounded from the neglect imposed by higher national priorities, primarily the building and maintenance of domes and related infrastructure and the process of building robots and automating industry and agriculture. In fact, in most areas, technology had advanced little since 2015 due to the tremendous resources and energy poured into doming America and automating industry.

General Beckett added that the troop strength estimates were based on a number of sources. One source was direct observation by a small number of Apache and Comanche scouts who penetrated deep into Sonora and Chihuahua. Another source was observation via camouflaged remote controlled optical sensors planted by the scouts. Small optical sensors, some with audio capability, were deposited by scouts in or near towns. Beckett marveled at how much information could be picked up from a sensor hidden in a local cantina. Remote-piloted Unmanned Aerial Vehicles (UAV's) like the

Predator made a few reconnaissance sorties into Mexican airspace but such incursions were rare in order to avoid giving the Mexicans undue provocation for initiating hostilities or to play the victim card in the UN. A few of the UAV flights used the new "spy-glide" device. The size and shape of a large bird, the spyglide camera package was towed via thousands of feet of wire at low altitude while the Predator flew high enough to mask its engine noise. Larger optical sensors where positioned on mountain tops near troop concentrations and near likely lanes of travel. The final source of information was the Central Intelligence Agency which didn't give Beckett detail on its human assets in the area but the agency did help tweak the troop estimates.

"Are we sure this won't be a two-pronged attack?" asked Pruitt. "You don't think those troops in Chihuahua will cross the Rio Grande and attack into Texas at the same time their western force moves against Arizona?"

"Can't be 100% certain. We have a couple of clues though. One, they have set up enough tents for 100,000 troops around Chihuahua and our scouts report the Mexicans light cooking fires by the empty tents—clearly a deliberate ruse to make us think there are a lot more troops in the area.

"Then there is the incident the other day with the Mexican scouts dispatched to probe our Texas dome farm. That was a suicide mission with expendable troops. I doubt those men even realized they were supposed to be caught red-handed. I suspect one of the goals of that mission was to make us think the eastern force is coming soon. Actually, I wouldn't be surprised if they moved their eastern force a day or two before the western force simply to reinforce the ruse. But if so, they would likely stop at the river. Worst case and they do cross the border; they will face Kathleen's army dug into the West Texas high ground."

"Spread pretty thin, though; that's a lot of ground to cover," said the Chairman.

"It's a risk to be sure. But do we take troops away from the west and go from being outnumbered 4 to 1 to being outnumbered say, 6 to 1 in Arizona?"

"How do you and your commanders plan to meet the threat?"

"First of all," began General Beckett, "We need the President to authorize our western force to cross the border, in force, into Sonora. We can't sit back and wait until the Mexicans cross first. The first Arizona domes are only two miles north of the Mexican border."

"Why the hell did they build so close to the border in the first place?" Hopkins asked shaking his head.

Beckett shrugged. "The specs for the dome farm locations were: large, flat land in a warm climate with little possibility of large earthquake."

The US Northern Command commander continued with a laundry list of concurrent preparatory activities. Every UAV flying drone available was being transported to the theatre. Not just the old Predator reconnaissance drones that could only carry two missiles, but the upgraded hunter-killer "Reaper" variant that was faster and could carry ten times the weapons payload. The newer jet powered Avenger UAV's were being funneled to the theatre as well.

Tomahawk cruise missiles were being prepared for ground launch at Tinker Air Force Base in Oklahoma. Two automated prepositioning ships in the Pacific where steaming toward San Diego, each carrying 400 brand new infantry robots complete with weapons, ammunition, support equipment, spare parts, and repair robots. Automated tractor trailer trucks that normally transported food would be waiting to drive the pre-loaded trailers of combots to Arizona. More combots stored in Galveston and at assembly plants in Kentucky would be shipped as well.

"This is going to be an infantry and horse cavalry battle, gentlemen," noted General Beckett. "Fortunately our side has aerial drone and cruise missile support. But we have no heavy armor, no fighter jets or bombers. After compiling reports from scouts, UAV recon photos, and mountaintop cameras, Mexico has an estimated 150 Chinese Type 59 tanks that must have been delivered within the last couple years. That is old technology but if I am an infantryman in the open with only a rifle, that is one scary deadly museum piece. Mexico has no offensive air force to speak of unless the Chinese have shipped in some aircraft we haven't detected. It's worth noting that all this troop movement in Mexico is being conducted without motor transport—more evidence of acute fuel shortages that we have suspected for some time."

"Any idea when Mejias will push the button and commence the attack?" asked Hopkins.

"No. Best guess is sooner rather than later. After all, we are talking about a battlefield contained within the Sonoran Desert. If I were the enemy, I would avoid waging war in the oppressive heat of summer.

"Also, the first thing that hit me regarding the battlefield was '*water*.' Not just the question of how do we get water to our troops, but how do we get enough water to as many as one hundred thousand horses. Half of our troops are cavalry and we are expecting each cavalryman to bring two or three horses."

"How do you plan to get that much water to a desert battlefield?" asked Pruitt with no attempt to disguise his skepticism.

"I am commandeering every milk tanker operated or stored by the automated dairy farms in Wisconsin and New York. So weekly ration packs might come without the normal ration of powdered milk for a while. We are also rounding up every 400-gallon military water trailer we can find and having the Cherokee mechanized infantry force tow them to the area. Trains with hundreds of grain cars are bringing down grain from emergency stores in Montana and North Dakota. I am also using the automated truck fleet."

"What combat assignments are Mark and Kathleen making regarding who does what?"

General Beckett enumerated the disposition of American forces. In round numbers the cavalry forces of Lt. General Mark Tanner's Western Army would consist of 4,000 Apache, 5,100 Comanche, 3,200 Cheyenne, 14,000 Lakota (Teton Sioux), 1,300 Arapaho, 2,000 Navajo, 1,200 Kiowa, and 1,000 Cherokee for a total of 31,800 light cavalry horse soldiers in the west.

Infantry forces of the American Western Army would include 2,000 Cheyenne warriors but the bulk of the foot soldiers consisted of 15,700 Navajo and 15,000 Cherokee. The Navajo infantry units were pure straight-leg, meaning when they moved, it wasn't via the luxury of air or ground transport—they marched on foot everywhere they went, just like the legions of ancient Rome. The Cherokee Nation went the other way and had mechanized their infantry forces with the iron horse. Cherokee units maintained over 600 M2 Bradley infantry fighting vehicles and over three thousand HMMWV's, a.k.a Humvee's. Every Cherokee rifle team proudly maintained their own Bradley or Humvee and made each vehicle unique by splashing war paint patterns (bright clan colors in the case of Oklahoma bands, black paint in the case of the Eastern Cherokee) over the original Army vehicle paint.

The smaller Eastern Army commanded by Lt. General Kathleen Singer consisted of a cavalry force of approximately 600 Apache, 1,800 Comanche, 900 Cheyenne, 3,000 Lakota, 1,000 Arapaho, 1,000 Kiowa, and 400 Cherokee horse soldiers for a total force of 8,700 light cavalry. The eastern infantry force of 5,800 men consisted of 5,500 mechanized Cherokee infantry and a contingent of 300 Cheyenne warriors on foot.

"Okay Beck, if I can get the President to authorize a preemptive defensive move into Mexico, when would that need to happen?"

"About three weeks. If we wait any longer, I am afraid Mejias will start moving north and we will lose the initiative. If we let him cross the Rio Magdalena unopposed, we could lose this fight. Mark Tanner's plan turns on occupying the hills around the town of Caborca, right here." General Beckett drew a circle around the Mexican town of 85,000 located ninety miles southwest of Nogales.

"Caborca is right in the middle of the travel lane from Hermosillo to the border. Look at these hills north and south of the town. The Mexicans have nothing up there. We can dig in on the high ground and keep Mejias from using Caborca as a resupply point as he moves north. "

General Hopkins interrupted, "But the troops you put in those hills will be flanked."

"Yes, but it keeps Mejias out of the town and forces his army to move along the coast west of town, or along the base of the Sierra Madre east of town. And our troops can use the hills as a base to harass his columns as they move north. It's a bold move to plant those troops in the path of the Mexican advance but we're heavily outnumbered so we need to get creative."

"And if the Mexicans don't flank but instead attack into the hills with a hundred thousand men?"

The consensus is that Mejias won't want to waste time and resources rooting out a well dug in force. Our men will have constant air cover provided by Reaper hunter-killer UAV's. And we do have an emergency evacuation plan that utilizes the Cherokee Bradleys if things really get desperate."

General Pruitt continued to press and play devil's advocate. "What if Mejias doesn't take the direct route through central Sonora and instead uses the Sierra Madre for cover to slip into southeastern Arizona?"

General Beckett was quick to respond. "We have considered that. The main highway north from Hermosillo comes up here to Santa Ana and at that point there are three options. The most direct route to our Arizona dome farm is the road west to Caborca. As I mentioned, our plan is to occupy the hills outside Caborca so that he is forced to veer more northwest before reaching the town.

"The other options at Santa Ana are to continue due north and cross the border at Nogales or veer northeast through Cananea and then turn north to cross the border between Fort Huachuca and the Chiricahua Mountains. The Cananea option increases the travel distance to the objective, slows your march, puts your men in rough terrain, and puts you on Apache home turf. There will be twelve hundred Apaches camped in the Huachuca Mountains ready to bottle up any Mexican advance through the mountains and fight delaying actions until reinforcements arrive.

"However…" General Beckett hesitated.

"Sounds like bad news coming," commented General Hopkins.

"Well, there is concern over the possibility that Mejias will split his forces and take one force along the expected direct route to the domes, while a second force crosses the border at Nogales to push up to Tucson, and then cut northwest to attack the Phoenix stronghold before turning southwest to join in the attack on the dome farm."

"How are you dealing with that contingency?" Pruitt asked.

"We have six thousand Comanche and Apache cavalry in the mountains east and west of the I-19 corridor to Tucson. They can harass and slow his columns while we run round the clock Reaper and Avenger sorties and send in cruise missiles from Tinker."

General Hopkins studied the map and interrupted with a concern of his own. "Beck, what keeps Mejias from crossing the border *west* of Sonoita? Couldn't he hug the coast and turn due north toward Yuma?"

"Terrain, Hop. That route means marching through the Altar Desert—possibly the most inhospitable area in all Sonora. No roads, no water, and unlike most of the desert battlefield, that portion of the desert actually has sand dune fields like you see in North Africa and Arabia."

"We are one minute from the President and the Secretary," noted General Pruitt. "It's agreed then, we are all going to push for the preemptive move into Mexico in order to establish a buffer between our dome farm and Mejias' army?"

"Agreed."

"Agreed."

16.

After breakfast Roving Wolf and Sun Rain left the house to make preparations for the journey to El Paso. Jenny and Tom set out moments later intent on exploring the Outside by taking a leisurely walk through the surrounding Pecos neighborhoods. The rising sun had already chased away the morning chill by the time the domer couple began their stroll down the paved street. The small town of friendly, unassuming character blossomed like a desert wildflower amid the dry brown brush and cactus fields of the flat Texas plain. The local neighborhoods were full of small, single story residences with driveways and sidewalks separated by an occasional lawn of dead grass, or rock garden, but more often by miniaturized versions of the sage brush prairie that surrounded the town on all sides.

Pecos was ideally situated as a waypoint for the thousands of Native American warriors pouring south from the Great Plains and coming west from Oklahoma. At Pecos, warriors assigned to the Western Army could resupply and turn due west through trans-Pecos Texas, then move through southern New Mexico and finally on to Arizona. The warriors assigned to the Eastern Army, upon reaching Pecos, were within a hundred miles of their assigned positions in the West Texas mountains along the Rio Grande.

The couple walked from one end of the small town to the other and back. Tom was exhilarated by the proximity of so many people, *in person,* and not merely as flat faces on a video screen. Word had spread quickly through the town that visitors from the frightened turtle place were guests among them. Tom and Jenny received friendly waves from the adults but for the most part, only curious children approached and engaged in conversation. The rest of the village was too busy rushing about in the preparations for war to be distracted by curious strangers.

Tom led Jenny by the hand to a bench on the covered porch of a small building along the 3rd Street thoroughfare on the north side of town. They had learned to lower themselves slowly onto such old cushioned benches, not because of their sore legs which were feeling better all the time, nor for fear the old benches would collapse, but because of the dust. There was desert dust *everywhere*. Only in permanently occupied homes like that of Roving Wolf was the dust under control and even then, it was a constant battle to remain free of the insidious buildup.

Tom held Jenny close as they rested. He unsnapped a canteen from its cover on the web belt that Roving Wolf had provided and offered Jenny a sip of water. Moments after sitting, their attention was drawn to the heavy rattling of a truck engine. They had seen a handful of automated tractor trailer transports rushing down Interstate 10 shortly after their rescue by Roving Wolf, but this was the first remotely driven rig they had seen close up. The eighteen-wheeler rolled slowly west on 3rd Street passing directly in front of Tom and Jenny. The truck cab was empty of course. The actual driver was in a dome somewhere—only a Dome Services computer knew exactly where. The trailer in tow was a large 9,000 gallon milk tanker that would carry precious water to the battlefield. A line of similar tankers followed behind. Even as they watched, the convoy slowed to a stop. The trucks would now shut down and wait to join a column of cavalry riding west across the desert.

After a short rest, Tom stood and the couple sauntered down Maple Street back toward the dwellings of Roving Wolf's family. Clouds on the western horizon obscured the solar disc as the sun set but the red and orange tinting of the cloud edges was still an amazing first time sight for the former domers.

Red Sky and Sun Rain were cooking the evening meal when Tom and Jenny returned. They exchanged friendly greetings with their hosts and sat at the table.

"Where is your brother?" Jenny inquired.

Sun Rain popped upright after a quick peek in the oven. "He is still preparing equipment and horses for the journey tomorrow. We will eat and sleep before he returns."

Tom absently watched Sun Rain flitter about the kitchen, her black hair now in a pony tail tied with a simple red bandana. Her movements were almost frenetic yet always purposeful and graceful. Tom felt Jenny squeeze his hand and he returned his attention back to the dinner table.

"We saw some Cheyenne and Kiowa cavalry come in and bed down on the east side of town," Jenny informed the other women. "Of course, some delightful young children pointed out their origin for us. We wouldn't have known otherwise."

"Yes," Sun Rain began while taking bread from the oven. "And more are on the way. They say 20,000 Lakota warriors are on the move again and will be here within a week."

After dinner Jenny and Sun Rain took food next door to Grandmother Angry Dove. The matriarch of the family had become temporarily bed-ridden due to a flare up of gout. Tom tried to help Red Sky with the dishes but was rebuffed.

Later in the evening Tom and Jenny met in the back yard of the house and laid down on an old blanket they spread on the ground. Tom had been waiting for an opportunity to get a better look at the stars. Finally they had a few quiet moments to themselves to lie down under a clear moonless night sky that was alive with thousands of shimmering lights.

Tom's eyes darted through the heavens with a curious excitement he had never known. "Jonny would really love this."

"It is amazing, isn't it?" commented Jenny, but she was not fond of lying on the hard ground—she had done enough of that lately. She longed for the mattress inside Angry Dove's house a few feet away.

"Yes," Tom agreed. "I can't believe I always thought the living space of the domes was so huge—twenty-two feet high, after all. But this..." Tom lifted his arms and spread them wide. "...there is no ceiling! We are looking out into infinity. Like you said honey, 'amazing.'"

"Ouch! Tommy!"

Jenny's painful cry surprised Tom who felt his fiancé jump to her feet. It was too dark for Tom to see Jenny slapping at her right arm.

"Tommy, make it stop!"

Tom scrambled off the blanket, fumbled for and grabbed Jenny's hand to pull her through the dark yard and around to the front door. Jenny's screams followed them into the house. Jenny jerked her hand violently out of Tom's grasp so she could rub her forearm. Sun Rain darted out of the kitchen into the hall and pulled Jenny along to the sink. Red Sky joined the action and held Jenny's arm under cool running water while Sun Rain quickly examined Jenny head to toe.

"What's going on?" Tom pleaded with concern.

"Fire ants," offered Sun Rain.

Jenny whimpered at the sink while Red Sky muttered to herself in her native tongue at the foolishness of her guest.

Sun Rain approached Tom and knelt down to examine him for any signs of the vicious red ants. Starting from his boots, then up to his jeans, Sun Rain probed with her eyes and fingers then pushed against one of Tom's legs while pulling his opposite leg. Tom got the idea and turned slowly so she could examine behind, then back around to his front. Sun Rain stood slowly while continuing to walk her hands over Tom's arms and torso. Her hands were up to Tom's broad shoulders when her eyes met his. Tom didn't notice the two-second pause in the examination.

Sun Rain stepped back and nodded.

"Am I safe?" Tom asked.

"From fire ants," Sun Rain smiled and turned to help Red Sky care for Jenny.

17.

"No!" General Juan Mejias, supreme ruler of Mexico, bolted out of his chair and pounded both fists onto his desk. Polished military service medals—some of them earned—dangling from the breast of his full dress uniform clinked together with each strike against the desktop. "Prison is unacceptable! Deserters must be hanged before a divisional formation!"

"Sir, Mr. President, one of the eight deserters was a regular, not a conscript," noted General Gutierrez, one of several general staff officers present in Mejias' office in the Palacio Nacional, in Mexico City. General Mejias had completely remodeled the presidential office in the National Palace. Now a vaulted ceiling towered thirty feet over an ornate, gold-inlaid desk of African ebony. The paint was barely dry on the newly completed oil collage overhead depicting scenes of the Mexican Revolution. More than one cynic believed the artwork had not been commissioned in order to honor Madero, or Villa, or Zapata but to remind Mejias what could happen to him if he lost popular support. Below the painting of the Revolution, wide fluted columns lined all four walls of the spacious office. More scenes of Mexican military history were boldly splashed between the columns. On the north wall, on either side of the massive window behind Mejias' desk, were scenes of General Mejias' triumphant overthrow of the civilian government. Also painted on the wall was a twenty-foot tall Mejias wearing army battle fatigues under his "Para Las Personas" (For the People) slogan. The face had been re-painted three times by three different artists before the General was satisfied that it depicted the proper level of 'fierce determination.' The artist who dared to allow a realistic representation of gray in the general's moustache no longer painted in Mexico—

Mejias learned from the experience too and now used hair dye.

"All the more reason for summary executions, General Gutierrez. I won't have conscript cowardice infecting the career troops. I expect everyone here to give me a disciplined army." Mejias resumed his seat. There were no chairs for his generals who were expected to render oral reports standing at attention. Mejias was the only one permitted to sit comfortably in this room.

"General Trujillo, the deserters were from your army. I will expect them to be dealt with within the next two days. Are there any other matters to discuss regarding our forces in Sonora and Chihuahua?" Mejias looked at his officers. The glare he gave each of them in turn was not a look designed to invite response. Predictably, the officers remained silent.

"We are adjourned, gentlemen."

All general officers present saluted in unison and abruptly marched to the main doorway. The pounding of their boots on the marble floor echoed through the stark chamber. The man in the black business suit had been largely hidden by the row of departing generals but now he stepped closer to Mejias. The stomping boots were gone, the heavy door closed and the two men were alone in the grand office.

"You are wise to insist on such measures, General." Lu Zhuàng's Spanish was much improved after two years in the country. "Your bold plans require much discipline."

Mejias turned his jowly face toward the slight, thin frame of Lu. The general resented that he was forced to rely on Chinese support for his plans to rebuild Mexico and return honor stolen by Spain and the United States. But his country was in deep financial trouble and not even the increased offshore oil drilling was helping. Oil prices had dropped sharply decades ago when the United States, once the largest importer of petroleum, no longer required imports of crude to fuel its economy. Mejias sold as much Mexican oil to the world as he could for cash—he didn't even leave enough crude behind for refining into fuel to move his army.

"My army will be victorious, of that I am certain, Señor Lu. Of course, the task would be much easier if I had planes for an air force." Mejias spat out the last phrase with contempt. His appeal to the Chinese for tanks and aircraft resulted in zero combat aircraft and two hundred ancient Type 59 tanks.

"My apologies, General. The generals in Beijing are too concerned with the military buildup by India to part with equipment essential to the defense of our nation." Lu didn't know if the Mexican tyrant believed that lie, but it hardly mattered.

Mejias scowled and turned his attention back to the material reports on his desk. "I hope your politicians realize that I will rule the entire North American continent in short order. I will remember those who assisted and those who did not, Señor Lu."

"Of course, General." Lu Zhuàng turned and took his leave of the irritated general. Lu's obsequious smile disappeared the instant he showed his back to the Mexican.

* * * *

Within an hour Lu was back in the Chinese embassy and in the office of the Ambassador.

"Do you still have control of the situation?" asked Ambassador Deng.

"Yes. Mejias is quite predictable. His army is still drilling and training. Significant numbers of conscripts are slowing the process. But he can field an army many times greater than can the Americans."

"Can we be certain of that given we have no intelligence on the ground?"

"Your Excellency, we know that less than 30,000 people remained outside when the last domes were sealed in the late 20's. Those people are widely scattered across the country."

"True, but what of the Indians? At least a million American Indians remain outside, is that not correct? I lament our long standing lack of intelligence regarding the new American frontier."

"I concur, Your Excellency. As for the Indians, they too are widely scattered. They also have a long history of fighting each other. I hardly expect a cohesive, organized defense."

Lu Zhuàng was unconcerned. The Americans had made this operation all too easy by building four lightly defended prison farms for themselves.

18.

Tom awoke when he felt Jenny sit down at the foot of his bed. He sat up quickly and swung his feet around to the floor. Before he parted from Jenny the prior evening, Red Sky had assured him that Jenny would be just fine but he was anxious to confirm that prognosis.

"Good morning, Jen." Tom hadn't seen that look on Jenny's face before. What was it? Disappointment? Resignation? "Are you okay, honey? How is your arm?"

Jenny lifted her injured arm. A fresh bandage applied by Red Sky covered most of Jenny's arm, wrist to elbow.

"Uncomfortable. It hurts and it itches."

"I'm sorry, baby. Did you get a good sleep?"

"Some," came her soft reply.

Outside a car horn sounded. Before yesterday, neither Tom nor Jenny could have identified the loud honking sound but their day-long stroll through town had given them quite an education in the outside environment. Tom also heard the muffled laughter of several men.

"What's the commotion about?" Tom asked.

"That's our ride to El Paso."

A bright line of light peeked under the blanket covering the window telling Tom that he slept through another sunrise.

Tom rubbed his eyes. "When do we leave?"

Jenny lifted off the bed, almost in slow motion. "As soon as you get dressed. I was sent in to get you." Jenny reached out with her good arm; Tom took her hand and rose from the bed.

Jenny pointed to neatly folded clothes on top of the dresser. "Red Sky gave us some clean clothes. Come on." Jenny managed a weak smile before leaving and closing the door behind her.

Tom dressed in a new pair of jeans; this time the tee shirt was black. After a bathroom visit he walked into the kitchen where Jenny and Sun Rain sat at the table. Roving Wolf leaned against the far wall with one hand, his other hand resting gently on Red Sky's swollen belly. The couple kept to their quiet, private conversation and didn't appear to notice Tom's arrival.

"Hi, Tom!" greeted a cheerful, smiling Sun Rain. "You ready to go?"

Without waiting for an answer, Sun Rain stood, snatched her desert camouflage boonie hat from the table and grabbed a plastic bag from the counter. She threw the bag to Tom. "Breakfast." In a flash she was out the door.

Jenny set down her cup and rose from the table. "I guess we have our orders." She led Tom away from the kitchen and out the front door.

Tom immediately noticed two armored Humvee's parked on the far side of the street. Both Humvees were hard top variants with .50 caliber machine gun turrets. One of the vehicle gun turrets was fitted with an automated CROWS system that permitted a gunner to aim and fire the heavy machine gun from inside the vehicle. Alternatively, the automated system allowed the gun to be controlled remotely by a domed soldier. The lead Humvee was painted in the Army's standard light tan desert ready paint. The trailing Humvee showed hints of the same desert tan paint but most of the vehicle body was covered by brightly colored stripes, dots, and swirls of red, yellow, and green that represented the clan colors of the Cherokee rifle team that owned and maintained the vehicle. Both Humvees towed 400-gallon water trailers ("water buffalos" to the troops) behind them.

The driver of the lead Humvee sat back casually in his seat, one arm draped loosely over the steering wheel. He looked to be a few years younger than Roving Wolf but in every other respect, Comanche hair braids, desert battle fatigue pants, et cetera, he seemed Roving Wolf's twin. The driver divided his attention between the animated monologue Sun Rain showered on him and the approaching ex-domers. The interior compartment of the second Humvee was empty. Tom and Jenny angled toward the three men standing near the second vehicle's water trailer. Two of the men wore desert camouflage pants and brown army tee shirts while the third man was naked except for a tan deerskin breechcloth and deerskin leggings; he also held the bridle of a fine black mane mustang.

"Hello," called Tom as he and Jenny walked through the front yard.

The men turned their heads to face the approaching domer couple. The large heavy set man in the middle returned Tom's the greeting and waved.

"Hello. I hear you were once frightened turtles. How is life outside your shell?"

"An adventure. I am Tom Corant. This is my fiancé, Jenny Salem."

The taller man on the left added his greeting, "*O si yo*, Tom and Jenny—that means 'hello' in the Tsalagi language. You know my people as 'Cherokee.'" He extended his right hand expecting to shake hands, a white custom many Native American nations adopted and still practiced, but ironically, Tom and Jenny didn't know what to make of the gesture.

The warrior laughed. "You have been in your shell so long you have forgotten some of your own customs! I am called Yonahdisi, "Running Bear" in your language. Take my hand in friendship Jenny Salem."

Jenny tentatively clasped Running Bear's large hand and let him pump her hand up and down several times.

"O si yo, Running Bear," said Tom while offering his hand.

Running Bear smiled. "Fast learning, Tom. Very good!" Running Bear vigorously shook Tom's outstretched hand.

"I am Awiusdi, 'Little Deer' to you," offered the heavy middle warrior who had first returned Tom's greeting. He exchanged handshakes with the domer couple and explained, "Like my brother, I too am of the Tsalagihi Ayili, but I am from the eastern band of the great Cherokee people. My brother is of the western band and stays in the Oklahoma land. Every year we meet at the All Nations Pow-wow and I try to convince him to come to the green hills of home."

"Meet our Lakota brother," continued Little Deer who gestured to the well-muscled man to his left. The shirtless third man stepped forward and offered his hand while still holding his horse with the other. Small strands of his free flowing black hair whipped about in the light breeze.

"You call me Shatonskah, 'White Hawk' using white words. My brother says true, I am Lakota. Maybe you know as Sioux."

Tom and Jenny took turns shaking hands with White Hawk.

"How is it that all of you are brothers if you are from different tribes?" asked Jenny innocently.

Running Bear explained the term 'brother' was not limited to defining men from the same mother but was a term denoting the larger brotherhood and fellowship among warriors within a nation or among multiple American Indian nations. All warriors of all tribes were 'brothers.' All older warriors were 'fathers' and 'grandfathers.'

Roving Wolf approached the group as Running Bear finished his brief lesson on culture. "So you have already met my brothers?" Roving Wolf asked.

"Yes," Jenny replied with new understanding. "But not the brother over there talking with Sun Rain."

"Come," commanded Roving Wolf. Tom and Jenny followed the Comanche scout to the first Humvee.

Sun Rain and the Humvee driver dropped their conversation as Roving Wolf approached. The driver climbed out of the driver's compartment and Sun Rain put her arm around his shoulder and tapped his bare chest with her other hand. "Tom, Jenny, meet our cousin, Kanaretah. In English that means 'Cloud Rider.'"

Tom and Jenny each shook the hand of Cloud Rider. The Comanche had the same high cheek bones, wide jaw and strong chin as Roving Wolf. The two men wore the identical kit: desert camo pants, no shirt, and web belt with pistol and hunting knife. The only difference was that Cloud Rider wore his pistol on his left side and he sported a desert boonie hat.

Roving Wolf removed a map from one of his cargo pockets and spread it out on the hood of the lead Humvee while the scout party members jockeyed for position around the improvised map table. The mission leader's hands floated over the map to indicate key navigation waypoints as he explained the plan that he and his US Army handler devised the evening before. The dual mission goals were one: deliver Tom and Jenny to the El Paso stronghold; and two: scout the U.S./Mexico border from Presidio up to El Paso for any sign of Mexican military activity.

Tom moved around to the other side of the Humvee for a better look at the map. The morning was brightening quickly under a clear sky and the usual pre-dawn chill was a memory. As he moved, Tom turned his head in the direction of a horse snorting to clear dirt from its nostrils. He noticed several other horses tethered to a fence a few buildings down the street behind the trailing Humvee. Immediately ahead of the lead Humvee, twenty feet up the street, a group of Comanche children happily played. Red Sky sat alone on her porch swing slowly rocking back and forth.

Roving Wolf pointed to Pecos and traced a route south down Texas Route 17 to Marfa, reversing the route taken by the Mexican kidnappers. From Marfa, three scouts would make for three separate deserted border towns. Roving Wolf would travel down US 67 to Presidio, White Hawk would scout down highway 2810 to Ruidosa and Cloud Rider would cut across country over the Cuestra Del Burro Mountains to Candelaria. After reaching their assigned town, each of the scouts would turn northwest and scout along the Rio Grande rendezvousing in Esperanza 65 miles south of El Paso. Meanwhile, Cherokee scouts Running Bear and Little Deer would drive the Humvees with Tom, Jenny, and Sun Rain northwest along US 90 to I-10 and then on to the rendezvous in Esperanza. The Humvee element and extra horses would spend two nights in Valentine and one night at Van Horn so that they didn't move too far ahead of the scouts traveling along the Rio Grande.

"Tom, other orders about you," Roving Wolf indicated. "You must begin weapons training and infantry rifle team movement and tactics."

Tom smiled broadly. "Really? Great!"

"But why do you have to do that?" Jenny asked.

Tom shrugged. "I am in the Army after all, honey."

"Well yes, but you drove combots remotely from your bedroom, sweetheart. Out here you could get hurt, or worse."

"And I recommend both of you start conditioning for more horse riding," added Roving Wolf. "Start with an hour in the morning and an hour in late afternoon. Increase saddle time each day as you can."

Roving Wolf folded the map. "Brothers, are you ready?"

A shrill burst of simultaneous Comanche, Cherokee, and Lakota war cries startled Tom and unnerved Jenny.

Little Deer put his hands on the brown tee shirt that stretched over his ample belly and rocked backward in laughter. "Don't be frightened Tom and Jenny. Those war sounds are meant to put fear in the hearts of our enemies, not our friends!"

"Tom, Jenny, follow me to the horses," said Roving Wolf. "You can get your one hour in the saddle then ride in a Humvee until afternoon. Sun Rain, you can drive but let our Cherokee brothers pull around in front and you follow."

"Yes, brother," responded Sun Rain with obvious disappointment about being relegated to the rear.

Little Deer put his hands on his hips and shook his head in mock disgust at Running Bear's brightly painted Humvee. "I can't believe I have to ride in this peacock with wheels."

Running Bear slapped his fellow warrior on the back. "I am not so happy about it either, brother. I know you will bite my ear with your nagging about wanting me to leave Oklahoma for North Carolina."

Roving Wolf and Cloud Rider helped Tom and Jenny onto their mounts and gave another brief lesson in horseback riding, important because this time the couple wouldn't be riding horses that were being led by a line. They had to learn to control the animals on their own.

Roving Wolf walked his horse around the vehicles to the front of the party. The Comanche children laughed and scampered out of the way. Cloud Rider and White Hawk helped the young domer couple move their mounts behind Roving Wolf's lead horse. Sun Rain and Running Bear pushed the starters of their respective machines and the Humvee engines roared to life.

The children waved as the convoy moved forward. Roving Wolf looked over his shoulder at Red Sky standing alone in the front yard resting both hands on her belly. He knew she wouldn't cry until he was out sight.

19.

The initial travel down Highway 17 passed slowly as the discomfort of the saddle reemerged within moments of setting out on the journey; but an hour later Tom and Jenny were much more comfortable sitting in the two rear seats of Sun Rain's Humvee with folded blankets providing extra cushioning for their sore posteriors. Much to their mutual disappointment they were not able to sit close together because filling the space between the rear seats was the driveshaft ridge and an equipment locker that doubled as a support for the turret gunner platform. The bullet resistant glass plates on their doors were unlatched and lowered into the door body to allow for better air flow. Mile after mile of dry desert and defiant sage brush drifted by as the Humvee rolled slowly behind the easy trot of the horses.

"How is your arm, Jenny?" Sun Rain asked.

"Itchy, but much better, thank you." She occasionally poked at the bandage to try and scratch the pesky itch but Sun Rain's tight cloth wrappings permitted only an unsatisfying rub that left Jenny in a state of perpetual annoyance.

"I will help you change the dressing tonight. It looked like you two are really learning to ride a horse!"

Tom nodded. "We're getting the hang of it thanks to your brother—and his '*brothers.*'"

"And cousin Cloud Rider. Now, does 'cousin' really mean cousin?" Jenny asked for clarification.

Sun Rain laughed. "Yes, Cloud Rider is our cousin by blood."

"Oh, wait!" exclaimed Sun Rain while stepping hard on the brake. Tom and Jenny lurched forward against their seat belts.

Tom leaned over to look through the windscreen for an explanation of the sudden stop but saw only the rear of the lead Cherokee Humvee plodding ahead. "What's wrong?"

"I'm sorry, Tom. I forgot, I am supposed to show you how to drive!"

Sun Rain cut the engine, pushed open the heavy armored door, and jumped out of her seat. Tom climbed out of the back and into the driver compartment as Sun Rain jogged around to the front passenger seat.

"Tom, are you sure this is a good idea? You've never driven anything before—in person anyway." Jenny's voice was heavy with concern.

Tom twisted to look in the back seat. "Are you kidding? This is going to be great!"

Jenny noted that her affable fiancé rarely beamed a smile so large or seemed so giddy. She settled deep into the back of her seat and let her head rest limply against the door frame which left her staring out at the wind-blown shrubs dotting the landscape.

Tom listened intently as Sun Rain explained the gauges, pedals, transmission, and how to use the rotary switch to start and stop the engine.

"Ready to drive, Tom?"

"Yes!" Tom turned the rotary switch to RUN. When the 'Wait-to-Start' light went out he turned the switch to START and released when the engine turned over.

Tom felt the engine vibration shake under his grip on the steering wheel; the movement transformed into a tingle of excitement that coursed through Tom's entire body. He pressed the button on the gear selector, pushed the lever to DRIVE, then moved his foot from the brake to the gas pedal and the Humvee rolled forward. He released pressure on the gas pedal and coasted to stop. Tom moved forward again and stopped but this time used the brake pedal. He soon had a feel for the sensitivity of both the accelerator and the brakes and began to turn the steering wheel in slow arcs back and forth, weaving the truck left and right as he drove down the highway.

"You are doing great, Tom. Give it a little more gas and catch up to the others. Don't close the distance too fast, take it easy. Then try to keep a smooth pace about 50 yards back."

Tom did as instructed by Sun Rain. "Honey, this is fun. You have to try this!"

"It handles much better without the water trailer we are pulling. We can try more things at the end of the day, even go off road once we unhitch the trailer," promised Sun Rain.

The mixed horse and truck convoy travelled without incident and stopped just after midday at Balmorhea for a short rest and to offer water to the horses. Both Tom and Jenny understood that they were near the place where their unbelievable adventure began. Tom's family dome was only four miles to the east. But, had the dome been merely an arm's length away, it wouldn't have mattered—they lacked the authorization codes to open the dome from the outside.

After lunch the party followed the highway as it climbed into the Barilla and Davis Mountains. Cloud Rider and White Hawk alternated responsibility for leading the four spare horses and for investigating their left and right flanks for any sign of the enemy. Catching up after a flank scout was hard work as Roving Wolf set a challenging pace for those on horseback in order to reach Fort Davis by dark. Late in the day Tom took another short turn in the saddle but Jenny declined and stayed in the Humvee.

As they neared town, White Hawk rode ahead to confirm the area was free of hostile forces. The balance of the party reached the Fort Davis crossroads of US 17 and Texas highway 118 half an hour before sunset. Roving Wolf located a brick house in better condition relative to the crumbling and rotting wooden homes and the team moved in to bed down for the night. The large house had all of its windows intact which meant less dust inside. Darkness came quickly because the small ghost town was tucked directly against the base of a 300-foot mountain ridge that blocked the view of the western horizon.

Tom slapped the fender of the Comanche Humvee only partly in jest when he learned that his night driving training would not be permitted at this time. The consensus among the professional scouts was that the area was too dangerous given all the cover that could be used by an enemy to approach undetected.

Once the Humvee's were hidden away in nearby garages, optical and seismic sensors planted, and the horses watered and grazing, the scouting party was able to sit down in the home's dining room to eat the evening meal.

"That was exceptional driving, Tom," joked Little Deer.

"I had fun," Tom responded. "I can't wait to see how fast these Humvee's can go."

"Faster than a horse trot," assured Little Deer. "But don't get your hopes up, they aren't race cars. They're too heavy and the transmission isn't built for speed."

Jenny sat down next to Tom who noticed the smell of smoke followed her to the table. She had been helping to heat the military rations on an old barbeque grill that White Hawk salvaged from one of the nearby backyards.

"Are you okay, sweetheart?" Tom inquired.

Jenny shook her head. "I don't know what's wrong. I have a headache, my nose is dripping, I have a sore throat. What is happening?"

"You are getting a cold," Cloud Rider interjected. "You will be fine in a few days."

Jenny shot Tom a puzzled look. "A cold virus, yes," she continued, "We learn about viruses in school. Not much in the way of communicable disease in our dome society."

White Hawk was the last person to join the crowd at the table. He emerged from the back rooms and sat across from Jenny who gasped in shock.

"My God, what is that you are wearing?!"

White Hawk's torso was no longer bare. Around his neck and shoulders he wore the hide of a small grey wolf. The wolf's lifeless head hung down onto White Hawk's right breast.

White Hawk was nonchalant. "Grey wolf is good luck to a Lakota scout. I can't wear this on the trail—much more dust here than in Lakota country in the north. My war shirt is also packed away. I won't wear until we begin battle—too much dust, too much dust and not enough trees in this place."

Jenny lost what little appetite she had, covered her mouth and left the table.

Fearing White Hawk's reaction to Jenny's slight Tom offered, "Please don't be offended. Your culture and ours are very different." With a simple wave White Hawk dismissed any notion that he was offended.

"So how did you two get along in the other Humvee?" Sun Rain posed her question to the Cherokee scouts Running Bear and Little Deer.

Running Bear grabbed the sides of his head in a comical, exaggerated movement. "Oh my ears, sister! It is a wonder I still have them. I heard nothing but 'green hills of North Carolina' hour after hour. I tried to tell my eastern band brother that we have hills and green trees in Oklahoma as well!"

Little Deer raised an arm to demand the floor. "Tiny bumps on the ground are not hills and the trees are so few, how can you stalk your game?!"

Roving Wolf joined a portion of the hearty laughter erupting around the table but he kept one trained eye on the sensor display panel he set near his plate. Seismic and motion sensors would flash an alarm if movement or localized ground vibrations were detected.

Tom reveled in the Comanche, Cherokee, and Lakota stories shared over the next few hours before dismissing himself to check on Jenny. He found her curled into a fetal position on the bed. Tom blew out the lone candle on the cobweb-covered dresser and eased onto the bed.

"It's about time you came to see how I was doing."

Jenny's cold tone took Tom by surprise. "I'm sorry, honey. I wasn't thinking. I got caught up in the party at the table."

"It's getting so hard to breathe, this is awful."

Tom reached in his pocket and pulled out a cloth handkerchief. He felt through the darkness for Jenny's hand. "Here, honey. Sun Rain said to give you this for your nose."

Jenny prickled at the name of the spunky Indian girl.

Tom laid down with an arm around Jenny. "Try to get some sleep, honey. We have another long day tomorrow."

Tom quickly fell asleep. Jenny lay awake for hours.

20.

Steven rubbed his aching eyes. Eighteen straight hours of Net surfing made it difficult for him to focus clearly on the wall-mounted display screen in his bedroom. He was logged in to the Net in his capacity as an FCC SNet investigator. He scoured the Net going deep into layer after layer of links, hidden server directories, micro chats that lasted only moments, and anonymous blogs. He searched the Net indexes for key words and phrases that might point to subversive content as defined by the Federal Communications Commission. But he also poured through the electronic nooks and crannies for anything that might relate to Tom and Jenny and their "accident."

He gulped coffee from his favorite oversized mug. It was cold but he didn't care—he just needed to stay awake. Steven set the mug back down in a slow deliberate motion, taking the extra care because he was tired and that's when nasty spills happened. When he turned back to the screen, that's when he noticed the message:

Tom lives on the Outside…

Steven squinted and leaned forward to be sure he read the tiny text correctly. The words were not contained within a standard message window. They were printed in the bottom bar of his main desktop border. How did words get written into there? he wondered. He had never seen that before. "So how do I talk back?" Steven said aloud. He hovered his cursor over the text and clicked. Sure enough, a text insertion cursor blinked within the border bar waiting for keyboard input. Steven typed:

"Who are you?" and pressed the enter key on his keyboard.

The answer came back immediately:

"Black Shine."

Two simple ordinary words yet when combined they represented an entity that was the government's Public

Enemy Number One. Steven stared at the words; his hands would not move to type on his keyboard. The next few breaths he took, he made a conscious effort to inhale and exhale as quietly as he could. He took an unnecessary look around his room to confirm he was alone.

Was this really Black Shine? Or was this a trick by a fellow Net cop to entrap him? How could he be sure? He couldn't. But he had to find Tom. If he guessed wrong, he heard the government could hit some sort of 'kill switch' on his family's connection to the Net and instantly make their dome into prison, cut off from everyone. Steven finally summoned the will to move his hands and type a return message:

"You know where my brother is?"

Up to a point Steven figured he could claim he was using his official office to flush out criminals or working to infiltrate an anti-government group.

"We do."

"You know I am FCC Web Police?"

"Of course we know that, Steven Corant."

"How can we trust each other?"

"We may be able to arrange for you to see and speak with Tom."

Steven brightened with the hope offered by those last words. He had to learn what happened to Tom despite the risk. Steven centered the keyboard on his lap and soon found his hands drifting slowly over the keys again. All the lessons from his training and his oath of fealty to the Federal Communications Commission dissolved away as he typed…

"Tell me more."

21.

At daybreak the next morning Cloud Rider jostled Tom awake. Tom woke Jenny who moaned in protest of lack of sleep and of the discomfort brought on by her cold symptoms. The couple slipped on their boots and stumbled through the darkness following the faint candle glow to the dining room. The floor of the old house creaked noisily as they crossed the wooden floor boards. Jenny walked with a blanket wrapped around her to keep the morning chill away. They sat down at the empty dining table and Sun Rain brought them two military ration packs and a canteen of water.

"Ten minutes for one quick cold meal, guys. Sorry, but my brother wants to get moving." Sun Rain exited the room and continued out the front door. Beyond the dining room window the eastern sky glowed with pre-dawn light.

"I need to go to the bathroom first," Jenny announced. "Start without me, honey."

Jenny left the room carrying one of the candles. Tom tore open both ration packets.

Jenny returned and Tom rose to take his turn in the bathroom. Jenny caught Tom's arm.

"Tom…I, well….," Jenny stammered with embarrassment. "I forgot there isn't any running water. I am afraid I left a bit of a nasty mess in there."

Tom laughed and kissed Jenny on the cheek. "No need to be so prim, darling. I won't think any less of you and if it helps, I won't bring a candle, that way I won't see anything."

"It's not just that, Tom. This is somebody's house. I feel like I am desecrating someone's home."

"Jenny, outside the domes the country is ten thousand ghost towns and millions of crumbling houses and buildings that don't belong to anyone any more. Don't worry. Eat up. I'll be back in a minute."

Tom returned and they hurriedly crunched through the rations. Sun Rain came in to collect the candles and everyone rendezvoused outside on the cracked sidewalk that ran through the front yard. The Humvee engines were running and the horses were collected, saddled, and bunched together on the street in front of the idling vehicles.

Still wrapped in a blanket against the chilly air, Jenny finished her latest fit of sneezing and, followed Tom to the horses. Roving Wolf helped Tom find his horse since the morning was still too dark to distinguish much detail. Before Tom could mount, Roving Wolf put a hand on his shoulder.

"Wait, Tom."

"Sure, what is it?" Tom asked and Jenny leaned in close.

"I heard something from my lieutenant that you should know. Your families were told that the accident that prevented you from reaching your dome was fatal, that both of you were killed."

"What?!" exclaimed Jenny. "Tommy, they can't do that! Why would they do that?"

"Do you have any other details?" Tom asked.

"No."

"My family thinks I am dead?" Jenny grabbed Tom. Her blanket fell to the ground but she barely noticed the cold. Jenny pressed her face into Tom's shoulder and wept. Then Tom felt Jenny's head lift abruptly and saw she was looking up at him, but it was too dark to read her face. He did hear Jenny gasp.

"Oh, Tom…Jonny!"

Tom nodded. He had already realized that his effervescent, carefree little brother must be devastated.

* * * *

The sun splashed orange fire along the eastern horizon but Tom saw only the cracking asphalt of the road ahead. He held the reins absently in his hand; Tom didn't notice that Roving Wolf led his horse with a lead line in the same manner that Cloud Rider and White Hawk took turns leading the spare horses. Tom felt nothing. He was numb from head to foot as he completed his saddle portion of the morning trek. The shock of being declared dead to family and friends had not yet worn off.

Tom dismounted and left his horse in the care of Roving Wolf. He did manage a half-hearted wave to Running Bear and Little Deer as they drove by in the lead Humvee. Tom again took up driving duties in the trailing Humvee. Sun Rain slid into the passenger seat and Tom rolled the Humvee forward to keep pace with the horses and lead truck. Jenny had skipped her horseback session again and was curled up under a blanket in the back seat.

"My brother told me the news. I am sorry, Tom."

"Thank you. How are you doing back there, honey?"

Jenny's head leaned heavily against the door frame. She answered Tom without taking her eyes from the slowly passing landscape. "We can never go home, can we Tommy?"

Tom knew Jenny was right. There was no point in denying that fact. "Yeah, they wouldn't have said we were dead if they were going to allow us back into a dome."

Tom sniffled. "If it makes you feel any better, I am coming down with your cold. You are right, not very comfortable."

"Oh, it gets worse." Jenny assured Tom.

"Tell me about your family, Tom. I made Jenny tell me about hers. Now it's your turn."

Tom obliged Sun Rain as he kept pace with Running Bear and Little Deer. It actually did help to talk about his family.

The small scout convoy rolled out of the Davis Mountains and the landscape once again resembled the flat sage brush desert like that which surrounded Pecos. Occasionally a mesquite plant rose above the scrub and developed into a ten or even twenty foot tree if its deep roots were lucky enough to find a source of ground water. Tom was intrigued by the sky which was crowded with a much greater number of puffy cumulus clouds that he had seen previously.

Sun Rain's short range radio crackled to life briefly to announce that Roving Wolf was breaking off from the group to scout ahead into the town of Marfa in order to confirm the town was free of any enemy ambush. Half an hour later the radio blared again with Roving Wolf's 'all clear' call. After another hour of travel the scout team assembled at an abandoned gas station on the primary Marfa crossroads of Texas Route 17 and US 90. Everyone gathered around the hood of the lead Humvee for one last map check.

"A change in plan as of last night," announced Roving Wolf. "The Humvees and spare horses going down Highway 90 to Valentine; you need to wait three nights in Valentine before beginning travel to Esperanza instead of two nights. The extra time is needed because me, White Hawk, and Cloud Rider will extend our scout into Mexico if we don't find enemy on US land. Scouts...avoid contact, work your way northwest. The meeting place for everyone will still be Esperanza in five days."

After farewells were exchanged, Roving Wolf, White Hawk, and Cloud Rider each took their mounts on three different routes to the Mexican border.

"That leaves us with five horses," noted Running Bear. I will ride one and lead the others. My eastern band brother is too fat to cover much land on horse."

"I am not fat, I am healthy!" Little Deer insisted.

Running Bear continued Tom's training by talking him through saddling one of the horses then Tom jumped back into the driver's seat of the trailing Humvee. The convoy bound for Valentine now moved northwest along the highway toward the Sierra Vieja and Van Horn Mountain ranges.

Shortly after setting off, Sun Rain loosed a curt laugh. "Look at that, Tom, Jenny. Running Bear could be out in front leading Little Deer's truck but he is riding along side so he can still talk to his brother. I knew his complaints about being forced to listen to Little Deer were empty. You can't separate those two now!"

Tom's mood had lightened and he was able to chuckle in agreement while he followed the usual fifty meters behind the Cherokee Humvee as it drove toward the mountains and the thickening clouds blowing in from the northwest.

22.

Tiny Valentine Texas didn't have many houses to choose from but Running Bear scouted the town ahead of the Humvees and found a serviceable house that had a small barn nearby for the horses. Jenny's stuffy nose, cough, and headache made her whimper in misery as she stumbled through the dark house looking for a place to sleep. If she could only fall asleep she wouldn't be conscious of the cold symptoms that made her feel as if she inhabited an alien body. Jenny found one of the bedrooms, pulled the dusty bedspread off the bed, and fell asleep moments after lying down. Sun Rain, Running Bear, Little Deer, and Tom ate cold rations by candlelight at the small kitchen table.

"Looks like there might be a storm tonight," observed Running Bear. "Not sure if there will be any rain but if there is, we should look to catch some of it, eh?"

"Good idea since we will be here for a few days," agreed Little Deer.

Running Bear stood and put his ration wrappers in a garbage can that would never be emptied. "That large warehouse building we saw coming into town…I will investigate. If the rain gutters are in place, that structure will capture a lot of water."

Little Deer rose from the table as well and announced that he would scout the opposite end of town for water collection opportunities in the event it did rain.

Tom and Sun Rain were left to finish their meal minus the jovial banter inspired by the friendly rivalry of the Cherokee warriors from different bands. Sun Rain rested her folded arms on the table and leaned forward. "So, Tom, what do you think of our adventure so far? Nothing like dome life, right?"

Tom watched the soft glow of the candle light dance across Sun Rain's face. Her manner betrayed no sign of the frenetic energy that normally radiated from the gregarious young woman. Tom wondered what had occurred to bring about the more composed demeanor. "It's overwhelming. I lived my whole life thinking my dome was the universe. Now I know just how small my world really was."

"Like a prison," suggested Sun Rain

"Yes. Exactly. Now I understand why the government wants to destroy anything that references the world outside. Everybody ran into the domes because of many terrible evils and I understand that. But the freedom we traded for safety…I don't think it was worth it.

"Sun Rain, if I can find a way, I have to get Jonny out of there, and anybody else who wants to come. But Jonny…he seems to *know* there is something better Outside. Some of that comes from Grandpa Frank's influence but I don't think that explains it all. That little boy has some sort of intuition most of us don't have."

Tom and Sun Rain talked well into the evening. Outside, wind gusts began to whip through the trees and cause the old house to creak from the strain imposed by the rushing air.

"I better turn in and check on Jenny," said Tom.

"Yes, that is a good idea. Your training starts tomorrow. You need rest."

A distant lightening flash shot through the window and caught Tom's attention. A moment later came the low rumble of thunder.

"A thunder storm is on the way. If the storm comes close, some of that thunder will be extremely loud, Tom, be prepared for that. There is nothing to fear as long as it doesn't spawn any tornados—that's less likely this time of year. Also, don't stand near any trees or metal objects when lightening is near."

Sun Rain stood and blew out all but one candle. Before Tom rose she bent down and kissed him on the cheek.

"Good night, Tom." And she was gone.

Tom fumbled his way to the far northwest bedroom to find that Jenny hadn't moved an inch since falling asleep. Tom quietly stretched out next to Jenny trying his best not to jostle her awake. He saw one more lightening flash and heard another few seconds of distant rolling thunder before closing his eyes and joining Jenny in the deep sleep of an exhausted traveler.

* * * *

The loud thunderclap woke Tom and Jenny but they were both too groggy and the thunderclap too brief for the couple to realize why they were suddenly awake. Then more bright lightening flashed through the window. Before Jenny could ask what was happening, a booming hammer of thunder pounded and shook the entire house.

Jenny screamed and held Tom tight.

"Relax, honey, just some thunder and lightning." Sun Rain was right, thought Tom. Some of that thunder could be really loud.

After more flashes and loud booms, heavy rain drops began pelting the roof. Tom pulled away from Jenny and got out of bed.

"Tom, what are you doing!?" Jenny was frantic.

Tom ran to the window. "I want to see. This is incredible!"

Wild gusts of wind raged against the house while the pounding rain drummed loudly in their ears. Another lightning flash generated a sharp crack of thunder as well as another fearful scream from Jenny. Tom stood at the window with eyes wide and mouth gaping in absolute awe of the power of the storm. More lightning and thunder sent his heart racing.

"Jenny, come on, let's go to the front porch for a better look!"

"Noooo!" came the desperate plea from Jenny. After another loud crackle and boom of a close lightning strike Jenny was crying. It was too dark for Tom to see the fear on Jenny's face but he heard the fear in her next plea.

"Please don't go!!"

Tom rushed back to the bed and held Jenny tightly. He held her for a long time, until the rain eased and the thunder became a distant low rumble instead of a nearby deafening blast of noise. Tom hadn't felt anyone tremble with shear terror before. Even the treatment she endured in the Mexican camp had not left her so affected. Jenny felt drained and cold in his arms and she sobbed and shook for a long time before drifting back to sleep.

When Tom woke, Jenny was not in the room. Concern for his fiancé made Tom quickly slip on his socks and boots and go in search for Jenny. He didn't have to go far. She was in the kitchen drinking hot coffee with Running Bear and Little Deer. Some of Tom's worry eased. The two Cherokee warriors had managed to put a slight smile on Jenny, but her eyes where puffy and red from crying.

"Morning, Tom," called Little Deer. "Come have some coffee."

"Sounds good. I will be right back." Tom walked through the house and out the door to the house next door that they were using for its bathroom facilities. The morning sun was already blazing in a crisp clear sky that showed no sign of the storm that savaged the town the evening before. Only the moist ground provided evidence of the passing storm. Much of the other moisture had already evaporated into the dry air.

Tom walked into the bathroom of the neighboring home and was startled by a cheerful "Hi, Tom!" from Sun Rain. The surprise was all the more profound as Sun Rain stood naked in the bath tub casually drying her hair.

"Little Deer is a genius. He rigged some half barrels on 'X' frames outside with fire pits for heating the water and a garden hose brings it in here to the tub!" Sun Rain rattled on without a shred of embarrassment while she dried.

Tom's shock wore off and he turned away quickly after staring for what he believed was an inappropriately long few seconds. "I'm sorry, Sun Rain...the door was open...I didn't realize...."

Tom rushed out of the house. The door of the next house was locked so he chose a spot between the houses to urinate onto the damp ground before returning for coffee with Jenny and the others.

Tom wore enough residual surprise on his face for Jenny to ask, "Everything okay, Tom?"

"Yes, yes. How about you, honey?" Tom leaned down to give Jenny a hug. "You were really spooked by that storm."

Tom sat down across from Jenny. Someone had already set a mug with hot instant ration coffee on the table. "Thanks for the coffee."

"You are welcome," replied Running Bear. "Yes, Jenny, I heard a couple screams from your way."

"Right, and it didn't sound like that was Tom's doing!" joked Little Deer.

Jenny smiled weakly. "I'm sorry, I had no idea what a thunderstorm was like, so powerful. It was frightening."

Sun Rain bounded into the room a few moments later dressed in a clean set of desert camouflage pants and brown army tee shirt. Her long hair was uncombed and still air drying.

"Jenny, you have to try Little Deer's plumbing!" Sun Rain didn't wait for an answer and was already helping Jenny up from the table. "Come on. I will help."

Sun Rain led Jenny out of the kitchen and Tom called after them, "Have a good soak, Jen!"

"You are going to need a good soak by the end of this day, Tom," said Running Bear.

Little Deer nodded and laughed. "That's right. I would never keep up with Sun Rain if she were my trainer!"

Half of Tom's coffee was gone when Sun Rain returned and announced that Jenny was happily soaking in a hot bath.

"Thank you for helping, Sun Rain."

"Glad to help, Tom. Are you ready to get started?"

Tom nodded. "Yes. I want to go check on Jenny real quick, then we can move out."

Tom retraced his earlier steps to the house next door. The bathroom door was closed but at least this time he knew what to expect inside the room. Tom knocked gently. "Jenny?"

"Come in, Tommy."

Tom entered and sat on the closed toilet next to the tub. "How do you feel, sweetheart?"

"Even with this stuffy nose I feel a thousand percent better than the last few days." Jenny's eyes closed and the smile on her face was proof of her statement.

"You do look much better, honey. Are you going to keep me company today?"

Jenny opened her eyes and shot a puzzled look in Tom's direction. "Are you still doing training? Why, Tom? You are dead as far as the Army is concerned. You don't owe them anything."

"Still, I am a soldier," Tom insisted.

"A soldier? You sit in your bedroom with a keyboard and control robot machine guns from half a world away. You kill from the safety of your home. You may as well be playing video games. That's not being a soldier. Tom, you can get hurt or you can get killed out here."

Tom stood to leave but hesitated momentarily at the threshold. Jenny's words delivered painful truth but the contempt with which they were spoken hurt even more. "Well, if we can't go back to the domes and we have to live out here, I better start developing some new skills." Tom left abruptly and rejoined the others in the main house.

"Okay, I'm ready. Brother Running Bear, brother Little Deer, please keep Jenny safe while we are gone."

Jenny's unsupportive comments still stung so much Tom found in them the motivation to beat Sun Rain to the tan Comanche Humvee. The brightly colored Cherokee Humvee would remain in town with its drivers.

Tom turned the truck engine over and pulled into the center of the road. No longer required to keep pace with trotting horses, Tom experimented with applying a lot more throttle.

"That's it, Tom!" encouraged Sun Rain from the passenger seat.

The truck was indeed much more responsive without the weight of the water trailer. Sun Rain signaled for him to slow down.

"Now let's take it off-road."

Tom left the paved roadway and drove a random pattern around the desert brush. Sun Rain provided training pointers about the dangers of rollover and about avoiding new growth mesquite and other plants that could sometimes sport thorns strong enough to puncture tires. Tom alternated his speed and tested different turn rates all to get a better feel for the vehicle. Sun Rain gave Tom navigation tips and cautioned him to remember waypoints and landmarks and keep an eye on the compass. Tom laughed and hooted and sported a grin from ear to ear; he couldn't remember ever having so much fun. In the seat beside him, Sun Rain laughed heartily and cheered him on at every turn.

Sun Rain pointed Tom to a line of small hills that rose twenty to fifty meters high two miles beyond the town. Tom slowed and listened to Sun Rain call the route that he was to drive up to the crest of the tallest hill.

As the Humvee topped the crest of the hill they actually found themselves on an old jeep trail. Sun Rain told Tom to cut the engine and they both climbed out of the cab. The small hill was only fifty meters high but clearly the highest point on the desert prairie for miles around. Sun Rain grabbed two pairs of binoculars and threw one pair to Tom.

"Check the east-west line sweeping south and I will sweep north, then we'll switch. Let's be sure we are alone," said Sun Rain as she climbed up through the gun turret removing the improvised wooden hatch cover—the original hinged metal cover had disappeared years ago for some long-forgotten purpose.

Tom probed his assigned sector with the high-powered binoculars. He had used the optics of infantry combots to do the same search task on many occasions but he had been restricted to using only infrared and ultraviolet EM bands. Tom confirmed what he always instinctively knew, that it was much more natural and comfortable scanning the outside environment using the visible light spectrum. Of course there were times when using other bands were indeed more useful, such as using infrared at night to see warm-bodied people contrasting sharply with the cooling surface of the earth. Still, Tom believed it was unfortunate that domers teleoperating equipment on the Outside weren't given the opportunity to perform their tasks using the visible light spectrum as well.

"Nothing," indicated Tom.

"Same here," confirmed Sun Rain.

Sun Rain climbed down and into the driver's seat. "Back away, Tom. I want to reposition a bit for a test fire."

Tom backed away from the truck as Sun Rain briefly turned the engine over and repositioned the Humvee a few feet further down the western slope to give the gun turret a better firing angle into the flat plain below the hill.

Sun Rain climbed back into the turret and removed the water proof canvas covering from the .50 caliber heavy machine gun.

"Come on up, Tom, don't be shy. Time for some weapons training!"

Sun Rain smiled and patted the big M2 Browning gun. Tom noted the obvious twinkle in her eye and the extra breadth of her smile. His trainer's enthusiasm was unmistakable; she was indeed in her element and clearly very much a soldier at heart. Tom climbed into the rear seat compartment while Sun Rain lifted herself up to sit on the vehicle roof toward the back of the turret. That position gave Tom room to stand up through the turret opening while Sun Rain's legs dangled inside the Humvee on either side of him. Tom stood in the turret facing the gun with Sun Rain sitting immediately behind him with her hands on his shoulders.

Sun Rain talked Tom through opening the gun's receiver and the attached ammunition can. He positioned the ammunition belt, locked the receiver and pulled the cocking lever to chamber the first round, all under Sun Rain's expert guidance.

"Perfect. Now, hands on the grips. You normally fire five to seven round bursts," instructed Sun Rain. "See that old storage shed, that's our target."

"I don't see a shed. Wait, over there? That's at least half a mile away!"

Sun Rain laughed and reached around Tom to put her hands on top of his as he grasped the left and right firing grips of the machine gun. She traversed the gun slightly and aimed. With her thumb she depressed the butterfly trigger and the gun barked loudly and tried to recoil against its mount with each round fired.

Tom watched dust kick up in front of the shed as Sun Rain walked the rounds into the tiny building.

Sun Rain released the trigger and let go of Tom's hands. "Now you try."

Tom mimicked Sun Rain's performance perfectly and the little shed collapsed in a heap of rubble.

The sound and power of the gun produced an adrenaline rush through Tom unlike anything ever caused by teleoperating a combat robot. "Wow! Now that's better than remote controlling from a dome any day!"

"Nice job!"

Tom turned around to face Sun Rain and realized immediately that she was uncomfortably close but he didn't have room to back away with the gun grips pressing into his back.

Sun Rain smiled then laughed at Tom's noticeable discomfort. She playfully jostled his boonie hat and then broke the tension by announcing, "Okay, you are checked out on the M2, now we move to the M240, then M4 carbine, and we will wrap with a heavy SCAR. We will need to get back to base well before dark so I have time to show you how to clean and oil whatever weapons we fire this morning."

Sun Rain continued Tom's weapons training and drills all morning and into mid afternoon without break. Tom didn't want a break—he was having too much fun.

Tom drove back into Valentine far more confident and in a much better mood than when he left. He parked the Humvee in the next-door driveway and helped Sun Rain carry the weapons. Jenny rocked in a porch swing as he approached with an M240 machine gun resting on his shoulder. He recalled the scornful manner with which she reproached him that morning regarding his pseudo soldier status. After only one day of intense training, he already felt like a different man.

Jenny jogged off the porch to Tom and gave him a hug.

"I am sorry about this morning, Tom."

Little Deer approached Tom. "I will take that," and he lifted the machine gun off Tom's shoulder.

"What's going on," Tom asked.

Little Deer pointed to the two saddled horses in the next yard. "You haven't had your saddle time today."

"No…" Tom protested. "I am beat."

"I'm going with you, Tom. We are going to ride out, have a picnic dinner, watch the sunset, and ride back." Jenny made a note to thank Little Deer again for this helpful suggestion.

"All right, I *am* hungry. I am also a dirty, sweaty, smelly mess. If you are sure you want to hang out with me in this condition, then come on, let's go."

The next day passed in similar fashion for Tom, Humvee maintenance and training in the morning, weapons training in the afternoon, dinner and horseback ride with Jenny in the evening. His tired and sore body was asleep not long after sundown.

On the morning of the third day, Running Bear led the "interior scout team" as Roving Wolf had referred to them, on the 40-mile trek from Valentine to Van Horn where they picked up Interstate 10 again. Except for the time needed to care for the horses, everyone had the night off and a friendly game of poker commenced after dinner when a deck of playing cards was found in their home for the night. Jenny's cold symptoms were abating and Tom wasn't as incapacitated by his cold as Jenny was by hers so all five members of the scout team stayed up late using toothpicks, dried beans and ancient shell pasta for betting chips. Running Bear monitored the remote sensors, just in case.

The team departed Van Horn before dawn for Esperanza despite the late evening card games. Everyone was anxious to reunite with their friends—and family in Sun Rain's case—who had undertaken the dangerous task of scouting into Mexico.

23.

Running Bear alternated his riding time among the horses because he had to press the animals hard to cover the sixty miles between Van Horn and Esperanza before dark. Most of the sun's face was buried beneath the desert when he led the Humvees off I-10 for a short 20-minute jaunt south to the Esperanza compound located near an old dirt landing strip. Running Bear confirmed by short range radio that Cloud Rider and White Hawk were already waiting at the compound. There was no word from Roving Wolf. Sun Rain wasn't discouraged but her cheerful disposition was muted somewhat and would remain so until she knew the status of her brother.

There were happy greetings all around outside the compound's main house in the last of the evening twilight. Little Deer started a camp fire in order to heat the dinner rations. Jenny and Sun Rain both searched for and found plenty of candles to brighten the dining room.

Dinner was a welcome event for the hungry scout teams. Tom thought the meal would have tasted better though, had Roving Wolf been there. He listened to Cloud Rider and White Hawk separately recount their scout missions into Mexico. Both men observed small groups of Mexican soldiers operating reconnaissance patrols in advance of the primary eastern force that remained encamped near the city of Chihuahua.

Another poker game was being contemplated when Roving Wolf's voice crackled over the radio. He was only half an hour away. Sun Rain's spirit noticeably improved and she worked to prepare a hot meal for her brother.

Roving Wolf opened the door of the main house and followed candle glow to the dining room. He was met with a chorus of greetings and a hug from Sun Rain.

White Hawk noticed the carbine slung across Roving Wolf's back. "You don't usually come armed to the dinner table."

"You say the truth my Lakota brother. Call it an abundance of caution. We are less than two miles from the border. A weapon in arm's reach eases my spirit."

Roving Wolf took out his map and spread it out on the table so that he could debrief his fellow scouts and prepare a report for his handler, Lieutenant Benson.

"Everyone get some rest," Roving Wolf advised. "Tomorrow we cover the forty miles to Fabens. That will put us less than a day's ride to El Paso.

"Tom, before you go I have something you need to see." Roving Wolf pulled his SATCOM transmitter out of the satchel he had carried to the table and turned on the power. He recalled the text of a saved message and showed it to Tom.

"I received this message of unknown origin two nights ago. I did not report it."

Tom read the message displayed on the satellite communicator's low-power auxiliary screen:

IS THOMAS CORANT WITH YOU? BUCEPHALUS WONDERS.

"Do you know what that means?"

Tom's eyes widened. "My God, it's Steven, my big brother! He is referencing a game we used to play together as kids. How could he do this?"

Roving Wolf shook his head. "I don't know. These communication devices are extremely secure. I am not certain one person could do this without help from others."

"Steve is one of the people who patrols the Net for subversive material. He does have access to things most people do not. Will you send a message back for me?" Tom knew he was asking Roving Wolf to break some laws with severe penalties, just as Steven was taking a big risk reaching out like this.

"Yes, Tom. I will send a message tonight. I live free. I do not fear the government. But if this message is from your brother, use caution. He thinks he lives free inside his dome because the government tells him he does. But I think you know the truth now?"

Tom nodded. He knew that Freedom was not a right *granted* by a government. Everyone on earth was born with the right to live free.

Tom typed a draft message on the device's small keyboard. "Send him this response. He will know it is from me."

YES. TOM IS WELL. ALEXANDER's GOLD IS STILL HIDDEN UNDER THE CRADLE.

* * * *

After a quick pre-dawn breakfast the El Paso scout party, now back to full strength, left the Esperanza compound for Fabens, Texas. They traveled the entire way on I-10, paralleling the Rio Grande which was never more than two or three miles away. The sky was overcast all day with low, light gray clouds but nothing that threatened rain. The trip was uneventful but the level of alert was high given the proximity of the border.

The scout team followed its usual procedure of setting up for the night in the most suitable (least dusty) house in the area. Also standard was the candlelight dinner well after sundown and after the horses were tended to. In a break from routine, however, Roving Wolf's SATCOM satchel vibrated to announce receipt of a message. Most of the calls were at scheduled times agreed upon by Roving Wolf and his handler so an unscheduled message at this time meant a possible emergency.

Roving Wolf pulled the SATCOM unit out of the satchel. The device was capable of two-way real-time video with a proper satellite link but most of the time, he and Lieutenant Benson used the simpler, more efficient text-only mode. The message was indeed marked urgent.

"What is happening, cousin?" Cloud Rider asked.

"The El Paso stronghold has fallen off the grid. They missed their daily check-in yesterday and attempts to contact them have been fruitless. We are warned to approach with caution and I am to make a detailed report tomorrow evening on the stronghold's status."

Roving Wolf declared the previous plan of following the Interstate into town was now too dangerous. There were still two million Mexicans immediately across the river in Juarez. If the people of Juarez started pouring across the border into El Paso, there was little the scout team could do about it. One of the primary missions of the El Paso stronghold was to monitor illegal movement of people from Juarez into the United States. The stronghold citizens considered it easy duty despite the tremendous disparity in numbers because, with the United States population under domes, there were no economic opportunities—legal or illegal—available to Mexicans who crossed the border. There was no market for illicit drugs and there were no longer any jobs available inside the United States. And then there was the shoot-to-kill order enforced by aerial drones and Apache and Comanche warriors patrolling the border. All these realities meant that, in the year 2080, there were no financial incentives whatsoever for Mexicans to cross the international border. A few still tried though, to escape an overcrowded city or to find more prosperous agricultural land.

Roving Wolf concluded that the I-10 corridor offered too many opportunities for ambush so he decided to approach from the east passing through Biggs Air Force Base and Fort Bliss. The tactical situation favored the use of the Humvees instead of horse cavalry. If they ran into a vastly superior force they would likely need the speed and range of the Humvees to evade the enemy.

Under the new El Paso approach plan, Running Bear, Cloud Rider, and White Hawk would crew the Cherokee Humvee and Little Deer and Roving Wolf would crew the Comanche Humvee. Both vehicles would drive eighteen miles north across country to park their water trailers in the Hueco Mountains then turn due west toward El Paso. Sun Rain, Tom, and Jenny would lead all the horses north to the hidden water buffalos and wait while the Humvee teams reconnoitered the city. The horse team would carry one of the longer range pack radios to stay in communication with the truck teams.

"Any message from my brother?" Tom asked hopefully.

"Yes," Roving Wolf answered. "A time scheduled for a video link. Tomorrow night, 11:30 p.m."

The weary travelers all found beds for rest. Jenny returned to the pitch black room she shared with Tom and lowered herself gently next to her fiancé. She felt his strong arm slip around her waist and pull her close. The last two evenings were the first two realistic opportunities for romance since their ordeal began but Tom still showed no signs of pursuing a romantic agenda. Jenny realized with profound sadness that she lacked much motivation to press the issue. Still, she needed to know Tom's heart on the state of their relationship and decided on a course of direct questioning.

"We always said we couldn't wait until we were together so that we could make love for real. Are you ready?"

Tom's answer did not come immediately. "I guess there haven't been very many opportunities for intimacy out here have there? Seems like we have been too tired, or in too much pain, or too sick for any romance."

"Yes, you're right, honey. Tonight might be the first decent opportunity we have had. What do you think?"

Tom held Jenny with one hand and adjusted his stale, musty pillow with the other. "I am thinking about my strict upbringing that stressed no sex before marriage. Of course, our dome society always made that moral choice a no-brainer by keeping men and women physically separated until marriage. Our current situation is obviously incredibly unique. Will you be terribly disappointed if I take a little more time?"

"No, of course not." Jenny gently moved her hand between her face and where she rested against Tom's shirt so he wouldn't feel her tears.

24.

The Humvee teams left the house before dawn. Running Bear and Little Deer used night vision goggles to drive the trucks into the mountains before first light. After unhitching the water buffalos, they drove the Humvees west toward El Paso with the sun rising behind them. The lighting conditions would help screen their movement and make the trucks more difficult to see. But they were off road now and kicking up desert dust. If someone was watching the eastern approaches, surprise would be difficult to achieve if their dust plumes rose high enough into the air before dispersing. Roving Wolf stood in the gun turret of the lead truck looking west through binoculars for any sign of life in El Paso. He instructed Little Deer drive up onto US Route 180 to reduce the telltale dust clouds kicked up by their tires, but the maneuver helped only somewhat because desert dust had been drifting over the rarely used highway for years.

South of the Humvee team, Sun Rain, Tom, and Jenny led the scout party's entire compliment of horses toward the mountain rendezvous point at the water trailers. Sun Rain had the pack radio's handset clipped to her saddle within easy reach. She expected to hear a status report from the Humvees before she reached the mountains.

The horse team was six miles from the water trailers when Sun Rain heard her brother's voice over the radio. She picked up the handset and held it to her ear. Even though the transmission was encrypted, Roving Wolf spoke in their native language as an extra precaution.

"Deserted. We are moving down Montana Avenue to the base of the Franklin Mountain ridge and the central stronghold fortifications. Next transmission in ten minutes. Out."

Tom watched Sun Rain as she listened. The relief conveyed by her smile set Tom at ease.

"No sign of anyone yet," Sun Rain announced to Tom and Jenny. "Certainly no massive influx of Mexican civilians or military."

* * * *

The Comanche/Cherokee Humvee tandem rolled through the city's northern business district with the brown, treeless Franklin Mountain ridge growing larger across its path. Little Deer followed Montana Avenue as it jogged southwest through mixed residential and business districts. The trucks turned north onto Cotton Street putting them on a more direct path to the bare mountain ridge. The bright sun over their shoulders warmed the air faster than the average spring day. Roving Wolf slowed to avoid an emaciated German shepherd that scampered across the street but there was still no sign of human life.

The Humvees dodged downed power lines near Rogelio Avenue. Several bare foundations and partially destroyed homes were evidence of a tornado strike in years past. The trucks turned due west onto Murchison Drive. After a few hundred feet they encountered a wall of stone erected across the roadway. The wall was part of the defensive perimeter of the central stronghold. Citizens of the stronghold had the run of El Paso but the core of the stronghold was the medical complex located at the base of the southern terminus of the Franklin Mountains. The complex was the fallback point, the heavily defended fortress built in the event of an attack.

The improvised entrance gate door of corrugated steel fastened to a wood frame had fallen to the ground. The Humvees easily climbed over the door and drove into the compound. Both vehicles pulled into an empty parking lot off Medical Center Drive and parked. White Hawk, Cloud Rider, and Running Bear dismounted and fanned out to investigate nearby buildings. Little Deer and Roving Wolf served as an overwatch covering the others with the heavy machine guns mounted atop each Humvee. While he stood guard, Roving Wolf called Sun Rain on the radio and told her to lead the horse party into El Paso.

After half an hour, Roving Wolf and Little Deer joined in the investigation of the perimeter. The complex was empty—none of the stronghold citizens could be found. Several buildings had clear signs of recent occupation. A freshly broken pane of plate glass and overturned chairs in one of the building lobbies evidenced a brief struggle, but nothing extensive.

White Hawk posted himself on the rooftop of the southernmost building in the compound. He was able to observe downtown El Paso and beyond that, the city of Juarez and the Sierra de Juarez Mountains south of the city. From his vantage point, he was also able to spot for Roving Wolf, Cloud Rider, and Running Bear as they scouted south outside the perimeter wall of the stronghold and into downtown El Paso. Beyond the perimeter there were additional signs of recent occupation. Several store fronts had newly broken glass that lay in the street with little or no dust blown onto them. Boot prints and tire marks in the dust were everywhere.

* * * *

The pervasive emptiness grew more unnerving the deeper they rode into the city. Tom mused privately that the dead, ghost town feel might even begin to wear the edges of his sanity if he dropped his guard. The El Paso metropolitan area was many times larger than any of the abandoned towns Tom had seen on the Outside. They rode mile after mile through endless rows of empty houses and empty shops. Even the horses sensed the strange air as they bucked and brayed in an unusually skittish fashion. Tom was pleased with the group's faster pace now that he and Sun Rain split between them the two nervous horses Jenny tried to lead unsuccessfully. Fortunately navigation was as simple as following the Humvee tire tracks pressed into the soil that accumulated on the vacant streets. Tom fought the anxiety and the dreariness conjured by the dead city with the happy anticipation of talking with Steven later in the evening. If the mysterious message sender was indeed his brother, that meant he could get word to his family that he was still alive. Anger still flared within whenever Tom imagined the emotional hammer-blow young Jonny must have taken upon learning the lie about his death. Tom used the smoldering anger to strengthen his resolve to find a way to break Jonny and the rest of his family out of their dome prison.

Sun Rain successfully guided the horse team to the inner stronghold compound. Roving Wolf was there to greet them as they trotted their horses into the parking lot occupied by the Humvees. With the horses secured in the shade of a small stand of pinyon pine trees, the scout leader brought Sun Rain, Tom, and Jenny to the compound's largest building which had a cafeteria area suitable for hosting a late lunch. While the group ate, Roving Wolf took Running Bear, Little Deer, and Cloud Rider on a high-speed Humvee run to recover the water trailers they left behind in the Hueco Mountains. White Hawk stayed behind to continue watching for any enemy movement in El Paso and Juarez.

The Humvees returned with the water trailers in under an hour. Roving Wolf quickly gathered the entire team for a strategy meeting on the rooftop where White Hawk maintained his observation post. Before the meeting convened, everyone lined up along the south edge of the building to get a good view of deserted downtown El Paso and a few hundred yards beyond that, the city of Juarez, teeming with over two million Mexicans.

Tom shook his head. "Anybody else a little nervous about this? Four hundred people just disappeared without a trace from this very spot and less than three miles away are two million of our enemy."

"General Mejias is the enemy," corrected Jenny. "Not the people of Mexico."

Cloud Rider agreed with Tom. "The General has enough soldiers in Juarez to kidnap everyone in the El Paso stronghold without a fight. We are certainly being watched from across the border. If we stay here tonight, we could find ourselves prisoners as well."

Roving Wolf lifted the binoculars from around his neck and gave them to his cousin.

"Look there," Roving Wolf indicated.

Cloud Rider lifted his sunglasses onto the top of his head, put the binoculars to his eyes and aligned his view parallel to Roving Wolf's extended arm and skyward-pointing index finger. Cloud Rider was able to fix on an odd-looking, far away aircraft following the Rio Grande river course at about 5,000 feet above the ground. Cloud Rider returned the binoculars and flashed Roving Wolf a puzzled look.

"What is that?"

"May I see?" Tom asked and Roving Wolf passed the binoculars. Tom locked onto the aircraft and smiled. "UAV, right? An Unmanned Aerial Vehicle. A Predator drone?"

"Some prefer RPV, Remotely Piloted Vehicle. Not a Predator, a Reaper. Looks similar to a Predator but flies faster and carries many more weapons.

"I was concerned in staying here at night also," continued Roving Wolf. "But there are two Reapers, both have fourteen Hellfire II missiles, and one Predator with two laser guided bombs all loitering in El Paso airspace looking for targets. They will cover us all night before returning to Holloman Air Force Base in Alamogordo, New Mexico."

"Well, I will sleep better tonight!" announced a much relieved Little Deer.

"They can fly all night?" Jenny inquired.

"Yes they can," confirmed Roving Wolf.

Tom turned his back to the town and sat on the low wall that ran the perimeter of the roof's edge. "So, what happened here? Any idea?"

"A large group of military from the south came and took everyone away," reported White Hawk whose eyes still scanned southward with distrust.

Sun Rain looked to her brother. "The Army chiefs you talk to don't know what happened?"

"No, sister. Probably the Mexicans targeted the stronghold leader first with special forces. He has the satellite phone. If you capture the phone, there is no communication with the government."

"Most, if not all, left here alive," added White Hawk. "There was no big fight—no bullet holes in buildings and no spent shell casings lying on the ground. There are...," White Hawk paused looking for the right white words. "...civilian shoe tracks mixed with Mexican boot tracks walking south."

Jenny turned and sat next to Tom. "What happens to us now that we have no stronghold citizens to stay with?" She shuddered upon realizing that if they had arrived in El Paso two days earlier, she and Tom would likely be in a Mexican prison at this moment.

"I have instructions on that," answered Roving Wolf. "I am to continue my scout along the border through New Mexico and Arizona. My Cherokee and Lakota brothers will accompany me as advanced elements of their nations' war parties. You and Tom will be taken to the Phoenix stronghold of Governor Jeffers."

Tears rolled onto Jenny's cheeks. "Tom, we just keep getting father away from home."

Tom realized that Jenny had long ago come to the end of being interested in the adventure on the Outside. "I know. We will talk with Steven tonight. Maybe he has a plan."

25.

For the first time since leaving Pecos, Roving Wolf's expedition had electricity and indoor plumbing. Like Pecos, El Paso was tapped into an auxiliary power grid charged by the nuclear power plants of the Texas dome farm. The travelers occupied one of the large medical office buildings that clearly served as one of the living quarters for residents of the El Paso stronghold. They found comfortable beds to call their own for one night but were careful to leave rooms as undisturbed as possible. Unlike the other structures they borrowed during their journey, this building was still someone's home.

By late evening, everyone had eaten and showered and dressed in clean clothes—Running Bear had discovered several sets of working clothes washers and dryers in the basement. More comfortable than the clean clothes, however, was the reassurance provided by the three armed reconnaissance aircraft that guarded the scout team from above. On the ground, local sentry duty had been turned over to Running Bear as White Hawk now joined Little Deer in getting some much needed sleep.

The balance of the team gathered in the third floor waiting area of what had once been a medical laboratory business. There was still a bucket of children's toys shoved in a corner near a small television set that hadn't received a broadcast signal in sixty years. Blackout curtains were drawn over the windows. The scouts saw no sense in advertising which building they occupied, although no one was under any illusions that they weren't being watched from across the river…or closer.

Roving Wolf setup his SATCOM device on a wheeled equipment cart and was able to plug into a power outlet to recharge the batteries and to draw on the AC power for the video feed that was expected to begin momentarily. Tom and Jenny sat holding hands on one row of waiting room seats while Sun Rain and Cloud Rider occupied the opposite row.

Tom watched Roving Wolf flip open the video screen of the SATCOM terminal which looked like Net pictures he had seen of antique laptop computers. The device connected wirelessly to the uplink/downlink antenna that Roving Wolf attached outside the window. The blinking red light on the lower right corner of the screen indicated an incoming signal. The light stopped blinking and held a steady red color as the video screen blinked to life.

Tom ceased the nervous tapping of his foot and the tension that held his body stiff drained away upon seeing Steven's face, concerned and serious though it was until the camera returned a picture of Tom to his brother's bedroom display screen. Steven smiled as he recognized Tom and Jenny.

"Hi, Tom! I knew you were still breathing!"

"Hi, Steve, it's great to see you! Thanks for believing."

"Hello, Jenny. How are you?"

"Hi, Steve. Doing okay. Wonderful to see you."

"Tom, before we get too far, I have someone else who wants to say hello..."

Tom watched his brother motion to someone off screen and suddenly Jonny's happy face filled the screen.

"Hi, Tommy! Hi, Jenny!" The young boy waved almost frantically at the camera.

"Hey, hi there, buddy!! How are you?" Tom stared at his little brother's bright face and had to make a significant effort to choke back the beginnings of tears—just as he had done two weeks ago as he left the family dome.

"Hi, Jonny," Jenny squeezed in a quick hello.

"I'm great, Tommy. Steven was right. He told me what they told mom about you being dead was crazy."

"Yes, I am just fine, Jonny. Don't you worry about me. But Jonny, don't tell anyone you have seen me, okay? None of your friends and not Grandpa Frank—promise?"

"Okay, Tommy."

"We will talk more another day soon, okay Jonny? Can you please go to your room and go to bed so Steve and I can talk now?"

"Oh, Tommy, I wanted to hear all about the Outside." Jonny's words were smothered in disappointment. "It's great, right?"

"It is." Tom turned deliberately to gauge the reaction of his fiancé and saw what he expected—disapproval. "But I will have to tell you all about it later. Okay, buddy?"

"All right, I guess I can wait if I have to. Bye, Tommy."

"Bye, Jonny. I will see you later!"

The brief exchange with his excited little brother left Tom full of calm, warm relief inside. "Thanks for that, Steven. What about mom?"

"I didn't want to get her hopes up until I actually confirmed you were alive. I will talk to her later. We don't have enough time for a family reunion right now. I was advised to keep this call short so that it doesn't raise a red flag somewhere. You say you and Jenny are okay?"

"Yes. Our transport was attacked by Mexican soldiers. We were rescued by the gentleman you see in the back, Roving Wolf of the Comanche Nation. Over here are his sister Sun Rain and his cousin Cloud Rider."

Tom gave Steven a fast summary of the last twelve days. "Steven, how are you able to communicate using the military encrypted system? Are you in danger?"

Steven nodded. "I suppose 'yes' to the danger part. I was wading through some of the dark, secret places on the Net looking for any information I could on what happened to you and Jenny when I received a clandestine text message on my screen telling me you were alive."

"The group we have talked about—it's real?" Tom deliberately avoided putting the words 'Black Shine' into the audio stream of the conversation—just in case the call washed through the automated software that hunted for seditious activity.

"It's real. Tommy, I don't know what you are learning about the Outside but I can tell you I am learning some troubling things about the '*Inside*.'"

Tom listened to his brother's brief political report and then asked, "Steve, does everyone know there is a war with Mexico coming soon?"

"The President addressed the nation last week saying Mexico was drilling troops and she felt the need to undertake additional security measures. But she downplayed any notion that war was coming."

"Steven, I don't know what the President is talking about. War is imminent. The Treaty Tribes are pouring tens of thousands of warriors into the Southwest. I am in El Paso right now. The four hundred people of the stronghold disappeared mysteriously two days ago. The scouts I am with say Mexican troops snuck in from Juarez and took them."

"You better get out of there, Tommy."

"Yes, we are pushing on to the Phoenix stronghold in the morning. We will be there in a couple weeks. Steven…"

"Yeah, Tommy?

"Grandpa Frank is right. The Outside isn't perfect, but it's special. You have no idea how much we lost by going into domes and letting the government 'protect us.'"

Steven didn't have long to consider his brother's remarks. He had to end the transmission before it was discovered by FCC agents. "I will contact you again soon, Tom."

"Steve," Jenny interjected. "Can you get word to my family that I am alive?"

Steve hesitated for a moment. "Jenny, will your parents and siblings keep that knowledge from leaving their dome? I am not telling my own grandfather. If word leaks out onto the Net about the Mexican attack on Tom and you and that you are alive despite the government indicating otherwise, that knowledge might get traced to me. If it does, the government might hit the kill switch on our dome as well as yours."

Kill switching a dome was one of the conspiracy theories that Steven was learning might not be just theory. The term meant cutting a dome off from the Net and the rest of the dome world. It meant putting a dome in solitary confinement. It meant the slow death of a family.

"I will see what I can do, Jenny," Steve promised.

"I better pull the plug, Tommy."

"Thanks, Steve. Call back soon, please. And say hello to mom. She is going to give you hell for not bringing her into the call. Also, Steve, in the meantime, give some thought about how I can break Jonny and the rest of you out of there."

The screen went black and Roving Wolf shut down the terminal immediately.

26.

General Mejias puffed his hand-rolled Montecristo A and lounged along the edge of the shallow end of his indoor pool, his bare legs dangling into the warm water. The Mexican dictator's opulent mansion was tucked away behind a large iron gate in the swanky western heights overlooking Mexico City. A heavy rain, rare for this early in the year, pounded the plate glass windows and obscured his view of the city.

Lu Zhuàng dabbed his forehead with a handkerchief and did his best to ignore the pool room humidity and the double assault of cigar smoke and chlorine on his nostrils.

"I did not realize you planned an operation against El Paso, General." Lu was furious about the reckless move but couldn't appear to question the volatile Mexican ruler's military judgment.

"I did that for you Señor, Lu. To show you proof of the weakness of the United States."

A young bikini-clad house girl strolled into the room and set a snifter of straight tequila on the pool ledge next to Mejias. Mejias grabbed her arm and the surprised girl shrieked as he pulled her into the pool. He laughed while the girl wrung the water out of her long black hair. Lu guessed the girl was all of fifteen—about the average age for a presidential mistress—but she had enough experience with the General to hide her annoyance.

"But is there danger that you show your intentions too early, General?"

Mejias waved to dismiss the girl who climbed out of the pool and jogged quickly out of the room.

"Keep your enemy guessing and off balance, Señor Lu. At the same time, it gives me some operational intelligence and some hostages that might be useful later."

"Have the Americans asked about El Paso?"

The Mexican president chuckled and made no effort to hide his disdain. "American embassies are nothing but a conference room with a secure satellite feed to an ambassador hiding in a dome. It makes them easy to ignore." Mejias smiled and sipped his tequila.

Lu had read a preliminary report of the raid on El Paso, only two men killed out of 420 men women and children. A rather remarkably restrained, well-executed action, thought Lu.

"Is your army ready, Mr. President?"

Mejias picked up the DVD remote control on the pool ledge and pointed it to the large screen mounted on the north wall. The video showed 15,000 men in parade dress uniform standing at attention and formed into neat company and battalion-sized rectangles of troops that surrounded a large raised stage. Eight wooden gallows lined the platform. Eight men stood on the platform each with a hangman's noose around his neck. In one instant, trap doors below each man sprung open simultaneously and the men dropped through the stage. There were no hoods covering the men's heads and no curtain screen below the stage. Mejias did not want any of the gruesome details hidden. Mejias was particularly pleased when the force of the drop decapitated the heavier soldier on the end.

"No desertions since this," Mejias proclaimed proudly.

Lu watched the video dispassionately, not giving another thought to the brutal display. "When can the invasion begin?"

"Two or three weeks, right on schedule. You want to trade your business suit for a swimsuit and jump in?"

"No thank you, Mr. President. I should be getting back to my embassy." The Chinese government minister offered a slight bow in the General's direction. Lu knew full well that Mejias wouldn't have asked him to stay if he thought there was any chance that Lu would agree. Lu found it amusing that their mutual dislike and distrust for one another had spawned a tit-for-tat display of false sincerity that continued unabated.

27.

Dawn transitioned quickly to full daylight in the crisp, clear, cloudless morning. Despite the protection from the armed aerial drones above, everyone was anxious to put El Paso behind them. The group had passed through many ghost towns and had stayed in a number of houses abandoned for half a century, but the El Paso stay was different. The building they slept in was full of people two days ago. Dinner plates in the building's tiny cafeteria had been partially covered with food when they arrived. The unknown fate of the missing stronghold citizens bred an air of mystery and unease over the entire compound.

Before resuming their journey, the scout team topped off their diesel fuel and water from the intact supply stores of the stronghold. Tom assisted with the re-supply operation then mounted his horse and maneuvered into a riding position behind Roving Wolf and alongside White Hawk. His saddle time had been increasing each day as he built his endurance and tolerance of horseback travel. Jenny lost ground as the lengthy saddle time required yesterday left another deep burning in her thighs and rear end. She found the back seat of Sun Rain's Humvee much more comfortable.

Situated only three miles north of the international border, the next deserted town on their route was Columbus, New Mexico, but seventy-five miles was too far to push in a single day on horseback. Instead, the westbound travelers planned to cover half the distance and then camp for the night under the stars.

Shortly after leaving the El Paso metropolitan area, the scout team crossed into New Mexico and following a late morning off road shortcut they picked up Columbus Road which would later become New Mexico State Highway 9 and take them to Columbus and beyond. The mixed horse and truck convoy pushed west down Columbus Road for over an hour when Roving Wolf and Cloud Rider peeled south to scout into Mexican territory per the instructions of Roving Wolf's US Army handler.

Tom continued his ride alongside White Hawk until the midday rest break then resumed his driving duties in Sun Rain's Humvee. The southern New Mexico desert was even drier and dustier and had fewer pre-dome signs of civilization than the desert of West Texas. The road was often arrow straight and the pattern of widely scattered sage brush and cactus varieties changed little as the miles drifted by.

Just west of the old Mt. Riley railroad stop, White Hawk found a tabletop hill that rose a hundred feet above the desert floor. Considering the small mesa to be the best camp location around, White Hawk led the horses to the base of the hill while the Humvees easily negotiated the moderate incline of the east slope and parked on the summit. Little Deer and Running Bear dug a fire pit to shield the campfire flames from view in the unlikely event hostile brigands were camped nearby on the desert plain. Tom drew upon his recent training to plant optical and seismic sensors around the hill while White Hawk, Sun Rain, and Jenny tended to the horses.

After dinner everyone planned his or her sleeping arrangements. For the first time since beginning their journey, the team wouldn't have the relative comfort of a roof over their heads or even an old creaky bed in which to lie down.

Jenny felt a strange alternating cycle of hot and cold running through her body and announced she was turning in right away. Her choice of sleeping arrangements was the familiar feel of a cushioned Humvee back seat. Jenny's experience with fire ants in Pecos was still too fresh in her memory to permit worry-free sleep on the ground like the others.

Tom slipped a desert camouflage shirt over his tee shirt to prepare for the night chill and then went to relieve himself in the area White Hawk designated for such business downwind of the camp. As Tom returned to the main part of the hilltop camp, he nearly tripped over Sun Rain who was lying on part of the hill's incline below the flat hill crest.

"What are you doing here instead of on top of the hill?" asked Tom.

"More comfortable for star gazing. Come try it, Tom."

Tom hadn't chosen a spot for the night yet. He certainly couldn't spend the night next to Sun Rain, but Jenny was out cold in the back of a Humvee so staying to talk for a few minutes couldn't hurt. Tom laid down next Sun Rain who moved over a bit to give him room on the blankets that she used to cushion against the hard ground.

The night was clear and cool like most. Below their mesa, the desert floor glowed in the moonlight cast down from a waxing gibbous moon that climbed into the eastern sky. Tom hadn't had a decent chance to lose himself in the stars since he tried to watch the sky with Jenny but that session was rudely interrupted by fire ants more than a week ago.

"How is Jenny?"

"She wasn't feeling too well," Tom answered. "She is asleep in the Humvee."

Tom marveled at the twinkling night. He had read about stars and seen small images of stellar fields in his school work growing up. He studied the spectral types, the life cycles of stars, read statistics on size and color. He learned about the energetic fusion furnaces that burned inside stars and fueled their bright beams. But he hadn't understood their power or appreciated their beauty until seeing that first sunrise or until the few brief glimpses of the night sky he had managed since emerging from the dome.

"I never get tired of looking up," said Sun Rain. "I can't imagine how terrible it was for you, Tom, never seeing the sky or feeling the earth."

Sun Rain grabbed the edge of the blanket covering her and threw it over Tom to protect him from the cold air. "Here, these things hold heat very well."

Tom noticed she was using one of the foil blankets Roving Wolf had taken from the Mexican patrol. "Thank you, Sun Rain."

They watched the sky in silence for a long time. An occasional meteor briefly streaked overhead. The warmth Tom felt under the foil blanket was not something he wanted to give up.

Tom felt Sun Rain roll onto her side to face him. "Tom, you shouldn't worry. A medicine chief from one of the nations can marry you and Jenny. In fact, I know…"

Tom leaned in and pressed his lips to Sun Rain's. Her words drifted away as she accepted, then returned his kiss. Sun Rain rolled onto her back and pulled Tom with her. Tom continued the kiss as he pressed into Sun Rain's warm chest. His eyes were closed but he still saw the stars. Tom felt Sun Rain's arms wrap tightly around him. A rush of emotion he never experienced before exploded through him like…like….his sheltered dome life didn't give him anything to compare it to. The closest comparison might be the powerful thunderstorm that crashed down on the group the other night.

But after another moment, a different feeling surged through Tom. Part of recalling the thunderstorm experience was remembering the fearful screams from Jenny. It was Jenny he held that night. She wasn't warm and sweet like this… Jenny had been cold and trembling. And Tom had told her everything was going to be all right.

Tom pushed away from Sun Rain and her strong embrace. He slipped from the warmth under the blanket and stood into the cold night air. He could only manage a whispered, "I'm, sorry," before stumbling up to the flat crest of the hill.

There was enough moonlight to clearly identify the Humvee silhouettes on the other side of the hill. Tom opened the rear cargo hatch as quietly as he could so he didn't disturb Jenny. The Humvee dome light glowed a deep red to preserve night vision. Tom pulled the sleeping bag from where he remembered packing it at the start of the journey. He closed the hatch and went around to the right rear door to check on Jenny through the open window. Her face was masked by impenetrable shadow but she appeared to be fast asleep. Tom tucked the rolled sleeping bag under his arm and walked toward the fire pit.

"She is a remarkable woman, isn't she?" Little Deer's voice surprised him.

As Tom walked closer to the fire pit, the small flame splashed a faint dancing glow onto Little Deer's seated frame.

"Yes, indeed. Have a good night, brother." Tom rolled the bag out on the ground near the pit and climbed in. Only then did it occur to him that he couldn't be sure for whom Little Deer's comment was meant—for Jenny, or did Little Deer know Tom was just with Sun Rain? Something told Tom that the observant Cherokee scout knew exactly who was where in the hilltop camp.

* * * *

Bright morning sunlight illuminated the team's hilltop camp and ran down the slopes of the mesa to wash across the desert floor. The dawn light nudged Tom awake and he greeted the warmth brushing his face with a warm smile of his own. A few yards away, Lakota words drifted east as White Hawk said his morning prayers. Tom recalled his talk with friend Ari weeks ago, in another world, questioning prayer and more. He quietly watched the land and its flora and fauna greet the new day. Tom was wide awake too and he no longer needed that talk with Ari's rabbi.

Tom shook what desert dirt he could from his sleeping bag then rolled it and slipped it quietly back into the Humvee. Through the open rear hatch he saw the top of Jenny's head just visible over the rear seat back and through the gear stored in the cargo bay. Tom pressed the door down softly so that he didn't startle Jenny. Looking his fiancé in the eye wasn't going to be easy so putting that awkward moment off as long as possible seemed a good, if somewhat cowardly strategy.

Running Bear warmed a small pot of water over the fire for the men to share for shaving. Tom still struggled a bit with shaving cream and disposable razor, but his face had fewer cuts and nicks this week than last. At least the process was quicker than the electric razor he had used since high school.

Tom wiped his face and folded his shaving kit when he noticed White Hawk and Little Deer both leaning into the rear passenger compartment from opposite sides of Jenny's Humvee. Sun Rain approached Tom; the concern written into her expression was unmistakable.

Sun Rain took Tom's hand. "Jenny is very sick." She led Tom to the truck.

Tom quickened his pace and ran ahead of Sun Rain. "What's going on?"

"High fever," White Hawk announced while stepping back.

Tom leaned in for a good look at Jenny. Sweat poured down her face. Tom touched her cheeks which felt as if they were on fire. He looked up at Little Deer who leaned in from the other side of the truck and saw concern there, too.

"Jenny? Jenny?" Tom couldn't get a response and backed away from the vehicle. "What do we do?"

"We keep her body covered, her head and hands cool, and get her to drink as much as possible," Sun Rain responded. "We have some fever reducer in the medical kits. It's probably viral but we should get her out of the truck and check her for any cuts or insect bites." Sun Rain explained that cuts and cactus pricks could get infected and the desert had black widow spiders and other poisonous insects whose bites sometimes caused severe reactions.

Tom helped White Hawk pull Jenny from the vehicle and lay her on a pile of blankets. Sun Rain performed the examination to confirm there were no infected cuts or problematic insect bites anywhere on her body. Jenny's fever was high enough that she wasn't very lucid during the exam. Sun Rain managed to get Jenny to drink a few sips of water that contained medicine to reduce fever.

Consensus judged that Jenny's condition would not likely be exacerbated by travel so Tom and Sun Rain bundled her up in blankets and put her in the back seat of the Humvee. Sun Rain sat in the back to monitor Jenny's condition while Tom drove. Later in the day, Running Bear took over the driving so Tom could continue working on his saddle endurance. An hour before sunset, the team rolled into Columbus and found a suitable house with a sick bed for Jenny whose fever lessened during the drive, but not dramatically so.

By morning Jenny was still weak with fever but she was talking more coherently and taking in sufficient amounts of water. The team held in Columbus for the day to account for Roving Wolf and Cloud Rider's deeper penetration into Mexico. Jenny rested in the care of Little Deer. Tom, White Hawk, and Sun Rain spent the day conducting more vehicle and weapons training.

In the afternoon, White Hawk began teaching Tom close quarters combat: hand-to-hand and knife fighting. After that session came the real treat for Tom when White

Hawk began Tom's instruction on stringing a bow and firing arrows. Tom followed White Hawk's example of catching one end of the bow on his ankle and using his body weight to help string the weapon. Tom also learned that arrows needed constant attention and tweaking to stay straight and fly true.

When Tom returned from the day's training, he found Jenny sitting up in bed but still very weak.

"Hi, baby, how are you feeling?"

"Tom, it feels awful. I am a little better now but my God, it felt like my body was on fire I was so hot."

"Is Little Deer taking good care of you?"

"Yes, he is a big sweetheart and a great nurse. What have you been doing?"

"I was out with Sun Rain and White Hawk doing more combat training. I can string a bow and fire an arrow now! Although, I admit that I need a lot more practice. You had me worried there, honey. Are you going to be okay traveling tomorrow?"

"I will be okay, Tom. Thanks."

After two more days of routine, uneventful travel, the horses and Humvees reached the old border patrol station at Antelope Wells, close enough to the border to get a radio signal from Cloud Rider. He and Roving Wolf would rejoin the scout team in the Cloverdale area in two days.

The trip from Antelope Wells to Cloverdale was relatively short and easy which suited Jenny just fine given she still fought against the stubborn fever that returned if she was late taking the medicine from the first aid kit. The nature of her illness was a mystery. Growing up in a sterile environment meant no exposure to common viruses loose in the world and that meant her body had no antibodies to fight off a viral attack. Fortunately, the symptoms of her illness were limited to fever, muscle weakness, and dehydration.

Cloverdale, New Mexico turned out to be nothing but an early twentieth century storage barn, and a small one at that, so the team laid out an outdoor camp near the building. Little Deer cleaned out the interior building space so that Jenny would have a roof overhead for the night. The team had a day to wait for their two companions sweeping through northern Mexico. Tom took advantage of the time by undergoing more training with Sun Rain in the morning and with White Hawk in the afternoon.

Tom devoted as much time as he could to learning multiple weapons systems—modern firearms with Sun Rain, and ancient lance and bow and arrow with White Hawk. Between the various instructional sessions, he and Sun Rain spent more and more time talking, about life on the Outside, about life on the Inside, about Life. Over time the subject matter became more and more personal. Tom was acutely aware of his deepening feelings for Sun Rain just as he was aware of his deepening conflict regarding his feelings for Jenny—but for Tom, a promise was a promise.

Half an hour before sunset, Tom sat on the hood of the colorful Cherokee Humvee with his freshly cleaned and oiled M4A1 carbine in his lap. Fifty yards to the south Running Bear faced their camp and slowly waved his arm over his head. Tom climbed up onto the gun turret for a better look over the desert brush. Dust plums from two riders on horse drifted east pushed by the light breeze. Tom jumped off the truck and joined the others as Roving Wolf and Cloud Rider were welcomed back into the company.

Sun Rain hugged her brother and cousin and led them to a meal waiting by the camp fire.

Cloud Rider took stock of the team and asked, "Where is Jenny?"

Little Deer pointed to the crumbling building. "Resting inside. She is ill with fever but is recovering."

"What of the Mexicans?" asked White Hawk.

"Nothing," said Roving Wolf. "No Mexican army forces anywhere within fifty miles of New Mexico."

The two scouts ate quickly in order to water and brush down their mounts. Running Bear continued Tom's equestrian training by having him remove the saddles and leading the horses north to the patch of prairie grass being grazed by the team's other horses.

As night fell, activity in the scout camp declined and everyone prepared for sleep except for Running Bear who had the first guard watch. Tom wished everyone a good night and disappeared into the old store building to sleep near Jenny. Tom stretched his sore muscles as he lay on top of the blanket and the sleeping bag unrolled onto the hard ground. He stared at the thin sliver of campfire glow that slipped passed the blanket Little Deer used to cover the doorway. His last thought before drifting to sleep was that, according to Roving Wolf's map, the trail to Phoenix was still a long one.

28.

Red Thunder's spirited mustang fidgeted beneath him. The energetic animal didn't enjoy being held in place but respect for his rider and the proximity of the cliff edge kept the horse on station, even if not absolutely still. The Lakota war chief surveyed the small valley before him. Carved by the Canadian River flowing two hundred feet below, the valley wound west to east across the great expanse of the Texas panhandle. A blanket of greenish-brown prairie grass covered the valley floor while creosote bushes and several varieties of sage climbed the moderate slopes of the valley walls. A quarter mile to his front, the plateau opposite his ran to the horizon under a blue sky heavily dotted with fair weather cumulous clouds. A mile downstream where the valley walls flattened, thousands of buffalo forded the river to move north and graze new land. From this distance, the herd was an undulating black mass that crept across the valley floor and splashed through the meandering river. Red Thunder grinned at the rambunctious pack of young wolves nipping and tussling with one another as they trotted down the river bank toward the migrating bison. If the skinny wolves wanted to keep wandering the plains, they would need to cut a buffalo calf from its mother soon.

Like the bison downstream, Red Thunder's army was moving again. A SATCOM call with the Secretaries of State and Interior had satisfactorily resolved the issue of the Black Hills. The massive Sioux cavalry column and support train had left Colorado behind and was now moving south through New Mexico. Red Thunder, however, had broken off from the army's main body and ridden east to see for himself the great bison herd reported to be migrating north out of Texas. His scouts indicated the herd's position as almost due north of Amarillo at the extreme northern limit of the Texas dome farm. In fact, the last row of domes glinted in the sun less than a mile over his shoulder. The largest of the four US dome farms, the Texas dome farm stopped at the Canadian River which flowed east out of New Mexico's Sangre de Cristo Mountains, through the Texas panhandle, and into Oklahoma.

Red Thunder had another reason for the quick diversion into Texas to locate the herd. Four young would-be braves who rode with his army had not been ready for the final test required to become an official warrior of the Lakota Sioux at the time the military expedition began the journey south. Despite significant training in both ancient and modern weapons, the sixteen-year-olds could not participate in combat operations with the rest of the Sioux warriors until they proved themselves by killing their first buffalo—unassisted. The anxious boys had completed their final instruction and received the final blessing of their band's medicine chiefs during the journey from South Dakota and the lengthy encampment in southern Colorado. This would be the last chance for hunting before reaching the desert where no buffalo tread.

The principal Lakota war chief lifted his US Army-issued binoculars for a better look at the tiny dust cloud a quarter mile away on the opposite plain above the river valley. Red Thunder watched the last of the hopeful boys race his horse alongside a large bull. The youngster was in proper but perilous position—nearly brushing against his prey's left flank—ready to deliver a crippling lance thrust just forward of the hind leg and ahead of the huge beast's groin. Buffalo hunting with firearms was forbidden by all nations.

With his hands already positioned close to his face in order to cradle the binoculars, Red Thunder couldn't resist moving a forefinger to rub the knot on his nose obtained when he was a boy in the exact same position. On that misty gray day long ago, his prey had rammed his horse sending Red Thunder tumbling to the ground and breaking his nose. Back in the present, the experienced warrior watched the teenager's thrust miss its mark and instead blunt against the buffalo's hip bone. The young hunter was forced to turn his horse and run briefly from the short but angry charge of the slightly wounded buffalo.

After another moment, the boy regained the initiative and used both his horse and well-placed arrow strikes to force the speeding bison south toward the river valley. Hunter and hunted raced directly toward Red Thunder who could hear the young man's war cry echo across the river valley. The harassed buffalo sped across the plain with the single-minded purpose of escaping its pursuer. The charging animal suffered from the same poor eyesight as the rest of its kind and saw the end of the flat prairie too late to prevent its 2,000 pound mass from careening off the cliff edge. The dark brown buffalo body tumbled down the slope like a loose boulder crashing through the scattered brush growing on the slope that connected the plateau to the valley floor. The beast rolled to a stop in a small clearing of prairie grass on the north river bank. The stunned animal lay on its side moving its legs as if it were still running across the plain. One of the powerful front legs flopped about in a grotesque unnatural fashion, obviously broken.

Red Thunder was pleased with the ingenuity and boldness of the hunter who overcame his botched lance strike with a stampede maneuver usually performed by an entire hunting party and reserved for hunting buffalo en masse. The boy was already off his horse and running down the slope to complete the kill with a knife puncture to the neck—a dangerous proposition given that one twitch of the animal's massive head could fatally gore a careless hunter.

Through the powerful lens, Red Thunder watched the young man successfully end the suffering of the wounded animal. But his thoughts drifted to his stern sister-in-law, Snow Wind, who led the support team that recovered the dead animals for butchering and other processing. He could hear her shrill complaints already in his head, expressing annoyance that the kill didn't occur on the more conveniently accessible plain. But the woman couldn't be too put out, thought Red Thunder because, while the hunt had to be conducted with ancient weaponry, he had permitted—since they were pressed for time—two large army trucks to accompany the hunting party in order to haul the game back to the war party camps in New Mexico—a much easier logistical operation than the usual reliance on pack mules and wagons.

Red Thunder slipped the binoculars back into a saddle bag. The buffalo hunt was over and four new Lakota braves would be inducted into the army in a sunrise ceremony that would signal their rebirth into the warrior brotherhood. With only the gentlest of prodding, Red Thunder had his mustang happily running at a hard gallop toward the distant herd of fording bison. He raced the swift panhandle wind east across the sunny, warm plateau and stole one last glance over his shoulder at the tragedy that was the Texas dome farm.

Red Thunder would have to remember to thank his ancestors again for refusing to forsake the earth and sky.

29.

"Damn it!" Lieutenant General Mark Tanner spilled a swig of coffee onto his baggy gray domer pants. The stain would not be lonely. The general set his coffee cup down on the end table by the bed. He had been checking and re-checking his staff's battle plans for the last fifteen straight hours.

The screen on the wall buzzed and Tanner looked at the Kathy Singer icon and blinked twice to take the call—he preferred that more deliberate method to voice commands which had gotten him into trouble before. Lieutenant General Kathleen Singer had completed the review of her battle staff's plans and called her colleague to compare notes and synchronize the plans.

General Singer flipped a portion of her full-bodied blond hair from the right side of her face and back over her shoulder. "Hello, Mark. Everything coming together?"

"Hi, Kathy. Yes, about as well as can be expected given the lack of resources."

"Quit your crying, Mark. I have it worse than you. I am the back door so I get the leftovers," joked General Singer. But the truth wasn't very funny, she thought. If the top brass was wrong and the Mexican army pushed into West Texas, she didn't have much of a defense force to stop them.

"Yes, I know, Kathy. Do we know any more about the fate of the El Paso stronghold citizens?"

"No. The Mexicans still don't admit to holding them. Now that we finally have more aerial drone assets in the area, a Predator has been tasked with flying over Juarez every night to search with infrared. If they are keeping the 400 people grouped together, we might get lucky. Big haystack though, Mark."

"True. I've seen the data from all the scout missions and UAV sorties and it looks to me that the immediate border areas are clear of enemy troops. Mexican troops are all still concentrated around Hermosillo west of the continental divide and around Chihuahua to the east."

Kathy Singer nodded. "Yes, that's my read. Mejias is probably keeping them grouped together to minimize logistical problems with delivering food and water."

"Right. Once this thing gets started, we'll need to make the destruction of resupply convoys—especially water transports—a priority."

Both battlefield commanders compared notes on the progress of the Treaty Tribe forces. Native American fighting units had been assigned to their places on the battlefield and had received movement instructions, but this was the first time the Treaty Tribes had been mobilized for war; planners had to be alert for signs of trouble. The biggest problem so far had been the large Lakota force that stopped their trek south to await word from the government on their demands related to the Black Hills. But the Sioux were moving again. They weren't getting all the land promised in the 1851 Treaty of Laramie because the government worried about setting a precedent for compliance with *all* the broken treaties with Native Americans over the years—that would lead to chaos. Instead, 4,200 square miles of the Black Hills proper and 6,000 square miles of immediately adjacent land would be ceded forever from US custody and control and that was good enough for the current Lakota leadership.

Generals Tanner and Singer were pleased to see the progress of mechanized Cherokee infantry streaming across Texas from Oklahoma and as far away as North Carolina. Waves of Navajo infantry were marching southwest down from their land in the Arizona high country into the hot, dry Valley of the Sun to take a position between the dome farm and the border with Mexico—they would be the last line of defense.

"Are all the Treaty Tribe war chiefs still endorsing the plans?"

"Yes, Kathy, we look good there. There was some resistance by the Apaches to the Navajos being assigned to the Caborca task force. That resistance wasn't the result of any bad blood, though. The Apaches wanted to take the assignment. They cited their history of raiding into Sonora going back 400 years. The Apache is still greatly feared among the residents of northern Mexico. Armed Apache units have been patrolling the border since 2013 and illegal border crossings dropped to near zero that year, long before the dome system eliminated the market for illicit drugs. Considering how difficult the Caborca assignment is, it was good to see two friendly rivals vying for the mission."

"How did you resolve the matter?"

"The Apache war chief is a practical man. I explained that the mission required troops to dig in and harass, that the mission was best accomplished by a relatively stationary force, that mobile Apache cavalry could be put to better use elsewhere. It also helped that I assigned a small Apache cavalry troop to the Caborca north and south mountain forces."

"You gave in," Singer smiled.

"A little compromise," Tanner shrugged. "Hey, a few hundred cavalry troops can extend the harassment and protect the flanks of a straight leg force doing a hit-and-run. Still one huge worry, though—despite all the cooperation and the movement of Treaty Tribe forces, until they convene their combined war council, we don't know if they are going to fight or if they are going to turn around and go home."

"They have to fight," insisted Kathy Singer. "This is about their survival, too"

"Let's hope they see it that way, Kathy. There is one new wrinkle here in the west," Tanner continued.

"General Malcolm is concerned Mejias might blitzkrieg us with his tank force, and the push might come further west than we have planned, through the Altar Desert. We dismissed the idea of infantry moving through there, but Mejias' old Chinese tanks might still slog through."

General Singer studied the map on her display and nodded. "Yes, I can see that possibility. That is a 250-mile sprint. He wouldn't have much fuel left for fighting."

"Exactly. I am requesting a drone flight to look for any sign of refueling preparations between Caborca and Puerto Peñasco. I am also rushing anti-tank mines from Utah weapons storage down through Yuma so the Navajo troops adjacent to the domes can plant some mine fields. We will have Reapers loaded with Hellfire II's ready for flight at Nellis, Creech, Holloman, and our forward base at Luke." All four US Air Force bases were prepped and ready to conduct around-the-clock drone operations.

"Still no sign of mobilizing motor transport, Mark?"

"Strangely, no, their motor pools are quiet. The reports of serious fuel shortages must be accurate. Either that or Mejias' eccentricities are manifesting themselves. Maybe he just wants to toughen his inexperienced troops by walking instead of riding."

The two generals continued synchronizing plans and running logistics scenarios regarding water, food, and ammunition resupply. Water and feed stations for horses were being setup along the border. Medical aid stations were being mapped and a forward field hospital near Gila Bend now had electrical power. Remote tractor trailer rigs with refrigerator trailers that normally carried harvested fruit to processing plants were coming in from the Great Plains and points east full of whole blood and plasma donated by many Native American groups, not just the Treaty Tribes. Blood came from as far away as the reconstituted Iroquois Confederacy in the New England area.

"This is going to be a difficult fight," observed General Singer.

"I agree, Kathy. I can't help thinking that Alexander rode into battle at the head of his army wearing splendid armor and a double plumed helm. I am going to lead an army from my bedroom while wearing gray pajamas."

"Warfare evolves, Mark, you know that. But I suspect victory tastes just as sweet wearing domer grays as it does with a bunch of metal and leather strapped to your body. And are you really so flamboyant that you would wear a garish double plumed helmet?"

Mark Tanner laughed. "My pretentiousness knows no bounds!" Tanner studied the map and the disposition of his heavily outnumbered forces. He recalled that Alexander faced some pretty long odds as well.

30.

Barbara Phillips called to order the National Security Council's regularly scheduled meeting. "Good evening, everyone. I know this is our second meeting in as many weeks but I didn't want to put this off given developments in Mexico. General, Pruitt, would you catch everyone up, please."

"Certainly, Madam President." Joint Chiefs Chairman Pruitt began with the situation in El Paso: over four hundred missing citizens. The satellite phone of their leader was silent. Indian scouts on the scene reported finding trace evidence that Mexican soldiers had approached from the direction of Juarez and marched civilians back across the border.

The President scanned the display screen windows for the face of Secretary of State Carter Mason. "Carter, still no response from the Mexicans?"

"No, Madam President. We have made calls to the Palace and broadcast to the US embassy conference box our request for an audience with the foreign minister but the Mexican runners hired to monitor the conference box are not at their post. We have asked the Swiss and the Brits to relay a message—they have done so, but again, no response at all from the Mexican government."

The "conference box" was the US government's link to nations on the Outside. The briefcase-like secure satellite communication device was a larger version of the SATCOM units used by the military. Like the SATCOM units, the conference box opened to expose a video display screen and could be setup anywhere with electrical power and space to setup a small antenna dish. A conference box and backup were placed in every US embassy around the world so that foreign governments, friendly or not, had contact with the domed government of the United States. To further facilitate communication with foreign governments, the case could be carried by a runner out of the embassy and directly into the office of the official with whom American officials wished to engage.

"We can't force them to answer our call, Madam President. I certainly recommend continuing the process you began with our United Nations ambassador to obtain a United Nations resolution condemning Mexico for the incursion," concluded Mason.

General Pruitt continued, "Meanwhile, Madam President, preparation of men and material for battle is progressing well now that the Lakota have resumed their journey."

Vice President Sullivan emitted an audible grunt of disapproval. He was already on record recommending against submitting to what he considered a blackmail demand that required the US government to cede the Black Hills and stop all mining of uranium in the area. Few were in the Vice President's camp however, as votes of three fourths of the House and the Senate were secured in less than three days. No one knew to which dome farm they belonged so the Senators and Representatives, not wanting to gamble with their own lives easily made the decision to trade the Black Hills for protection by the Sioux army.

"Two matters still need your approval, Madam President. First, we would like to penetrate Mexican airspace with reconnaissance drones as necessary to monitor their movements and preparations."

"I say yes, General. Mexican recalcitrance regarding their obvious move against El Paso makes that decision easy and justified. Anybody disagree?"

With no dissent voiced, General Pruitt continued. "Second, Madam President, we are still awaiting your decision about the preemptive move into Mexico to keep Mejias off balance and to gain the initiative before his forces are too close to our domes."

"Yes, Joshua, I have considered that request. We can't move into Mexico unless a more provocative move is made by Mejias. If we go in now, Mejias can make a case that we initiated hostilities and therefore any Mexican military action is justified. The UN doesn't consider the stunt pulled by the Mexican patrol in Texas to be sufficient provocation for us to cross the border."

General Pruitt noted the head nods of Secretary of State Mason and Attorney General McInnis. "What type of provocative action will allow us to move, Madam President?"

"If Mejias starts moving significant forces further north, I would consider that provocation." The President shifted her gaze to the window containing the face of the Secretary of Defense. "Belinda, just so we are clear, we will follow the normal chain of command on this. Any order given to move our troops over the border starts with me, then goes to you, then to General Beckett."

"Thank you, Madam President." General Pruitt was gracious but he couldn't help wonder if the President's comment was an intentional or an unintentional slight. Pruitt knew full well that as JCS Chairman he wasn't in the combat chain of command and could not order an attack. Perhaps his question about provocation betrayed a tone he hadn't intended to convey.

"If I may cut in," sounded National Security Advisor, Alan Sayles. "General Pruitt, with the El Paso stronghold deserted, what happens to the wayward dome couple now?"

"They are being escorted to the Phoenix stronghold as we speak. They obviously can't be allowed back under dome," said the General who did his best to hide any lingering annoyance at the President's last comments.

"Thank you, General Pruitt. Does anyone else have thoughts on Mexico before I move on to other security matters?"

"Just one thought, Madam President," answered the Secretary of State. "General Pruitt, will we win the fight that is coming?"

General Pruitt scanned all the faces on his display then returned to the expectant glare of Secretary Mason. He gave the only answer he could.

"I don't know, Mr. Secretary."

31.

The flurry of noise outside the rotting old storage building jarred both Tom and Jenny from a deep sleep. Tom sat up, his back sore and stiff from the hard ground. Early dawn light streamed through the broken window glass. He leaned over to Jenny.

"How are you feeling, honey?"

Jenny covered her mouth to cough. "Groggy, but at least my head isn't on fire." Jenny lifted gingerly into a sitting position.

"What's going on outside, Tom?"

"I don't know." Tom pushed off the ground and stood.

"Help me up, Tommy."

Tom reached out to Jenny's outstretched arms. "Are you sure you want to do this, Jen?"

Tom pulled Jenny upright and she leaned heavily onto his body, her arms wrapped around his back to help her stand, but it was Tom's arms around Jenny that kept her from sliding back to the ground.

Tom tucked an arm under Jenny and helped her keep an arm around his neck as he walked her forward. When they reached the doorway, Tom pushed aside the blanket acting as a makeshift door. The couple stepped through and found the rest of their party standing near the campfire watching a group of galloping horses and riders approach from the west.

Over forty Indian riders screamed loud war whoops as they galloped in a circle around the camp and the old storehouse. Jenny cringed at the continuous thunder of nearly two hundred horse hooves pounding the ground and at the piercing hoots and yips from the warriors. Most of the warriors wore standard desert camouflage pants but their upper bodies were a mix of desert camouflage shirts, tan Army tee shirts, or bare skin. They didn't wear their long black hair in braids like Roving Wolf. Instead they wore their hair loose and used a beaded headband to keep it from obscuring their vision. Many of the men pumped steel-tipped lances menacingly over their heads.

The circling horses slowed to a trot, then a walk, and finally stopped. One of the Indians walked his horse to the campfire.

"He doesn't look very happy," Jenny whispered.

Sun Rain and all the scout party's men stood their ground. Roving Wolf took two steps toward the rider. There was enough morning light for Tom to read the scowl on the rider's face. He hugged Jenny tighter.

Finally the rider spoke. "I see Numunuh (Comanche). I see Lakota (Sioux). I see Tsalagi (Cherokee). All of you must be lost. This is Chiricahua (Apache) country!!" He pumped his lance overhead and a new round of yells erupted from the circle of warriors. The rider dismounted and his men stopped their chants. The boisterous group leader slid his lance through straps on his saddle then approached Roving Wolf who appeared unaffected by the haughty display.

The Apache leader broke into a hearty laugh and clapped both his hands down onto Roving Wolf's shoulders. "Brother, good to see you again!"

Roving Wolf smiled and the two men embraced while another short round of whoops burst from the men.

"Chachu! Brother. Good to see you," said Roving Wolf, returning the greeting of his friend. There was no hint of the vicious and deadly Comanche/Apache rivalry of centuries past. "You look much older and fatter than I last saw you!"

Certainly a jest, thought Tom. Chachu looked to be in his early thirties and didn't appear to have an ounce of fat on his tall, lean body. The Apache leader was the only one in the group who wore deerskin leggings but like the others, a beaded headband held his long, unbraided black hair away from his face.

"Come meet my fellow travelers," Roving Wolf insisted.

"Everyone, meet Chachu. He is a scout for the Army like me. We see each other sometimes at the All Nations Pow-wow. Chachu, meet my companions."

The men exchanged respectful greetings and handshakes.

"This is my sister, Sun Rain. You have never had a chance to meet during the All Nations festivities."

Chachu smiled. "Sun Rain, you are as beautiful as your brother said. Also, I see in your eyes you have a warrior spirit. Good for you!"

Chachu concluded his introductions with Tom and Jenny. "You two are the domers I have been hearing about. I have never seen skin so white!" Laughter resounded through the circle of Apache warriors.

"Tom Corant," said Tom while offering his hand.

"Good to meet you, Tom Corant."

"Jenny Salem," said Jenny and shook Chachu's hand.

"You don't look well Jenny Salem. Do you need a medicine chief?"

"No thank you, Chachu. That is a kind offer but I seem to be over the worst of it. I just need a few days rest."

Chachu stepped back to Roving Wolf. "Brother, you received the updated instructions last night?"

"Yes. I am ready."

Tom stood close enough to overhear the conversation. "What is happening?"

"Tom, I go with Chachu on a scout deep into Mexico. The rest of you go to Phoenix."

Chachu mounted his horse while Cloud Rider led Roving Wolf's readied mount forward and handed the animal off to his cousin. Roving Wolf jumped on his mustang and Chachu raised a fist high in the air prompting more wild war screams that once again assaulted the quiet desert morning. Chachu pointed his horse west and charged ahead. Roving Wolf and the rest of the Apaches followed. Seconds later, the war party was out of sight with only a slowly drifting cloud of dust in their wake.

Everything was happening quickly for Tom who had been in a deep sleep only moments ago. Sun Rain approached and felt Jenny's face for signs of fever.

"Tom, Jenny, we should be on our way."

"Sure, Okay. I need a moment behind the shed first," said Tom.

"Me too," added Jenny.

"Do you need any help, honey? You are a bit weak and I wouldn't want your bottom to drop into some prickly pear cactus."

Jenny smiled. "I can manage. Thank you."

Tom helped the others pack camp equipment into the Humvees. It wasn't until everything was loaded and the last rear hatch closed that Tom realized there were no horses left in the camp.

"Where are the horses?" Tom asked Little Deer who was busy extinguishing the campfire.

"No more horses, Tom. We go to Phoenix using Humvees only."

Tom smiled as Jenny staggered up to him. "Did you hear that, honey?

"What?"

"We are all driving the rest of the way to Phoenix. I didn't even notice that the Apache party took all the horses with them."

"Why so happy about that?" she asked.

"It means we will be in Phoenix in one day instead of four or five days. It will be a much easier trip."

Jenny gave a slight nod. Reaching Phoenix sooner made little difference to her. Whatever the method of transport, she was only getting farther from home.

Cloud Rider unfolded the map his cousin had given him and the team conducted another of their typical navigation briefings gathered around the hood of a Humvee.

"Running Bear, Little Deer, and White Hawk will drive the lead vehicle. The rest of us follow in Humvee number two. Easy route. We follow this road number 338 through the Animas Valley between the Animas and Peloncillo Mountain ranges, all the way to Interstate 10. We take I-10 west to Tucson and then northwest into Phoenix."

White Hawk nodded approval of Cloud Rider's route.

"We should be in Phoenix by early afternoon," noted Running Bear. We could have made it before noon if we didn't have to tow the water buffalos."

* * * *

The two-truck convoy worked its way northeast dodging the larger plant life and occasionally breaking through an old wire fence as they searched for State Route 338. When they found Route 338 it was evident that the estimated time of arrival in Phoenix would need pushed back a couple hours. The road was unpaved and at times made unexpected course changes with little warning forcing a slower rate of travel. But the convoy did travel faster than the speed of a horse trot and that meant the trailing Humvee followed at a longer distance than previous travel procedure both to minimize dust and to allow more stopping distance in the event the lead vehicle had to stop or slow down suddenly.

A few miles south of Animas, the road became a paved two-lane highway. There were a few portions of roadway cracked enough to require slow speed but most of the road was serviceable despite fifty years of neglect. The Animas valley was one of the warmest and driest locations in the United States so weather-related road damage was minimal and damage by vehicular traffic was nonexistent. They were the first people to drive this stretch of road in decades.

The vast expanse of desert seemed to have no end. Tom was still amazed at how big the Outside really was. Jenny slipped in and out of sleep in the rear seat opposite his. In the driver's seat in front of Tom, Cloud Rider kept pace with the lead Humvee. Sun Rain watched the dust cloud ahead and watched the mountains roll by out the right front window. The group kept conversation to a minimum to allow Jenny some rest. Tom continued to study the terrain that zipped by the left rear window. He also watched Jenny curled up and trying to sleep. But he discovered that his gaze always seemed to wander back to Sun Rain in the front passenger seat. He hoped she didn't notice his blissful stare from behind.

After a couple more hours of travel, Running Bear drove his lead Humvee onto the overpass that bridged Interstate 10 and stopped the engine. Cloud Rider pulled behind and killed his engine as well. Everyone climbed out of the trucks to stretch their legs. Even Jenny managed to climb out of her back seat cocoon.

Tom jogged around to the right side of the Humvee and helped Jenny walk to the guardrail. When they reached the edge of the bridge Tom understood why Running Bear chose to halt here briefly. On the Interstate below the bridge, along the westbound lanes of the highway, two parallel columns of Lakota cavalry stretched as far as the eye could see on either side of the overpass.

White Hawk grabbed his bow and one arrow from the rear cargo area and climbed onto the top of the Cherokee

Humvee. He notched the arrow in place on the bow and raised it high overhead while yelling a Lakota war cry.

Lakota warriors approaching the bridge seemed surprised to look up and see a Lakota-speaking man atop a western band Cherokee Humvee. Several of the Lakota riders walked their horses out of the column to converse with White Hawk.

Jenny surveyed the roadway below and was awestruck by the size of the cavalry force riding west. Two columns of warriors stretched from the eastern horizon to the western. "Wow, Tom. Sun Rain was right. Thousands of Lakota really would follow soon." The immense size of the Lakota army brought home for Tom and for Jenny just how significant the fight with Mexico was going to be.

After a few moments, White Hawk jumped down from the roof of the Humvee.

"Your people look like they are prepared for a big fight," Tom said to White Hawk.

"We are anxious to meet the enemy and put our years of training to the test in a real battle."

"Let's mount up, everybody," ordered Cloud Rider. Brother Running Bear, follow me. I will turn around and take the ramp onto eastbound I-10, but I will be driving west."

Cloud Rider planned to drive west on the eastbound side of the highway until they were clear of the Lakota columns. That path would be less disruptive to the horse cavalry riders because the clean road surface meant the Humvees would not kick up choking clouds of dust that the Lakota warriors would have to contend with. Fortunately, I-10 was well-travelled by automated big rigs carrying agricultural products from California to processing plants in each of the four dome farms. All that traffic meant the road surface didn't have the accumulation of dirt and sand that most desert roads did.

"But stay alert, brother," warned Cloud Rider. "We may run into eastbound automated truck transports. If we do, we will need to get off the road in a hurry to let the trucks pass."

Everyone jumped back into their places in the Humvees and motored west. White Hawk stepped up into the gun turret of the lead Humvee and Tom followed White Hawk's example by stepping up through the turret of the trailing Humvee for a better view of the Lakota columns moving west.

After a few minute's drive, the Humvees were adjacent to the lead element of the Lakota. Red Thunder, principal Lakota war chief, rode with stately majesty at the head of his army. The leader's conspicuous, ornate attire was designed to leave no doubt as to who was in charge. The enormous ceremonial war bonnet held a regal band of flowing eagle feathers that streamed down both sides of the chief's head and continued down passed his feet that were tucked into stirrups. The chief's proud mustang strutted confidently along the roadway, seemingly aware of the high station of its master. White Hawk had Cloud Rider slow the Humvee so that he could give a respectful salute as they pulled ahead of the war chief and the army he led.

A half mile beyond the Lakota warrior train, Running Bear veered off the eastbound side of the Interstate and rolled up onto the westbound lanes to continue the trip to Phoenix. The trucks were able to travel at a much faster rate now but the water trailers still forced them limit their top speed. The team hoped to be in Phoenix within five hours.

32.

With their vehicles now traversing the well-maintained road surface of Interstate Ten, the drive to Phoenix became significantly smoother and easier. Coincidently, Cherokee advance teams had just completed the refueling station north of Tucson so the last refueling stop before reaching the Phoenix stronghold was a simple matter. Tom was back behind the wheel so that Cloud Rider could read the maps and navigate. When the team passed Sky Harbor Airport, Tom took up the lead position in the convoy since Cloud Rider was the scout who possessed the most detail about finding the stronghold which was located on the grounds of the Arizona Biltmore Hotel. The airport was also the waypoint the team marked to signal their approach to the stronghold via short range radio. Of course, stronghold spotters hidden in the South Mountains noted the team's approach long before they reached the airport.

Cloud Rider guided Tom to North 51, then east onto Camelback and north onto 24th Street. A short jaunt on Biltmore Estates Drive brought the team to the main parking lot in front of the Biltmore complex. A young woman dressed in a stylish tight skirt, blouse and matching navy blue jacket stood outside between the lobby doors and the edge of the parking lot.

With ignition switches off, the weary travelers pulled themselves out of their trucks to meet the woman prepared to welcome them to the stronghold. Jenny was still weak and needed Tom to help her keep up with the others.

"Hello, I am Lindsey Stokes, executive assistant to Governor Jeffers. Welcome to Phoenix and to the Biltmore." Lindsey smiled politely but not warmly—inhibited by a natural distrust of strangers.

Greetings and introductions were made all around and Lindsey was glad to see that she had received an accurate count regarding the number of guests. She detested inaccurate information.

"Everyone follow me and I will get you to your rooms. Dinner with Governor Jeffers will be at 8:30 tonight so that gives you almost three hours to rest and prepare. We have volunteer valets who will be stopping by your rooms to help you find dinner wear and to provide any other assistance you may require."

Cloud Rider led the expedition members as they followed in Ms. Stokes' turbulent wake. As they walked they heard detail on everything from the hotel's beginning in 1929 to how they could request laundry service. The efficient assistant ushered the group passed the lobby, back outside and then into the Paradise Wing of guest rooms situated near the swimming pool of the same name.

"Lindsey, you mentioned 'Governor' Jeffers?"

"Yes, Mr. Corant."

"Please call me Tom.

"Yes, Tom."

"I thought that ever since the country went under domes, there really were no governments at the state level. How is it the Arizona has a governor?"

"You are correct. All legislative, executive, and judicial authority has been consolidated into a central, national government. State governments no longer exist."

"So how did Mr. Jeffers become Governor Jeffers?"

"Lane's father organized this stronghold around the Biltmore with the permission of President West before the last domes were sealed. His father assumed the title when the last elected governor went into his dome. Neither Lane nor his father approved of the way state government just melted away. Lane uses the title now in the same spirit as his father did, as a protest and as a reminder of what has been lost. Of course, the title is functional too since Lane is the chief executive of the stronghold and his influence extends well beyond Phoenix."

Lindsey showed the group how to use their keycards to open the doors to their rooms. "Dinner is in the Gold Room just passed the main lobby. You may ask the security guard at the front desk for help if you need it." Lindsey flashed her efficient half smile and seeing no one with questions, vanished with her clipboard down the hallway.

Jenny thanked Tom for helping her to her room then promptly dismissed him in order to take advantage of the indoor plumbing and hot water that were rare luxuries since leaving her family dome. Her room was clean and the bed soft and inviting. Maybe if she went to sleep, they would let her skip the planned dinner with the leader of the stronghold.

* * * *

The shower did wonders for Tom's disposition. The strong stream of hot water soothed his aching muscles as it rinsed away days of desert grim. Tom felt clean and dust-free for the first time in a long while. He dressed in the dark suit dropped off by one of the Biltmore staffers but after several attempts, he gave up trying to tie the necktie. He had seen pictures on the Net of men wearing them, but he had no idea how to actually tie the thing.

Tom left his room to explore the grounds before dinner. There was no answer when he knocked on Jenny's door so he set out alone. The sparkling clear water of the Paradise Pool looked cool and strangely inviting despite the fact that he had never seen a swimming pool before and he certainly did not know how to swim.

Tom walked west in the direction of the main building but jogged right to the area signs titled the Squaw Peak Lawn. Lamp posts, spotlights, and other decorative outdoor lighting fixtures cast their glow into the evening twilight. The lush grass lawn was a beautiful deep green and immaculately maintained. The flower garden encircling the water fountain bloomed with vivid color in a hundred hues. Towering date palms lined the grounds providing an air of tranquil majesty. And rising from the desert behind the hotel, the sharp darkening lines of Piestewa Peak made a dramatic backdrop for the whole estate. Everywhere Tom looked, whether inside its buildings or out, the Biltmore was an open, bright pallet of vivid color.

He scanned the perimeter of the grounds and caught sight of Sun Rain on the far side of the lawn waving and walking in his direction. He met her in the middle of the lawn.

"Tom, isn't this beautiful?!"

Tom knew what Sun Rain meant but he was momentarily rendered speechless over her change in wardrobe. He had only seen her in jeans and army desert camouflage pants. Now Sun Rain wore a strapless white cocktail dress that didn't cover much of her smooth shapely legs. Her valet had obviously gathered an array of cosmetics: lipstick, mascara, eye shadow—all items familiar to young Comanche women but completely foreign to domers like Tom.

Tom struggled to recall her question then finally offered, "Yes, a true oasis amidst the millions of acres of desert we've been blowing through over the last couple weeks. I must say, it's not just the Biltmore grounds that are exploding with beauty this evening. You are quite stunning yourself, Sun Rain."

Sun Rain laughed away the compliment. "And look how handsome you are, Thomas."

Tom chuckled. "I'd look better if I knew how to tie this…" Tom pulled the tie from his jacket pocket.

"Funny," said Sun Rain. "And I can't wear these shoes they gave me." Sun Rain held up a pair of white high heeled shoes.

Tom gazed curiously at the heels. "I've never seen anything like that. How can someone walk wearing those?"

"Exactly!" exclaimed Sun Rain.

Above the courtyard the sky was darkening quickly and more and more lights were beginning to turn on and strategically illuminate trees and buildings and patios.

"Shall we find this fancy dinner that we have been invited to?" Tom asked.

"Yes, let's." Sun Rain happily slipped her arm around Tom's.

Tom led Sun Rain off the lawn and cut toward the Paradise Wing.

"I thought it was this way?" questioned Sun Rain.

"It is, but let's see if Jenny is ready. She didn't answer when I checked a little while ago."

"Sure, Tom. I will meet you two in the dining room."

"No, come on, let's get Jenny."

Near the pool Tom and Sun Rain met Little Deer. He had dressed in the slacks and jacket set out for him though both were somewhat snug for his large frame. His necktie was draped around his neck, untied.

"Hello, you two! This is a really fancy place, huh? It is good to see some *green*! Hundreds of miles of brown desert, tumble weeds, and angry cactus were all starting to dishearten me. Forgive me, sister, I know the desert and prairie are home for Comanche. To me, it is an alien world."

"Don't apologize, brother. I would be just as lost in your mountains and forests."

"Both worlds are alien to me," Tom noted. "But they both have sunshine and freedom so you should consider yourselves blessed."

Little Deer smiled and nodded once. "Wise words, Tom Corant.

"I see you can't handle these things either?" Tom held his folded tie then draped it around his neck to match Little Deer.

"No, I gave up. What are you two doing?"

"We are going to get Jenny, then head for the dining room."

"We both just missed her," said Little Deer. "I just saw her enter the main building. She's probably already in the dining room."

The trio turned back to the main building and walked through the lobby and into the hotel's Gold Room. The elegant dining room was well lit by light from dozens of decorative lighting fixtures lining support columns. Between the columns, windows as tall as the fourteen foot high ceiling let in more light from the outdoor patio fixtures now burning to keep the evening darkness at bay. Topping the opulent appointments was the splendid sheen of the gold leaf that covered the slightly vaulted ceiling and gave the room its name.

Executive assistant Lindsey Stokes was there to meet them but she had traded her clipboard and business attire for evening wear. Her conservative black gown nearly brushed the carpet. Her brown hair was clipped and bundled high on her head and diamonds sparkled on her ear lobes.

"Good evening. Let me show you to your seats."

One medium length dinner table was centered in the dining room. Tom saw Jenny sitting near one end of the table next to Cloud Rider. He walked over and bent to kiss his fiancé on her cheek.

"Hi, honey. I stopped by earlier but must have missed you."

Jenny nodded once and cast a suspicious glance in the direction of Sun Rain.

"You look beautiful." Tom noted that Jenny did not experiment with cosmetic use and had chosen to wear a red, knee length cocktail dress.

"Tom, your seat is right across from Jenny," directed Lindsey. "Sun Rain, you are next to Tom. Little Deer, you are between Stan and Running Bear there.

"While we wait for our host and co-host, I would like to complete the introductions."

Ms. Stokes proceeded to introduce the travelers to Stan Felker, security chief, Daniel Jeffers, son of stronghold leader Lane Jeffers and Dr. Sara Saunders, medical director.

"Governor and Mrs. Jeffers and chief of staff Briggs and his wife will be with us momentarily," Lindsey said as she took the seat next to Cloud Rider.

"Are we expecting someone for the place between you and Dr. Saunders, Ms. Stokes?" Running Bear inquired.

"Yes, an Army officer, Colonel Holland."

"Nathan Holland?" asked White Hawk. All four Native American guests looked to Lindsey and seemed intensely interested in the answer.

"Why, yes. The Colonel just arrived. Do you know him?"

Cloud Rider nodded. "Nathan Holland is well known to us, Ms. Stokes. The Colonel and his men war game and train with us every year at the All Nations Pow-wow in Oklahoma."

"Wonderful. Oh, your ties!..." Lindsey stood and circled around Tom. "I can help you with those." She reached down to Tom's dangling necktie and expertly fashioned a Windsor in seconds. She moved on to Little Deer and in seconds he was as uncomfortable as the other men unfamiliar with such fashion accessories.

"Thank you," said Tom. "I see you have already assisted my other Cherokee, Comanche, and Lakota friends."

"My pleasure."

"Unfamiliar clothing for us," said White Hawk who tugged at his uncomfortably tight shirt collar.

Tom looked around the table at each of his companions sitting stiffly and fidgeting with their attire. He realized that his Indian friends were as uncomfortable and unfamiliar with suits and ties as he was.

After a few minutes of small talk around the table the host and the remaining dinner guests strolled into the Gold Room.

"Hello, good evening, keep your seats everyone. I am Lane Jeffers. This is my wife, Melanie. Walking to the other end of the table are my chief of staff, Bob Briggs and his wife, Amanda. I think some of you know Colonel Nathan Holland."

Jeffers was sixty years old and trim and fit as a result of his mountain climbing hobby. His deep suntan was distinctly evident and made more so by his thick but completely white hair. Melanie Jeffers was ten years younger but just as well-tanned as her husband. At the opposite end of the table the Briggs' were clearly not sun worshipers. Bob Briggs was a bit portly and most of his graying dark hair was long gone. His wife was dressed as stylishly as Mrs. Jeffers but was noticeably less social.

White Hawk rose from his seat on the approach of Colonel Holland who wore his Class A Army uniform rather than more formal dress blues.

"Greetings, Colonel."

Nathan Holland embraced White Hawk. "Good to see you brother White Hawk. Your father will be here in three days."

"Yes. We passed his columns this morning near the Arizona border." The two men took their seats.

Tom looked down the far end of the table and addressed White Hawk while the Jeffers' and Briggs' took their seats. "What do you mean, your father's columns?"

"My father is Wahkeyunshah, Red Thunder, principal war chief of the Lakota."

Jenny leaned forward and looked to White Hawk. "The chief we saw today—with all the eagle feathers—is your father? Why didn't you stop to say hello?"

White Hawk smiled. "That wasn't the time to exchange family pleasantries, Jenny Salem. I will see my father soon enough."

Jeffers cleared his throat. "I hope everyone is feeling welcomed here in Phoenix?"

Tom nodded. "Very much so, thank you."

"This place is beautiful," added Sun Rain.

"It is so good to be off the road," said Jenny.

"Good. Good." Jeffers stood as an elderly Mexican gentleman in fine evening dress entered the room. "Emilio, come. Everyone, this is my friend Emilio Gonzalez." Jeffers put an arm around the much shorter man. "Emilio and his staff run the Biltmore for me. Emilio and his father both worked for my father when the stronghold was first established. Thank you, Emilio, you may begin the service now."

The old man gave a shallow head bow and left the room.

Jeffers chortled. "Emilio and his staff are the only hotel staff in the history of the world to live in million-dollar estate homes surrounding their workplace.

"It is a pleasure to have all of you here," continued Jeffers. "We have welcomed Navajo and Hopi and Tohono O'odham and Apache, but we have never had Comanche or Cherokee or Lakota guests. And we certainly have never had domer guests. The Biltmore is the headquarters of the Phoenix stronghold although most of our 2,000 residents live in homes within a mile radius where water and sewer service is still provided. Others live farther away and fend for themselves when it comes to sanitary services."

After Jeffers' completed his introduction, Bob Briggs spoke from the opposite end of the table. "What do you think of the Outside, Tom and Jenny?"

"It's beautiful, but it's hard...and scary sometimes," Jenny offered.

"It's wonderful," said Tom.

Melanie Jeffers turned her head back and forth, alternating her gaze between Jenny and Tom. "How can you live all cooped up with no windows and no way out? I couldn't stand something like that. But I can see how the nickname for domers came about."

Tom shrugged. "When you are born into a dome and know nothing of the Outside, you don't know what you're missing. Nickname? You mean 'frightened turtles?'"

"No, I am sorry, I thought you knew." Melanie Jeffers was suddenly embarrassed.

Bob Briggs came to the rescue. "Veals. Outsiders sometimes refer to domers as veals."

The word meant nothing to Tom or Jenny since veal cows hadn't been raised in decades. After Briggs' explanation, the concept comparison definitely registered with Tom. Jenny was appalled, not by the nickname, but by learning the historical details of veal farming.

"Do you think the people in domes would want out if they knew what the Outside was like?" Briggs queried Tom.

"I think they would, yes. I have certainly changed my mind about things in the last few weeks. But domers have been sold so much fear their entire lives, I don't think the choice would be easy or automatic for everyone without experiencing the Outside, or at least without knowing a lot more about it."

"Would you prefer the domers never come out, Mr. Briggs?" asked Running Bear.

Jeffers spoke before his chief of staff could answer. "Sir, you should know that among the residents of the

Arizona stronghold you will find we all share the sentiment that what has been done to this country is disgraceful, criminal. Our proud republic that once celebrated the unique and free spirit of every man and woman is now a socialist democracy that treats everyone like sheep—or veal as Bob so eloquently described. What about you, sir? I would think Native Americans would want to keep the domers in their shells."

"No," came the quick answer from Running Bear. "I would expect the domer people to respect the land and respect our rights in a manner better than their ancestors. But I certainly can't countenance my cousins of every race and color being trapped in a prison that withers the spirit. Our medicine chief says the spirit inside every man that animates his body will never know truth if it stays inside a dome cut off from the earth and sky."

"Domers are looked upon with pity by my people." White Hawk added. "Separating a man from the earth is the same as death for us. Of course, some of my people would be concerned if the domers ever emerged. Would they destroy the buffalo herds again? Would they encroach on sacred land and be bad neighbors again?"

"My brother presents good questions," said Colonel Holland. "I happen to think we can learn from mistakes made long ago. But all this talk about the end of the domer society is moot if we lose the coming fight. I submit that war with Mexico is the first order of business."

"I agree, Colonel," Jeffers said as the wait staff arrived and began the dinner service.

"How do things look in that regard, Colonel," Briggs asked.

"Hostilities are likely to begin within three or four weeks."

"And our chances of winning, Colonel?"

"Mr. Briggs, I wish I had better news there. Our troops are better trained and equipped. But General Mejias has many more soldiers than we have—many more."

"Does the word: 'Alamo' mean anything to you, Colonel?"

"As an Army officer, I have studied my military history, Mr. Briggs. The comparison you make is valid. Rest assured, I am going to do everything I can to ensure a different outcome this time."

33.

Five days after her arrival in Phoenix Jenny was exhausted. She trudged down the hotel hallway with legs so heavy she wondered if she would make it to her room before collapsing. She had barely recovered from her fever when she was pressed into service to help the stronghold prepare for war. Every able-bodied citizen was likewise pressed into service. 'Pressed into service' was probably the wrong phrase, Jenny thought. Everyone was a volunteer because everyone knew that if they lost this battle, they truly would become slaves. Everything she learned growing up about the Outside being a dangerous place was true. She missed her family and she missed her clean, safe, comfortable dome.

Jenny found herself assigned to Dr. Saunders' hospital prep team. Her days were spent setting up beds and stocking the local hospitals that were being setup on the west side of the Biltmore and the larger facility in the Phoenix Mountains Park half a mile behind the Biltmore. The Phoenix Mountains were being prepared as the emergency, temporary fallback position for the Biltmore-area stronghold residents in the event Mexican troops penetrated the city far enough to require evacuation of the hotel grounds. Trucks, buses, and automobiles were waiting in and near the mountains to transport citizens to the backup stronghold in Flagstaff, if things really got desperate. Jenny also stocked transport vehicles with medical supplies. The trucks took the supplies sixty miles south to the forward field hospital established at Gila Bend. Other vehicles drove even deeper into the anticipated battlefield areas to stock battalion aid stations—stations that were especially important because the United States had not yet automated helicopters that were traditionally used for medivac operations that transported wounded soldiers to medical facilities.

The exhausting work kept Jenny busy from dawn to well into each evening. She saw Tom only once in the last five days. He was extremely busy as well but his work involved preparing fortifications in the city's residential and commercial areas between the Biltmore and the expected line of advance of Mejias' soldiers. A combined force of stronghold residents and a small Navajo infantry detachment planned to give the Mexican army a strong dose of house-to-house urban warfare if they were inclined to try and capture the heart of the stronghold at the Biltmore.

Jenny also understood that tomorrow was an important day for overall war preparations. All the Treaty Tribe war chiefs had arrived in Phoenix to conduct a joint war council meeting. The President of the United States and her domed military commanders would be present via video.

As she plodded through the Paradise Wing to her room, Jenny's thoughts turned to Tom and the future. If they survived the war, what happened then? Would they live here in Phoenix and hopefully avoid terrorist bombs or nerve gas or man-made genetically altered bacteria or a deadly strain of a natural virus, or wait for another attack from Mexico—all those were very real threats from everything she had seen on the Net. Would she even have Tom by her side? Jenny's breathing shallowed and her teeth clenched when she thought of the pretty young Comanche girl flirting with Tom.

Instead of opening the door to her room, Jenny walked three more doors down to *her* room. Jenny didn't even want to think the name, much less hear it. She saw Tom and Sun Rain laughing, arm-in-arm on the lawn before dinner their first day in Phoenix. That sight hurt then and the memory hurt now. Exhaustion and pride were heavy weights that nearly prevented her from raising her arm to rap on the door, but Jenny managed three heavy knocks. Maybe she isn't here, thought Jenny. Sun Rain was busy with war preparations like everyone else. Second thoughts of regret sprung forth immediately and suddenly Jenny found herself hoping desperately that Sun Rain wouldn't be in. Luck was not on her side.

Sun Rain opened the door. She wore one of the hotel's white terrycloth robes and her hair was wet from a recent shower. She smiled at Jenny. "Hi, Jenny."

Somehow the cheery hello lightened the load on Jenny's arm and before she realized what she was doing the vindictive slap snapped viciously into Sun Rain's cheek. Shock stayed any immediate retaliation from Sun Rain. For the briefest moment the look of surprise in Sun Rain's wide eyes satisfied Jenny, then remorse flooded in.

Jenny stepped forward and tried to embrace Sun Rain but the wounded girl's instincts took over and her arm swung like a club against Jenny's head knocking her onto the floor of the hotel room. Jenny sat up and brushed the hair and tears from her face. She offered up a weak "I'm sorry" and wept as she sat on the carpet.

Anger replaced the look of surprise on Sun Rain's face but she didn't continue the counter-assault against her attacker. "I know why you do this, Jenny, but you cannot tell a man what woman to love."

Jenny knew that. Sun Rain's lack of compunction wasn't helpful but Jenny understood that too. She picked herself up off the floor and stared back at Sun Rain.

"My fiancé hasn't been intimate with me since we've been together. There haven't been many opportunities for romance the last few weeks, but now Tom isn't interested because of you. That isn't your fault, I know that. I am sorry." Jenny didn't make the uncomfortable confession because she felt she owed Sun Rain an explanation, but rather out of a necessary cathartic exercise—she desperately missed sharing her thoughts and feelings with the scores of close on-line friends back home.

"You are foolish, Jenny. Tom is loyal to you regardless of his other feelings."

Jenny walked briskly out of the room and down the hall, tears still flowing. She didn't acknowledge Little Deer's hello when she rushed passed him and into her room. Little Deer turned and was about to call out after Jenny when he heard Sun Rain's door slam shut.

"Well, that was bound to happen," the tired warrior muttered to himself before wandering into his room and collapsing for a few hours rest.

34.

Bob Briggs paced the Squaw Peak Lawn and grumbled as the grounds crew hurried to set up the tent to protect two large flat panel video screens from potential rain. Plans for the war council meeting in the Grand Ballroom had to be scrapped abruptly when the medicine chief in the Cheyenne delegation declared the interior spaces were unsuitable for hosting the meeting of the war chiefs. According to Lindsey Stokes, the hastily arranged alternative on the Biltmore lawn had a fifty-fifty chance of being ready by the 10:00 a.m. call with the President. At least the clouds were beginning to break up and more often than not, bright morning sun beamed onto the grass, so the tent would help more with glare than with rain.

A small fire pit had been dug and consecrated on the west side of the lawn much to the horror of Emilio Gonzalez. The Biltmore caretaker did manage to have one of his staff save the sod so that with any luck, the damage could be repaired the next day. Briggs noted that activity around the fire pit was on the increase as Biltmore staffers mixed with the entourages of the war chiefs to make certain all was well before the leaders began the council. Moments before the ten o'clock hour, the staffer connecting the electronics flashed Briggs the thumbs up sign.

"Thank God," muttered Briggs.

At that moment, Lindsey Stokes emerged from the main building with Governor Jeffers, the war chiefs, and the Treaty Tribe delegations following. Colonel Holland brought up the rear with the domer couple and the Indian scouts with whom they had arrived the previous week.

The war chiefs took their seats on blankets spread in the grass while two of the medicine chiefs chanted and prayed and lit the council fire. A few men in the delegations wore US Army desert battle fatigues but most wore traditional, ceremonial dress. The chiefs of the northern and central plains had donned war bonnets with hundreds of flowing eagle feathers. They wore deerskin war shirts with colorful bead patterns sewn in, deerskin leggings, and moccasins of buffalo hide. The chiefs of the south and west wore simpler, less colorful accessories. One or two eagle feathers were either tucked into a headband or dangling from hair braids. No weapons, modern or ancient, were brought to the council fire.

Briggs made his way awkwardly down onto the blanket with the Governor and Colonel Holland, wincing at the twinge of pain shooting up his bad back. He glanced again at the monitor placement to confirm everyone had an adequate viewing angle. The equipment looked good. The video screen on the left blinked on with the image of General Tanner on the left and General Singer on the right. The war chiefs continued the council by taking turns passing a tobacco pipe among themselves while exchanging pleasantries expressed with varying degrees of English fluency. Briggs took a puff when the pipe reached the blankets of the stronghold leaders and guests. His occasional indulgence in cigars of Southern tobacco brought west by independent traders allowed him to avoid the smoke-induced coughing fits that overtook the non-Indian novices at the council fire. As the pipe passed down to the domer couple and the scouts, the presidential seal on the right video screen disappeared and was replaced with the live image of Barbara Phillips, 58th President of the United States.

Governor Jeffers took the lead in opening the council; he considered himself to be the host given that the council convened on land he administered. "Welcome, everyone, to this Council. We gather on this occasion to discuss the safety and survival of our combined nations. Let us begin with some introductions." Jeffers introduced the war chiefs of the Treaty Tribes with whom he had met separately over the course of the previous day:

Wahkeyunshah, "Red Thunder," War Chief of the Lakota,

Kwinashano, "War Eagle," War Chief of the Comanche,

Yonahequah, "Big Bear," War Chief of the Cherokee (Western and Eastern bands),

Cabello Amarillo, "Yellow Hair," War Chief of the Navajo,

Minninnewah, "Whirlwind" War Chief of the Cheyenne,

Itzachu, "Great Hawk" War Chief of the Apache

Koatyka, "Wolf Outside" War Chief of the Kiowa,

Nahanahcha, "Chief in Everything," War Chief of the Arapaho

Bob Briggs studied the eight leaders of the largest armed force gathered in the country since the American Civil War over two hundred years ago. To a man they were deliberate and confident. There wasn't the smallest spark of fear in any of them.

Jeffers completed the introductions of the war chiefs with what he hoped were no major gaffes in pronunciation. "Madam President, I turn the floor over to you to introduce your staff."

"Thank you, Governor. I have the entire Security Council staff with me today." President Phillips introduced each member of her staff and as she did so, the staffer's face briefly flashed on the right hand video screen:

Donald Sullivan (Vice President of the United States)
Carter Mason (Secretary of State)
Belinda Ashmore (Secretary of Defense)

General Joshua Pruitt (Chairman of the Joint Chiefs of Staff)

Anthony Covelli (Director of National Intelligence)

Alan Sayles (National Security Advisor)

Betty Saville (Chief of Staff to the President)

Cecil Harbaugh (Deputy National Security Advisor)

Judith Zaranski (Secretary of the Treasury)

Daniel McInnis (Attorney General)

Mary Loveland (Secretary of Homeland Security)

Matthew Smith (Counsel to the President)

Dennis Newbury (White House Press Secretary)

"Thank you, madam President," said General Pruitt. "I would like to conclude with the introductions of the military portion of the team." General Pruitt listed the general officers present:

General Bruce Beckett (US Army) - Commander, USNORTHCOM

General Roy ("Hop") Hopkins (US Air Force) - Commander, USSTRATCOM

Lt. General Mark Tanner (US Army) – Commander of the Western Army

Lt. General Kathleen Singer (US Army) – Commander of the Eastern Army

The faces of the military leaders cycled on the left hand video screen.

"Finally, sitting at the council fire in Phoenix, Colonel Nathan Holland, commander of our Outside Special Forces unit. I believe the Colonel is known to all of the war chiefs present. Madam President, I turn the floor back to you."

"Thank you, General Pruitt. It is an honor to meet all of the war leaders at this council fire. As President of the United States, I also want to be clear that my duty is to protect all citizens of this country, whether they live in domes, strongholds, or Native American villages.

"The threat posed by Mexico is real and war is imminent. I am committing all available military forces to the defense of our country. I understand that the battle staffs of Generals Tanner and Singer have been coordinating defensive and offensive plans with appropriate leaders within each Treaty Tribe and consensus on the conduct of all forces has been reached. Does that mean I have the official commitment from each Treaty Tribe to provide military forces to defend the United States?"

Itzachu (Great Hawk), War Chief of the Apaches was the first to speak. "To the Great Chief of America, I promise all Apache divisions and bands will fight, no matter what the other nations decide. None of my people want Mexican boots walking upon Apache land."

"President Phillips, I hope there is nothing ominous portended by the presence today of General Hopkins," commented Wahkeyunshah (Red Thunder). The experienced War Chief of the Lakota was well aware of the responsibilities of the commander of the US Strategic Command. "You know the position of the Lakota people on the use of nuclear weapons on or near US land."

"I am very aware, Chief Red Thunder. I consider the use of nuclear weapons a very last resort and for only the most desperate situation. But I will not lie or mislead you, use of nuclear weapons, while a last resort, is not off the table but as I say, only in the event of an extremely desperate situation might they be used."

"I understand, President Phillips. And you understand that the Lakota will follow me home if nuclear bombs fall?"

"We understand each other, sir."

"The Cherokee will fight to remain free," promised Chief Yonahequah (Big Bear). "What the frightened turtles hiding in their shells fight for, I do not know."

President Phillips deftly ignored the derisive quip referencing the lack of liberty inherent in dome society. "Many thanks Chief Big Bear, and Chief Red Thunder and Chief Great Hawk."

"Chief Barbara Phillips, if the war is won, will your people come out of their shells?" asked Cheyenne War Chief Minninnewah (Whirlwind). "The Cheyenne lament the fate of our imprisoned cousins but that lament is tempered by the fact that our cousins imprisoned themselves and by the fact that the imprisonment has permitted great herds of buffalo to graze the plains once again."

"Chief Whirlwind, the aggressive actions of Mexico only underscore the dangers we see on the Outside. A victory over Mexico doesn't solve the dilemma of many missing nuclear warheads, or terrorists with nerve gas, or the lurking danger of natural and man-made killer bacteria and viruses, or the impending ravages of climate change. I don't see us abandoning our domes, sir." President Phillips kept that rote response handy at all times over the years, ready to use as a shield against any jab at the new American way of life. She knew very well however, that no one present at the Council or any of their people had ever experienced any of those terrors.

War Chief Cabello Amarillo (Yellow Hair) who led the large Navajo infantry force looked away from the video screens to Colonel Holland. "Nathan Holland, do you believe the words of your government and military leaders are true? Do you vouch for their truthfulness? I do not know your far away chiefs. They are only heads in a box to me. You I know for years. You are a fellow war chief. We have shared meals, and the pipe, and many council fires. I want to know your words on this."

Nathan Holland was not completely surprised about being put on the spot in this manner. He knew the war chiefs and the cultures they represented. Trust had to be earned with deeds, not words.

"I do trust them, brother. And I will be on the battlefield with you."

Colonel Holland's words satisfied the Navajo war chief who affirmed the Navajo commitment to the war effort.

One by one, the remaining war chiefs committed their nations' armies to the defense of the United States. Bob Briggs bristled whenever the President used the short simple phrase: 'United States.' That phrase was in many ways meaningless these days. Americans no longer lived in a republic; they lived in a socialist democracy. Briggs wondered if the domed citizens would ever wake up to the fact that having a vote didn't necessarily mean you were free.

35.

"Damn this crap bucket!" Sergeant Rodriguez pounded the hammer violently against the armored engine cover and jumped down from the old Chinese Type 59 main battle tank. When Rodriguez recovered from the landing he stood face to face with General Juan Mejias, President of Mexico and commander-in-chief of the Mexican army. Rodriguez snapped to attention and saluted the general.

"Is there a problem, Sergeant?"

"Yes, there is, sir. Some of the spare parts for these tanks just don't fit together properly. How the Chinese kept these hundred-year-old tanks from rusting into dust, I will never know."

"So you are not impressed with the equipment, Sergeant?" Mejias strutted with his hands clasped behind his back; his eyes scanned the sergeant from head to boots and back again.

"It was impressive in 1960, sir—not in 2080." Rodriguez wiped his hands on his greasy coveralls.

Mejias was in a good enough humor at the moment to approve of the young sergeant's candor. "Still, Sergeant, the Americans have no heavy armor so wouldn't this tank prove to be an asset for us?"

Rodriguez thought for a moment. Images of his wife and daughters flashed in his head long enough to quash any rash response to the General's question. "I see your point, sir. Yes, if utilized properly, I can see where a working tank like this could be helpful. We received 150 of these vehicles but only 119 are healthy enough to drive and fight."

"That will be all, Sergeant."

Rodriguez saluted and left the garage thankful that he survived the encounter with the most feared man in Mexico.

Mejias turned to his military aide, Colonel Jorge Sanchez. "Jorge, the Chinese must think we are idiots."

"They are clearly showing contempt and disrespect, General, by dumping inferior equipment on us."

"At least they came cheap, Jorge." Mejias directed his irritated scowl from one end of the busy garage to the other. "Where is that fool, Trujillo? He should know by now that I am here."

General Mejias had arrived on the outskirts of Hermosillo an hour ago from his headquarters in Mexico City. The general thought a snap inspection was in order given that his window for launching the invasion of the United States was at hand. Mejias wore camouflage battle fatigues rather than the dress uniform he normally wore when touring military facilities. The fatigues made it easier to surprise unsuspecting officers and soldiers. The cap and sunglasses helped him get even closer before his face was recognized.

Mejias stomped to the far end of the motor pool garage, one of many where the Chinese tanks were being readied for battle. The young sergeant had been incensed that one-fifth of the Chinese tanks were unserviceable. Mejias actually expected as much despite the complaints he shared with his aide.

Mejias exited the garage as General Trujillo's staff car arrived and parked across the street. Trujillo climbed out of the sedan with two junior officers, walked quickly toward Mejias and flashed a crisp, precise salute.

"Mr. President, welcome to Hermosillo."

Mejias answered with a sloppy, disdainful return salute. "Are you ready to move, Trujillo?"

"Yes, sir. All elements are ready. A number of the tanks won't..."

"I already know about the tanks." The General whipped his hand through the air in a dismissive gesture that resembled swatting at a pesky flying insect. "Are the men ready to march?"

Trujillo nodded and bellowed, "Yes, sir!"

"I would like to address the lead element. Have them form up."

"Already being done, sir." General Trujillo knew the President's *modus operandi* well enough to anticipate such a request. "Your driver can follow us to the parade field."

Mejias nodded his approval and stepped into his command car along with Colonel Sanchez. The dozen men serving as Mejias' armed escort climbed back into their truck and followed. In less than five minutes the small motorcade arrived at an improvised parade field where a brigade-sized formation of men in battle fatigues stood at attention behind unit identifier flags that fluttered in the moderate breeze.

Mejias, Trujillo, their aides, and presidential bodyguard all dismounted and marched under the hot noon-time sun to the formation of soldiers. Mejias walked slowly down the front rank of one of the formations. Every man stood tall and rigid, maintaining the position of "attention" which also required all eyes to stare straight ahead and not wander to either side. He carefully observed the condition of uniforms and weapons, alert to any sign of sloppy maintenance. The men appeared fit and ready until Mejias approached a baby-faced private in the middle of the front rank who fidgeted uncomfortably. Mejias stopped and stood toe-to-toe with the boy.

"What is wrong with you, soldier!?" Mejias snarled.

The young, inexperienced conscript muttered a barely audible, "Nothing, sir."

Before Mejias challenged the boy to deliver a more confident response, the general noticed a wet spot growing in the front of the private's trousers and running down his leg. Mejias backed away and anger flushed his face red. The members of Mejias' bodyguard had seen the general's deep red complexion before and things never turned out well.

"Boy, how do you expect to defeat your enemy in battle if you are too afraid to stand for a simple inspection?!" Mejias shouted his angry challenge and at the same time deliberately suppressed a grin that would have betrayed the fact that he felt pride in invoking such fear in the recruits. Without question he was indeed genuinely angry. Men like this were cowards whose actions, or more likely inactions, could cost other men their lives during combat.

"Come here, private." Mejias pulled the frightened soldier out in front of his unit. "Turn around. Let them see you!"

Mejias addressed the formation and pointed to the private. "Look at this coward! He pisses himself during an inspection! How can you trust this man to fight with you?"

The wet private began to tremble but did his best to remain at attention.

"You." Mejias pointed to the soldier still in formation who had stood on the boy's right. "What's your name?"

"My name is Estrella, Mr. President."

"Estrella, if you were in battle next to this coward and the enemy was approaching, would you trust him to stand with you?"

"No, sir," stammered Private Estrella.

Mejias unsnapped the cover on the leather holster that hung over his right hip and removed his Ruger Redhawk. The general handed the revolver to Estrella. "Private Estrella, I order you to immediately execute this man for cowardice." Mejias stepped away from the condemned man who was too frightened to move.

Estrella stepped forward out of formation and lifted the heavy pistol but then hesitated.

"Squeeze the trigger, man!" demanded Mejias.

Estrella's hand began to tremble and the young soldier shook his head from side to side when Mejias looked him in the eye. Mejias lurched forward in frustration, grabbed the pistol from Estrella, and immediately turned the weapon on Estrella and fired into his chest. The soldier snapped backward like he had been hit with huge invisible hammer and fell to the ground. The tremendously loud report of the pistol shot reverberated through the formations and across the parade field.

Mejias turned and pointed the side arm at the forehead of the wet recruit and squeezed the trigger. After another ear-splitting bang from the powerful weapon, a second soldier collapsed in a bloody heap on the parade field.

Mejias was not finished. The general pointed the pistol at the company commander who stood thirty feet away in front of the men he led. The army captain had relaxed his posture of attention enough to turn his head toward the scene of Mejias' rampage. When he saw Mejias bearing down on him, the officer's discipline broke down completely and he turned to run. Mejias fired and hit the officer square in the back knocking him onto the grass. The general fired another shot into the man's prone body when the dying officer failed to stop moving after the first bullet.

For the most part, the discipline of the formations held. Mejias noticed some slight movements as men in rear ranks tried to sneak a peek around the men lined up in front of them. His armed escort had unslung their rifles and held them at the ready. Mejias tucked his revolver back into his holster and snapped it shut.

"Colonel Sanchez, mark this man as executed for failing to carry out an order, mark this wet man as executed for cowardice, and mark the company commander as executed for incompetence in command." Mejias barked out the instructions loud enough for most men in the formations to hear.

"Yes, sir," answered the aide.

Mejias approached General Trujillo. "Begin the march to Arizona in the morning, general!"

"Yes, sir!"

Mejias lowered his voice for the final instruction to Trujillo. "General, break up this unit immediately and sprinkle the men through as many other units as you can. I want word of this action to spread through the army tonight." Mejias and his escorts returned to their vehicles and sped away.

Trujillo turned to his aide. "Good thing we are moving out tomorrow. If we spend much more time in Mexico, we won't have enough troops left alive to fight."

36.

Chachu's "reconnaissance in force" as his Army handler referred to it consisted of forty- three Chiricahua Apache light cavalry and one Comanche guest scout—his good friend Roving Wolf. They left Roving Wolf's Phoenix-bound companions in Cloverdale and rode southwest through the Guadalupe Mountains whose rugged slopes and valleys would provide good cover for moving over the border. Before crossing the international border near Rancho Guadalupe and striking southwest toward Mexico Highway 17, all members of the scout team changed out of their US Army or native clothing and into their Mexican scouting kit—jeans, tee shirts or casual button shirts, cowboy boots, and cowboy hat or baseball caps. The vaquero clothing and accessories (including hand stitched ostrich and armadillo leather boots) were absolutely authentic, collected by the Apaches from the bodies of dead Mexicans who were killed violating US territory, or in some cases, just getting too close.

Successful disguise was crucial because any Apache caught in Mexico could expect torture and death as revenge for the policy of summary executions of Mexicans found north of the border. Their flowing, long hair would betray their identity instantly so they tucked their long locks inside their shirt collars. When they were forced to move near populated areas, they took the extra precaution of tucking their hair under their hats and caps. The scouts hid their rifles under strategically placed saddle bags, extra bits of saddle blankets and whatever other accessories they could. The deception wouldn't survive a close inspection, but would pass casual observation well enough.

Chachu's men made liberal use of encrypted short range radios to coordinate their movements. Travel by horse in the rough terrain of the Sierra Madre Mountains was common and would not arouse suspicion. A band of over forty men riding together, however, was indeed unusual so Chachu's command split into teams of three or four men each. The radios and the GPS units they carried made navigation a simple matter. Most professional scouts, Chachu and Roving Wolf included, only used the GPS units as a double check for their old fashioned method of map reading—maps didn't run out of batteries.

Their mission was dangerous. Chachu's orders were to scout into the heart of the Mexican military buildup around Hermosillo. The overcrowded city of three million people had tripled its population since the doming of America just as many other cities of northern Mexico had swelled in size due to the millions of Hispanic illegals—Mexican and non-Mexican—deported by the US as she forced her citizens into domes. The United States gave billions to the Mexican president and key members of the corrupt government when Mexican officials threatened to use the army and the federal police to close the border and prevent the illegals from crossing back into Mexico. The money that actually made it passed corrupt officials and into the Mexican treasury wasn't enough to deal with the population influx and both governments knew that, but the fund transfer served its purpose—preventing an ugly and violent scene at the border during a tumultuous transition period in American history.

The Apache scout team traveled for five days through the difficult mountain terrain of the Sierra Madre to reach Hermosillo. All of Chachu's men were experts at traversing mountain terrain by horse and by foot thanks to their upbringing in Arizona's Chiricahua Mountains. Not all were trained scouts, however. Chachu had wanted to minimize risk of detection by having only himself and Roving Wolf on the mission but he was overruled by his Army handler. The Army wanted a force that could defend itself. With war imminent, the US was not concerned about political ramifications if a small American military force, in the form of Apache scouts, was discovered operating inside Mexico. Mexico had obviously already been caught sending in a small patrol of its own. Still, Chachu implored his men to be discrete and to avoid all contact with Mexican citizens.

Chachu positioned his men in makeshift observation posts on high ground northeast and northwest of the city while he and Roving Wolf explored the large arid plain northwest of Hermosillo where the bulk of Mexican forces gathered. Initial observation of the target area did not show any use of horses in the area so Chachu and Roving Wolf conducted a quiet, early morning raid on one of the Mexican army motor pools to commandeer a Humvee. They scrounged gasoline where they could and for two days the scouts drove through hundreds of square miles of assembly area without being challenged once—no doubt due to their care in avoiding close approaches to well-guarded positions such as ammunition supply points. Chachu used his small handheld radio to report troop concentrations and equipment inventories to the man he left in the hills who was trained to operate the SATCOM unit. The satellite communications gear was safer in the hills than on Chachu's person where it wouldn't give away Chachu's identity or slow him down if he needed to move in a hurry. Chachu also instructed the man entrusted with the SATCOM gear to transmit the curious information collected by his other teams hiding in the hills above the city, information on large numbers of Mexican troops billeted with civilians among the city's residential districts. The news about troops quartering with civilians meant that US intelligence analysts might be underestimating Mexican troop strength by a significant margin.

On their eighth evening in Mexico, Chachu and Roving Wolf discovered large numbers of men and a small number of supply vehicles staging themselves along the roads that led north. All signs pointed to the Mexican army beginning to move north in the morning. Chachu radioed a report to the operator of his SATCOM unit while Roving Wolf drove through the northern limits of Hermosillo and toward the Apache teams in the northeast hills. Their scout of the city was over and it was time to recover their horses and start working back toward Arizona—spying on the Mexican army as it moved north.

Chachu slipped the small radio into the simple leather case clipped to his belt. "Another successful mission, brother!"

"Yes, but not over yet. We will follow the army north and report," said Roving Wolf as he drove the Humvee through the dark streets of north Hermosillo. The truck had no top cover so the cool night air whistled over the windscreen but wasn't hitting their cowboy hats with enough force to dislodge them. They wore their hats low and tight on their heads to keep their long hair out of sight even though the sun disappeared long ago.

The scout team was almost out of the city when Chachu noticed the small neon sign of the cantina: "Ricardo's Café Mexicana." Chachu slapped Roving Wolf's arm and pointed to the small, non-descript building. "I am thirsty."

Roving Wolf pulled off the road and stopped. "Chachu, are you always this reckless on your scouts?" Roving Wolf knew the answer to that already. He had never run a mission with his friend but Chachu's exploits were well known in the scout community. Roving Wolf subscribed to a more conservative mission posture than his Apache friend.

Chachu smiled broadly. "Come on, brother. This is how we test current skills and develop new ones. My Spanish is better than yours, just let me do all the talking."

Roving Wolf surveyed the surroundings. The small, one-story cantina was isolated; the next closest building was a one-pump gas station fifty meters down the dark street. The only vehicles parked at the cantina were an old pickup and an even more ancient Volkswagen beetle. There couldn't be many patrons inside. The operation was not Roving Wolf's style but it was indeed an interesting challenge. He had made very brief visits into cantina's to plant listening devices but those were quick, in-and-out drops—he suspected Chachu planned to stay a while.

"Alright," Roving Wolf acquiesced and stepped out from behind the steering wheel. He mentally ticked through his weapons inventory. He had a knife in each boot but each under a pant leg so they were not what he considered "instantly" available. On the other hand, the 9mm pistol tucked in his pants under his shirt was definitely readily accessible, but also very loud. He packed a nylon garrote in the lower left pocket of his guayabera shirt but he doubted the device's application in the cantina environment.

The men stepped onto the creaking floorboards of the covered porch.

"You know, if anything gets us into trouble it's going to be your boots," Chachu chuckled.

Roving Wolf had never been a fan of gaudy Mexican cowboy boots and he didn't appreciate being made more self-conscious than he already was over his black ostrich leather boots each with a long-stemmed red rose stitched from toe all the way up the medium length side. It was the only pair he had yet come across that fit his size 12 double wide feet. Roving Wolf coped by keeping his pants leg over the boots instead of tucked inside.

"I will do the talking. You are already drunk." Chachu pushed open the left and right saloon-style swing doors that covered the middle portion of the cantina entrance.

Roving Wolf followed close behind and quickly mapped the environment. At the pool table at 10 o'clock, a thin, short old man of 65-plus years played a stocky forty-something pot-bellied man in jeans, stained white tee shirt and brown leather vest. Both men had cigarettes that seemed permanently inserted between their lips. The other pool table at 2 o'clock was empty. A set of two café tables were pushed near the left and right cantina walls. Directly ahead, beyond the pool tables was a seven-seat bar counter. To the left of the counter was the door to the unisex bathroom and to the right was a partial kitchen and cooking station. An open door near the kitchen led to a storeroom. The low, eight-foot ceiling didn't leave much clearance for the three ceiling fans, only one of which turned and had its lamp lit. A single, bare, low-wattage light bulb over the bar provided most of the illumination in the poorly lit cantina.

Two "boys" barely out of their teens worked on a bottle—probably tequila, Roving Wolf assumed—at one of the tables along the left wall. The one man sitting at the bar in jeans and checkered shirt turned in their direction. From the bleary look on his heavily sun-beaten face, he was only one drink away from passing out, or vomiting—even money on which. The woman stood looking directly at the cantina newcomers; her back was to the bar and she stood with one stool between her and the seated drunkard. She wore a conservative, solid red broom skirt that nearly touched the dirty, unkempt floor. The white camisole top wasn't conservative at all and left the dark brown skin of her arms and upper chest exposed. Her full-bodied dark hair flowed in waves passed a face that was pretty ten years ago but was now beginning to wrinkle and hang loosely from her high cheekbones.

Behind the counter the bar tender wore a dirty apron over a once white, now gray tee shirt. The seemingly casual glance he gave them while he wiped the countertop was anything but casual. The dark eyes above his bushy mustache and puffy, tanned cheeks had been trained over many years to fully observe minute detail of a cantina patron's appearance and behavior in only milliseconds—were they dangerous?, drunk?, troublemakers?, big spenders?, poor tippers?, etc...

Chachu waved two fingers at the barman, ordered two Coronas, and then led Roving Wolf to the empty tables on the far right side of the room. He made a show of pulling a chair out for Roving Wolf and guiding him into it. Roving Wolf leaned forward, elbows on the table and head tilted down to where he could just peek out under the brim of his cowboy hat to continue to observe the activity in the bar. Chachu sat to his left in the very corner of the room and angled directly toward the row of bar stools twenty feet away.

A television screen mounted high on the wall behind the bar displayed a Mexican news program. The volume was kept respectfully low. Roving Wolf caught enough of the Spanish broadcast to know a local citizen was complaining about all the army troops living in his neighborhood. Occasional boisterous laughter erupted from the two young men at the table on the opposite side of the room. The two men wielding pool cues said little as they played. The only noise from their direction was the sound of cue ball strikes, billiard balls clacking together and a groan here and there marking a missed shot.

Roving Wolf realized the only one who seemed to be paying much attention to him and Chachu was the woman. He hoped this was the type of place where everyone minded their own business—some cantinas were just the opposite.

Chachu leaned close and spoke softly in English. "Typical neighborhood cantina, eh brother? The smell of alcohol, cigarettes, fried food, unwashed men, and one lonely hint of cheap perfume." Chachu laughed conspicuously and slapped Roving Wolf on the back, obviously having fun playing the role of cantina patron.

The bartender set two open beer bottles on the counter and used a slight tilt of his head to tell the woman to deliver the bottles. Now the act really begins, thought Roving Wolf.

She held a bottle in each hand as she sauntered to the table, expertly dodging the cue stick draw of the old man along the way. "Hello, boys! I am Rosita." She set down the Corona bottles and Chachu produced the proper amount of pesos based on the sign above the counter, plus a moderate tip.

"Hello, Rosita. My name is Juan and as luck would have it, my friend here is also named Juan. Unfortunately, he is feeling a little tired."

Rosita sat down in the chair beside Chachu. "Where are you boys from?"

"We are from up north. The army hired us as mountain guides."

"Ah, yes, they are finally leaving tomorrow, thank God. It was so terrible that the soldiers were not allowed in the cantinas."

"Thankfully, we are not soldiers!" Chachu raised his bottle and gulped a portion of his beer. Roving Wolf lifted his bottle slightly for a quick sip then returned to a posture of keeping his face down and his head low over the table.

Rosita and Chachu traded questions as well as less meaningful conversation for several minutes with Roving Wolf grunting a word or two occasionally. Rosita drifted back to the bar. The bartender—"Manuel" according to Rosita—wiped the countertop in front of her and listened to Rosita's report on the strangers.

Roving Wolf mumbled quietly, "Manuel wipes down that counter much. Must be the cleanest bar top in Hermosillo."

"Yes. From the look he just gave us, I don't think he believes what we told Rosita. Let's watch him closely to be sure he doesn't pick up a telephone or a cell phone."

Rosita finished her conversation with Manuel with a nod then turned to the scouts. "How about a game of pool, boys?"

"Sure," agreed Chachu.

Roving Wolf stood and moved to the far end of the empty table which put him near the bar. Chachu stood at the opposite end of the table while Rosita distributed cue sticks that she pulled from a wall rack near the cantina entrance.

Manuel stopped wiping the countertop. "According to the soldiers in my house they are going to Nogales by the highway, not by the mountains. Why would the army need mountain guides?"

Chachu shrugged and laughed lightly. "I have no idea the army's plan for me."

"Your friend doesn't speak Spanish?" Manuel asked Chachu.

Roving Wolf actually understood Manuel's question clearly.

"Of course I speak Spanish!" Roving Wolf went on to assault the bartender with the Spanish he knew best—Mexican cantina vulgarities—and questioned the size of Manuel's manhood, questioned his ancestry, and questioned his sexual orientation, all in a Nogales accent.

The profane tirade actually seemed to satisfy Manuel, but only momentarily. The other patrons barely flinched—typical cantina banter as far as they were concerned.

Manuel regarded both men carefully. "You say you are from Nogales? I say you are from a little further north." Manuel nodded to Rosita.

Rosita snatched Chachu's hat from his head. The scout's long hair tumbled down passed his chest.

"¡Dios Mio! Apaches!" Rosita hissed the word and lifted her leg and long skirt to retrieve a six-inch stiletto. Chachu didn't hesitate—a woman like Rosita might have experience with a knife—he delivered a right cross that dropped the Mexican woman unconscious to the floor.

Manuel repeated the scream at nearly the same moment as Rosita: "Apaches!" and ducked under the counter.

Roving Wolf acted instinctively too. He ran toward the bar and launched himself over the counter just as Manuel popped up with a shotgun. The scout's momentum toppled Manuel backward against the wall. Glass from the back counter shattered under the impact. Roving Wolf wrenched the shotgun from Manuel's hands.

"I am Comanche, not Apache!" exclaimed the usually more sedate Roving Wolf as he smashed the shoulder stock of the gun onto the bridge of Manuel's nose knocking him unconscious.

Rosita's initial startled cry attracted the attention of all five cantina patrons but it was Chachu's fist to her face that inspired the two pool players and the two young men to action. The only move made by the lone drunkard at the bar was a shot glass to his lips—even Roving Wolf's nearby acrobatics hadn't interfered with that important movement.

The old man was closest. Chachu blocked the swinging pool cue with his arm and side kicked the man with a cowboy boot heel to the gut, sending him back against the wall near the swinging saloon doors. The old man's pool partner lowered his head and barreled straight for Chachu but his fat belly made his movements sluggish and the scout easily juked left and side-stepped the charge, delivering a powerful elbow to the jaw of the Mexican as he stumbled passed.

The young men from the far table rushed to the action. One of the youths charged around the first pool table to the right while his friend ran left around the same table; that route took the young man near the bar counter. Roving Wolf leapt over the bar as the youth passed. The

Comanche scout used his left arm to pivot over the counter leaving his right arm free to grab at the neck of the Mexican and take him down with a horse-collar tackle.

The second youth ran into a stiff jab from Chachu but the man's flailing arm managed to grab Chachu's outstretched arm and momentum took both combatants to the floor. Both American scouts were now on the ground, each pummeling one of the younger patrons. The pot-bellied man shook off enough of the dizzying effects of the elbow to the jaw to lunge for Chachu. The middle-aged man threw a roundhouse left into the back of Chachu's head. Chachu smiled when he heard the man's hand crack. The Mexican was on his knees holding his broken hand and whimpering when Chachu's right fist broke the man's already cracked jaw and sent him slumping to the floor.

Roving Wolf regained his feet and stood over the semi-conscious body of the man he incapacitated. Chachu's last two opponents where in a similar state moaning and bleeding on the ground.

During the commotion, a young pre-teen Mexican boy emerged from the rear storeroom and grabbed a pan from the cooking station.

"Brother!" Chachu's warning shout came too late for Roving Wolf who felt the frying pan slam into his buttocks. Roving Wolf whirled around but pulled his punch when he saw his grade school attacker. Instead of throwing the punch, he shoved the boy to the floor and told him not to move. The boy fixed on Roving Wolf's Comanche hair braids swinging free after his hat was lost behind the bar in the attack on Manuel. Roving Wolf didn't see any fear in the child's eyes—and the boy still held the frying pan over his head ready to strike.

Chachu turned just in time to take a surprisingly powerful punch to the face from the old man who had been doubled over catching his breath after the kick to his stomach. The senior seized the initiative and shoved

Chachu awkwardly through the swinging saloon doors. Roving Wolf saw the action and couldn't help the grin that formed. His friend deserved that one. He recovered and reseated his hat, not bothering to hide his braids. Roving Wolf picked up the shotgun and used it to club the old fashioned phone into pieces. He took a tequila bottle from the rear counter and set it on the bar in front of the inebriated patron who quietly sat through the entire affair. The man grunted a thank you.

Roving Wolf, shotgun in hand, stepped over the youth he had beaten and walked toward the swinging doors. He felt for his pistol to make sure it hadn't fallen loose and watched the old man, now in his path, back away and give Roving Wolf the room to exit, but not without spitting forth a slew of anti-Apache epithets. Roving Wolf didn't bother correcting the old man's misidentification of his tribal affiliation and instead walked around the two patrons and Rosita, all still unconscious on the floor between the two pool tables and near the cantina entrance. He turned to survey the damage and throw one last icy glare at the old man and little boy, then pushed through the doors and jogged to the Humvee which Chachu already had running.

Roving Wolf threw the shotgun into the night and climbed into the passenger seat. Chachu laughed as he pulled back into the roadway.

"I don't know why you laugh, brother. You were just beaten by an old man. And were you not the one who lectured the men about being discrete?"

"I guess we just don't look much like Mexicans. Better take a look behind us, brother."

Roving Wolf turned to look over his shoulder. The Mexican boy was running after them. He threw the frying pan which impacted the Humvee with a harmless but loud clank. Roving Wolf looked at Chachu's dark, laughing silhouette and he couldn't help but break into uncontrollable laughter of his own.

The two US Army scouts, fresh from their bar brawl, raced into the hills to plan their return scout that would shadow the right flank of the Mexican army as it marched north to invade their country.

37.

"Hurry up, baby. They are pulling out." Tom stood in the Biltmore parking lot holding the heavy passenger door of the Humvee open for Jenny. Jenny jogged out of the lobby with baggy jeans—she couldn't stand the feel of tight jeans like Sun Rain wore—sneakers and a tee shirt. In her hand she brought a light jacket for use in the cool later evening hours.

"Thank you, Tommy." Jenny slid into the passenger seat.

Tom lowered the door's ballistic glass panel for ventilation since the Humvee was not a fully up-armored version equipped with air conditioning. He shoved the door closed, its hinges squeaking in angry protest against the weight of the improvised armor—a rusty half inch iron plate bolted onto the door panel.

Tom and Jenny were alone in the truck. They were set to follow the two Humvees driven by Running Bear and Cloud Rider who between them carried as passengers Sun Rain, White Hawk and Little Deer. The group was part of a larger convoy transporting the war chiefs and their parties down to the primary Treaty Tribe gathering area at Casa Grande, fifty miles south of Phoenix. Tens of thousands of the Treaty Tribe warriors had camped at Casa Grande to await the results of the war council. Now that the council confirmed all eight Treaty Tribes were committed to battle, the warriors of the various nations planned a massive war dance at Casa Grande before deploying to their assigned areas on the battlefield.

Jenny noted the late afternoon temperature was near eighty degrees as the convoy motored down I-10. "This short drive is going to be the longest period we have had alone together in quite a while."

"Yes, I know, honey. It's been crazy with all the war preparations. Is everything coming along okay with the medical support facilities?"

Jenny didn't want to talk about the coming war. "Tom, is there really no chance we can go home?"

Tom shook his head. "No, they aren't going to let us back into a dome, or if they do, we would be cut off from the Net. How could we live like that?"

Jenny sat back and watched the dry desert flora drift by. "So, no honeymoon dome for us?"

Tom looked at Jenny and smiled. "I am afraid not, baby. We can have one of the empty big estates in Phoenix or Scottsdale. Governor Jeffers will perform the wedding ceremony."

"You already arranged that?"

"No details, but I confirmed that he would be happy to do the ceremony if we want him to."

Sun Rain was right, Jenny thought. Tom was committed to her. He was also committed to fighting in the war. "Tom, do you really have to fight? Why fight for the government that is taking away our life?"

"I am not fighting for the government, honey. I will fight to remain free in the land outside the domes. If the Mexicans win, there will be no freedom outside. We already know there is no freedom inside."

Tom followed the convoy west on State Route 287 through Casa Grande. The small town was crowded with warriors of all Treaty Tribe nations. Beyond the town, tipis blanketed the land in every direction. The convoy stopped at the edge of the giant tipi city. The large, former agricultural land west of town had been selected as the site of the dance. Great makeshift horse corrals were setup throughout the area as were feed and water stations. Fire pits had been dug over several square miles and firewood gathered, cut, and stacked at the ready by each pit.

Tom hopped out of the Humvee and helped Jenny out as well. The couple caught up with their friends from the trail.

"Too bad your brother can't be here, Sun Rain," Tom said.

"Yes, his scout took him deep into Mexico. I am sure he and his old Chiricahua friend will return with many bold and bawdy tales of their mission."

Jenny climbed up onto the hood of the Humvee to get a better look at the buzz of activity and the sea of people everywhere. "It's wonderful to see so many people in one place—and so many women? I thought only men traveled to the battle zone."

"Women keep the warriors in the field by helping with the distribution of food, water, and ammunition supplies. They also help mend weapons and nurse wounded warriors. Women are an important component of the war party," explained Sun Rain. "Some even do a little bit of fighting," she added with a grin.

Jenny smiled too when she noticed White Hawk standing in front of his father near Running Bear's Humvee. The Lakota war chief's hands rested on his son's shoulders. She wondered what a father says to his son as they are both about to go to war.

Jenny bent down and grabbed Tom's shoulders and he caught her as she jumped off the truck. "Looks like you are feeling better, Jen."

"I am. Thank you."

As the sun set on the western horizon, the fire pits were lit throughout the dance area. Medicine chiefs chanted away any mischievous spirits. Most of the warriors had stripped down to breechcloths and little else. Most also carried one or more traditional weapons—an axe, or war club, a lance or bow; the modern rifles, machine guns, and grenade launchers where left in vehicles or tipis.

The mix of so many different cultures led to a wide variety of dress and accessories among the warriors. Many of the men had applied war paint to their faces and bodies. The Lakota and Cheyenne chiefs and sub chiefs sported war bonnets flowing with eagle feathers as did the Kiowa and Arapaho. Comanche warriors had one or two eagle feathers attached to their braided hair. Apaches wore personalized beaded head bands. Some of the Navajo were draped in splendid hand-woven capes full of symmetrical patterns of color. Cherokee warriors wore eagle or turkey feathers and bear claws and painted their faces and bodies in menacing patterns of black war paint designed to intimidate and frighten their adversaries.

At dusk the war dances began. The style of dance and accompanying song and music varied by culture. The meaning and reasons for the dance varied by culture too. None of the dancing was intended to intimidate the enemy. For some cultures the dance was used to solidify the bonds among the warriors, for other cultures the dance built up a supply of strength and courage for use on the battlefield, still others danced the war dance to prepare the warriors' hearts for participating in the disharmony caused by war.

With everyone deploying to their battlefield assignment after the ceremony, the scout party companions said their goodbyes before jumping into the fray. Running Bear and Little Deer wished Tom and Jenny luck and left to find one of the Cherokee fire pits. Cloud Rider took his leave, then White Hawk bade the couple goodbye and followed his father into the maze of fire pits and dancing.

"We should return to the stronghold in a couple hours," Sun Rain suggested. "I will meet you two back here?"

"The dance will be completed?" Jenny asked.

"No, Jenny. The dancing will continue until dawn," answered Sun Rain.

"Oh, okay. Then yes, we will see you back here in two hours." Those were the most words Jenny and Sun Rain had shared since the incident in Sun Rain's room at the Biltmore.

Tom and Jenny left Sun Rain by the Humvee and wandered passed many of the bonfires. Every fire seemed to have a different style of dance, even among groups of the same nation. Some of the war dances were conducted at a fast, energetic pace, others were slower and more solemn. Sometimes only a single dancer moved to the rhythm of many singers and musicians; around other fires the opposite held true—dozens of dancers moving to the sounds of only one singer of lyrics.

The music of war song filled the night. Buffalo skin drums pounded out beats fast and slow. Bells and rattles clanked and shook rhythmically around the fires. Everywhere flutes of wood and others of eagle bone pushed out tunes from happy to haunting. According to the medicine chiefs, the smoke and wafting embers generated by the Dance of a Thousand Fires would cover the army with a blanket of courage and hope.

Tom helped Jenny drape her jacket around her shoulders as the day's desert heat fled from the cool night. They were surrounded by the chanting and the dancing of tens of thousands of warriors that generated continuous pulses of energy—like electricity in human form. Tom felt an unexplainable glow inside himself, like he was being recharged by the mystery and magic of the moment. After two hours he and Jenny rejoined Sun Rain for the drive back to Phoenix. The beauty and spirit and fellowship they left behind were inspiring. It was difficult to believe that the brutal business of war would soon scar the hearts everyone.

38.

Steven stepped through his bedroom door into the clean gray cavern of the dome central living space. The nighttime lighting had been tweaked to a slightly brighter than normal glow. Through the gloom he saw his mother sitting alone in her usual seat at the family dining table. He assumed the cup from which she sipped held her nightly hot chocolate made from the powder of a ration package.

Steven approached the table and Cynthia turned her head toward her son. "Up late again, Steven?"

"Yes." Steven walked around the table to the kitchen intent on accomplishing his coffee resupply mission. "I'm sorry we haven't had much time to catch up, mom," said Steven, with his back to his mother as he prepared his cup. "I have been busy searching the Net for more Black Shine signs and more insight about the motives of our government both now and earlier this century."

Steven microwaved the instant coffee and brought his cup to the table. Instead of taking his usual seat across from Cynthia, he sat in his father's seat at the head of the table closer to his mother.

Cynthia set down her cup. "You know, I am still upset you didn't let me talk to Tom two weeks ago."

Steven hunched over his coffee and blew into the rising steam. "Come on, mom. You were asleep and I didn't even know I would actually see Tom on the other end and I only had moments before the connection had to be terminated for the safety of all of us." Steven also knew that his mother took her anti-depressant before bed because the drug made her drowsy and it was difficult to rouse her to wakefulness once the pill took effect.

"Steven, please be careful on the Net. You don't know who could be watching or listening."

"Mom, I'm a Net cop for the FCC. I know the tricks. I am part of them."

"Yes, but don't assume you are privy to all the powers of the government."

"Understood. But so you know, mom, I have seen no evidence that the government routinely pries into personal email or spies on individuals using hidden microphones and cameras. I know you are saying that such activity might occur, but I am not sure of that. It's true that content about the Outside is censored but that is done for health reasons. We know how hard doming was on the first generation."

"Steven, what has Tom found on the Outside that has him so intent on taking us out of here?"

"I don't know, mom. There wasn't time to go into that. He said the world out there is beautiful."

Cynthia scoffed. "Beautiful?...yet here he is about to go to war and maybe die? I don't understand that. I don't see the beauty in that."

"I don't either. Tom was happy in here. Something significant had to happen to change that."

"Is the world outside really so special that brief exposure to it can change your whole life and alter one's thinking in such a profound fashion?" Cynthia wondered.

"If it is, maybe the government is justified in scrubbing pictures and references to the Outside in order to prevent Dome Syndrome."

"If it's that wonderful out there, why are we in here, Steven? Why would people let anything chase them into a dome if the Outside is so beautiful? I don't understand that."

"Maybe they didn't appreciate the beauty and freedom they had? I don't know, maybe Black Shine has some answers. They don't fully trust me yet—and the feeling is mutual by the way—but I am beginning to make some headway. Much of the discussion I encounter on the Net seems to center on the question: Is it Man's nature to be free, or no? I am also seeing the framing of an argument pitting Individualism versus Collectivism. It's all enough to make my head spin, really."

"Can you give me the gist?"

Steven explained as much to his mother as he understood himself. Collectivists believed in the laudatory goals of everyone in the world having enough to eat, everyone having a home, everyone having medical care, and no more war. Individualists believed in personal liberty and responsibility, in freedom of choice in all things, in a mind and spirit free to follow any road unrestricted by another's rules and conditions. The collectivist vision depended on an all-powerful government redistributing resources evenly to everyone. The individualist vision depended on just the opposite, as little government as possible. Collectivists believed individualists were selfish, irresponsible anarchists. Individualists thought collectivists were arrogant oppressors of liberty. Not surprisingly, the two diametrically opposed worlds clashed with each other often in dramatic fashion. The differences were so striking and so engrained and so intransigent, Steven was beginning to wonder if there was some genetic factor that determined which path a person followed rather than a set of environmental factors guiding the choice.

"Tom asked me to start working on a plan to get all of us out of here."

Cynthia mulled the life-changing significance of Steven's words. She looked into the eyes of her oldest son and wondered how effectively her doubt moved from her heart onto her face.

"Do you know when you will speak with Tom again?" Cynthia asked hopefully.

"No, I don't. Black Shine says the Army scout who has the communication device we were using is on a spy mission deep inside Mexico. Tom should be in the Phoenix stronghold by now. My Black Shine contact doesn't want to risk making contact through the stronghold leader's satellite phone because he is concerned the stronghold leadership might be too close to the domer government."

"You be sure to let me see Tom next time, Steven."

"Yes, mom."

39.

The alarm applet popped onto every display screen in the dome. The thick yellow border around the message window blinked on and off and was accompanied by three urgent sounding beeps that repeated every five seconds from audio speakers.

Brian Phillips had seen the alarms before. The fact that his wife hadn't answered the call told him she was asleep in her office—not surprising since Barbara wasn't getting much sleep during the overnight hours lately. Occasional insomnia was just part of the job. He quickly crossed the dome interior and entered the presidential work space.

"Barbara," he called while shaking her shoulder.

Barbara Phillips felt the tug of her husband's hand then heard the distinct sound of the message alarm. She rose into a sitting position on the couch while trying to shake the fog from her head.

"Thank you, Brian. Sorry."

Brian Phillips left and closed the door behind him.

President Phillips picked up the keyboard that had fallen to the floor and issued a verbal command to: "Answer alarm." Seconds later a window framing the face of her chief of staff, Betty Saville, opened on the screen.

"Hi, Betty, sorry about that. What's going on?"

"You are going to have me worrying about your health again, Barb."

"Nonsense. Just didn't get much sleep last night. Now, what's up?"

"Mexican forces are on the move. Take a look."

President Phillips watched as a series of aerial photographs flashed onto her display.

"General Pruitt just sent these. Surveillance photos from the Global Hawk unmanned aerial vehicle we have flying 60,000 feet over Sonora and Chihuahua."

"Thank you, Betty. Better set up an NSC meeting for this evening."

* * * *

Sam Yazzie and several of his Navajo infantry brothers sat in the shade of a large mesquite tree whose deep roots had found water that had managed to percolate down through the desert floor after running off the Sierra Pinta Mountains and onto the Mohawk Valley of southern Arizona. Sam was accustomed to the relatively cooler desert of Arizona's high country in the north. He thought the heat here in the Valley of the Sun was oppressive considering it was only spring.

Sam watched his squad leader, Pete Avalina, jog toward him and his resting rifle team buddies. "Everybody up!" ordered Sergeant Avalina. "We're going to form up back at the battalion command post south of Hill 1498. Come on, let's go men!"

"What's going on, Sarge?" asked Sam while placing his desert boonie hat back over the bristles of his close-cropped black hair.

"We are marching east toward Lukeville to get on the transport trucks."

Sam and the rest of the battalion had already been briefed on their dangerous mission to occupy the hills around the Mexican town of Caborca, but that operation wasn't supposed to happen for another couple weeks.

"But Sarge, we still have two weeks." Sam yelled at Avalina's back as he jogged away.

Sergeant Avalina halted abruptly before disappearing over the ridge and looked over his shoulder to bark at the young soldier. "Private Yazzie, the Mexicans are not operating according to your timetable. They are on the move sooner than expected. Pack up and get down to the company assembly area asap. We move out in ten mikes."

Their squad leader vanished below the ridge into a rising cloud of dust. Sam and his rifle team shared looks of surprise for a split second then every man rushed to throw on his desert battle fatigue shirt and rucksack.

The war was on and they had a leading role in it.

* * * *

Every evening Generals Tanner and Singer conducted their daily synchronization briefing, but this meeting was different—Mejias' forces were on the move. That fact was clearly documented by Global Hawk reconnaissance photos and confirmed by clandestine Apache scouts operating near Hermosillo.

Mark Tanner stood in front of his display screen with input stylus in hand arranging the newest Global Hawk pictures. Kathy Singer's eyes examined the pictures on her screen even as her colleague positioned them for analysis.

"Three Mexican army elements moving in Sonora, just like we figured," said Tanner. "The left flank is a tank force moving north along the coast toward Puerto Libertad; in the center is the main body infantry force marching toward Caborca; and there is a right flank infantry force moving north along the base of the Sierra Madre toward Nogales. There is no sign that they are using motor transport for troops, no doubt due to fuel shortages and lack of spare parts."

"Yes," affirmed Kathy Singer. "And I see two large infantry forces in Chihuahua marching northeast toward the Rio Grande and my sparse lines."

"Yeah, we expected that, too."

"Still think they will stop at the river, Mark?"

"I sure hope so, Kathy. Look at this right flank force moving up to Nogales. That's got to be almost a hundred thousand men—twice the size we expected. He must have been garrisoning more men than we thought in houses among the citizens of Hermosillo. That last Apache scout to Hermosillo called it right."

"Why do you think the tanks are moving so slowly? I assume he doesn't want to outrun his infantry in the center?" Singer mused.

"Probably."

"Do you think he will top off fuel in Puerto Libertad? There is a refinery in there."

"No, that's still 150 miles from the border. They are clearly preparing for a massive refueling here at Puerto Peñasco. That's only forty miles from the border so topping off there will give his tanks plenty of fuel to fight with and to terrorize the dome farm."

"Still planning a warm reception for them, Mark?"

Tanner smiled. "Oh, yeah." The coordinates of the power plant and refueling station at Puerto Peñasco were already programmed into three Tomahawk cruise missiles ready to ground launch from Tinker Air Force Base in Oklahoma City. Reaper drones loaded with Hellfire II's were standing by at Holloman Air Force Base in Alamogordo, New Mexico and Creech Air Force Base near Las Vegas, Nevada—a warm reception indeed.

* * * *

President Phillips and the other members of the National Security Council each watched their wall-mounted video screens in their dome homes as JCS Chairman Pruitt drew colored lines and arrows to indentify General Mejias' forces and indicate their expected lanes of advance.

"So when does the fighting begin and how is this going to unfold, Joshua?"

"Madam President, we are at the end of Day One of the Mexican march north to Arizona and northeast to Texas. The columns are all stopping for the night after moving about thirty miles. Except for the larger than expected right flanking force, the Mexicans are behaving according to our expectations. At this pace, Mejias' Sonoran forces will be in Caborca in three days and on the Arizona border three days after that. Mejias' forces in Chihuahua will be on the Texas border in only three days from now."

General Pruitt cleared his throat and continued, "If nothing changes, we are about two and a half days from first contact with the enemy because our plans still call for sending in the Navajo strike force into the hills around Caborca before Mejias reaches the town. Our strike force isn't quite ready for transport because Mejias is moving sooner than anticipated but troops and transports are on their way to Lukeville for staging right now. The run to Caborca by the tractor trailer troop transports shouldn't be more than two hours drive down Mexico Highway 2 so we should have plenty of time to catch up with our plan's timetable. We do have to keep an eye on those tanks along the coast. We expect them to stop in Puerto Peñasco to refuel before attacking into Arizona. If they decide to let their tanks get ahead of their infantry, first contact with the enemy could happen sooner because we absolutely must hit their armored force as they reach Puerto Peñasco. We can't let them re-fuel."

Vice President Sullivan addressed the Chairman. "General, do we still think Mejias won't be expecting our infantry strike into Mexico or our airstrike on Puerto Peñasco?"

"We can't be certain, Mr. Vice President, but I personally think Mejias doesn't expect us to cross the international border in a preemptive strike because of all the condemnation that will come our way from the United Nations."

"Carter, is our UN ambassador ready to make our case on that?"

"Yes," confirmed Secretary of State Mason. "Ambassador Barnham will address the full Assembly tomorrow and will tell the world that Mexico has two large armies moving to the border and that the United States intends to defend herself."

"You would think we would already have the upper hand," commented Vice President Sullivan. "I can't believe the UN bought the Mexican story that those troops who snuck into Texas and attacked the dome transport were merely renegade deserters acting on their own."

"Don, I can't believe that you can't believe the UN let Mexico slide on that," chided his old friend Judith Zaranski, Secretary of the Treasury.

"Thank you for the briefing, General Pruitt. You will let me know when it is time to move our troops across the border into Mexico, won't you?"

"Absolutely, Madam President."

40.

Mark Tanner propped his legs up on the coffee table and leaned back into his couch to view the real-time video feed from the Predator drone flying south from Sonoita to Puerto Peñasco above Mexico Highway 8. The road was virtually deserted thanks to the US Army Psychological Warfare (Psyops) Division's pamphlet drop yesterday warning Mexican citizens near the border that provocative action by General Mejias forced the United States to take defensive military measures.

Tanner watched the drone loiter briefly over the port town flying at 15,000 feet to avoid any portable anti-aircraft missiles that Mexican troops might have in the area. Mexico wasn't supposed to have anti-aircraft missiles in its inventory but General Tanner lost a Predator yesterday on Day Two that was flying at 5,000 feet while keeping a watch on the same tanks moving up from Puerto Libertad. Evidence pointed to a shoulder-fired SAM, something akin to a Stinger. Tanner believed the missing drone was more evidence of Chinese involvement. The US stopped selling Stingers decades ago. The batteries on old US-supplied Stinger missiles would be dead by now. China, on the other hand, had been producing Stinger knock-off's for many years.

The pilot controlling the Predator drone turned the unmanned aircraft east and then southeast to follow Highway 3 that paralleled the coast along the Gulf of California—that's when Tanner saw the first tank. The Predator operator saw it too and zoomed in on the armored vehicle.

Tanner sprang upright and leaned closer to his screen. The tank had a small rounded, low-profile turret and five road wheels under its tracks with a gap between the first and second wheels. Looks just like an old Russian T-54, thought Tanner. That meant it had to be a Chinese Type 59 which was based on the Russian design. Instead of the red communist star, the turret of this tank sported the red, white, and green flag of Mexico.

The camera zoomed out again to show a long line of tanks traveling behind the first. The heavy war machines drove beside the highway rather than on it to avoid further damage to the road surface. A quick mental calculation put the lead tank in Puerto Peñasco in half an hour.

Mark Tanner smiled. Cruise missiles from Tinker and a squadron of Hellfire-laden Reapers from Creech were already in the air and on their way to the Mexican port city. Tanner suspected that Mejias had rushed the tanks forward after learning that the original observing Predator had been shot down. Clearly Mejias thought to gain the advantage of surprise by moving the tanks through the evening, unobserved. Not a bad plan thought Tanner but luckily for the Americans, the tank column hadn't escaped the notice of a high-flying US Air Force Global Hawk UAV—Tanner was ready.

The video feed from the Predator suddenly went black.

General Tanner jumped off the couch and tapped the link to Brigadier General Barney Malcolm, his chief of operations and chief battle planner.

"Barney!"

"I see it too, sir. My team is contacting the UAV pilot as we speak."

"Damn it, Barney, if the Mexicans have portable Chinese AA, that's going to put a serious crimp in our operations."

Barney Malcolm read the report just coming in. "General, the Predator pilot reports sudden loss of signal and all telemetry consistent with an enemy missile strike on our bird."

Tanner paced back and forth and chewed on his input stylus.

Malcolm watched the video camera track his pacing boss and then continued, "General, we have drone contingency plans in the event of enemy portable SAM's but that drone was flying at 15,000 feet which means the Chinese have an improved missile with an unknown ceiling."

"Recommendations, Barney?"

"Sir, they are unlikely to hit the three inbound cruise missiles—they travel too low and too fast. But those Reaper UAV's coming down from Nevada might be vulnerable. Hellfire II's have a range of five miles, but that's pushing it. We better have the Reaper pilots fly in at 22,500 feet and hope the Chinese missile can't climb that high."

"Alright, pass the word. Is the Global Hawk close enough to observe?"

"No sir, it's doing its run over Chihuahua right now."

"So I have to hold my breath for an hour before we know if we can use our missiles to hit those tanks?"

"Yes, sir"

"Perfect," replied the angry commander.

* * * *

The Kenworth T700 diesel raced down Mexico Highway 2 with a trailer jammed full of anxious Navajo foot soldiers. Their destination was the high ground surrounding the Mexican town of Caborca, a key re-supply point for the Mexican army as it marched north. Two thousand Navajo and 300 Apache men were being planted in the path of two hundred thousand Mexicans. The idea was to force the Mexicans to divert around the town instead of topping off supplies. American planners were gambling the Mexican leader was impatient and rash enough to write off Caborca and drive on to Arizona which was less than 90 miles and three days march north of the town.

Sam Yazzie had been standing for an hour and a half because the men of his platoon were packed into the trailer too tightly to sit. Their rucksacks were either piled near the rear door or hung out of the way on hooks that dangled from the trailer ceiling. The trailer wasn't air conditioned so its poor ventilation was augmented by holes punched hastily through the thin metal skin. The driver remotely piloting the truck down the highway was doing her best to steer around potholes in the poorly maintained road but the men in the truck would be hard pressed to believe such care was being taken considering how often they bounced, sometimes violently, up and down inside the trailer. But speed was of the essence. They had to reach the cover of the hills and dig in before the Mexicans arrived or they would be crushed by the advancing army.

There were a number of other big rigs in the fast moving convoy. Some of the trailers contained nervous horses of the small number of Apache and Navajo cavalry that accompanied the infantry force. Eight large water tankers also followed in the convoy. The water tankers were critical to keeping the strike force operational in the field far from friendly forces.

Sam looked up with envy to Sergeant Avalina who sat on top of a group of large plastic crates piled against the forward end of the trailer. The squad leader's perch kept him free of the crush of men below.

"What's in the boxes, Sarge? That isn't ammo or food."

The squad leader leaned over and pointed to the tiny markings stenciled on the front side of the crate. The label contained a lot of numbers and abbreviations but only one group of words that Sam readily recognized: "PSYOPS."

"Psychological warfare stuff?" Sam was puzzled.

"We will be briefed later," said Sergeant Avalina.

Sam knew that was the sergeant's way of saying he didn't know either so just shut up and leave him alone.

A few minutes later they were slowing down noticeably, then came the big crunch and the trailer rocked back and forth almost to the point of tipping over. The tractor-trailer rig continued forward at a much slower and bumpier pace.

Sergeant Avalina cupped his hand and yelled over the noise in the trailer, "We are off the road and climbing into the mountains as far as the terrain will permit this truck to go. After that we pile out and hump it the rest of the way."

After an hour of gut-wrenching bounces and scrapes the truck's 700-horsepower diesel shut down. Platoon sergeant Galen threw open the rear doors; he was as anxious as anyone to escape the stuffy overcrowded trailer. Men grabbed their packs and scrambled out into the hot sun. Dusty hills nearly devoid of vegetation surrounded the men. One of the water tankers had backed into a ravine and was being camouflaged with desert tan tarpaulins. Further down the line of trucks, Apache cavalrymen were dodging angry horses bolting out from their transport trailers.

Sam was one of the unlucky men close enough to the Psyops crates to be volunteered to unload the heavy crates and carry them to a staging area. The balance of the day was spent unloading supplies and helping to dig a company command post into the side of the mountain. Sam was hot, and tired, and hungry—and the shooting war was going to start at any moment.

* * * *

General Kathleen Singer stood in front of her large display screen and tapped her finger on the "Mark Tanner" link to join her colleague for the showdown south of the Altar Desert with the Mexican tanks. She anxiously followed developments at Puerto Peñasco and with the advancing armored force.

"How soon, Mark?"

"Two minutes, Kathy. Here is the video link from the lead Reaper."

"Thanks, Mark." Singer tapped the link when it appeared on her display a second later. "Still too far away for much detail but I see…maybe two dozen tanks neatly lined up for refueling?"

"Yeah, that looks to be about right. I see from the Global Hawk that the Chihuahuan troops are holding at the river—-so far, so good, eh?"

"I am keeping my fingers crossed there, Mark."

"Stand by, Kathy. We are about to mark Day Three with the first American shots of the war."

The three Tomahawk cruise missiles launched from Oklahoma sped across the Mexican desert at over 500 miles per hour and only 110 feet of the ground. Computer controls and GPS signals guided each missile to its target. The armament package of each missile was a 1,600-pound load out of "Mega-T" high explosive that packed a punch twelve times that of the same weight of TNT.

"Missile, missile!" General Tanner shouted as the Reaper drone's video camera caught the engine glow of the streaking Tomahawk. One second later a huge ball of orange flame erupted over the petroleum sludge burning electric power plant on the coastline.

Another cruise missile detonated directly over the refueling point, then a third powerful explosion seconds later. The power plant and fueling station were both engulfed in a raging sea of hot flames fanned by desert winds.

"Nice!" Mark Tanner jumped up and punched the air. "Take that, Mejias!"

Video from the cameras of multiple airborne Reaper drones continued to roll. The drones were flying almost five miles high which meant the Reaper hunter-killers would have to be right on top of the remaining tanks before launching any Hellfire missiles that would be operating at the extreme limit of their range.

"Hey, Mark, I am seeing Hellfire launches...good news!"

General Tanner watched video of multiple Hellfire II's rain down onto the Mexican tanks. The neat column of tanks south of the refueling station broke apart as individual tanks scattered in all directions. Tank crews already stopped near the fuel depot were desperately restarting their engines and trying to flee the deadly rain of missiles. Several tanks were now burning from Hellfire impacts.

Mark Tanner had just started a dead tank tally when the first Reaper video camera went black. "Damn it! There's one Reaper destroyed."

The UAV pilots had been briefed on the possibility of high flying portable SAM's. Each of the Reaper pilots pushed their throttles hard over and targeted and fired on as many tanks as possible as fast as possible. Fortunately the version of Hellfire they were using was a fire-and-forget missile that needed no assistance to home in on its target once fired.

The long white streaks of Hellfire missile contrails filled the desert sky over Puerto Peñasco, but so too did high altitude explosions of Mexican missile impacts against US Reaper drones.

* * * *

"So what's the casualty report, Mark?" asked General Singer.

"Only three Reapers out of twelve survived. One is loitering in the area for recon purposes; the other two are flying to Luke Air Force Base instead of returning to

Creech since Luke has a good supply of laser guided bombs and JDAM's which can be dropped from much higher altitude."

Both commanders were fully aware that the Reaper airframe only allowed for three 500-pound bombs whereas they could carry fourteen Hellfire II's. That fact meant far fewer enemy targets could be engaged per Reaper sortie—not a good turn of events for American forces.

"We took a big bite out of the tank force, though. One hundred twenty one tanks reached Puerto Peñasco but only thirty-nine made it out."

"I see that, Mark, but they haven't turned around. They are driving north despite not being able to refuel?"

"Yes, they have obviously been ordered to conduct a one-way mission, a kamikaze blitzkrieg across the Altar Desert. We may lose a few domes—correction, we may lose a few families." Tanner's stomach twisted into a painful knot—again. "I have already alerted the old man who will relay the situation to Pruitt, the Secretary, and the President."

41.

Major Fernando Gomez-Ruiz was now *Colonel* Fernando Gomez-Ruiz, promoted during the last radio transmission by none other than General Mejias himself. The Colonel was now the commander of the remaining Mexican tank force and had just been ordered to rush his tanks through any further enemy contact and destroy as many American domes as possible. Fernando knew it was a mission of no return but he was a career soldier and despite the despotic reputation of his President, Fernando, a loyal army officer, was compelled to follow orders. He believed Mexico would prevail in this war and he was proud to play a part in defeating the United States.

The Mexican army had little experience maneuvering with main battle tanks. Gomez-Ruiz was doing the best he could to keep the formation together as they crossed through the sand dunes. He kept his tanks close together so all could benefit from the protection provided by the three trucks loaded with infantrymen who stood ready to fire their Chinese SAM's at American aerial drones as directed by Mexican air defense radar that still operated in Puerto Peñasco despite the devastating cruise missile strikes.

Twenty minutes later, two more tanks in his task force had broken down leaving him with thirty-seven tanks positioned a mere twenty-five miles from the Arizona border and the first domes only two miles beyond that. They were out of the sand dune field now and able to cover ground faster. The Colonel stood with his torso jutting up out of the commander's hatch when he saw a tank on his right flank explode and jerk to a halt. Excited chatter filled the tank commander frequency. American Bradleys and Humvees armed with TOW anti-tank missiles were approaching his group from the right at roughly 2 o'clock.

Per General Mejias, Gomez-Ruiz urged his men forward at top speed. They were not to stop and engage the Americans. More American TOW missiles flew in from the right and found additional victims. The Colonel ordered a course change twenty degrees to the left hoping to avoid the brunt of the American force.

Twenty miles from the border he lost another tank but this one was on his far left flank. The Colonel shook his head while he scanned the desert, that casualty couldn't have been caused by an American missile, the range was too great. According to his anti-aircraft escort, only one aerial drone trailed them far to the rear—probably weaponless. Then another tank on his left flank exploded. Gomez-Ruiz cursed and realized the Bradleys and Humvees had pushed him into a mine field.

The Colonel ordered a course change 30 degrees to the right and charged on to Arizona, minefield be damned. He used the commander's frequency to order all tank commanders to fight into the domes and if they lost their squadron commander, to maneuver independently and destroy as many domes as possible.

His driver opened the throttle all the way and the radio headset he wore over his ears did little to muffle the sounds of the straining motor and the squeaking and clanking of the tank tracks that scraped over the road wheels. The border was getting closer by the minute but tanks continued to be lost to mines and missiles. The dust cloud to his front that had obscured the horizon was now thinning—bad news for Gomez-Ruiz because that meant the size of his attack force was dwindling fast. The Colonel's heart pounded a faster, stronger beat from the adrenaline surge created by the sight of the first rounded domes through his binoculars.

"We are over the border!" Gomez-Ruiz heard the excited voice of his driver rattle through his headset.

"Alberto, do you have a target?"

"Yes sir, ready to fire!" his gunner announced.

"Shoot!"

The 100mm main gun blasted a high explosive round down range. The Colonel was more confident that the limited vertical stabilization of the main gun would better ensure a hit on a stationary target than on the American vehicles chasing them. The few fellow tankers left in the formation followed his lead and began firing their main guns as they raced forward.

Gomez-Ruiz watched two domes explode under shell impacts and gleefully slapped his gauntleted hand against the armored skin of the tank turret. But the Colonel did not see the TOW missile that slammed into his tank robbing him of the chance to enjoy the moment—and ending his life.

42.

The cell phone Tom had been given buzzed in his pocket. The Phoenix stronghold operated only one communications cell that routed phone calls so Tom knew the call originated nearby.

"Hello?"

Jenny's voice sounded through the receiver. "Hi, Tom. Are you doing okay?"

"Just fine, honey." Tom was three miles away setting up safe houses, mapping escape routes, and plotting coordinates of likely enemy firing points in preparation for the heavy house-to-house urban warfare that was coming their way. "What's up?"

"Governor Jeffers is having a dinner and staff meeting and we are invited. Can you be back here in an hour?"

"Sure, Jen. Will do."

* * * *

Tom walked across the front parking lot toward the Biltmore lobby and noticed through the large patio windows that the Governor and guests were already arriving for dinner in the Aztec Room. Running late, Tom increased his pace to a jog and veered right toward the pool and the Paradise Wing so he could grab a fast shower and a change of clothes. Once dry and dressed in slacks, polo shirt, and shoes that were a bit too large, he quickly moved through the main building and into the dining room.

Jeffers was the first to greet Tom as he entered.

"Sorry for being late." Tom took the empty chair next to Jenny. The small party at the table was the same group as dinner that first night, minus their Indian friends who had deployed south to fight on the front lines. Mrs. Jeffers and Mrs. Briggs were absent as well.

"No, problem, Tom," said Jeffers. "You must be getting to know your way around Phoenix quite well now."

Tom laughed. "Well, this small section of the city anyway. How goes the hospital business, honey?"

"Busy."

Jenny looked tired but Tom didn't want to make that observation in front of the others.

"Jenny has been a great help," said Sara Saunders. "After dinner we are heading back to the hospital complex in the mountains."

"Preparations are going well all over the city," offered the younger Jeffers. "Sun Rain has been a big help to me setting up defenses on the eastern approaches in case the enemy swings behind Camelback Mountain and comes at us through Paradise Valley." Dan Jeffers lifted his glass to Sun Rain. "And thanks for all the hands-on weapons training." Dan winked at Sun Rain and set down his glass.

Tom glanced at both Dan Jeffers and Sun Rain and wondered what that exchange was all about.

Governor Jeffers took a quick sip of wine. "Yes, well, I want to thank everyone for all their hard work. I have made many rounds over the last few days thanking various teams of stronghold citizens but I haven't taken the time yet to appreciate my small core staff—which now includes our three guests from Texas!"

"Thank you, Governor," said Sun Rain. "You have so many wonderful people in your city. They are certainly dedicated to preserving what they can. Is there any chance the Mexicans won't come this way?"

Jeffers shook his head.

Bob Briggs had seen the reports from the field and offered a summary of the action in the south. "There is a large column of troops heading due north from Hermosillo directly to Nogales. From Nogales, terrain and roads point them right to Tucson where they pick up I-10 to Casa

Grande. Some of the force will likely turn east on I-8 and attack the northern domes. But some of that force will follow I-10 right into Phoenix—the military thinks so anyway, and so do I."

Security Chief Stan Felker added to the war briefing. "Some domes in the south were destroyed today."

"What!" Jenny's eyes widened as they fell on the security chief's dour expression but the rest of her body was frozen by shock. Destroyed domes meant murdered families. "I hadn't heard that. What happened?"

Colonel Holland nodded and explained what he knew from his Army contacts about the US attack on Puerto Peñasco and the suicide tank charge through the Altar Desert. The tanks had been attacked from the air at the refueling station, then harassed by Cherokee TOW missiles which pushed the tanks into a mine field. Two high flying UAV's with JDAM's (drones with GPS-guided bombs, Holland clarified) arrived at the last minute from Luke Air Force Base near Phoenix. Despite all the defensive measures, four of the 121 tanks battled close enough to lob armor piercing explosive rounds into the domes nearest the border. Navajo infantrymen smashed the last four tanks with shoulder-fired anti-tank missiles but not before the Mexican tanks destroyed twenty-two domes. The number of shattered dome homes was miniscule given the six million domes in the Arizona dome farm, but the fear generated by the suicide tank attack gave Mejias and the Mexican forces an important propaganda victory over the Americans.

A somber mood hung over the remainder of the dinner. Dr. Saunders and Jenny left for the mountain hospital and their departure broke up the rest of the party. Dan Jeffers lingered to talk with Sun Rain so Tom found himself walking alone, and annoyed, back to the Paradise Wing. He kicked off his shoes and dropped onto his bed. Tom didn't think about Jenny up in the hills, or about his defense work in the streets. His thoughts did not go to his family or to the war. All he could think about was Dan Jeffers flirting with Sun Rain.

* * * *

Tom was just beginning to drift toward sleep when the knock sounded on his door. His body was a sore, weary mass from head to toe and for a moment he wondered what harm would be done by ignoring the tapping. Tom sat up with a groan then shuffled to the door still dressed in his dinner slacks and shirt but minus the oversized shoes. Tom swung the door open and stopped breathing mid-breath at the sight of Sun Rain in a thong bikini that left little to the imagination.

"I came to take you for a swim."

"I don't know how to swim." Tom barely managed to complete the sentence then cursed himself for saying something so stupid. "And I don't have a swim…"

Sun Rain brought one hand from behind her back and dangled a tiny Speedo from her finger.

"…suit. Are you, kidding?" There wasn't enough cloth hanging from her finger to make a decent eye patch.

Sun Rain laughed and brought her other hand forward holding more modest mid-thigh bathing trunks.

Tom smiled. "You are a bad girl."

Sun Rain winked and threw the swimming trunks to Tom. "I will teach you how to swim—by the pool in five minutes." Sun Rain turned and sauntered down the hallway while Tom stood paralyzed and watching her in happy amazement. He was dressed in the swim trunks in under sixty seconds and even more amazing—he wasn't sore at all anymore.

Tom set a brisk pace for the short walk from the Paradise Wing to the pool right outside. Sun Rain was already in the pool, standing in three feet of water with her long black hair bundled and clipped on the top of her head.

The twilight air was beginning to cool when Tom walked to the edge of the pool. He certainly couldn't swim—or, more accurately, had never tried to swim—but he did have to admit that the shallow end of the pool had looked quite inviting on more than one occasion after coming back to the Biltmore tired and sweaty and sore from a long hot day preparing for war.

"Come on. Jump in!" exhorted Sun Rain.

Tom leaped from the ledge into the water. The coolness of the water was so unexpected; he stumbled forward and actually went completely under the surface—providing further shock, but exhilaration too.

Sun Rain waded forward, laughing at the surprise on Tom's face.

"Wow, that's cold! Why didn't you tell me?" Tom wiped the water from his eyes.

"I'm sorry, Tom. I forget that so many things are completely new to you."

"I don't know..." He looked suspiciously at Sun Rain's happy smirk.

Tom lowered his torso into the water as Sun Rain advised. He was soon accustomed to the cool water and experimenting with his buoyancy and moving his arms and legs under the water. Sun Rain had him dog paddling in only minutes. The couple splashed and played and Tom soon found himself hanging onto the edge of the pool ready to go into deeper water.

Sun Rain swam up to Tom and stood on her toes to keep her face above the water. Tom still reached the bottom flat-footed so when he saw how she struggled to keep her chin above the surface, he wrapped both his arms around Sun Rain's waist and lifted her off her toes and to a more comfortable height above the surface.

Sun Rain put her arms around Tom's shoulders, looked into his eyes and flashed her characteristic broad smile. "You know, you really looked cute this evening when Dan winked at me."

"You saw me? And just how did I look?"

"I think a little jealous."

Tom looked back into Sun Rain's warm, sparkling eyes. He couldn't argue with her spot-on intuition.

"There is nothing between me and Dan or me and anyone else. You know my heart, Tom. And I think I know yours."

Tom had drifted away from the pool wall and now felt Sun Rain pull her legs up to wrap her smooth, toned thighs around his waist. The hands she cupped on either side of his face warmed his cheeks. Sun Rain bent down to press her lips to his and the cold chill of the water and of the night air was lost to the passion of the long kiss.

Tom pulled away to catch his breath. He tried backing away but only pulled Sun Rain up the slope of the pool floor. Tom looked into Sun Rain's dark eyes that burned questions back at him, but he was too far down his chosen path. After a time Tom gripped her arms just below the shoulders and gently pushed Sun Rain backward; she responded by dropping her feet back onto the pool bottom.

Sun Rain looked away, her tears hidden among the droplets of pool water splashed onto her face. Chlorine burned Tom's eyes but a much sharper pain knotted his chest. He felt Sun Rain shiver at his soft, plaintive words.

"I am so sorry." Tom turned, he wanted to run but the heavy resistance put up by the water didn't allow him to do anything but struggle clumsily toward the steps. He climbed awkwardly out of the pool and walked cold and dripping and heart-sick back to his room.

43.

White Hawk walked his horse away from the water and feed station that friendly forces had prepositioned in the hills on the Arizona-Mexico border just east of the small Mexican border town of Sonoita. The Lakota scout climbed back onto his mount and began moving south with other members of the forward element of his father's army. Scores of his friends and anxious fellow soldiers rode on either side of him. The harsh environment of the hot, barren Sonoran Desert was completely foreign to all the Sioux warriors, nothing like the forested hills and grass-covered prairies of home—even the Badlands of South Dakota was more hospitable than this place where dust was born.

The lead element of Chief Red Thunder's army would join dismounted Cherokee mechanized infantry to form a defensive line many miles long midway between Caborca and the Arizona border. The line would face southeast which meant the warriors on the far right flank like White Hawk, would be the deepest into Mexico—about forty-five miles south of the international border. The warriors on the left flank would occupy positions twenty miles south of the international border.

Immediately forward of the Lakota and Cherokee line was the northern boundary of the "Kill Zone." The Kill Zone was a forty-mile deep, sixty-mile wide section of desert north of Caborca that the main body of the Mexican army was expected to traverse on its way to Arizona. No friendly American forces were permitted to operate in the Kill Zone. The only potential exception was a standby emergency relief force ready to charge to the rescue the Navajos at Caborca but only *if* such a risky maneuver was deemed necessary. Otherwise, everything moving in the Kill Zone would be considered a target and subject to attack by unmanned aerial vehicles, artillery, infantry, cruise missiles, or any other weapon scheduled for use on the battlefield by American forces.

White Hawk trotted his horse forward alongside his Lakota brothers. Many of the warriors, like White Hawk, still had their hand-decorated deerskin war shirts packed away out of the desert dust. If all went according to plan, he would be able to don his war shirt two days from now when first contact with Mexican forces was expected. White Hawk realized that by the time he faced the leading Mexican troops, he would be fighting an enemy that would have slogged through forty miles of US cruise missiles, Reaper and other UAV bombs and missiles, and massive artillery bombardment just for the privilege of reaching the line of dug-in, motivated Lakota and Cherokee warriors. It was hoped from there, a series of delaying actions would slow the Mexican forces enough that missiles, bombs, hunter-killer UAV's, and artillery would take a heavy toll and attrit the Mexican force to the point of ineffectiveness.

The desert air grew hotter and drier the farther south White Hawk went. Brittle sage brush tumbleweeds and eye-stinging dust blew across the cavalry column's path. Even his horse complained with annoyed grunts and sneezes to blow the dust from his nostrils.

During the mid-day rest stop, White Hawk's troop caught up with battlefront rumors that the Navajos at Caborca would soon be engaged by the enemy. As they neared the end of their march south, White Hawk's band of warriors passed through a long thick line of Cherokee Bradleys. The armored infantry fighting vehicles were busy emplacing M777 howitzers into firing position. The light weight, 155mm cannons were capable of extremely accurate fire and could shoot Excalibur GPS-guided rounds 25 miles into the Kill Zone within 5 meters of their targets. Colonel Holland swore by the big guns and White Hawk had witnessed the incredible long range accuracy of the guns for himself during the annual combat training at the All Nations Pow-wow in Oklahoma.

The scout noticed one of Colonel Holland's Special Forces officers rolling along in a Humvee setting and marking defensive fighting positions. White Hawk dismounted and began constructing the defensive position that would be his home for the next two days. His horse would be moved with the others back toward the rear for safety since this wasn't going to be the kind of battle that required cavalry charges—at least not if everything went according to plan.

* * * *

According to the topographical map issued to Sam Yazzie, the defensive fighting position he and Jim Bahe just dug near their hilltop was the southernmost position in the entire American army. No Diné brother was deeper into Mexico than Jim and he. While the sun set on his right, Sam squinted through binoculars at the cloud of dust miles ahead that marked the first of 200,000 Mexican soldiers coming his way. Jim piled heavy rocks around the lip of their foxhole for cover, oblivious to the approaching horde. Sam chose to let Jim's ignorance of the massing Mexican troops last for a few more peaceful moments.

It was still unclear if the Mexicans would try to push into Caborca during the night or wait until the morning. After one and a half days, the Navajo infantry force was well dug in on top of the southern range where Sam was camped as well as in the northern range where the balance of the Navajo force waited. Sam had watched a mounted Apache patrol gallop past the base of his hill a couple hours ago. The eager Apaches smiled and whooped wildly as they rode south to harass the lead Mexican element. Behind Sam, food, water, and ammunition was stored in hidden pockets through the hills and to his front, the

Psyops crates were placed several hundred yards down the hill away from American troop concentrations. As yet, no one had a clue about the mysterious contents of crates. Sam and his buddies hoped whatever was in the crates, it was something lethal and not just a bunch of propaganda leaflets.

Sergeant Avalina stopped by one last time before nightfall to check his squad's positions. "Yazzie, Bahe, if the Mexicans try moving into Caborca tonight things are going to get very crazy and very loud around here. There are four howitzers behind you that will fire around the clock. UAV's will be flying in dropping bombs. There will also be a few cruise missiles coming in. When those Mega-T charges let go, that whole valley is going to shake."

"What's in the Psyops crates, Sarge?"

"I still don't know. The platoon leaders and platoon sergeants have the controls that open the crates. From where we were told to position the crates, it must be something that is for close range and for a last resort. Don't worry about it. You guys stay alert. Fifty/fifty security. I want one man awake in every two-man position at all times. I heard your radio check but is your night vision working?"

"Checks out okay, Sarge."

"All right, I will see you guys in the morning." Avalina delivered the line with confidence to bolster the spirit of his brave men but he knew very well the odds were against his statement coming true.

44.

General Mejias took his dinner in the refurbished grand dining room of the private presidential residence in downtown Mexico City near the Palacio Nacional. Mejias preferred his home in the hills west of the city but the war was on and he wanted to be near the communications center in the Palace. As Mejias ate, the four general officers at the far end of the table stood in a semicircle and provided oral reports of the war's progress. The only other person seated at the large dining table was Lu Zhuàng who Mejias had invited for the evening meal.

Mejias stopped chewing his shredded pork tortilla long enough to listen to the account of the sprinting column of armor that obeyed his order to charge into the dome farm at all costs. The reporting officer heavily emphasized the destruction of multiple domes while only lightly touching on the fact that every Mexican tank was destroyed. Mejias was unconcerned about the losses and expected as much. The tanks hadn't cost the Mexican Treasury anything so he wasn't out any money. Nor was he concerned about the tankers who died in their machines—not even the brave Colonel who managed to hold things together long enough to destroy a few domes.

The destruction of at least one dome was all Mejias had hoped for. According to the last radio report, two or three dozen might be destroyed, but he needed video that he could show the world and he didn't have it. On the promise of reward money, several people from the nearby city of San Luis Rio Colorado had set out by car and by Cessna to shoot video but no one had yet returned with proof of the destruction. The success of the Chinese SAM's against the American aerial drones was another bright spot reported by his generals. Loss of power and petroleum infrastructure in Puerto Peñasco to cruise missiles, however, was indeed unfortunate.

The onset of hostilities had not gone according to his plan and Mejias had to credit the American President with having enough cajones to be the first to move across the international border. That outlaw action would give Mejias the upper hand in the United Nations although nothing immediately practical would come from being the "victim" of American aggression.

"General, my flanking force is on schedule to arrive at the border in two days. I will travel to Nogales for the crossing," reported General Trujillo.

"Very well, General. General Melendez, what is the status of the center column? Have you followed up on just what these American forces were that drove to Caborca?"

"Sir, we are five miles from Caborca but might be only two or three miles from contact with the American force that drove down from Arizona. The estimates by several civilian sources on the number of trucks vary widely but the Americans may have put 2,000 to 3,000 Indians around Caborca—depends on how many of those transports contained horses. Witnesses say some of the trucks were pulling cannons."

"What are the Americans planning, General?"

"Mr. President, I think they are trying to disrupt our supply chain. The Americans believe they can interfere with our progress north by denying us a resupply at Caborca. Obviously we can still move north without taking on supplies at Caborca but I refuse to allow the US control the agenda like that, sir. I plan to move into Caborca at dawn regardless of what is laying in wait between me and the town."

"Don't wait for dawn, General Melendez. You are only five miles out—move into town now."

"I could sir, but the men will be tired from the long march today. Wouldn't it be better to attack when they are better rested?"

"Nonsense. We have overwhelming force and I don't want those Indians harassing our columns as we drive north."

Melendez quickly relented. "I will order the attack, Mr. President. I am also getting scattered reports of other Indian forces coming across the border east of Sonoita. Regular reconnaissance patrols using commandeered private aircraft will begin at first light."

"Dismissed!" snapped Mejias. The generals were all too happy to leave the President to himself and his Chinese guest. Mejias had heard enough and wanted to finish his meal undisturbed, at least as undisturbed as was possible with his Chinese shadow in the room. One part of Mejias didn't want his generals seeing how close he was to the Chinese. The Mexican President could almost hear the scoffs and feel the disdain the generals must harbor over the influence of the Chinese. But Mejias hoped the smarter generals understood that Mexico needed strong friends right now. He believed there was another benefit to having Lu around. The presence of the powerful minister from China would hopefully deter an overly ambitious general from staging a coup as Mejias had done. Of course, he would have to monitor Lu's movements to be sure the minister didn't approach any of his generals with offers too good to refuse.

"Are you satisfied with the war so far, Señor Lu?"

"From the sound of the reports, matters are unfolding largely as you planned, Mr. President, even the strike against the domes that cost you your entire fleet of main battle tanks."

"A necessary sideshow, Señor Lu. How are your stuffed peppers?"

"Excellent and tasty as ever, Mr. President."

Mejias smiled. He knew Lu hated stuffed peppers, and tonight the Mexican leader had his chef prepare the dish with spices even more potent than the last time.

45.

Sam Yazzie and Jim Bahe nervously watched the enemy columns through night vision goggles and neither young soldier expected to get any sleep. The Mexican army continued its march through the darkness without pause. Mejias clearly was not waiting until morning to move into Caborca. Sam considered the situation rather comical—that only two miles of desert separated their 10-man infantry squad from the entire Mexican army. He addressed best friend Jim Bahe who wasn't as amused.

"Damn, Jim. I guess you won the bet. The Mexicans are still coming."

"I expect you to pay up, Sam—one million Krugerrands."

"Sure thing, I'm good for it."

"What is the artillery waiting for, Sam? The Mexicans are only a couple miles away for God's sake."

Sam didn't have a chance to answer his impatient friend. The soft booms of distant howitzers firing behind them where soon followed by bright flashes that exploded right on top of the Mexican troop columns.

"That's more like it!" exclaimed Jim, who was suddenly reenergized by the sight of artillery shell impacts that scattered the advancing Mexican army.

The barrage continued unabated through the night. UAV pilots joined the fray with Reapers, Predators, and Avengers loaded with GPS-guided bombs. Every fifteen or twenty minutes a "special" delivery was made by a Tomahawk cruise missile fitted with a hammerhead anti-personnel package. The hammerhead was a shaped Mega-T charge attached to the missile tip that made the missile resemble a hammerhead shark. The large shaped charge blasted shrapnel through a 300-yard kill radius and produced overpressures outside the kill radius that caused concussions, broke bones, collapsed lungs, and a host of other injuries.

Sam watched the terrifying scene unfold on the desert floor just two miles from his position. The bombs, missiles, and artillery rounds kept falling and lighting up the night but somehow the mass of Mexican troops crept closer every hour.

* * * *

Mark Tanner and Western Army chief battle planner, Brigadier General Barney Malcolm poured over the reconnaissance reports from the Navajo strike force and video from UAV flights.

"You're right, Barney. It looks like your plan worked." Predator surveillance clearly indicated the main body of the Mexican army was splitting into two large flanking forces that were moving to the west and east of Caborca, but not through the town. The advancing columns had tried breaking off small units to move into Caborca and test the willingness of American forces to intercept and block access to the town. Each attempt met with strong resistance from Navajo infantry backed up by Apache and Navajo cavalry.The US artillery commander and UAV coordinator contributed to the success of the plan by following the tactic of hitting hard any Mexican elements that tried to reach the town while allowing the flanking columns that ignored Caborca to move north unmolested.

"Yes, sir, but that does leave the problem of this center column that seems to be forming up right here. It looks as though Mejias has assigned a smaller force to stay behind to try and dislodge our troops regardless of possible Mexican losses."

"So we are up against his ego now, Barney?"

"His ego plus a subordinate general who has probably been ordered to take back the ground at all costs and fears the consequences of failure. You do realize we are nearing the limit of our ordinance budget for supporting the strike force, sir?"

"We can't leave our men hanging, Barney. Is it time to pull the trigger on the emergency plan and send in the Bradleys to extract the force? They have already emplaced the howitzers for Kill Zone operations and for supporting the Lakota and Cherokee defensive lines."

General Malcolm did know that the Bradley armored personnel carriers were available at this point to dash south and rescue the Navajo task force—that's the way he designed the battle plan, after all.

"Sir, let's wait for the results of the Psyops experiment. Our troops in the hills south of Caborca are now exchanging missile and small arms fire with the Mexican infantry that is beginning to move into the hills. The timing and conditions are perfect."

"Okay, do it," ordered Tanner.

* * * *

Pete Avalina dove headfirst into Sam's defensive position as machine gun bullets skipped off the rocks near his feet. The squad leader lifted himself up from the dirt floor of the foxhole and stood between the two privates manning the position. The winded sergeant strained to gulp air into his lungs while he scanned the condition of his men.

"You guys okay?" Avalina noticed the blood and bandage on Jim Bahe's face. "Jim?"

"I'll be okay, Sarge. A bullet hit one of the rocks we piled up for cover and a chip of stone shot into my face. Sam pulled out the piece that was sticking into my forehead."

Sam nodded. "Yeah, it was pretty disgusting, Sarge. You owe me, Bahe."

"I've got that piece of rock in my pocket. Do want to see it, Sarge?"

"No, keep it. Look you two, keep up intermittent rifle and grenade fire to keep the Mexicans' heads down. We've been given the order to pop the lids off the Psyops crates. Don't leave this hole under any circumstances—got it?"

"Sarge, we're not going to get out of this. There are a million Mexicans down there."

"Bullshit, Bahe. We are going to be okay. If the Psyops stuff doesn't work, they will send in the Bradleys to evacuate us."

"Sarge, we heard Wauneka is dead. Is that true?" asked Sam.

Avalina looked into the eyes of both men and nodded. "Look, you guys get back to work. They pull the trigger on the crates in less than ten minutes."

Private Bahe watched their squad leader climb out of the hole and crawl to the next two-man soldier team while Yazzie fired his rifle at movement 400 yards down the hill—just a token shot to keep heads down, he wasn't likely to hit anything at that distance.

* * * *

Mexican infantry private Jorge Salazar was almost on top of the strange green plastic case before he knew it. The box looked like a large footlocker or an over-sized drink cooler you brought to the beach or a picnic. He hadn't noticed the crate earlier because someone had hidden it behind a thick clump of creosote bush. For the moment the crate was providing good cover for him as he slowly crawled up the hill toward the Indians who had invaded his country.

Intermittent rifle fire echoed across the hillside and an occasional 40mm grenade launched from above blasted through air much quieter than that of the previous evening. There had been no devastating cruise missile strikes in the last two hours. No bombs fell from remote piloted aircraft and the once continuous artillery barrage had lifted. The Mexican infantry was finally able to concentrate at the base of the hills to begin the assault against the American Indian soldiers who were dug into the high ground.

Jorge lowered his head until his helmet dug into the dirt then used his arms and legs to pull and kick his body over the ground. His stomach scraped painfully across loose rock, but he had to keep his body pressed to the hillside as closely as possible to avoid enemy bullets and grenade shrapnel. As he crawled passed the mysterious plastic crate he witnessed the unexpected sight of the lid sliding open all by itself. Even stranger was the buzzing noise from inside the crate that grew louder and louder. After another few seconds, the toy helicopter—that's what it looked like—levitated out of the box, its main rotor whirling rapidly. The thing spun in almost a full circle then darted off down the hill. Jorge lifted his head to watch the opening of the box that still buzzed loudly; he was completely perplexed.

Another toy helicopter emerged, and then another. Each small flying machine wasn't much larger than a football. The fourth mini helicopter drifted over Jorge and it dropped lightly onto the back of his thigh as he lay prone in the dirt. The tiny aircraft rose back into the air a second later and buzzed away like a bumblebee.

Jorge soon felt a painful burning in his leg. He reached behind his thigh and found the small needle the machine left behind. He stared at the curious object until his hand and arm dropped to the ground uncontrollably. His arms and legs would not move and his helmeted head fell into the dust. Disjointed thoughts of all kinds raced through Jorge's mind which was the only part of him that still functioned, then his mind froze too—it froze in terror when Jorge realized that he could not breathe. Jorge focused his every thought and willed his chest to move. Inside his skull his mind screamed...*Breathe!* but his lungs would not fill.

He still heard the sporadic gunfire popping across the mountain slopes. He saw the parched dirt on the desert floor and the yellow flower blooms on the creosote bush. He felt the throbbing in his thigh and the pain of the rocks under his stomach. But not one muscle responded to his fully conscious commands. With his lungs unable to pull in or expel air, he couldn't even cry out to his comrades.

Jorge knew he was dying, but didn't understand how. At least he was able to collect his thoughts long enough to start thinking one last Hail Mary before he lost consciousness forever.

The gruesome death struggle of Jorge Salazar was repeated several thousand times in the hills around Caborca as the fully automated Psyops micro air vehicles (MAV's) located human heat signatures and delivered their poison stings. Every MAV could deliver up to 40 lethal injections of synthetic curare and return to its launching crate if it wasn't destroyed first.

* * * *

Sam Yazzie waved at the men in the next defensive position. They exchanged shrugs as well as theories about why the Mexicans hadn't fired a shot in the last hour.

"Jim, I think the Psyops stuff worked—whatever it was."

"Yeah, maybe."

Sam was secure enough to pull the binoculars from their case and lift himself above the lip of his foxhole to survey the desert floor. Everywhere he looked he saw Mexicans retreating back to the south—fast.

46.

White Hawk and his Lakota brothers threw up a withering barrage of bullets and grenades against the advancing Mexican troops. Casualties among the Mexicans were high but they pushed forward anyway. The men White Hawk fought were tired and desperate. The Mexican soldiers had spent two days crossing through the Kill Zone where artillery shells rained down with deadly accuracy, where Reapers and Avengers dropped GPS-guided bombs on troops massing behind cover, and where strikes by the hammerhead-fitted cruise missiles shredded entire companies of men at once. Now the exhausted Mexicans fought the unwavering line of Lakota warriors who were fresh, well-armed, and anxious for the fight.

But the Mexican soldiers advanced despite the current and past hardships. Overwhelming numbers made the advance inevitable regardless of the fierce fire by the Lakota. The Mexicans had no choice but move forward. Their fellow soldiers pushed them from behind, driven on by the twin terrors of the Kill Zone blasts and of their own ruthless commander.

In late afternoon the order flashed along the Lakota lines to retreat northward two miles to their pre-planned fallback position. One mile north along their path of retreat the Lakota would pass through a fresh defensive line of Cherokee warriors dug in and waiting to engage the advancing Mexican force in order to slow it down and cover the retreat of the friendly Lakota force. The retreating Lakota would then reestablish another line of defense to cover the Cherokee when they executed their planned withdrawal. If necessary, the cycle of fight-and-retreat would repeat until American forces were again in Arizona with their backs against the dome farm.

White Hawk and his fellow troop of warriors fought their own mini-delaying action until they were far enough from Mexican fire to sprint behind a nearby knoll and mount their horses. The forty men had just climbed into the saddle when the urgent call came over the troop radio reporting that the neighboring squadron of Lakota were about to be flanked by a bulge in the local lines before they could reach their horses.

White Hawk rallied the warriors around him and led the rescue charge from the knoll toward the break in the line. The Lakota war cry, pounding hooves, and automatic weapon fire from horseback surprised and scattered the Mexican soldiers. The lightening attack closed the breach in the line and permitted the trapped squadron to begin a safer, more orderly withdrawal.

White Hawk whirled his horse around to attack a small group of Mexicans attempting to reform. Unfortunately, a horse was a large target and vulnerable even to the poor shooting of inexperienced recruits. White Hawk felt his mount's legs buckle and he jumped free of the tumbling horse. He hit the ground with a painful thud and rolled into a thicket of thorny brush. The injured warrior crawled to his wounded mustang to find the animal covered all but the tip of his rifle.

With his primary weapon trapped under his horse, White Hawk pulled his bow and quiver from the exposed side of the saddle. Using the body of his dying mount for cover, White Hawk loosed arrow after arrow into the enemy ranks until a burst from a Mexican assault rifle found its mark. White Hawk slumped against his horse with his bow still gripped tightly in his hand. The deafening din and pandemonium of the desperate battle raged around him yet White Hawk felt he was on an island of peace among the tumult. His head rested just below his mount's shoulder and White Hawk felt the last beat of the proud animal's heart. Then the bright desert day dimmed to black and the fierce Lakota war cries faded to silence.

47.

The exhilaration General Victor Trujillo derived from standing on American soil was soon extinguished and replaced with deep concern. The mountaintop perch just north of Nogales offered the general a commanding view of the valley through which his troops now marched. His army discovered that the hot, inhospitable ground had been heavily mined on both the east and west sides of US Interstate Highway 19. Troops concentrated tightly along narrow lines of passage cleared by Mexican army engineers. That's when the crippling strikes by the cruise missiles came. It was no wonder that by the end of the first day's march into American territory, the region was dubbed the "Valley of Death" by his men. But Trujillo had more men than the Americans had ammunition so the march to Tucson continued.

On the following day artillery barrages by American 155mm howitzers and bombs dropped from unseen UAV's ripped into his dwindling army. In addition to the artillery barrages and bombs, Apache and Comanche warriors began a campaign of hit and run raids that decimated the fringes of his formations and bred fear in the hearts of his soldiers.

General Trujillo's men halted each evening for rest but they found little. Darkness brought no refuge from the deadly ordinance the Americans flung against the Mexican troops. Worse than the bombs and missiles were the chilling Apache and Comanche war screams that shot from the darkness and spread more fear among the men than did the fire of a machine gun.

The raids by the Indians stopped as Trujillo's soldiers approached the city of Tucson. The reason for the lack of Indian attacks became all too apparent when multiple cruise missile salvos exploded above the men as they concentrated together on the outskirts of Tucson. Water supplies were running short forcing the general to reassign groups of men from combat duties to instead focus on the task of foraging for well water resources in the area. Mexican Air Force cargo planes attempted to drop supplies but many were destroyed, not by Stinger-firing UAV's but by missiles fired by the Apache and Comanche raiders. American Predators and Reaper drones had to keep their distance because of Mexican troops wielding Chinese-provided surface-to-air missiles. The presence of Chinese SAM's forced the Indian soldiers to arm themselves with Stingers and assume the responsibility for air defense where needed.

Trujillo's bruised army finally passed beyond Tucson but resumption of the march north also meant resumption of vicious attacks by Apache and Comanche forces. The leader of Mexico's flanking army worried that the scarcity of food and water resources was taking an ever increasing toll on the morale of the men. Trujillo paced back and forth outside his command tent and mulled the fact that the road to Phoenix was long, but the road home was longer.

* * * *

"You don't look like you are getting much sleep, Mark," Kathy Singer observed. "Not that I blame you, of course. I feel a bit useless here with no action on my front."

The weary US Western Army general struggled to summon a smile. "Count yourself lucky, Kathy."

Both battlefield commanders discussed current status and war-gamed possibilities. The main body of the Mexican army took heavy losses in the Kill Zone before hitting the first defensive line formed by the Lakota and Cherokee. The Cheyenne, Arapaho and Kiowa were now fully engaged along with the Cherokee and Lakota against the Mexican main body. The Mexican right flank "Phoenix Force" likewise took heavy losses upon the initial border crossing and was now suffering constant harassment by Apache and Comanche forces.

Tanner still believed the American defensive plan was sound but the shrinking supply of bombs, missiles, artillery rounds, and UAV aircraft threatened to put this war in the loss column in two or three days—about when Mexican forces would reach Phoenix.

"Kathy, just so you know, I plan to ask the boss for permission to dip into the ordinance reserves for your Eastern Army—at least those that can be secured immediately, cruise missiles and JDAM's mostly."

"Understood, Mark. Of course you know I will fight that. If Mejias attacks across the Rio Grande, I will need that ordinance."

"Understood, Kathy, I would do the same."

"Thanks for the heads up, Mark."

"You know, what I could really use is more of those poison-laced MAV's but Psyops shot their whole wad at Caborca."

"I saw the reports, Mark. That was an amazing success. Is the Navajo advance force doing okay?"

"More than okay. They are coming down from the hills at night and chipping away at the Mexican forces flanking left and right around the town. And, yes, I would say the Psyops goal of terrorizing the enemy was achieved in outstanding fashion."

"Mark, I know matters look bleak because of the lack of ordinance but I have to say, the Treaty Tribe forces are performing exceptionally well against some very long odds," noted General Singer.

General Tanner nodded. "Best army since Philip's and Alexander's Macedonians."

Singer echoed the sentiment, "Here, here."

48.

The past two weeks of intensified war preparations took their toll on all the stronghold citizens but nothing was as sorrowful and emotionally draining as the activity in the bus convoy now parked along Biltmore Estates Drive in front of the hotel. This was the departure point for the "Flagstaff Convoy." Tears flowed freely as parents hugged children and put them onto the buses. Elderly and infirm citizens were helped aboard as well. The buses would drive due north to the safety of Flagstaff in the Arizona high country. Two of Colonel Holland's special operations team would accompany the convoy that would take the most vulnerable stronghold citizens out of harm's way.

Tom watched the emotional early morning scene before jumping into his Humvee and driving to his assigned sector just north of Sky Harbor Airport. Jenny was with a medical supply team that was rushing material to the forward hospital at Gila Bend. Sun Rain was somewhere in Paradise Valley doing duty similar to Tom—marking safe houses, helping build roadblocks, planting cameras and sensors; he even learned to rig Claymores and other explosive surprises for Mexican forces. He hadn't seen much more than glimpses of either Jenny or Sun Rain in the last seven days. Jenny split her time between the Biltmore medical facilities, supply runs to Gila Bend, and setting up the hospital in the Phoenix Mountains behind the hotel. Sun Rain sometimes returned to the Biltmore for a short rest and shower as did Tom but he stayed in his room and hoped there would be no knock on his door. He also hoped the cowardice he showed in facing his feelings didn't translate to cowardice on the battlefield. He wouldn't be in his bedroom controlling a robot thousands of miles away with a keyboard and joystick, he would be firing a rifle of his own—and people would be shooting back at him.

Tom's Humvee sat idling in the intersection of Van Buren and 40th street over the Grand Canal. He shut of the engine and surveyed the area for camera and explosive placement and noted only two nearby buildings had any height worthy of potential sniper positions. As Tom scanned the local terrain he heard several muffled booms similar to distant thunder that marked the opening salvo of the Battle of Phoenix. Tom looked north first to Camelback Mountain then a few more points north to the Phoenix Mountains. Tom knew from the briefings and from radio traffic that the distant booms were cannon fire from the 155mm howitzers that Cherokee artillery crews setup behind Piestewa Peak. The commencement of the artillery barrage meant that Mexican forces were less than one day's march away—maybe 25 miles.

* * * *

Jenny's medical supply delivery run to Gila Bend turned into full scale evacuation help. The Mexican force advancing on Phoenix had detached a column of troops that turned due west at Casa Grande and that meant the enemy was a day and a half march from the hospital down Interstate 8. A mixed nation blocking force made up of Cherokee, Lakota, and Cheyenne reserves was on alert in the event the Mexicans made such a move. The mechanized Cherokee force arrived first and began a delaying action similar to the action on the main battle front but on a smaller scale. Lakota reserves would ride in and setup lines two miles behind the Cherokee, then the Cheyenne would dig in and create a third defensive line.

Dr. Saunders organized a string of Cherokee Humvee ambulance convoys to move the wounded to the Piestewa Peak hospital behind the Biltmore. A portion of the medical staff would transfer to Phoenix while other volunteer medics and nurses and doctors would take on the dangerous duty of moving to battalion aide stations closer to the main war front along the Arizona-Mexico border.

Several ambulances from the front arrived as Jenny checked supply stores. With an evacuation planned over the next 24 hours, there was no sense in unloading too many of the medical supplies just to load them again tomorrow. Unlike her first trip here, Jenny was no longer afraid of the wounded soldiers or overcome by all the blood or smells from the abdominal wounds. Admittedly, her stomach did remain queasy near triage areas but she spoke with and engaged the wounded men now and she reassured them as best she could.

Jenny passed through a patient staging tent and was amazed to hear seriously wounded Lakota and Cherokee joking and comparing wounds. Not all the wounded were conscious and able to speak. Jenny hoped the medics and doctors could help them. The coming evacuation would be difficult timing for some of the wounded as communication and remote surgery performed by doctors from their domes would have to be suspended during the two-hour transport process.

"Jenny?"

Jenny turned when she thought she heard her name but the whisper was so soft she couldn't be sure what she heard.

"Jenny."

She definitely heard the call that time and crossed over to the far side of the triage tent—it was not the side of the tent one wanted to be placed.

Jenny walked to the large man lying on a stretcher supported on both ends by steel drums. Her heart sank when she recognized Little Deer, sweating profusely and clearly struggling with intense pain.

Little Deer managed a weak smile. "I thought I heard you Jenny, talking with my Lakota brother. Don't waste time with him. I am much more handsome."

Jenny took Little Deer's hand and with the other wiped the tears from her eyes. "What would your wife say if she knew you were flirting with the nurses?"

"She would say her husband, Little Deer, will never learn. Fortunately, I am too far away to be struck with a tent pole or a cooking pot—I have some experience with both, you know."

Jenny tried to smile. "I am sorry that I can't stop crying. I am supposed to provide better comfort than this."

"You are doing an excellent job, Jenny, don't worry. It's good to see you again. How is Tom?"

Jenny shook her head. "I haven't seen him much this past week."

"You are worried he has other interests."

Jenny wiped more tears. "How do you know that?"

"Jenny, I am a trained scout. I observe much."

"Little Deer, this is no time to worry about me."

"I know why they put me here out of the way. I think it means I shouldn't waste time worrying about myself, so that gives me time to worry about you."

"You are going to be fine, Little Deer."

Little Deer laughed despite the pain. "Ah, see, now you are remembering your training on comforting the wounded."

Jenny sniffled and squeezed Little Deer's hand. On the other side of the canvas tent wall she heard the squeaking brakes of another ambulance arriving from the front.

"Jenny, some advice you can take or leave...you will feel better about *yourself* if you let Tom follow his heart."

"Wise advice from a Cherokee scout?"

"I think so." Little Deer winked. "Do you know anything about my friend Running Bear?"

"No, I don't. I'm sorry."

"He promised me two days ago that after the war he would bring his family all the way home—to North Carolina. Will you find him and tell him my ghost will haunt him if he doesn't keep his word?"

"I will."

Jenny stayed with Little Deer for almost an hour, learning about North Carolina, from the lush green hills to the favorite stream he fished with his sons, until Little Deer closed his eyes and finally drifted home.

49.

Joint Chiefs Chairman Pruitt concluded the war briefing for the President and the Security Council members who were logged into the meeting,

"Unfortunately, Madam President, the situation with our Western Army is rather desperate. Mexican forces have reached the southeast suburbs of Phoenix. The main body of Mejias' army has pushed our forces to within four miles of the nearest domes here in the Mohawk and Growler Valleys. There will be no more delaying actions. We have drawn a line in the sand here where the domes are just out of range of Mexican mortars. Of course our defensive line is now strengthened by the bulk of the Navajo infantry reserve that was assigned as dome perimeter security for just this circumstance.

"There is still no movement by the eastern Mexican forces against Texas. General Beckett has authorized Lt. General Tanner to use most of the bombs and cruise missiles reserved for Lt. General Singer's Eastern Army."

"And if Mejias attacks Texas?" asked President Phillips.

"There is that risk, Madam President. We did have over 8,000 Crow and Blackfeet warriors arrive in Pecos four days ago. That arrival was quite unexpected as those nations are not officially among the Treaty Tribes. They do attend the All Nations Pow-wow and are therefore trained and equipped to assist. Kathy Singer is having the new forces move onto the battlefront here at the northern limit of the Mexican line and she is moving them in conspicuous fashion to the southeast in full view of the Mexicans so they know another significant force has arrived."

"Do we still think Mejias won't buckle under the threat of nuclear strikes against Mexico City?" asked National Security Advisor Alan Sayles.

DNI, Anthony Covelli, entered the discussion. "CIA says Mejias and family and mistresses, have evacuated their residences—same with his generals. Mejias thinks he will own the United States next week. He doesn't give a damn about Mexico City or any other place in Mexico despite his rhetoric about restoring Mexican nationalist pride."

"I concur," said Secretary of State Mason. "We know the minds of the Treaty Tribes about the use of nuclear weapons on or near US territory. Nuclear strikes deep into Mexico, such as on Mexico City, I think they might forgive. But Madam President, I believe such nuclear strikes deep into Mexico would be futile and would not deter Mejias. His sights are trained on bigger things than Mexico."

President Phillips paused to contemplate the consequences of dropping nuclear weapons on Mexico—she was doing that more often lately.

"Meanwhile Madam President," Carter Mason continued. "You see the stink Mejias is raising in the UN about Mexico being 'invaded by the United States.' That was to be expected. My greater concern is the support he is rallying against our use of micro air devices to deliver lethal poison on the battlefield."

"Is Ambassador Barnham relaying our position that based on our understanding of the Biological Weapons Convention of 1972 and subsequent treaties, the weapon we tested in Mexico is not covered by any treaty or convention?"

"She has done so, Madam President. Linda skewered the Mexicans by explaining that the weapon actually saved lives because the Mexican army fled the battlefield in terror."

"Thank you, Carter. Anything else, General Pruitt?"

"Only that, while the situation is desperate, the war is not yet lost. We will have a clearer picture in the next day or two."

"Thank you, Joshua. If strikes with strategic nuclear weapons on Mexican cities won't deter Mejias then we will not follow that course; however, General, please alert the Strategic Command that we may need to call on them to deliver *tactical* nuclear weapon strikes against Mexican army units within our borders and immediately south of the Arizona and Texas borders."

"Yes, Madam President. Will do."

50.

Tom tossed and turned in his bed throughout the overnight hours. The deep booming sounds of howitzer muzzle blasts slowly faded through the course of the evening as the guns were towed further away to the north. But the sharper, deadlier explosions of shell impacts were getting louder as the Mexicans advanced closer to Phoenix. The bulk of the Mexican force was stampeding through the deserted suburb of Tempe. American cannon and missile fire rained down onto Mexican forces from the hills in Phoenix's South Mountain Park.

Tom dressed in a clean tee shirt and jeans and buckled on the body armor that would help protect his chest and abdomen. He chose not to use the plate designed to protect his back or the arm and leg armor bands—it was all just too heavy and he expected to be on the move often. After strapping on the armor over his web gear, he buckled his web belt with canteens, knife and pistol, then grabbed his radio and rifle and stepped into the hallway to knock on Jenny's door.

Jenny opened her door; she wore the same type of casual clothes that Tom wore under all his infantry gear. Her eyes were puffy from crying much of the night. Concern welled up through Tom at the numb, glazed look on his fiancé's face, but he expected to be fighting for his life in an hour or two—what more could he say?

"Hi, Jenny. You said you were going to wake me when you got in last night."

"You need your sleep, Tom. We all do."

"It must be rough at Gila Bend, huh?"

"Yes it is. I saw Little Deer. He's dead."

Tom dropped his head and waves of grief pounded against him. That explained some of the crying, thought Tom. But he knew there was more to Jenny's sadness than the tragic passing of Little Deer.

"Jenny, I know we planned to have breakfast before things got hot but the Mexicans are about to cross the Salt River. I have to go."

Jenny nodded. Tom stepped forward and wrapped Jenny tightly in is arms. The body armor stole much of the tenderness of the embrace. After a long kiss, Jenny's tears resumed. He wondered if he would ever see her again.

"You be careful today, baby. It's going to get a lot rougher here than Gila Bend. Keep your head down. I hear you make a great nurse, by the way."

"Tom, just come back alive, please."

After another powerful squeeze, Tom slung his rifle across his back, ran down the hallway and pushed through the doorway of the Paradise Wing and into the war.

* * * *

Outside the Biltmore the morning sun burned brightly in the clear east while in the west the sky roiled with dark, menacing rain clouds that churned over the desert. Tom adjusted the canteen on his hip to a more comfortable position as he walked through the parking lot to the small bridge over the Arizona canal. Thirty seconds later he jogged up Telewa Trail to the top of Wrigley Hill whose crest was dominated by the Wrigley Mansion built one hundred fifty years before. The 100-foot knoll was the only high ground in the immediate area and served as Colonel Holland's special operations team command post. Multiple machine gun bunkers and defensive positions for riflemen had been dug into the hillside and reinforced with concrete.

Dan Jeffers' battle station was on the hill and Dan was Tom's ride to his assigned defensive area. A stiff breeze from the west blew in rain from the dark clouds. Tom was getting soaked even as the morning sun blared brightly. It seemed odd to Tom for rain to fall from a sunny sky, but then he had little experience with the wonders of the Outside.

Tom rounded the curve at the southern tip of the hilltop and his heart leapt at the unexpected sight of Sun Rain. Strangely, she wasn't trying to avoid the rain; instead she was in the grass twirling around with arms wide apart, dancing with the energy of a young girl. She smiled and laughed as if she didn't have a care in the world.

"Sun Rain, are you okay?" Tom asked with concern. They were minutes from going to war after all.

"Yes, Tom!" came the happy reply between giggles.

Tom was still confused by her apparent joy. "What is going on? Am I missing something?"

Sun Rain stopped twirling briefly; sunlight reflected in a thousand bright sparkles from the rain drops that ran down her smiling face and outstretched arms. *"This is me!,"* she exclaimed.

Tom thought for a moment and the flash of comprehension hit him like a hammer. He had never really given any thought before—about her name or what it actually meant. Now he finally understood the meaning of *Sun Rain.*

Tom smiled. Sun Rain saw he understood and gave him and his armor a wet hug.

"This will bring you good luck, Tom Corant."

Tom stepped from her embrace and he asked what brought her up to the Wrigley. He also noticed Dan Jeffers approaching from the main building.

"I had to give my last Claymore coordinates to Dan."

"I hope you aren't thinking of going out there into the fighting, Sun Rain."

Dan Jeffers was close enough to hear Tom's last remark. "She damn well better not be thinking that! Hi, Tom, how are you?"

Tom shook Dan's hand. "Hi, Dan. I heard your radio call that we were leaving early."

"Yes indeed. Jump into the Humvee." Jeffers gestured toward the main Wrigley entrance.

"You want a ride down the Hill?" Tom asked Sun Rain

Sun Rain shook her head. "You two be careful today." She was grateful the rain camouflaged her tears. "I will race you down the hill!" With that, Sun Rain turned and ran through the cleansing shower of water.

Tom joined two of Colonel Holland's men in the Humvee and Dan Jeffers drove all passengers to their initial defensive posts. As each man deployed into the city he was issued a GPS transmitter and wireless ear piece for his hand held radio so that he could receive direction on where to fire and when to fall back in order to avoid being surrounded.

Tom jumped off near McDowell and 44th Street. There was an abandoned hotel nearby that offered a commanding view of the likely avenue of approach of the Mexican troops. Tom found the second floor room that had been prepared with concrete block and steel partitions that would provide cover from small arms fire. A full rucksack lay on the bed among the bandoleers of ammunition and Kevlar army helmet. The backpack contained food and water and radio batteries and Tom would have to grab the bag if he needed to move to a new firing point. He had been reminded several times by men in the special operations force not to forget the bag and bandoleers when he moved. The supplies would be easy to forget in the heat of battle with bullets and grenade shrapnel chewing into his defensive position.

Tom seated the helmet over his head and sat down on a small crate near the window. In front of him was a steel door laying on its side and concrete blocks ahead of that. All the glass had been removed from the window frame to reduce risk of injury from flying glass fragments.

Tom cradled his rifle in his lap and waited. Reports of enemy progress rattled in his earpiece. As expected, the house-to-house urban warfare slowed the enemy advance considerably. Tom found himself hoping the small Navajo infantry detachment assigned to Phoenix would be able to stop the Mexicans before the less experienced stronghold citizens encountered them.

The shelling by the Cherokee artillery had eased significantly, but that was for lack of ammunition more than anything else. They had to save a few rounds for priority targets like Mexican mortar crews and the rare armed Humvee. Fortunately, all the Mexican artillery pieces and most of their limited vehicles had been destroyed since crossing into the country. Predator UAV's patrolled above the reach of Chinese shoulder-fired SAM's looking specifically for the dangerous mortars that could lob explosive shells up to three miles way.

Tom heard several loud explosions to his front. Moments later an excited forward observer shouted into his radio the confirmation that Mexican mortar shells were indeed falling in the area defended by Navajo infantry and stronghold citizens. Depending on their location, Mexican mortar crews were launching up to a dozen rounds before they could be targeted by UAV's and destroyed with a JDAM bomb.

Tom listened and watched by the window. Automatic and semi-automatic rifle fire burst in all directions in front of Tom. The rattle of small arms fire was occasionally accentuated by the angry barking of heavy machine guns.

The urgent popping of gunfire over the next hour steadily increased until loud rifle cracks reverberated through the nearby streets. Tom gave up trying to pinpoint the origin of the rifle reports since the noise bounced off multiple buildings by the time it reached him. The radio updates confirmed that the battle line was slowly moving north toward his position. Anxiety increased by the minute. Tom's earpiece buzzed with a message for him and his neighbors on his right and left flanks. Navajo infantry would be falling back behind Tom to setup new firing positions. That meant Tom would be covering their retreat and he was about to enter the war.

Unidentifiable shouts sounded from behind a nearby building then several bursts from a rifle in full automatic mode sprayed bullets through the streets in desperate fashion. Tom gripped his rifle tightly and tucked the stock into his shoulder. Sweat dripped inside his helmet. His hands were slick with sweat as well and his fingers were starting to cramp when Tom realized he was holding his weapon much too tightly. He tried a few deep breaths to relax. On his third breath a soldier came scrambling down the street and crouched by the corner of the building across the street from Tom.

The man wore US Army desert camouflage fatigues and had a yellow band tied around his left arm identifying him as Navajo infantry. The soldier saw Tom waving in the window and lifted his rifle overhead with magazine facing skyward followed by moving his hand and arm in an arching gesture. Tom's correct interpretation of the signals meant the enemy was right around the corner. Tom gave the soldier a thumbs-up then pointed at him and gestured over his shoulder telling the man to move and Tom would cover.

Tom sighted down his rifle barrel ready to fire at whatever rounded the corner. The Navajo warrior understood Tom's gesture and sprinted across the street in Tom's direction. His fellow combatant would fall back to a new defensive position and probably cover Tom's retreat shortly.

Tom watched the corner as well as the small building across the intersection diagonally from his position. He noticed the tip of a rifle barrel protrude from around the corner where the Navajo soldier knelt moments before. A

Mexican soldier had obviously stopped at the corner to survey the situation before continuing. The enemy soldier crept forward and Tom was able to confirm the uniform and weapon were Mexican military. Tom squeezed the trigger. Nothing. He cursed himself and flipped off the safety switch with a flick of his thumb. The hesitation allowed another Mexican soldier to come around the first man who now knelt and aimed his rifle to cover the moving man. Tom switched his aim to the moving man and squeezed the trigger. The range was short, forty yards. The man fell writhing in the street. The cover man aimed at Tom's window and fired.

While Tom crouched low and aimed, he heard the enemy soldier's bullets thud against the outside wall. More bullets dug into the concrete block and still others clinked against the metal door and ricocheted up into the ceiling. Adrenaline coursed through Tom and he felt energized beyond anything he had ever experienced. The feeling was wildly different than sitting in bed controlling a robot with a keyboard and joystick. Tom was so charged with adrenaline that, instead of ducking the enemy fire, he kept his rifle sighted on the Mexican soldier and fired two shots. The soldier dropped his rifle and slumped to the ground.

Tom also watched the man he wounded continue to twist and scream with pain. Had Tom been driving a combot he wouldn't have thought twice about ending the man's misery. For some reason, Tom couldn't bring himself to fire on the injured man. Two more Mexicans ran to the house across the street. Tom fired but didn't believe he had reacted in time to hit either of the men. Moments later, Tom was taking fire from the house.

Tom ducked behind the steel door long enough to open the breach of the grenade launcher attached to the barrel of his carbine and loaded a 40mm high explosive grenade. He peered out the window over the steel door cover and aimed just like Sun Rain had taught him. Tom squeezed the trigger and couldn't believe his eyes, and his luck, when the grenade flew through the very window at which he aimed. The grenade blast blew out window glass and buckled the roof of the small building. Tom returned his attention to the corner where the first Mexican soldier had appeared. He guessed there were more soldiers lined up out of sight, not yet daring to make the dash across the street.

While Tom scanned for advancing enemy, the special operations man assigned to coordinate the house-to-house fighting in Tom's sector issued an urgent order for him to retreat. Mexicans were moving to flank him on his right. Tom didn't hesitate. He strapped on the rucksack, draped the ammunition bandoleers around his neck and rushed out the rear entrance of the building.

Tom ran north and sure enough, the Navajo soldier he covered earlier was waving at him from the window of the next house. Tom ran passed the Navajo's position—and passed the next line of houses which were rigged with explosive surprises for the Mexicans—and into a south-facing house a block behind the Indian soldier. The same 'shoot and hold' if you could, or 'shoot and scoot' if you couldn't, went on in that same fashion all morning.

51.

"What do you mean there is no water in the canals? That's impossible." General Trujillo rocked with surprise at the news relayed by his chief of staff. Trujillo clasped his hands tightly behind his back and paced nervously in the front yard of the private residence just off Highway 101 in the Phoenix suburb of Chandler. The modest home had served as the general's temporary headquarters since early last evening.

Trujillo's army needed the water that should be coming into Phoenix via the Salt River. He had been prepared for the Gila River to be dry, but not the Salt. It was now painfully clear that war preparations by Arizona stronghold residents included closing the locks on the dams along the Gila and Salt Rivers in order to deny invading forces precious supplies of water.

General Trujillo was already facing critical supply problems. Most large freight trucks and water tankers were not getting passed the constant UAV patrols. The ancient jet aircraft maintained by the Mexican air force were useless against them. Apache warriors with portable missiles used hit and run guerilla tactics and watched all the roads that crossed the border. The general had already activated his emergency supply plan which entailed loading food, water, and ammunition into a fleet of small private planes massed in Hermosillo and then flying them to Phoenix to land among the city's plethora of long, wide, arrow-straight streets. Unfortunately, the small planes were capable of carrying only a very limited amount of cargo and many planes were destroyed by ground-based Stingers launched by the Indians. Trujillo had already tried landing larger C-130's at Sky Harbor Airport but the Americans detonated explosive charges on the runways as the first aircraft touched down.

Further complicating his operations, the general had to walk everywhere he went. His soldiers thought he was a hero and compassionate leader who wanted to share their pain. In reality the general feared that traveling in a motor vehicle would make him an instant target of a laser-guided bomb. Trujillo silently cursed General Mejias for allowing him only enough fuel for supply trucks, trucks towing artillery, and a few ambulances. As a general officer he certainly could have found enough fuel for a staff car or Humvee but again, the small number of vehicles in the theatre would make such a personal transport vehicle a conspicuous target—and he was not going to lose face before his men by riding in a Humvee ambulance with a big red cross painted on the side.

Trujillo bristled upon hearing that the advance on the Arizona stronghold had slowed significantly as the American forces became more concentrated and harder to flank due to the shrinking amount of territory that remained to be defended. The Mexican commander realized the morale of his troops was low for a number of reasons including the high casualties in the 'valley of death' near Nogales, the lack of sufficient water, and the ceaseless bloody raids by Apache and Comanche warriors on his army's flanks.

"Colonel Herrera, dispatch a force east through the Salt River Valley immediately and get the locks on those dams open! We must have water! Also, have Colonel Gonzales give me a quick plan for taking a force north to come in from behind these mountains and attack the Americans from the rear."

"Yes, sir," answered the skeptical but obedient officer.

* * * *

Tom ran toward the next pre-prepped house that would become his eleventh defensive position of the long, difficult day. Fatigue made his legs feel almost too heavy to lift, on the other hand, his rucksack of supplies and ammunition was becoming alarmingly light. He was so tired, he seriously contemplated abandoning the armor strapped to his chest and stomach the next time he moved.

The sudden stab of pain in his right thigh took him by surprise. Tom crashed onto the street and his rifle slid along the pavement. He rolled onto his back while blood started soaking through his desert camouflage pants. Tom grimaced and gritted his teeth against the excruciating pain. It was an effort to refrain from screaming his agony. He touched his hand to the exit wound on his thigh and felt his damaged quadriceps muscle protest with intermittent spasms.

Tom stopped moving and stared for one moment at the bright blue mid-afternoon sky while trying to focus on slowing his rapid breathing. His thoughts flashed to the Mexican soldier he left in a similar condition on the street this morning and to the combot shooting game he played so cavalierly with Meg. If he only got out of this alive, that game was going to stop. Tom resolved to take two more deep breaths to gather himself before making what he assumed would be a painful attempt to get out of the street. He rolled over and crawled on his stomach toward his rifle. Tom pulled with his left arm and pushed with his left leg. His right hand was busy trying to staunch the flow of blood from his thigh. Throughout the painful crawl he prayed another bullet wouldn't find him. More shameful images of less glorious combot actions flashed through his mind. While he prayed for safety and courage, he prayed for forgiveness, too.

Tom reached his weapon when the bark of the enemy's AK-47 sounded again and a chip of concrete curbing blasted away. Tom crawled over the curb toward the front door the small Spanish ranch style house. Tom kept as low as he could during the painful maneuver but now he would have to lift upward to turn the doorknob. Despite the danger, Tom had no other choice. He raised his heavy torso and used his right hand, slick with blood from his leg, to turn the knob. Suddenly he was re-thinking the decision to leave behind the armor plate that could have been covering his exposed spine right now. The enemy rifle blasted again and the bullet bored straight through the door as it swung open.

Tom scrambled inside and crawled to the reinforced living room window. A trail of blood followed Tom wherever he went. He quickly fished his radio out of his backpack and was finally able to report that he had been shot. While fumbling for the radio he found a length of all-purpose nylon cord and used it to fashion an emergency tourniquet around his bleeding leg. Tom pulled himself up to the window and aimed his rifle at the window down the street that hid the Mexican soldier who was doing the shooting. Tom had to get suppressive fire on that structure as soon as possible to keep the enemy from moving forward.

Tom fired a quick burst, then another. He felt suddenly very light headed but kept firing short, controlled bursts—until he passed out.

* * * *

Bob Briggs huddled with Dan Jeffers in a concrete machine gun bunker on Wrigley Hill. The men watched in stunned disbelief as their quiet North Phoenix home transformed into a boiling cauldron of war. Assault rifle and machine gun fire rattled through the city. Black smoke rose from several pockets of flames burning amid the grim hell of the urban battlefield. Briggs looked out over the Biltmore golf course and fumed at the large number of craters blasted into the greens by Mexican mortars.

"Those bastards! Look at what those sons of bitches have done to our beautiful golf course, Dan! They are going to pay for that!"

A hundred yards away in the opposite direction, the Arizona Biltmore structure and grounds showed signs of mortar damage as well. Palm trees toppled to the ground and into buildings, shattered window glass glinted everywhere, several villas had taken direct hits—one was on fire.

"Let me have that gun, Dan." Briggs reached for the bunker's tripod-mounted .50 caliber machine gun but Dan Jeffers stopped him.

"No, Bob. The Mexicans are close but not that close. You might hit one of our people."

Briggs checked himself. He knew Dan was right. Still, he wanted someone to pay for ripping up the beautiful greens. Briggs had run up to the Wrigley for a quick personal look around and to get an assessment of the situation directly from Colonel Holland.

"Mr. Briggs, you see me checking the inventory of the ammo pouches on my web gear, right?" queried the Colonel.

"I guess so."

"I do so because I expect to be fighting for my life in not long. You better get back to your boss and start thinking about proposing surrender terms."

"Things are that desperate?"

"I am afraid so, Mr. Briggs. Our urban street fighters who aren't dead or wounded will soon have no fallback position other than the Biltmore. The decision to surrender rests with Mr. Jeffers. Tell him that until I hear differently, I plan to stay on this hill and take down as many of the enemy as possible."

52.

The booming blast of the Mexican mortar round jarred Tom back to consciousness. He lay with several other wounded men in the nearly empty McArthur Ballroom building at the Biltmore. Tom smiled when he recognized Jenny running to him. She knelt next to him. Blood stains smeared her clothing; there were even a few dark red smudges on her face.

"What happened, Tom?" Jenny asked.

"Shot while running house-to-house—about what I expected would happen. But at least I managed to go most of the day without getting hit."

Jenny grabbed Tom's hand. "I heard on the radio that you were shot and being sent here. Oh, Tom, this is horrible!"

Tom realized that Jenny wasn't speaking merely of his wound. He knew what she meant. The Mexican aggression, Little Deer, the death and destruction in Phoenix and in the southern part of the Arizona, the explosions increasing in frequency around the hotel, those were the horrors to which Jenny referred.

Tom noticed his body armor was gone and his pant leg had been cut away and a large bandage was wrapped tightly around his thigh. "How is my leg?"

"I was going to ask you that, Tom. The medics say no permanent damage other than you will have some ugly scars."

"I say, sexy scars, honey," Tom threw a playful wink at Jenny despite the intense throbbing in his leg. "How long was I out? What's going on? Where is everyone?"

"The evacuation order was given before you got here. Everyone at the Biltmore is falling back to Piestewa Peak and the mountains. Some buses have already left for Flagstaff."

The mortar round landed outside but the powerful blast punched through the wall. Shrapnel hit Jenny in the back and she slumped over onto Tom. Tom coughed and used one arm to shield his eyes and nose from falling debris and choking dust. His other arm held Jenny. The amount of blood that wet her back was alarming. Tom called for help then realized several of Dr. Saunders' hospital volunteers were already lifting Jenny off him and onto a stretcher. Tom heard a shout ordering someone to hold the ambulance that was about to depart so that Jenny could be rushed to the surgery center in the mountains.

Tom struggled painfully to his feet. Among the debris he found a broken piece of PVC pipe with an elbow joint still in place so it made a serviceable makeshift cane. He limped outside, but Jenny's ambulance had already raced away. A hospital volunteer helped Tom into the passenger seat of the next Humvee ambulance waiting to depart.

Mortar shells fell more frequently now. The small arms fire was dangerously close. Tom saw enemy machine gun rounds chew into the side of the main Biltmore building near the Arizona Ballroom. Colonel Holland's machine gun bunkers on Wrigley Hill poured heavy fire into the estate homes on the far end of the Biltmore golf course. Tom thought if the Mexicans were that close, it wouldn't be long before the Biltmore fell to the enemy.

It took only moments to travel down Lincoln Drive and then turn onto Squaw Peak Drive. The route soon had the first range of peaks between them and Biltmore. The intense noise of the shells and small arms became mercifully muffled on the backside of the range.

The Humvee radio gear seated between Tom and the driver crackled with static and with the excited voices of urban street fighting teams falling back to the Biltmore while Colonel Holland and a few brave troops up on Wrigley Hill provided cover fire for the final retreat. Two Reaper drones from Creech Air Force Base dropped the last of the JDAM munitions onto Mexican mortar crews but that left two other mortar crews still conducting their deadly business. The Cherokee howitzers were silent—the ammunition was gone.

The next voice streaming through the radio static was Nathan Holland's. The Colonel was warning all friendly forces that ammunition on Wrigley Hill was almost exhausted. Mexican troops had marched up 24th Street and were circling behind the Wrigley, cutting Colonel Holland's command post off from the Biltmore and leaving the soldiers fighting on Wrigley Hill surrounded.

The asphalt pavement of Squaw Peak Drive ended but Tom's Humvee driver continued rolling forward and up the hiking trail to the hospital on the northeast side of Piestewa Peak. The hospital was nothing more than a series of simple corrugated steel Quonset huts set on hastily poured concrete pads.

Tom climbed out of the truck with the aid of his PVC cane and grimaced as he planted the bare foot of his wounded left leg onto the ground. He noticed an M2-equipped Humvee parked on the eastern side of the hospital. As Tom limped toward the truck Sun Rain emerged from the hospital with other volunteers to assist the wounded in transferring from the ambulance to the hospital. Sun Rain recognized Tom and ran to him. She looked remarkably similar to Tom's last picture of Jenny, blood-stained clothing and disheveled, unkempt appearance. Her characteristic smile was nowhere to be seen and her clear, sharp eyes beamed concern.

"Tom, I heard you were hurt."

Tom kept an arm around Sun Rain's shoulder for support after a quick hug.

"Jenny is going into surgery. I am so sorry, Tom."

"Sun Rain, is there a supply of ammunition nearby?"

"Yes, food, water, ammunition, medical supplies are in storage huts behind the hospital. Why?"

"I need you and anyone else who is able to help me load ammunition and a bit of water onto that Humvee over there. Colonel Holland just radioed that the ammunition supply up on Wrigley Hill is exhausted. I think I can change that."

Sun Rain looked at Tom and saw he was determined to undertake the dangerous mission. Part of her wanted to stop him, but refusing battle was not the Comanche way.

"All right, Tom. Can you get to the Humvee and drive it around back?"

"Of course, I am not that hobbled!"

There was at least a brief flash of a Sun Rain smile. "I will find some people to help with the loading."

"Great, I will meet you in back."

Sun Rain ran back into the hospital while Tom commandeered the Humvee. With the help of Sun Rain and three hospital volunteers, Tom's Humvee was loaded with ammunition and water in only minutes.

Tom climbed into the driver's seat and Sun Rain jumped in the back. This particular Humvee was an up-armored model with a CROWS firing system that allowed the gunner to aim and fire the machine gun from inside the vehicle instead of exposing himself, or herself, to direct fire by standing up through the gun turret.

"What are you doing, Sun Rain? Get out!"

"You don't have time to argue, Tom. Drive."

She was right; there was no time to lose. The radio operator at the hospital was able to get a message to Colonel Holland that a resupply Humvee was on its way. Tom drove the truck off the mountain and sped up when wheels were back in contact with paved road surface. Tom wound his way through the local Biltmore neighborhood until he was on Telewa Trail. The first enemy bullets began clanking against the armored truck as they approached the small bridge over the Arizona canal. Sun Rain used the CROWS remote firing system to point the gun westward and rake the area with heavy machine gun fire. The local streets were an excruciatingly loud conflagration of mortar blasts, machine gun bursts, grenade blasts, and rifle fire.

Tom made a hard left immediately after crossing the canal and sped another hundred yards before making a hard right that nearly rolled the Humvee over. Mexican small arms fire peppered the Humvee armor from every direction. Soon the Humvee was racing up Wrigley Hill which put friendly forces to their left but enemy fire still punched at them from the west.

Tom made five quick resupply stops on the crest of the hill, all within a few yards of each other. Each stop had a man standing by to unload ammunition for his particular bunker. After the last resupply stop, Tom drove the Humvee around to the main Wrigley Mansion entrance. Colonel Holland had two men who were too injured to fight and he wanted them taken to the Piestewa Peak hospital if Tom would volunteer to run the gauntlet again.

Since Tom wasn't very mobile and required the use of a cane, he stayed in the Humvee while Sun Rain jumped out to help load the wounded for the return dash to Piestewa. Seconds after Sun Rain exited, the Mexican missile slammed into the back of his Humvee and, once again, the lights went out for Tom Corant.

53.

"What the hell?" Mortar fire ceased and the once continuous small arms fire suddenly diminished to near nothing across the entire battlefield that surrounded the Biltmore. Nathan Holland was puzzled by the lack of enemy fire. He leaned his chest against the wall of his bunker on Wrigley Hill and focused his binoculars on the middle of the Biltmore golf course. Someone was driving a golf cart down one of the fairways and waving a large white flag.

Colonel Holland snapped up a radio. "Who is that idiot? I didn't authorize any sort of surrender or parlay and neither did Governor Jeffers as far as I know."

One of Holland's team leaders answered, "It's not our flag, sir—those are Mexicans."

Nathan's radio buzzed again, this time it was the Governor.

"Colonel Holland, this is Lane Jeffers, over."

"Holland here, go ahead Governor, over."

"Colonel, I am still in my sector at the northeast tip of the golf course. I am coming out onto the course now—waving my rifle—can you see me, over?"

Holland trained his binoculars east. "I see you, Governor, over."

"Colonel, I am going to see what this is about. I will let you know, over."

"Understood, Governor. Where is Mr. Briggs? Wasn't he with you, over?"

"He is here but wounded, over."

"Okay, let me know. Holland out."

Nathan Holland watched Governor Jeffers walk across the golf course and intercept the golf cart flying the white flag. Less than a minute later, Jeffers was back on the radio.

"Jeffers to Holland, over."

"Holland here, over."

"Colonel, the man in the cart is, Colonel Roberto Herrera, chief of staff to General Victor Trujillo. The Colonel indicates that General Trujillo wishes to surrender his army, over."

Nathan Holland wasn't sure he heard that right. "Say again? The Mexican army is surrendering to *us*, over?"

"Affirmative. The general does not command the troops fighting in the south, only forces from Nogales to Phoenix and the force moving down I-8 to Gila Bend, over."

"Sounds like we should have the general over for dinner in the Gold Room if it's still standing, over?"

"Sounds good, Colonel. Let's get out the cease fire word asap from here to Gila Bend, over."

"My pleasure, Governor. Let's endeavor to confirm this thing asap. Holland, out."

* * * *

"He did *what*!" Mejias' scream echoed through his presidential office. The general officer who just delivered the news of the surrender was genuinely fearful for his life and stepped back in line with his colleagues.

Juan Mejias rose slowly from his chair and tried to control the murderous rage boiling inside him. "General Lopez, tell me why and how this happened!"

Alberto Lopez briefly broke eye contact with Mejias to spend half a second contemplating the leather holster on the President's hip, then he reengaged his commander's burning glare. "Mr. President, General Trujillo's..."

"Stop!" Mejias shouted and dropped his head to stare at the communiqué sitting on his desk. "The coward Victor Trujillo is no longer a general. Trujillo is never to be referred to as 'General' again."

"Yes, sir," came the instant, obedient reply from Lopez who began again. "Mr. President, Trujillo's messages indicated his army was suffering thousands of casualties from heat stroke and debilitating dehydration. The Americans cut off the water flowing into the region and when Gen—, when Trujillo dispatched a force to open the locks on the dams, they were stopped in the canyons by Apache forces. His reserve forces not fighting in Phoenix were unable to forage for alternative water supplies because of constant harassment by Indians. Water tanker transport trucks had clearly been made priority targets by American Predator and Reaper remotely controlled drones. Morale among the Phoenix Force plunged upon reports of the stalled main body force in the south and the high casualties being inflicted on the force dispatched to Gila Bend. Rumors of the Americans preparing to release more poison micro air vehicles caused large scale desertions."

Mejias lifted his head and stared at the small group of officers. "And the status of all forces?"

"Sir, our main body has surrendered their weapons and is marching back to Hermosillo. Our Phoenix flanking force has surrendered their weapons and is marching back to Nogales under Apache and Comanche cavalry escort. The Americans are releasing all POW's and are providing drinking water as well as some medical assistance."

"What happened with our southern force, General Melendez?"

"Mr. President, when the men learned of the surrender of Trujillo's flanking forces and the simultaneous rumor of more flying poison robots from Caborca, coupled with stalled forward progress, lack of water, and the platoons of combat robots that arrived at the front yesterday, morale and discipline sank to unrecoverable levels. Entire units refused movement orders. We tried to disengage and retreat back across the border but the Indians pursued and forced a surrender."

"Trujillo?"

General Lopez had the last word from Trujillo and shared it with the group. "My last communication from Trujillo indicates he has been granted political asylum in the United States."

Mejias gave all four generals the same cold stare. "I want him dead. I don't care if we have to hire a Japanese ninja, I want him dead!" Mejias pounded his desk and violently pushed the stack of communiqués to the floor. "Lopez, get with the special operations group and have them start planning the mission."

"Yes, sir." Lopez changed the subject. "What about our forces in Chihuahua? Another division of Indian reinforcements has arrived as have additional infantry robots." Lopez hoped Mejias wouldn't try to attack across the Rio Grande just for spite. "We may want to pull the men back to the city. Supply logistics will be easier and cheaper close to the city rather than keeping them deployed to forward areas along the border."

Mejias appreciated the face-saving device of repositioning for 'cost' reasons and seized upon the idea. "I don't think the Americans will attack across the river but you are correct that it makes good logistical sense to pull back to Chihuahua. Make it happen."

"Will do, Mr. President," answered Lopez. Thank God Mejias was walking away to fight another day. Of course, Lopez did have to research the ninja idea because, if he knew Mejias, the general wasn't joking about that.

* * * *

Mark Tanner pulled out the foot rest on his game room recliner and leaned back, exhaling a satisfied sigh as he did so.

"Congratulations, Mark."

"Thank you, Kathy. I hear the Mexicans are beginning to withdraw from their positions on the Rio Grande so the pressure is off you, too."

"Yes, looks that way, thank God. You can get some sleep now and take a shower and wash your clothes, and get reacquainted with your wife."

"Right. It will be good to get back to a normal life."

"You realize that you are the first general in history to wage and win a major war from your easy chair?"

"You said it yourself, Kathy—warfare evolves. Still, we came within hours of losing this thing. If Mejias knew we were out of ordinance, he could have encircled Phoenix as well as the dome farm and picked us apart."

"The President would have ordered the release of tactical nukes before that happened."

"Yes and it would have been a shame to lose the support of the Treaty Tribes over that, especially now that we know how effective a fighting force they are. That multi-nation force of Native Americans just saved this country from the Mexicans *and* from ourselves."

"That they did. Take care, Mark. Say 'hello' to Sara for me." General Kathleen Singer signed off and turned to the business of standing down her army.

54.

Tom opened his eyes and recognized his old room in the Paradise Wing of the Biltmore—he considered that was a good sign. He lifted off the pillow and sharp pain shot across his wounded shoulder and down his left arm. The pain forced him to drop his pounding head back to the pillow. He tried bending at the elbow and that didn't hurt as much. Clean white bandages covered his wrist and hand. The last two fingers were missing.

After further self-inventory Tom discovered he had pain in more places than he could count, but the rest of his body was accounted for. He knew he was luckier than many others.

Tom wondered how long it had been since the explosion that turned out his lights. His sense was no more than a day or two. Tom put his unbandaged hand up to his face and rubbed—clean shaven. A peek under the sheets confirmed all he wore were cotton briefs. He had clearly been bathed somehow and there was no offensive smell under there either. Someone was taking good care of him. It couldn't be Jenny; she had been wounded too badly.

Jenny...where is she and how is she? He had to find her. And Sun Rain...*please, God, let her be okay.*

Tom threw off the sheet and blanket, rolled onto his right side, swung his legs off the bed and sat upright. He spied clothes piled neatly on the dresser on the far side of the room. The walk to the dresser was almost as painful as dressing but he managed both...slowly. After what seemed like hours, he stood wearing jeans—he skipped the belt—tennis shoes that he left untied, and a tee shirt that his head and right arm slipped through, but it was just too painful to get his left arm through the sleeve. In that awkward state, Tom set out to find Jenny.

He remembered lying in the McArthur Ballroom with a freshly bandaged leg after being shot during the house-to-house fighting in the city. He remembered the mortar shell that blasted shrapnel through the wall, and he remembered the terrible feeling of Jenny lying unconscious across his stomach bleeding from a serious wound caused by that blast. He hadn't seen her since the Cherokee medic and hospital volunteers carried her away.

Tom limped to the door and found that the card reader latch was disabled which suited him just fine because he didn't have a room key and he wanted to be sure he could return to the room. Also at the door, someone had thoughtfully placed an old wooden cane, battered and nicked but definitely serviceable. Once in the hallway Tom turned left and walked out the nearby door to the outside. To his left the waters of the Paradise Pool were full of blast debris and a palm tree that had toppled into the deep end. Beyond the pool, several of the Fountain Court villa buildings had been heavily damaged by Mexican mortar shells and subsequent house fires.

Before Tom entered the East Wing of the main Biltmore building he surveyed the damage to his right. The once immaculately maintained Squaw Peak lawn was littered with downed palm trees and debris blasted from nearby structures. Everywhere building walls were scarred by bullet strikes. Neat piles of broken glass swept from the walkways and patios were evidence that someone had begun the cleanup process. But the hotel grounds were strangely quiet and he had yet to see a single stronghold resident.

Tom walked through the East Wing, passed the café, and into the lobby to discover the reception desk was dutifully manned by a security officer as he hoped. Tom recognized the face but couldn't remember his name.

"Good morning, Mr. Corant. Glad to see you up and around. What can I do for you?"

"You are....?" Tom looked expectantly at the duty officer.

"Sorry, Jack Tatum."

Tom took Jack's extended hand. "Tom Corant, but I see you already knew that."

"Yes, sir. Everyone's still talking about your charge through enemy fire to resupply the troops up on Wrigley Hill."

"Call me Tom, please. Where is Ms. Salem?

"She is in the hospital—that is in the Frank Lloyd Wright Ballroom, the big ballroom in the back. Unfortunately, the McArthur Ballroom in front has been destroyed."

"Yes, I was there when it took the first shell."

"Has Ms. Sun Rain been taking good care of you?" Jack added.

Hearing her name and the realization that she must be okay brought an instant warm smile to Tom. Now he knew why he was so cared for.

Tom nodded. "What about the Mexicans? Where is everybody?"

"Mexico surrendered, well the Mexican army surrendered—three days ago, not long after your Humvee exploded. Most everyone is out combing the neighborhoods looking for survivors who might be incapacitated. Many have traveled to Gila Bend to help the wounded from the main battle front near the dome farm."

"Thank you, Jack." Tom backed away from the reception desk and limped away in the direction of the hospital. He quickened his pace as he discovered that his wounded leg, though painful, was strong and not necessarily completely reliant on the support of the cane.

Jack called out after Tom. "I will tell the Governor you are awake."

Every step, however, did send a burst of pain surging through his shoulder. Thankfully he needed his right hand for holding the cane and not his left. Tom slogged through the Grand Ballroom weaving a path through piles of rubble that had crashed down from the partially collapsed ceiling. He pushed through the damaged door and emerged again into the morning sunshine, then crossed the service road to the doors of the Wright Ballroom.

Inside the scene was still chaotic three days after the battle for Phoenix ended. Groups of people laid on carpet or sat against walls waiting for wounds to be treated while the more seriously wounded were assisted first. Army medics from multiple Indian nations acted as the hands of doctors who remotely viewed patients from their dome homes. A Navajo medic assisting with triage pointed Tom to the rear of the ballroom which served as a surgical recovery area.

Tom walked through the triage operation in the foyer to a perimeter hallway that led to the rear row of conference room salons. Tom looked into three salons before finding Jenny lying on a cot in Salon J.

Over twenty cots, all occupied, were crammed into the small twenty-by-thirty foot room. Most patients were sleeping while two volunteers kept watch on I.V.'s and patient vital signs.

Tom knelt beside Jenny's cot and gently clasped her left hand. Jenny opened her eyes and smiled.

Relief warmed through Tom's sore body upon seeing the strength of Jenny's smile. "Hi, honey. I have been quite worried about you, Ms. Salem. Of course, I just woke up after being unconscious for three days. Sorry for not getting here sooner."

Jenny managed a weak nod to accompany her smile. "Sun Rain has been keeping me informed."

"Yes, the duty officer just told me she has been looking after me, but that is news to me. I haven't seen her since my Humvee was hit up on the Wrigley." Tom remembered Sun Rain dancing happily in the rain on top of Wrigley Hill. "I still don't know how the war turned out but I assume things went well if everybody has returned to the Biltmore. How is it you are here? The last I knew you were in surgery on Piestewa Peak."

"They brought me here two days ago. The most serious cases are being handled at the hospital on Piestewa and they needed more room so some of us were brought down here. They couldn't put me back into my room in the Paradise Wing because I still have this I.V. going." Jenny looked into Tom's eyes. "Show me your hand."

Tom reluctantly lifted his wounded arm and showed her his bandaged hand. Jenny saw bandages covering stubs where fingers should have been and tears welled up then dripped onto the cot.

"Hey, it's just a couple of fingers. It could have been worse. A lot of people lost everything, honey.

Jenny turned away and tears flooded onto her face.

"You're thinking of Little Deer?" Tom asked.

Jenny nodded. "And White Hawk."

"What? White Hawk is dead?"

"Yes. Killed on the front in Mexico. The news just made it here yesterday. And Cloud Rider…he is badly wounded, up on Piestewa."

Tom rocked back on his heel and grabbed the edge of Jenny's cot to steady himself. The news about his former traveling companions was like a punch in the gut that he didn't see coming.

Tom was almost afraid to ask the obvious follow up question but did anyway, "Roving Wolf and Running Bear?"

"They are okay. Roving Wolf is here in Phoenix. Running Bear stopped by yesterday to say goodbye; he is taking some dead Lakota warriors to South Dakota for burial then heading home to Oklahoma."

"How about you, do you know when you will be able to get out of here?"

"I can leave in the morning. No infection, they say I will be fine. I just need to stay quiet and get a few weeks of bed rest."

"That's great, Jen."

Tom sat with Jenny for over an hour, alternating his kneeling knee when the discomfort became too great. Fortunately, kneeling on his injured leg wasn't too uncomfortable, walking on it hurt more. Long periods passed where they didn't say anything. At other times conversation drifted to how their dome families were doing.

Sun Rain appeared at the salon door. She waved and crossed the room.

"Hi, Tom, so good to see you awake!" Sun Rain put a hand on his uninjured shoulder. "Hello, Jenny. How are you today?" Without waiting for an answer, she continued. "See, I told you Tom would be fine. He can't stay long, though."

Tom gave Sun Rain a quizzical look.

"You are due to meet with the Governor in the Conference Center. He heard you are awake and he wants to thank you."

"Okay." Tom leaned over and kissed Jenny's cheek. "I will be back. Sun Rain, can you help me up, please?"

Sun Rain went behind Tom so she could lift him from his good shoulder.

Tom groaned as he lifted to his feet. "Thank you!"

"Get some sleep, Jen."

Jenny's eyes were already closed.

Tom followed Sun Rain through the ballroom and back outside. As soon as they walked through the doors Sun Rain pushed Tom against the wall with no regard for his injuries. She clasped her arms around Tom's neck and pressed her body hard into his. Tom was caught off guard. Her embrace hurt like hell but he put his good arm around

Sun Rain's back and hugged her tight. He quickly lost track of the pain.

Sun Rain looked up after a few sobs and sniffles. Tom realized he had never seen her bright green eyes glisten with tears. The sight knocked the wind from his lungs as thoroughly as a body tackle from Steven when they wrestled as boys. He looked into her eyes and ached to kiss her full lips, but he didn't dare. Instead he forced a smile.

"Thanks for taking such good care of me. I am sorry I slept through it all."

Sun Rain stepped back and rubbed her eyes. "You are very welcome, Tom." Her smile was tentative—another first.

Tom followed Sun Rain through the main building ballroom complex to the Conference Center that Governor Jeffers used as the stronghold administrative offices.

"Sun Rain, how are your brother and cousin?"

"My brother is well and is helping with the searching of neighborhoods for wounded and for Mexican deserters. My cousin died from his wounds this morning."

Tom shuddered with the realization that Cloud Rider was dead. He was surprised at Sun Rain's lack of emotion. Maybe she was still in shock. Maybe she reverted to her ancestors' tradition that revered death in battle. He thought it best to pursue the subject another time.

Sun Rain led Tom to the Grand Room where Lane Jeffers kept his office. "I will wait here for you."

"You don't want to come in?"

"I don't think I am invited."

"Nonsense, come on." Despite the shoulder pain, Tom took Sun Rain's hand with the three fingers he still had on his left hand and walked through the open door.

Lane Jeffers stood up from behind his desk. "Hello, Tom. Glad you are feeling better."

Tom handed his cane to Sun Rain and shook Jeffers' hand. "Thank you. Not really feeling better though. I have a pounding headache, my thigh is throbbing, and my shoulder feels like it is going to implode."

Sara Saunders sat in an overstuffed chair along the wall and made note of Tom's complaint. "Sorry Tom, there are not enough painkillers to go around. We have to save them for the severe cases."

"I understand completely, Doctor. Sun Rain here has been nursing me back to health."

"Good to see you again, Sun Rain," offered Jeffers. "Tom, I thanked Sun Run three days ago but I wanted to thank you too, for saving my son, well, for saving all the men up at the Wrigley."

Tom shook his head. "There are thousands of heroes from here to Caborca. Don't single me out." Tom noticed Bob Briggs, arm in a sling, leaning against the north wall of his boss' office. "Bob, looks like you could use a rest. Why don't you sit down?"

"Can't Tom," came the gruff reply. "Medics took a giant palm tree splinter out of my ass. I can't sit down and I can't run from the hazing I get from Lane."

Jeffers smiled; he hadn't done much of that the last few days. "*Giant* splinter? It was this big." He held up his thumb and fore finger about an inch apart.

"Well I am going to sit if you don't mind," said Tom. "I am still a bit unsteady." Sun Rain helped Tom to the empty couch and they both sat.

"So what has happened since I went to sleep?"

Bob Briggs gave a quick summary of the war. The few domes destroyed by the suicide run of the blitzkrieging tanks were the only dome casualties. The Lakota, Navajo, and Cherokee dome defense force, aided by the Cheyenne, Kiowa, and Arapaho, stopped the Mexican main body just four miles from the dome farm. The remnants of the main body were currently retreating through Caborca back to

Hermosillo. General Trujillo's defeated Phoenix attack force was disarmed and retreating under Apache and Comanche guard along the same route they entered Arizona. The bulk of the force was just passing Tucson. General Trujillo was granted asylum in Phoenix since he surrendered against Mejias' orders and would be executed if he returned to Mexico. All Native American nations had already begun their journeys home. Cherokee mechanized units were helping the other nations by transporting dead and wounded via Humvees and Bradleys.

Briggs was interrupted by three loud electronic beeps chirping from the SATCOM case on the credenza behind Lane Jeffers' desk.

"Bob, you expecting a call?"

"No, sir. We have been transmitting daily reports to our military liaison but no other contact with the Administration since your last call with the President."

Jeffers opened the case and the display screen blinked to life. President Phillips stared back at the stronghold leader.

"Good morning, Madam President."

"Good morning, Lane. How are you doing out there?"

"Mop up and clean up and burying the dead continue, Madam President."

"I just wanted to extend my thanks to you and your staff, Lane. Interior Secretary Morgan has been tasked with coordinating cleanup and infrastructure repair. You should feel free to work directly with his office on that."

"That will be helpful, thank you Madam President."

"Anything else we can help you with, Lane?"

"No. We are managing okay, thank you."

"I can think of something, Madam President." Tom had risen from the couch and was leaning across Jeffers' desk so the SATCOM camera could find him.

The stronghold leader noted the puzzled look on the President's face. "This is Thomas Corant, Madam

President. He was a very active part of the fight for Phoenix."

President Phillips recognized the name. The voice of her Chief of Staff came over a private channel.

"Madam President, I would advise against engaging Mr. Corant. It would be best to end the call here."

Jeffers and Tom saw the President shake her head, clearly in response to some advisor or administration member on the call but using a private channel so his or her words to the commander-in-chief were not overheard by the other call participants in the Governor's office.

"Mr. Corant, you have been through quite an ordeal since your transport was attacked. I am sorry that the incredible dangers of the Outside have disrupted your life so tragically."

"Madam President, why are my fiancé and I not being allowed to move into our designated dome?"

"That just isn't possible, Mr. Corant."

Tom couldn't press the point by asking why his family had been told that he was dead; knowledge of that fact could possibly compromise Steven. He took another tack and hit hard with the core belief of Black Shine. He had never expected to be in the position of directly addressing the President of the United States, so what the hell…Tom clumsily blurted out the core claims of the renegade group as he knew them and as Steven's investigation seemed to be corroborating.

"Madam President, is it true that the US government used Fear to herd citizens into domes in order to advance the progressive agenda of creating a socialist government, replacing capitalism with communism, and reducing everyone's carbon footprint?"

The President's slight hesitation and complete lack of expression told Tom what he wanted to know. He certainly did not expect an honest, direct answer to his accusation.

"Mr. Corant, I don't see how conspiracy theories about the nature of our condition contribute anything helpful to that condition. Our citizens live free from fear and are protected from the evil in the world. Everyone has food and shelter and instant communication with all fellow citizens. There are no squabbles over money, no poor and homeless in the streets, no decay of mind or body from drugs, alcohol, or fatty food.

"You *were* happy in your dome, weren't you, Mr. Corant?"

Pangs of shame washed through Tom because 'yes' was the answer to that question. But life on the Outside had shown him there was more to a person than mind and body, there was *a spirit, a soul* in there too. His Indian friends believed it. The reawakening of faith inside him was real.

Tom knew he didn't have long and that he had no chance of changing the President's mind, but maybe he did have a chance for a compromise that would give him what he wanted.

"Madam President, would you release my family from their dome so they can come live with me out here?"

"That is just not possible, Mr. Corant. Lane, thank you again. Goodbye." President Phillips ended the call abruptly in order to avoid further useless debate on the matter.

"That was ballsy," commented Jeffers.

"And ill-advised," added Briggs.

Tom returned to his seat next to Sun Rain who flashed Tom a look of concern.

Briggs continued. "You should be careful, Tom. You are a double threat to them now. You know that the beauty and truth and freedom on the Outside far outshine any fear and evil out here. You also understand the ugly nature of the oppressive domer government that has destroyed liberty."

Sara Saunders spoke from the easy chair opposite the couch. “Tom, my advice is to forget the domes and live free, with us, or anywhere you choose.”

Tom stared back at the medical director. “I can’t forget my family.”

55.

The setting sun was already resting on the western horizon when they reached the summit of the small butte. The natural stone monument jutted dramatically 200 feet above the desert floor. Sun Rain led the horse while Tom and Roving Wolf walked on either side of the spirited animal. The two men held steady the tightly bound blanket bundle sitting atop the saddle. Under the blanket and bindings, the fallen Comanche warrior Cloud Rider made his final ride.

Sun Rain calmed and steadied the horse when it balked at walking so close to the crevice that opened in the ground near its feet. Roving Wolf detached two of Cloud Rider's lances, as well as his cousin's bow, axe, and three arrows from the side of the saddle.

Waves of apprehension surged through Tom as he watched Sun Rain gently stroke the neck of the nervous horse. The group was dangerously close to the edge of the butte but the location permitted an unobstructed view of the spectacular desert valley landscape, now full of the long shadows of the day's end. The darkening sky contrasted starkly against hundreds of rock outcrops that rose randomly across the miles of desert floor below, each with its rust-red western face brightly lit by the last rays of the sun.

"Take good care of my brave cousin," Sun Rain whispered and stroked the thick black mane one last time. She stepped back and reached out to take Tom's hand and guide him away.

Roving Wolf walked slowly around to their side of the horse, one hand lightly stroking and patting the animal, the other hand grasping one of the lances, still blood-stained from battle. Tom deliberately looked away toward the valley that would soon embrace the night. Sun Rain's hand tightened noticeably around his.

Roving Wolf plunged the lance through the first and second ribs with one strong thrust. The front legs of the horse simultaneously buckled under the shock of its pierced heart and Roving Wolf's shove helped the dying mount topple into the crevice taking its rider with him.

Roving Wolf picked up the axe and used one swift strike to cleave the bow in half. Next he set the axe head on the ground and, still holding the handle, stomped on the handle neck to snap off the axe head. He broke the shaft of the second lance in the same manner. Finally, he picked up the arrows and broken weapons and walked to the crevice.

Sun Rain led Tom forward as Roving Wolf tossed the broken lance and axe into the crevice. The grieving warrior handed an arrow to Sun Rain and another to Tom. Each took turns snapping the arrow shaft and tossing the broken arrows down into the dark fissure.

Tom studied Roving Wolf's solemn expression. The warrior's eyes reflected the orange light of the last sliver of solar disc before it disappeared beneath the desert.

"He died in battle. For a Comanche, there is no higher honor." Roving Wolf turned to begin the short twilight hike to the base of the butte and to the horses they would ride back to Phoenix.

Before Sun Rain followed she glanced one last time at the spot Cloud Rider disappeared through the ground. His mother would be happy about the traditional Comanche good-bye, but she would also be glad to know Sun Rain had slipped a gold cross and a bible under the funerary bundle.

With Tom's hand in hers, they followed Roving Wolf off the butte.

56.

Four weeks had done much to advance the recovery of the Biltmore and of Jenny. For the past two days she was finally able to leave her sick bed on her own. As Jenny walked out of the Paradise Wing she winced when one of the occasional stabs of pain shot out from the middle of her spine. She found that she needed to lean to the right a bit to escape some of the dull throbbing of the more persistent pain in her lower back. Still, her second day of walking was easier than her first.

There were still plenty of scars visible as she walked the Biltmore grounds but the broken glass and toppled palm trees were gone, and the restoration of damaged buildings and bomb-chewed landscape was well underway. The Paradise Pool beside the Cabana Club was once again sparkling clean and available for use. Most importantly, Bob Briggs was driving and putting again on a patched and recovering Biltmore golf course.

The spring day was gray and cooler than average but Jenny had donned a bright white sundress anyway. She had originally planned to have breakfast with Tom at the Cabana Club restaurant for the second time in as many days. For the past month their time together consisted only of brief late night visits to say goodnight after Tom's long days of doing what he could to help with stronghold repairs. But instead of breakfast today, Jenny and Tom were meeting Roving Wolf and Sun Rain because Roving Wolf had received another text message on his SATCOM unit from Steven scheduling a video call. Jenny walked by the water slide and into the empty spa building. The group planned a private meeting because they were too fearful of exposing Steven's clandestine operations.

Everyone was already in the spa office when Jenny arrived.

"Hi, Jenny," said a smiling Sun Rain.

Jenny acknowledged her greeting with a nod. She thankfully hadn't seen much of Sun Rain these past few weeks. While Jenny recuperated at the Biltmore, Sun Rain spent her days and nights helping nurse wounded warriors while she waited to accompany her brother back to Pecos.

Jenny sat down by Tom who leaned over and kissed her cheek. "Good morning, honey."

"Hi, everyone. Sorry if I am late. They left too many choices of clothes for me this morning."

Roving Wolf tested the wireless connection from the main SATCOM unit to the antenna he set outside the window and grunted his approval of the signal strength. Now they would wait for Steven.

They didn't wait long before the indicator light signaled the incoming conference request. Roving Wolf entered the accept code he and Steven had agreed upon and within two seconds Steven Corant's face filled the top half of the SATCOM case.

Tom was anxious to start the call. "Hi, Steven."

"Hello, everyone. Roving Wolf, thanks for the debrief you sent on the war. I am sorry about your cousin and your friends. Hey, Tom, sorry it has been so long since our last call. I have learned from my contacts that these hijackings of the secure SATCOM units are not easily accomplished. But I also learned that military SATCOM traffic isn't monitored."

"Ok, thanks, Steven. Look, I spoke directly with the President when she called Governor Jeffers after the Mexican surrender. Jenny and I have no chance of going into our dome or any other dome. Frankly, Steven, I couldn't live in a dome ever again knowing what I know and after seeing what I have seen. I asked the President if she would permit all of you to come out from under the dome but she refused, so I want to come and get you and mom and Jonny, and the girls, and Grandpa Frank out of the dome and back here to the stronghold. You said you had a contact in Black Shine who could help make this work, right?"

"Yes, Tom. But it's hard to know who to trust. I could be talking with an undercover Net cop for all I know. My source says there is an emergency tool attached to every tenth dome that can be used to open the outer dome door provided the people on the inside have opened the inner dome door. But that procedure alerts Dome Services and could trigger an armed response by a combot. The safer procedure is for my Black Shine hacker contact to send a signal to open the outer door through one of Dome Services' own computers. We are ready to do that, but can you find our dome? We have no way to help you with that yet. Black Shine says they can send the door unlock signal to our specific dome, but they still don't have enough knowledge of Dome Services computers to identify the physical location of a given dome."

"I can find the dome," confirmed Roving Wolf.

Tom nodded a silent thank you to his scout friend. "We should do this as soon as possible while there is still a lot of movement by returning combat forces and while the military has a large deficit of flying drones due to war losses," Tom explained.

Roving Wolf added his own thoughts. "Yes, I agree, the sooner, the better. We can drive two Humvees tomorrow and make the rescue tomorrow night. You are back in Phoenix before the next night." Roving Wolf had completed his temporary one month assignment to help with tracking Mexican deserters and he was anxious to return home before Red Sky delivered their first child.

"Steve?"

"Yes, Tommy?"

"What is the window of opportunity regarding the hacker security by-pass that unlocks the outer dome door? I mean, how much time do we have to open the door, get everybody out, and shut the door before alarms start going off?"

"The door can't remain open more than forty seconds or we risk detection."

"Only forty seconds? Wow, okay. Well, everyone can be in the airlock ready to go, I guess."

"Tom, conditions have to be just right for the hackers to activate the by-pass. My contact suggested we be ready to open the door every hour on the hour. I don't know if we are going to get another chance to speak before we attempt this. We better set the timing right now."

Roving Wolf checked the digital time readout on the video display. "Make the first by-pass attempt at 23:00 hours tomorrow night. We will monitor through the night if necessary."

"Okay, 23:00 hours tomorrow night. Will do. I better cut this comm. link. Good-bye and good luck everyone."

"See you tomorrow night, Steve."

Jenny waved at the display screen. "Bye, Steve."

* * * *

The rescue party set out at sunrise. The two Humvees raced down I-10 through miles of flat, scrub-filled desert punctuated at intervals by majestic gatherings of solemn mountain sentinels rising over the arid plain. Tom followed the lead Humvee driven by Roving Wolf and crewed by Sun Rain. Bob Briggs had loaned them the second Humvee on nothing but the promise to bring it back someday. Both trucks carried ten five-gallon cans of diesel fuel so they could make the 650-mile trip to Pecos. They had to carry their own fuel because the Cherokee soldiers had already dismantled the refueling outposts that they had established while preparing for war.

Tom tried several times to start conversations with Jenny but the talks died out quickly as she seemed to be in a strangely pensive mood. He attributed her condition to her continuing recovery from battle wounds and, perhaps, the idea of returning so close to home but still not being able to see her family.

Near the New Mexico border they slowed for a small convoy of Cherokee Humvees and Bradleys that were escorting a mixed group of Cheyenne and Arapaho warriors east across the desert and toward the bison-filled plains of home. Most of the Treaty Tribe warriors had already made the trek home. Many of the members of this small party were wounded soldiers who had required some convalescence time to recover from serious battle injuries before making the journey back to their families.

An hour beyond the ambulance convoy, Roving Wolf made a short stop in deserted Lordsburg, New Mexico to refill the Humvee fuel tanks with diesel. The brief refueling operation passed without incident. Three hours later the team found themselves in familiar territory in El Paso. The atmosphere on the return trip was much different. Fear and concern were gone, replaced by confidence and hope via the victory over General Mejias and the subsequent return of the four hundred stronghold citizens unharmed except for the two men who had attacked the Mexican captain leading the raid. The travelers topped off their fuel tanks so they could reach Pecos without another stop. They decided against checking in with the citizens of the El Paso stronghold, there just wasn't enough time.

* * * *

Before embarking on the last 200 miles to Pecos, Roving Wolf made a scheduled SATCOM call to his fellow scout, Chachu. The Army had relaxed radio restrictions and allowed scouts to communicate directly with each other during the war to permit better command and control and better information sharing during the conflict.

Two hundred miles west of El Paso near Douglas, Arizona, the Apache scout sat on his mount atop the summit of D Hill. Four hundred feet below him on the desert floor, thirty warriors of his Chokonen band of Chiricahuas waited for him to lead the raiding party.

Chachu touched the wireless headset clipped on his right ear.

"Greetings brother!"

Roving Wolf could *hear* his friend's smile—they weren't using a video feed, only audio. "Good evening, brother. Are you well?"

"Very well," came the enthusiastic reply from Chachu. "My Mescalero brother from Las Cruces confirms your information. There is no significant security build-up directly on the Texas dome farm southern perimeter. I suspect this is because General Singer has kept a large number of Apache and Comanche patrols operating in the mountains that parallel the Rio Grande. With eyes that far forward, they are not so worried about watching their rear."

"Thank you," replied a grateful Roving Wolf. "What are your plans, brother?"

Chachu laughed heartily into the SATCOM headset. The brazen, battle-hardened warrior was about to revive the four-hundred-year-old Apache tradition of raiding across the border. On his right, the sun would soon set. Directly ahead, only a half mile away, was Sonora, Mexico. Chachu grinned as his eyes scanned the southern horizon. A gentle breeze nudged him from the north and he felt the spirit of his ancestor on the hilltop. Two hundred years ago, Cochise sat on his mount in this very spot, looking deep into Mexico—Chachu was certain of that.

"My brother, thirty brave warriors and I are about to ride beyond the frontier and make a little noise."

Roving Wolf smiled too. With the war won, the government had basically given tacit approval for Apache and Comanche forces to "aggressively" patrol along the border and enter Mexican territory as necessary. Word—and fear—spread quickly through the villages and towns of northern Mexico as it became known that armed Apache and Comanche warriors had free reign to enforce border security and protect the Homeland and they could cross into Mexico at their discretion.

"Have fun, brother," Roving Wolf said with all sincerity.

"I will. And I expect you to join me soon, brother!" Chachu screamed a piercing war cry which his men below imitated as they kicked their horses into a fast gallop due south. Chachu recovered his SATCOM gear and raced down the more easily traversed northern slope of D Hill and then wheeled his mount south to join his men—the Chiricahua were on the ride into Sonora once again.

57.

They reached Pecos just after 9:00 p.m. Very few lights lit the streets of the small town. Only a few electric bulbs shining from private houses and a handful of flickering camp fires near tipis broke up the dark night. But Roving Wolf was in home territory and easily found the refueling station near I-20 and State Highway 17.

Tom saw Roving Wolf exit the lead Humvee and watched as he exchanged welcome embraces with several of his Comanche colleagues who manned the refueling station. Tom and Jenny stepped out of the truck to stretch their legs but the rest stop would last only moments. Everyone took a few minutes with the restroom facilities before jumping back into the Humvees.

Roving Wolf approached Tom's driver door and opened it.

"Tom, this is Neraquassi, "Yellow Horse" in white words. He will join us and be your turret gunner in case of trouble."

Tom shook the warrior's hand and introduced himself. "Tom Corant. Pleased to meet you, Yellow Horse. This is Jenny Salem."

Jenny reached across Tom to clasp Yellow Horse's hand. The dome light of the Humvee didn't offer much illumination but there was enough light to see Yellow Horse was much younger than Roving Wolf.

"Well to see you Tom and Jenny." Yellow Horse stepped back and entered the rear compartment. Roving Wolf shut the driver's door and Tom leaned out the open window.

"Not going to say hello to Red Sky?"

"No time," replied Roving Wolf tersely. "Go to night vision."

Tom turned to Jenny. "You ready for this, baby? Are you sure you don't want to wait here where it is safer?"

"No, I am ready."

Tom switched off all interior panel lights and donned night vision goggles. The convoy would use blackout lights the rest of the way. The tiny, dim lights were almost impossible to see through the windscreen with the naked eye but through night vision goggles their pinpoint glow was distinct and obvious. Tom followed Roving Wolf and Sun Rain as they wound their way back to the highway.

The rescue team soon made the turn east onto I-10. After half an hour they were adjacent to the portion of the dome farm that contained the Corant family dome. Tom followed Roving Wolf when he turned off of the highway and into an adjacent arroyo that acted as part of the road's drainage system. The arroyo was deep enough to conceal all but the topmost portion of the canvas coverings of the .50 caliber machine guns.

Everyone piled out of the Humvees and scrambled up one of the sidewashes to climb out of the arroyo. All but Jenny had carbines slung across their backs. Tom continued to use the night vision goggles to follow Roving Wolf, then Yellow Horse, then Sun Rain. He held Jenny's hand tightly so she wouldn't get lost and because her gait was still unsteady due to her injuries.

Roving Wolf led the party eight dome rows deep and stopped to examine the surface of one of the many service roads that ran along the rows of domes. Gouges in the pavement matched Roving Wolf's memory of the toppled transport truck.

Roving Wolf pointed to the dome just west of the marred road surface. "That's it, Tom."

Tom removed his goggles and stared at the imposing black silhouette that arched high above the ground and obscured a good portion of the night sky. He walked forward slowly with halting, uncertain steps and laid both hands gently on the dome's outer skin of photovoltaic cells that converted sunlight into auxiliary electrical power. He smiled with the knowledge that his family was only a few feet away inside the dome shell. Tom resisted the urge to tap on the dome outer door to signal his family who would be waiting inside the airlock. They had been warned that unnatural vibrations on the dome's outer skin could trigger alarms by Dome Services computers.

Tom backed away from the dome and looked at the adjacent, neighbor domes. He wondered who lived in the domes just a few feet from his? There was no way to know.

With only a few minutes to spare before the first rescue window at 11:00 p.m., Roving Wolf brought the group around to the outer dome door. As the eleven o'clock hour approached, Roving Wolf grabbed the door lever that would open both the upper and lower dome door in unison. No one spoke. All eyes watched the area on the door that contained the recessed indicator light, currently glowing red. A change to green meant the door could be opened.

Eleven o'clock came and went. Roving Wolf tried putting gently increasing pressure on the door lever anyway but to no avail. The twelve o'clock window passed, again with no change in the color of the status light.

"Looks like we could be here a while?" Tom said rhetorically.

Roving Wolf and Yellow Horse returned to the Humvees to retrieve some bedrolls and rations to make the wait easier. One person from the group would take a one-hour observation shift while the others rested. If the indicator turned green, whoever was on duty was to wake the others immediately.

Tom awoke two hours after his 3 to 4 a.m. shift. He was too excited to maintain a restful sleep for long intervals. The eastern sky was bright and the sun would soon rise above the level of the domes. He wandered between two nearby domes and relieved himself against one of the dome foundations. He joked shamefully to himself that the President was in that dome.

After the 7:00 a.m. window passed without incident the group began to wonder if Steven Corant's contact was legitimate, or maybe the contact had been compromised. The speculation didn't help the time pass any faster.

Tom asked Roving Wolf if he was certain Steven hadn't tried calling the SATCOM unit.

Roving Wolf held aloft a remote key fob. "I have the SATCOM antenna setup. This key shakes if an incoming signal is detected."

With his back against the dome wall, Tom slid down to the ground near Jenny, resigned to the fact that he could do nothing but wait.

58.

Red Thunder (Wahkeyunshah), war chief of the Lakota, climbed down from his mount. The morning was crisp and cool and the first rays of the sun peeked through the treetops on the eastern hills. Small remnants of the last snow hid in the shadows. The war chief took a knee beside the rock marker. He approved of his wife's choice for White Hawk's burial site. The warrior's hillside grave was positioned to meet the morning sun regardless of season. In the shallow valley two hundred feet below, a small stream swollen with snowmelt sparkled in the morning sunlight as it wound through the band's village encampment.

Red Thunder hadn't been in attendance during White Hawk's funeral ceremonies. A Cherokee truck convoy had carried White Hawk and other fallen Lakota warriors home for burial ahead of the main body of the returning Lakota cavalry that had taken another three weeks to find home. The grieving father pulled an eagle feather from his belt and placed it carefully under the rocks that marked his son's grave.

The victorious leader of the Lakota army returned to his feet and led his horse down the small hill. The peaceful valley was surrounded by thick evergreen forest that had shaken off winter and was now deep into the spring season.

At the base of the hill, the local band's medicine chief stretched his arms overhead holding a baby aloft to meet the morning sun. The child was White Hawk's newborn daughter. Red Thunder listened as the medicine chief repeated his new granddaughter's name seven times. Laughing Bird's spirit was being welcomed and introduced to the world.

The proud war chief stood strong against the rush of emotion that blew across him like a hot summer wind.

While he watched the naming ceremony his hand felt for the deerskin map case tied to his belt. He gripped the case tightly; inside was a newly drawn map of the United States created by a domed cartographer working for the United States Geological Survey. The map defined the boundaries of a 10,000 square mile hole in the northwestern Great Plains of the United States that surrounded the Black Hills. The sacred Pahá Sápa were no longer claimed by a foreign state.

Little baby Laughing Bird was the first child of the Lakota Sioux Nation to be born into the *free* Black Hills in almost 300 years. Red Thunder could not hold back his tears as Laughing Bird's hungry cry rode with the wind into the rustling green pines.

59.

At 8:00 a.m. the door indicator light turned green.

"Green light!!" Sun Rain had just started her watch. Her excited call brought Tom and Jenny running to the dome door.

Roving Wolf stepped forward and rotated the door lever. Both the top and bottom portions of the dome door slid away into the wall.

Tom hesitated and it took Jenny's tug on his arm to pull his mind back to the moment. Tom entered the airlock where two months before he waved his last goodbye to his family and awaited the ill-fated transport vehicle that carried his bride-to-be.

The light in the chamber was dim compared to the bright sunlight of the Outside. His eyes found his mother first. Cynthia Corant smiled and welcomed Tom into her arms.

Tom broke the embrace. "So great to see you, mom! Come on, let's go, we have less than a minute."

Steven stepped forward and hugged his younger brother. "No, Tom. Take Jonny, but the rest of us are staying. We have all discussed our options. It's best if we stay."

The words struck Tom like the kick in the ribs he had taken from the Mexican raiders. "What? You can't mean that."

His teary sisters walked forward and hugged him tightly for a few seconds before stepping away. They nodded their heads in affirmation of Steven's words.

"Mom?"

Cynthia put a hand on her son's shoulder. "My life is here, Tom."

"It's too scary out there, Tommy," Lucy said through her sobbing.

Tom felt Jonny thrust his hand into his but Jonny's attention wasn't on the desperate conversation in the airlock; he stared at the faces of Roving Wolf and Sun Rain in the doorway and looked with fascination at the bright light beyond the strangers.

Jenny hugged Cynthia, then Lucy and Linda. She hugged Jonny who said hello but only half-heartedly since he was still distracted by the commotion in the doorway.

Tom glanced down as Grandpa Frank wheeled his chair forward.

"You are a brave man, Thomas. I am proud of you. I know what I've said about the Outside, but I wouldn't be any good to anybody out there. I don't have many years left and I don't want to leave my little girl. I will fare much better now that I know you and Jonny are free."

Steven reached out and grabbed Tom's arm. "Tom, Black Shine says they can help cover Jonny's absence. As for the rest of us, either we all go, or we all stay—too dangerous otherwise. The resistance to the government is real, Tommy. I am part of it now. We have to get everyone out, Tom, not just Jonny or our family. You and me, we need to stay in touch. We need to keep working this—you from the Outside, me from in here."

Jenny slipped an arm around Cynthia who hugged the young woman tightly in return. Tears gushed uncontrollably from Jenny's eyes. "Tommy, I am going to stay in here too. I can't stay Outside."

Tom stared back at Jenny in bewilderment—another kick in the ribs.

"I'm sorry, Tommy. In here it's clean, it's safe, it doesn't *hurt,* it's comfortable." Jenny threw her arms tightly around Tom and sobbed.

"But what about us, Jen?"

Jenny lifted her head. "Oh, Tommy, "us" hasn't been developing very far out here, has it? Turns out that lust can transmit over the on-line wire, but love can't, at least not in our case. I am not blind, Tom. You have other opportunities and interests Outside. That's okay, don't feel guilty." Jenny remembered Little Deer. He was right. She did feel better about herself.

Tom glanced back at Sun Rain who waited anxiously in the doorway.

Cynthia Corant cast a circumspect glance in the same direction.

Jenny pulled away from Tom and approached Steven. '"Steve, can you fit me in?" Jenny asked with more than a hint of desperation in her voice.

"Sure, we'll make it work." Steven smiled and hugged their new family member.

Tom's head was spinning. The rescue was unfolding in a far different manner than he had planned.

"We need to close this door." Roving Wolf's decree jarred Tom back into action. He pulled Jonny by the hand toward the door. Tom felt Sun Rain rush passed him into the dome. She gave a quick hug to Jenny and all the Corants but lingered a moment longer with Cynthia.

"I am Sun Rain."

Cynthia smiled. She sensed a strong, bold woman.

Tom guided Jonny to Roving Wolf then reached out and pulled Sun Rain toward himself and the door. He glanced back to a scene much like the one he saw before the inner airlock door closed two months ago, his family all standing close together, many tears and waves goodbye.

Tom darted across the threshold pulling Sun Rain with him. Roving Wolf pulled the door lever and slammed the door closed with a heavy metallic clank.

Back in the daylight of the brightening morning, Tom leaned on the dome and took a few deep breathes to clear his head and shake off the shock of the moment. He looked at each of his companions, but was unable to say anything. From his rear quarter he heard an excited yelp.

"Wow, Tommy, look at that! The sun is so awesome!!" Jonny Corant shielded his eyes with one hand and pointed the other to the sun rising between a row of domes stretching off to east.

Tom felt and heard the joy radiating from his little brother. He had no doubt that he was doing the right thing bringing Jonny into the Outside. "Careful, Jonathan, don't look directly at the sun, it can damage your eyes. You will get better views during sunsets and sunrises."

Roving Wolf looked along the nearest dome service road that led south. "We should back off to the Barilla range and watch to see if our activity generates any response from security forces, then we can drive back to Pecos."

"Sounds good," replied Tom. "I will take Yellow Horse and Jonny and follow you. Jonny, come here. Meet my friends. This is Roving Wolf and Sun Rain and Yellow Horse."

"Nice to meet you, Jonny." Sun Rain smiled and offered her hand.

"Wow, real Indians! I read about you in class."

"We are Numunuh, little boy, not Indians," corrected Yellow Horse.

Sun Rain saw Jonny's brow furrow with confusion. "Maybe you learned about the 'Comanche?'"

Jonny smiled. "Oh, yes—okay."

Tom put an arm around Jonny. "Hey, Jonny, do you want a ride in my truck?"

Jonny's eyes widened. "Oh, boy, would I!"

Roving Wolf led the team south at an easy jog, out of the dome farm, down a drainage channel, up and over I-10, and down into the arroyo to the parked Humvees. Young Jonathan Corant kept up the pace well despite the handicap of gray domer pajamas and dome slippers on his feet.

"Jump in, Jonny." Tom opened the passenger door.

"Fantastic!" Jonny climbed up into the seat and Tom showed him the safety belt.

Yellow Horse climbed into the back and then up onto the gunner platform. Jonny's curious eyes darted everywhere as Tom started the engine and drove after Roving Wolf toward the nearest high ground in the Barilla Mountains.

60.

Running Bear pulled his Humvee over to the roadside east of Chattanooga on US 74 and halted the convoy. They were nearing the border of North Carolina driving through the Cherokee National Forest. Little Deer was right. The land radiated enchantment and wonder.

Running Bear kept his promise to his fallen friend. His family gathered their belongings and announced the move they were making to the Cherokee homelands in the east. To his surprise over twelve hundred other families packed up and followed.

He traced the reverse path of the northern route of the Trail of Tears as faithfully as he could. They traveled slowly, taking two weeks now to traverse 900 miles. Every evening when stopped for the night, they prayed and paid homage to their ancestors who in 1838 were forced by the government to leave their homes and to walk or take wagons along the same path but back then they moved west from North Carolina through Tennessee, Kentucky, Missouri, and Arkansas to reservation land in Oklahoma.

Two of the travel days were spent rolling their vehicles along at walking speed so the young could walk alongside the vehicles and experience just a small taste of the forced relocation that resulted in the death of thousands of Cherokee, Creek, Seminole, and Choctaw. Unlike their ancestors, the teenagers that walked on this trip had enough to eat and didn't have to sleep on winter's frozen ground with no fire.

Running Bear popped up through the gun turret and surveyed the mountains and valleys that stretched in all directions—green with the fresh new growth of spring. He estimated half an hour of sunlight remained for making camp and starting dinner. In the morning they would set out and not stop again until they reached the valley of Little Deer's family. He patted the breast of his deerskin shirt. The pocket inside held the last letters Little Deer penned to his wife and each of his children. His heart leapt as his friend's boisterous laugh bounded into his thoughts. Running Bear hoped the warm smile he brandished in this moment was something close to the smile Little Deer would have flashed to greet these beautiful green hills of home.

61.

Roving Wolf sat concealed below the military crest of the small hill. Elbows on his knees steadied the binoculars that he held to his eyes and trained on the dome farm across I-10.

Tom approached from the south side of the hill where the Humvees were hidden. "Anything?" They had spent the day scouting the area and watching the dome farm. Tom was anxious to leave.

Roving Wolf answered without taking his eyes from the scene. "No, it is quiet all day. Our raid is successful. It is safe to drive back to Pecos."

Tom stared at the countless mounds of concrete, steel, and manufactured composites crowding the land across the highway. The domes absorbed the orange light of sunset into their dark solar panel skins like a leech sucking blood. "We've got to find a way to get everyone out of there."

Roving Wolf lowered his binoculars in serious contemplation of Tom's wish. The powerful irony was not lost to him. The Numunuh and all other Indian nations were free once again and it was the newcomers to the land who now lived on spirit-killing reservations.

Tom smiled and dismissed his friend's concerned glance. "Don't worry, brother. We will get it right this time. I know we can be better stewards of the Outside and better friends to your people. You just saved *our* country—yours and mine—after all!" Tom saw Roving Wolf didn't look entirely convinced.

"So, now that there is no fighting to be done you two are going to sit around clucking like chickens?!"

Tom looked over his shoulder and up at Sun Rain who stood confidently with hands on hips at the highest point of the hilltop.

"You know that isn't very sound infantry procedure standing at the top of the hill like that," teased Tom.

"Are you saying I am not safe, Tom?" Sun Rain smiled mischievously.

Tom snapped to his feet and climbed to meet Sun Rain. "You're safe from the bad guys, but not from me."

Sun Rain smiled while a few loose strands of long black hair whipped over her face in the gentle evening breeze. Tom brushed the rogue strands aside and pulled Sun Rain close. Sun Rain returned his embrace and eagerly pressed her lips to his. The kiss was interrupted almost immediately.

"Hey, Tommy, do you really know how to shoot this?!"

On the back side of the hill Yellow Horse had pulled the canvass cover off one of the machine guns to show the curious Jonny Corant.

"Forget about that, Jonny. Come here, you are missing your first sunset."

Jonny jumped down from the Humvee and ran up the hill.

Tom grabbed his little brother with his left arm and pointed him west. "Keep your eyes on that, Jonny."

The brilliant splashes of color on the horizon caught the happy young boy's attention—for a moment. "Wow, Tommy, that is super! Hey, look, another rabbit!" With that, Jonny scrambled gleefully down the hill.

Tom kept Sun Rain close while he looked once more at the vast sea of domes that stretched to the horizon. He thought of all the souls trapped inside without knowledge of the *real* world. His first emotion ran to sorrow but the laughter of a little boy chasing rabbits quickly transformed the sorrow into hope. Tom would pray tonight for those who, out of fear, built for themselves a colorless world that shut out far more than fear; it shut out liberty and it withered the spirit living within everyone.

I will work to change that.

"*I was born upon the prairie where the wind blew free, and there was nothing to break the light of the sun. I was born where there were no enclosures, and where everything drew free breath. I want to die there, and not within walls.*"

– Paruasemena (Ten Bears), Comanche Chief (1790-1872)

mistakes ll